CAPE BAY CAFE MYSTERIES

Books 1 to 3

HARPER LIN

Harper Lin Books

ISBN-13: 978-1987859621

ISBN-10: 1987859626

www.harperlin.com

Book 1: Cappuccinos, Cupcakes, and a Corpse

Chapter 1

I WAS BENT OVER A CAPPUCCINO, carefully moving my milk pitcher to etch a design into the foam, when Mrs. D'Angelo burst into the café.

"Francesca!" she exclaimed so loudly that I jumped, pouring milk across the center of my design and out onto the saucer and counter.

I sighed and put down the milk pitcher, then plastered on a huge smile before looking up at her. "Mrs. D'Angelo!" I tried to sound happy despite having ruined my almost-finished cappuccino.

"Francesca!" she said again, coming around the counter. She grabbed my hands. "How *are* you, dear? Oh, you poor thing! I've been so worried about you!" She put one hand on my cheek, still managing to grasp both of mine in her other hand. She was exceptionally strong for an older woman. "You precious dear!"

I tried to keep the happy look on my face as I took half a step back, but some glimmer of distress must have flickered through my eyes because Mrs. D'Angelo pulled me into a tight hug.

"No, no, no, you dear girl, you come here!" She held me in such a way that my hands were pinned up by my shoulders, as if I had been raising them in surrender when she moved in.

I patted the woman's shoulders feebly with the slight range of motion I had in my wrists.

"You don't have to be strong, Francesca! You don't have to be strong!" she murmured.

At that moment, I wished I was strong—strong enough to break away from her grip. I caught the eye of one of my employees coming out of the backroom and sent her a "help me!" message with my eyes.

"Mrs. D'Angelo? Is that you?" Sammy asked, putting her hand lightly on Mrs. D'Angelo's back.

Mrs. D'Angelo mercifully let me go and turned her fountain of emotion in Sammy's direction. "Oh, Samantha!" She put one hand on Sammy's upper arm and her left one gripped mine. Her long red fingernails dug enthusiastically into our flesh. She looked between the two of us. "Samantha, I'm so glad Francesca here has you to help her through this difficult time. She needs good friends like you now more than ever." She rubbed my arm as she spoke, a welcome relief from her talon-like grasp.

"I'm doing all I can to help her out." Sammy smiled at the older woman.

"I'm sure you are, dear," Mrs. D'Angelo cooed. She turned back to me. "Do you need anything else? If there's anything you need, you know you can come to me or to any of us in the Ladies Auxiliary, and we'll do absolutely whatever we can to help you. We owe it to your dear mother's memory, God rest her soul, to help her dear Francesca." Mrs. D'Angelo crossed herself reflexively as she referred to my mother, releasing Sammy in the process.

Sammy took advantage of the freedom and stepped quickly over to the register, where customers were getting impatient, leaving me to deal with Mrs. D'Angelo and her monologue and grasping hands. I gave Sammy a look, and she smiled at me. She'd hear about it later, that was for sure. But for now, she was the lucky one getting back to work.

Out of the corner of my eye, I saw the tourist whose cappuccino I had been working on when Mrs. D'Angelo rushed in, impatiently tapping his fingers on the marble-topped table where he was sitting.

I looked helplessly at him then back at his cappuccino. "Mrs. D'Angelo—"

"Now, now, dear," she went on, oblivious to the fact that I was trying to escape. "No objections. None of us would have it any other way. Anything for our dear Carmella's daughter. Now, what time is it?" She looked at her watch. "Oh, heavens, I didn't even realize! I'm due at the library for our Genealogy Society meeting! I have to run!" She hurried back around the counter toward the door. "Now, don't forget what I said, Francesca dear! Anything you need!" And she was gone, in as much of a whirlwind as she'd arrived, leaving only a cloud of her floral perfume and some red fingernail prints in our arms.

I sighed as I began a fresh cappuccino for the man who was still waiting impatiently for his drink. Not that I could blame him.

"I need a nap after that!" I whispered to Sammy as we moved around each other in the small drink prep area. "That woman has more energy in her seventies than I've had in my entire life!"

Sammy giggled. "I think she gets it from exhausting other people."

I bent over the steaming cappuccino, carefully crafting a rose in the foam. I tried not to rush, but I could feel the man's eyes boring into the top of my skull as I worked. I finally put down the milk pitcher and stood back to assess my handiwork. Certainly not my best, but it was still better than a person could find anywhere else in town, or in most places on the Massachusetts coast.

I picked up the mug and saucer and carefully walked them around the counter to the man who had ordered the drink. I set it gently on the table in front of him, positioned perfectly so he'd have the best view of my creation. "So sorry about the wait, sir. My apologies." I gave him my very best café-owner smile.

"I hope it don't always take this long," he grunted. He took a drink without even glancing at the rose I'd crafted.

I smiled sweetly. "I really am very sorry, sir." *Rude.* I turned to go back around the counter. *I should have known that when I saw the Yankees jersey.*

Despite living in New York City for years before moving back home, I've always been a Massachusetts girl at heart, and during baseball season, I bleed Boston Red Sox red. Well, I suppose everyone bleeds red, but that just shows how much better the Red Sox are than our rivals to the south. No one *literally* bleeds Yankee blue.

I took up my post in front of the espresso machine, wiping things down while I waited for the next order.

Sammy worked the cash register and called out the next drinks to make just seconds later. "I need two lattes, please!"

I set about making the drinks, brainstorming what I would design in their foam as I worked. I steamed the milk for the first drink, getting it about halfway finished before I pulled the espresso. The timing had to be perfect or the espresso would get bitter. Fortunately, I'd been making cappuccinos since I could see over the counter, so it was second nature to me. I decided on coordinating sun and starburst patterns. I made the sun design first, pouring the center circle of foam then using a toothpick to draw out the rays. Finishing that, I moved on to the starburst.

Work, except for Mrs. D'Angelo's interruption, was a cherished distraction from the circumstances that had brought me back to my hometown on the Massachusetts coast. This café had been in my family for three generations. First it had belonged to my grandparents, who opened it shortly after arriving from Italy almost seventy years ago. My mother grew up here, making coffee and cannoli alongside her parents. It was her sanctuary when her marriage fell apart and she needed a way to support herself and her young daughter. Now it's my sanctuary.

Like a lot of people who grew up in this town, I left for college and didn't come back. Not for a long time, anyway. I went to school in Boston and got a job working in public relations in New York. The hours were long, and the competition was fierce. I was happy at first, but it wore on me over time. I managed to carve out a personal life in what little free time I had, dating then getting engaged to a guy I thought was the man of my dreams. *Thought* being the key word.

He broke my heart, removing his things from the apartment we shared, the apartment I couldn't afford on my own, and running off with a girl from his office. I'd cried for days, pulling it together just enough to go to work, then coming home and crying some more while I packed up my own things so I could move into a new apartment when I found one. I spent hours on the phone with my mother.

"Francesca, come *home*," she'd say and tell me how the café had saved her when she'd been in my position so many years ago.

But I didn't listen. I stayed in New York to fight for what was left of my life.

And then my mother died.

I quit my job, broke my lease, and moved back to the Massachusetts coast. I buried my mother, moved into the house where my grandparents had raised my mother and me, and stepped back behind the counter at Antonia's Italian Café as if I had never left.

So there I was, two weeks later, back in the place where I had spent the better part of my thirty-four years, creating intricate designs in the artisan cappuccinos our café had always specialized in. It wasn't a terribly big place, just ten two-top tables along the exposed brick walls and ten oversized armchairs arranged in groups and nestled into cozy corners. All the tables and chairs were mismatched because my grandparents hadn't been able to afford coordinating furniture when they first opened the café. My grandmother had frequented estate sales and auctions, picking up one table or chair at a time until the space was full. They're pretty old, but my mother had maintained them by reupholstering any that needed rejuvenating. It was an eclectic mix, but it gave off a surprisingly cozy, homey feel.

Compared to Antonia's, the stylish coffee shops I'd visited in New York seemed sterile and severe. And of course the burnt dirt water they served and tried to call coffee was even worse than it sounded when compared to the drinks my family proudly made. Don't get me wrong, plenty of little family-owned diners in New York can make a great cup of coffee, but when you got into the espresso drinks the fancier places tried to serve, that was when you got bilge water. My grandparents would roll over in their graves if I ever even thought about bringing in pre-roasted beans, let alone pre-ground ones. That was part of the magic of Antonia's—we did every-thing, from start to finish. Our milk even came from local dairy farms.

Our coffee wasn't the only thing that kept people coming in. We served some food, mostly desserts and sandwiches, but it was really the way we catered to our customers that kept us busy. The café was popular with book clubs, partly because of our coffee, partly because of the comfortable chairs, and partly because we let them drag the tables and chairs around however they wanted. As long as they bought something and didn't violate fire code, we were more than happy to accommodate them. My mother had even encouraged them to place their orders ahead of time so we could have everything ready when they came in. Even without the book clubs, we stayed busy, especially during the summer tourist season.

I finished the second drink and passed them to Sammy to deliver to the customers' table. Finally, I got a moment to catch my breath.

As Mrs. D'Angelo had said, Sammy really had been a lifesaver since my arrival back in Cape Bay. She had worked alongside my mother for years—since Sammy was in high school actually—and she knew the café like the back of her hand. In my first few days back, she had helped me learn the new cash register, taught me the stocking and ordering procedures, and generally followed me to make sure I didn't make a mess of things. Now I relied on her the same way my mother had, working side-by-side to keep the café humming along smoothly. We had some part-time help from a couple of teenagers out of school for summer vacation, but the two of us, plus our two bakers, carried the bulk of the load, and it was going great. Except, of course, when someone came along and started talking about my mother. At those times, the reality and freshness of her death hit me, and focusing on my work became infinitely harder.

"I'm going to take a break," I told Sammy as she came back around the corner.

She looked at me, her eyebrows drawn together. "Are you okay?"

I usually took a lunch break and not much else, so this was unusual. "Yeah, I just need to get some air."

I pulled off the apron I wore to protect my sleek black clothing, which was the uniform of the New York City public relations world, as I stepped into the back-room. Outside, I took a deep breath. We were in town, but the tang of the salt air was still strong. It felt good in my lungs. It was the smell of my home and childhood. It made me happy to be back and nostalgic for what I had lost. I closed my eyes and leaned back against the café's brick wall. I must have been out there longer than I thought, because the next thing I knew, Sammy poked her head out the door.

"Francesca?" she called quietly.

"Hmm?" I murmured, my eyes still closed.

"Why don't you get out of here? You've been working nonstop since you got back. You deserve some time off."

I'd been in the café from open to close since the day after my mother's funeral, but that was the way I wanted it. If I stayed busy enough, I couldn't think. "I can't. I can't leave you here alone."

"I won't be alone. I already called Becky to come in. You need the rest."

I opened my eyes and looked at her. She had one hand on her hip and was holding the door open with the other. Wisps of her long blond hair had escaped the low ponytail she always wore at work and were swirling around her head in the breeze. Despite the golden halo effect her hair was giving her, she had a stern expression to go with her assertive posture. She didn't look as if she would take no for an answer. I sighed and looked at my watch. Three hours to close. Going home now wouldn't be the end of the world. I could make myself some dinner, take a long bath, maybe go to bed a little early. It would be a treat.

"Are you sure?" I asked.

"Yup. In fact"—she leaned to look around me at the parking lot on my other side—"I think I see Becky pulling up now." She waved at me. "So go on, get out of here."

I had to admit she was right. I sighed and pushed myself off the building. "Okay, you got me. I'll go home. Let me just get my purse."

Sammy patted my back as I walked past her. "You'll thank me for it tomorrow."

I fished my Italian leather purse out of the cabinet

where we kept our personal belongings while we're working and slid it onto my shoulder. My mother and grandmother had never cared much for fashion or labels, but they had instilled a firm belief in Italian leather in me. Shoes, bags, belts, wallets—all leather goods had to be imported from Italy. Nothing else was good enough. Even after all my years in New York, surrounded by devotees of French red-soled Louboutins, I still swore by Ferragamo, Prada, Gucci, and Bottega Veneta.

I straightened a few boxes of supplies that weren't lined up properly on their shelves against the wall. Then I noticed that a couple of them were empty enough that their contents could be combined and the boxes thrown away, so I started cleaning them out.

"What are you doing?" Sammy asked.

"I'm just straightening things up a little bit. I don't want to leave everything all over the place for you to clean up tonight." I knew I was making excuses not to go home.

"Things are not a mess. Those boxes are fine the way they are, and they're certainly not something you need to take care of now!" Sammy took me by the shoulders and turned me toward the door that Becky was walking through.

"Hi, Francesca!" Becky said as she walked in.

"Hi—" I started.

"Francesca was just leaving," Sammy said, cutting

me off. She guided me to the door and walked me outside. "Go! We have everything under control. The café will still be here for you to fuss over in the morning." She released my shoulders, walked back to the door, and kicked out the doorstop. "Bye now!" She waved.

The door thunked closed. I sighed, staring at it for a minute. There was no way Sammy would let me back in today, even if I did own the place. And a long, hot bath really did sound pretty good. I adjusted my purse on my shoulder and started on what I thought would be an uneventful walk home.

Chapter 2

IT WASN'T A LONG WALK—JUST a few blocks. My grandmother had never learned to drive, so when she and my grandfather decided their family needed more space than was available in the apartment above the café, they needed to look close by. The house they found was a Cape Cod that was old even when they bought it. It was nestled among other Cape Cods on a street two blocks over and perpendicular to Main Street, where the café was. The previous owners had adapted the house so that it had one downstairs bedroom and two upstairs bedrooms—one for the boys and one for the girls, my grandparents thought. But no children came along, besides my mother, and the third bedroom stayed empty until I moved into it as a child.

I decided to take a shortcut across a few backyards,

the same shortcut I used to take when I was a kid running back and forth between the house and the café ten times a day. I hadn't taken it since I'd been back because I'd still been wearing my New York stilettos, which weren't exactly suited to grassy wandering, but my aching feet had finally convinced me to dig some of my mother's loafers out of her closet. Fortunately, her obsession with Italian leather, combined with regular visits to Cape Bay's cobbler, meant that her nearly twenty-year-old shoes were still in great shape and comfortable to boot.

I turned off the sidewalk and stepped onto the grass. The shade from the trees was a nice break from the summer heat. With how humid Massachusetts summers could get, I had learned long ago to keep my thick mass of hair in a chignon pretty much the entire season. As a teenager, I had argued with my mother that black hair made me hotter in the summer sun and I would be so much cooler if I could just dye it blond. She refused, insisting that it would turn orange. I didn't believe her and bleached it at a friend's house one summer day when I was avoiding working at the café. It turned orange. Very, very orange. After that, I listened to my mother's beauty advice.

I trekked across a few yards, reminiscing about all my childhood adventures. As I got close to my house, I saw Mr. Cardosi, the town barber, sitting on his back porch.

He had lived two doors down from my grandparents my entire life, and I had played and gone to school with his son Matteo, or Matty as I had always called him. It was unusual for Mr. Cardosi to be home at that time of day, but it was unusual for me to be home at that time of day too.

"Hello, Mr. Cardosi!" I called, waving.

Mr. Cardosi didn't move. I thought that was strange, but when he sat out back, he usually had his radio turned to the Red Sox game, so maybe he just couldn't hear me. I decided to wait until I was a little closer to call out again.

I waved again as I got into his backyard. "Hel—"

I stopped, noticing that Mr. Cardosi's chin was resting on his chest. Was he sleeping? I cut across his yard to check on him. This had always been the kind of neighborhood where everybody watched out for everybody else. I appreciated it now, but I'd hated it when I was a kid and Matty and I were running around, causing trouble. I'd never once made it home before the news of whatever mischief we'd gotten ourselves into had reached my grandmother's ears.

I walked across the lawn, wondering if I should call out to Mr. Cardosi so as not to startle him or stay quiet to let him keep sleeping. Not wanting to scare the old man and give him a heart attack, I called out again. "Mr. Cardosi! Mr. Cardosi!"

He didn't move. I slowed down as I got to the porch.

"Mr. Cardosi?" I said more quietly. Still nothing. I nudged his shoulder. "Mr. Cardosi?"

He slumped farther over, and I got a sick feeling in the pit of my stomach. Mr. Cardosi wasn't asleep—he was *dead*. I backed away slowly, reaching for my phone in my purse so I could call for help.

I lurked at a distance while I waited for the police and ambulance to arrive. I knew I couldn't leave, and really, I didn't want to just abandon poor Mr. Cardosi, but I didn't want to hover too closely either. I didn't know how he'd died, but I knew the police would want to look around, and I didn't want to mess with things. Besides, being so close to a dead body was a little unsettling.

I wasn't too surprised that the police car arrived first —it's a small town, and the police station is just across the street from the café. The ambulances have to come all the way from the next town over. I heard the cruiser pull up, and I poked my head around the house and waved. The officer climbed out of the car and approached the house. He was a big, imposing man. Not overweight, just very tall and broad.

"You the one who requested police?" he called when he spotted me.

"Yup, that's me!" I yelled.

He strolled a little bit closer then motioned me

toward him. "How 'bout you come over this way for me?"

He sounded suspicious. His brow was furrowed as I walked toward him. He was clearly trying to figure out who I was and what I was doing there. While everyone pretty much knew everyone else in town during the off-season, the summer brought a lot of tourists, and the officer seemed to think I had wandered off the beach and into trouble. We recognized each other simultaneously.

"Mike!" I exclaimed.

"Francesca!" he said at the same time.

He held out his arms, and I hurried to give him a hug. Mike was another former classmate of mine. It wasn't really surprising to run into him, but it was pleasant all the same. I hadn't seen him since I'd gotten back.

He held me out at arm's length. "You look great!" Then a shadow passed over his face. I knew he'd remembered why I'd moved back. "I'm really sorry about your mom. She was such a great lady. Sandy and I would have come to the funeral, but we had booked a trip to Disney with the kids..." He seemed to realize how awkward it was to go from talking about my mother's death to his trip to Disney. He grimaced and looked at his shiny cop shoes.

"It's fine, Mike, really. You have your life to live."

Mike smiled, grateful for the out. "So I heard you're sticking around for a while?"

"That's the plan. I was kind of in a rut in New York, and I figured coming home would be a good change of pace."

"That's great! That's really great. We're happy to have you back in town." He chuckled. "I'm sure you'll see it hasn't really changed all that much over the years."

I laughed with him. "I've noticed! It's like stepping right back into high school! All the old neighbors are living in the same places—"

All of a sudden, I remembered the neighbor who had prompted the call that had brought Mike out here. The look on Mike's face told me he had just remembered too. He rubbed a hand back and forth across his high-and-tight hair.

"So, uh, you were concerned about Mr. Cardosi?" he asked.

I nodded. "Yeah, I was walking home, and I took the old shortcut through the back. When I was coming across the yard, I yelled to say hello, but he didn't move, so I went over to check on him, and, well…" I gestured toward the back of the house.

"He's around back?" Mike asked, starting in that direction.

"On the patio."

Mike took a wide path toward the back of the house,

I guessed so he could get a good look before he got close. When he got to where he could see Mr. Cardosi sitting in his lawn chair, he held a hand out to me, motioning for me to stop. He glanced back. "You check his pulse or anything?"

I shook my head. "No. I just nudged him, and he— he kind of slumped."

Mike nodded and continued across the back of the house toward Mr. Cardosi. He rested his right hand on his gun. A cop habit, I assumed.

"Mr. Cardosi?" he called softly. He took a couple of steps closer. "Mr. Cardosi?"

There was no movement from the lawn chair. Mike reached out a hand toward Mr. Cardosi's neck and held it there for a moment, checking his pulse. He withdrew his hand and pushed the button on the walkie-talkie on his shoulder.

He spoke quietly, but I could just hear, "You can let the ambulance know there's no rush. He's gone."

Hearing that, I realized I'd been holding out some hope that Mr. Cardosi really was just sleeping very soundly, or maybe even had passed out. Not something I'd normally wish for, but given the options, I would have preferred it.

Mike walked a wide circle around Mr. Cardosi's chair, leaning down to look from all angles. I wondered if that was standard procedure or if he'd seen something suspicious. I hadn't noticed anything, but I also hadn't lingered once I'd realized the situation. Mike walked back toward me with a grim expression. I felt tears unexpectedly fill my eyes. So much had happened in my life recently, and this was just one more thing on top of it all.

Mike must have noticed my expression because he put his hand awkwardly on my shoulder. "I'm sorry, Francesca. I know you knew him well growing up."

I sniffled. "It's not just that. Everything has changed so much lately…" I covered my face with my hands. "Sammy made me leave early today because she thought I needed a break and now—" I waved toward Mr. Cardosi.

Mike patted my shoulder. "It's a lot." He seemed very uncomfortable.

I took a couple of deep breaths then shook my shoulders. It was what I always did when I was trying to cheer myself up—literally shake the bad feelings off me. I wiped my eyes and forced a smile. "Whew—sorry about that. Just got a little overwhelmed there for a minute."

"That's all right." He seemed happier now that I had regained my composure. "Now, uh, I know you told me you were taking a shortcut home. Is this a way you come often?"

I shrugged. "Kind of. I mean, it's the way I always walked to and from the café growing up, but I think I've only done it once or twice since I got back in town."

"Uh-huh." Mike reached in his breast pocket and pulled out a small notebook with a pencil through the spiral at the top. "And is this the time of day you usually come home?"

"No," I said. He must not have heard me say that Sammy had sent me home early. "Usually I stay until close at eight, but today—" I thought about telling him about Mrs. D'Angelo's visit but decided against it. "Today, Sammy thought I should leave early and get some rest." I paused while he scribbled, then I thought of something. "Wait, why? Did you see something? You don't think someone—" Crime was virtually nonexistent in Cape Bay, and murder was practically unheard of. Surely he didn't think someone had killed Mr. Cardosi!

Mike looked up from his notebook and smiled at me. "Just trying to make sure I have all the details right for my report." He resumed writing, looking at me again when he was finished. "Now did you see anybody nearby? Anybody coming or going? Anything suspicious?"

I shook my head. "There were a couple of tourists out on the street when I left the café, but once I got on the side streets, I didn't see anyone."

Mike grunted and wrote something else. "Sammy can confirm what time you left the café?"

"Yes, and Becky had just gotten there. Mike, you're

not telling me something. You don't think I did some-thing to him, do you?"

Mike smiled at me again. It wasn't the friendly smile from when he first recognized me. It was more of a cop-placating-a-citizen smile. "No, I don't. I'm just estab-lishing a timeline so they know what they're working with when they do the autopsy." He waved toward Mr. Cardosi. "Case like this—no one around, no obvious cause of death—they always do an autopsy, just to figure out what happened."

I nodded. That sounded reasonable. Still, Mike's tone made me a little anxious, as if he wasn't quite telling me the whole truth.

"Helps the family rest a little easier too," he said.

The family! I remembered Matty. Poor Matty! His mother had died when we were kids, and now his dad was gone too. He'd be all alone in the world. *Like me.* I brushed the thought away. This wasn't about me, and I'd already had my breakdown for the day.

"Do you know if anyone's called Matty?" I asked.

"No, they haven't," he replied quickly. "Not unless one of the neighbors has seen my car out front and called him. Which is actually pretty likely."

It was. In a neighborhood where everybody watches out for everybody else, something like a police car parked out front was unusual enough to raise interest.

"Should I call him?" I reached for my phone that I'd

shoved in my pocket. "I'm not sure if I have his number. Do you have it?"

Mike held out a hand. "No, no. I'll call him in a bit. Just want to finish getting some things down." He looked at his notepad. "When you left for work this morning, did you take the shortcut or go another way?"

I sighed. All his questions about my day were a little frustrating. "I took the main road. Out the front, down York Street, and out onto Main."

"What time was that?"

"About seven."

"And did you see Mr. Cardosi?"

I sighed again. All I wanted to do was get out of there. "This morning? No, I didn't."

"When was the last time you saw him?"

"A couple days ago. Maybe more. He was out getting the paper when I was on my way to work."

"And you haven't been around the back since that time?"

"You don't think he's been dead that long, do you?" I exclaimed.

Mike smiled his vaguely patronizing smile again. "Just asking questions."

"A lot of them!"

He chuckled. "Just doing my job. Now, have you been around the back since then?"

"No, no, I haven't."

"Have you seen Matt since then?"

"Matty? No, I haven't seen him since the funeral."

Mike looked at me sympathetically then back at his notebook. He seemed to be reading over what he had written. "I think that's about it." He flipped it closed then flipped it back open almost immediately. "Almost forgot—what's your cell phone number? That'd be the best way to reach you, right?"

"My cell or the café," I said before rattling off both numbers.

He jotted them down and flipped the notebook closed again, then he slid it back into his breast pocket. "Thanks for your help, Francesca." He looked toward the street. "Ambulance is sure taking its time, isn't it?"

It did seem as if it had been forever since I'd called. Just then, we saw the ambulance coming down the street, and at the same time, from the other direction, a car pulled up to the curb. The driver hesitated a moment then opened the door. Flying toward us with a panicked look on his face was Matty Cardosi.

Chapter 3

"MATTY!" I shouted, stepping toward him.

He didn't even hesitate, just kept running toward where we were standing at the back of the house.

Mike, in full cop mode, walked forward to intercept him. "Matt!" He caught Matty as he tried to run by and held him in place.

"What's going on? Where's my dad? Let me go! Tell me what's going on!" Matty fought against Mike's grip, but Mike held on.

"Matt, Matt, you gotta calm down, man," Mike said as he struggled to keep Matty from running past him.

Matty made a few more attempts to escape before he gave up. "Okay, okay." He raised his hands in surrender, and Mike let him go slowly. Matty ran a hand through his hair. "What's going on? Where's my dad?"

I didn't know whether to reach out and comfort Matty from the pain I knew was coming or keep my distance. I ended up stepping closer so that I was barely an arm's length away, close enough to reach out and touch him but far enough away that I wasn't crowding them. It had been less than a month since I'd gotten the news about my mother that Matty was about to get about his dad, and I knew how much it hurt.

Mike took a deep breath. "Matt, I'm really sorry to have to tell you this—"

Matty stepped back, shaking his head rapidly. "No, no, no, no."

Mike stepped toward him and rested a hand on Matty's shoulder. "Matt, your dad passed away."

"But—he can't—" Matty glanced at me.

My eyes filled with tears I struggled to keep from pouring down my face.

"No, no, no," he repeated and ran around Mike.

Mike caught him as Matty got around the corner of the house to where he could see his dad slumped in his chair on the patio.

"Dad," Matty cried out as he collapsed to his knees.

Mike grasped Matty's shoulder. "You can't go over there, Matt. We have to process the scene."

"'Process the scene'?" Matty exclaimed. "What do you mean, 'process the scene'? Did someone kill my dad?" He looked frantically toward his dad's body as if he were searching for blood or bullet holes or some other sign of foul play.

"We don't know," Mike said. "In cases of unexpected deaths, we need to make sure we document everything just in case."

Matty sat back on his heels. Mike looked at me and nodded toward Matty. I knelt beside Matty and took his hand.

"They're just covering their bases, Matty," I said quietly.

Matty looked at me as if he were just noticing that I was there. "Franny," he said quietly.

I smiled at him sadly. I hadn't heard anybody call me "Franny" in years. We heard motion behind us and turned to see the paramedics we'd forgotten about wheeling a stretcher across the lawn.

"Uh, Francesca, how about you take Matt inside?" Mike suggested.

I looked at Matty, and he nodded. We both stood, our knees wet from the damp grass. Still holding hands, united in our orphan sorrow, we started toward the front of the house.

"Try not to touch anything!" Mike called after us.

I glanced back and nodded as Matty's hand tightened on mine. The added reminder that someone may have killed his dad pained him.

Mike said to the paramedics as we passed them, "Let

me get my camera out of my car, then you can take him."

Matty and I walked to the front door. I reached for the knob, but Matty shook his head.

"He always keeps it locked," he said, reaching in his pocket for his keys.

But my hand was already turning the knob. I looked at Matty and saw him crumple.

"I'll make sure to tell Mike," I said. I knew we both hoped that his dad had just forgotten to lock it this once. As painful as my mother's death was for me, I couldn't imagine how much worse it would be if someone had taken her from me deliberately.

I glanced around as we stepped inside the house. Nothing looked disturbed or out of place. Everything was as quiet and in its place as if Mr. Cardosi had just stepped out to run to the store. Matty and I sat on the sofa in the front room, where we'd sat many times to watch TV in the afternoons. His house was a mirror image of my own, with the master bedroom on the right of the entrance instead of the left. Unless they'd been remodeled, Capes were all pretty much the same.

We were quiet, neither of us feeling the need to put our pain into words. That was all I had wanted in my first days back in town—to sit quietly and think about my mother. I stole a few glances at Matty. I'd only seen him briefly on the day I got back then again at my mother's funeral. I wasn't in much of a state of mind to pay attention to how he looked either time. I could see that, despite the tension and anguish in his face, he had been aging well. He had grown his thick, dark hair longer than he wore it in high school, but it was still a preppy, business-like length. He still had the same warm brown eyes. Back in school, those eyes could make me melt. We'd never dated, but that hadn't stopped us from flirting, and he'd been an expert at using those big brown eyes for that.

I didn't know how long we sat there. After my mother died, I'd felt as though I'd barely sat down on the train in New York when we arrived in Boston, so we could have been on that couch for five minutes or two hours. Time passed differently when your life was falling apart. There was a quiet knock on the door before it opened. I popped up off the couch, ready to fend off any prying neighbors, but it was just Mike. I sat back down next to Matty, who was staring off into space.

"Just going to take a few pictures," Mike said, nodding at us.

I nodded back as Matty continued staring.

Mike stepped into the master bedroom, and I saw the flash from his camera as he moved around the room, taking pictures. He went up the stairs next, and I heard his heavy shoes moving around the floor above us. Matty glanced at the ceiling then looked back at the spot on the carpet he seemed focused on. I leaned back on the couch and crossed then uncrossed my legs.

Mike came down the stairs a few minutes later and nodded at us as he passed through the living room to the back rooms of the house. I heard the click of the camera and saw the flash as he took more pictures. He seemed to be spending more time in the kitchen than he had in the other rooms. Finally, he came back into the living room and took a couple of pictures before sitting on a chair across from us. Matty didn't look at him until Mike cleared his throat.

"Did you find anything?" Matty asked, his voice hoarse.

"There were no visible marks on the body," Mike said professionally.

I cringed at his reference to "the body." That body had been Matty's dad just hours earlier. At least I hoped it had only been hours.

"They'll want to do an autopsy. Standard procedure to determine cause of death."

Matty nodded.

"Nothing appears disturbed in the house," Mike said.

"Can you tell me if your dad drank coffee throughout the day or just in the morning?"

"He makes a pot in the morning," Matty said, forgetting to use the past tense. "He drinks most of it before he goes into the shop then takes a travel cup with the last of it." Matty wrinkled his forehead, looking more alert. "Did Dad make it into the shop this morning?"

Mike shook his head. "I don't know. We'll check on it. Would you normally hear if he didn't go in?"

Matty sank back on the couch, shrugging. "Who knows? Dad would get in a mood sometimes and just decide he wasn't opening the shop that day. I'd drive by and see it closed and freak out, but when I'd call to check on him, he'd say he just didn't feel like cutting hair that day." He shrugged again. "Who knows? You know how Dad could be."

Mike nodded as he scribbled in his notebook. I wasn't sure what recent events Matty was referring to, but I remembered that Mr. Cardosi could fly off the handle at perceived slights. I remembered one time when the paper boy had delivered the Boston paper but not the local one and Mr. Cardosi went on a tirade. He had been certain the paper boy had done it deliberately, that the editor of the local paper had told him not to deliver it, and that there must be something negative about Mr. Cardosi in that day's paper. My grandfather had taken him our copy of the paper to show him that there was nothing about Mr. Cardosi in it at all, but Mr. Cardosi just accused him of being a part of the plot against him. He'd looked suspiciously at my grandfather and the paper boy for months after that.

"Do you know if there was anyone who had a grudge against your dad? Who might want to hurt him?" Mike asked.

Matty scoffed. "My dad's enemies are more in his imagination than in real life."

"Any close friends? Girlfriends? Anyone your dad might have been close to? We probably won't need to talk to them, but it's good to go ahead and get it in the notes."

Matty shook his head. "No, I mean, there're the guys at the barbershop—the employees and the regulars—but I don't think he really socialized with anyone outside of work."

Mike nodded and scribbled. "When was the last time you talked to your dad?" He was starting in with the same questions he'd asked me.

Matty visibly crumpled. "A couple of days ago. I've been so busy. God, I wish I'd called him. I just—I just had no idea it was the last time I'd talk to him."

"Did you see him that day or just talk on the phone?"

"The phone. I haven't seen him since last weekend." Matty bent forward and put his head in his hands. "If only I'd known it was the last time. I would have hugged him, told him I loved him."

"Were you and your dad close?"

"As close as he was to anyone. He's not a real

sociable guy. *Wasn't.*" Matty caught himself referring to his dad as if he were still alive. "He *wasn't* a real sociable guy." As if using the past tense hurt him all over again, Matty made a choking sound and covered his face with his hands.

I rubbed Matty's shoulder. I suddenly realized how lucky I was that I'd spent the hours after I found out my mother was dead on a train instead of being questioned by the police.

"I'm sorry, Matt." Mike looked over the notes he'd been scribbling as he talked to Matty. "Just a couple more questions. Did your dad have a will?"

"Yeah, I think so. It'd be in the safe in his closet."

Mike looked up with his eyebrows raised. "There's a safe in the closet?"

"Yeah," Matty said. "You didn't see it?"

"I just took pictures of what was visible. I didn't open the closet." Matty started to stand, but Mike raised his hand for him to stop. "Whatever's there or not there isn't going to change while we're sitting here. Let's wrap this up, and then we'll go look."

Matty sank back onto the couch.

"What about life insurance?" Mike asked.

"Yes," Matty said. "He got it after my mom died, so I'd have something if anything happened to him. The paperwork should be in the safe too."

"You're the sole beneficiary of both of those?"

"Yeah." Silence fell for a few seconds, then Matty snapped his head up to look at Mike. "Wait, you don't think—"

Mike held up his hand again. "No! No, no, no! Just making sure I have all the information. Like I said, we probably won't need to use any of this, but it's better to go ahead and get it all now."

Matty nodded.

Mike looked between his notebook and us several times then made a face and took a breath. "So you, uh, you showed up here at the same time as the ambulance, Matt."

I looked at Mike sharply. Despite his denial seconds before, the way he was talking to Matty made me suspicious.

Matty either didn't notice or ignored it, nodding in response. "Yeah, I did."

"Were you just driving by?"

"No, Mrs. Howard across the street called me. She saw Franny hanging around, and I guess she called here and no one answered, so she called me. She saw you pull up while we were on the phone and told me to hurry."

"And where were you when you got the call?"

"I was in the car, on my way home from work."

"So you just drove over here instead," Mike said.

"Yeah."

Mike nodded and scribbled some more in his notebook. "I think that about wraps it up for me. What's the best number to reach you?"

Matty gave him his cell phone number.

Mike jotted it down then looked at us. "Okay, want to show me the safe?"

Matty nodded and pulled himself up off the couch. Mike followed him across the room, and I brought up the rear. I lingered in the doorway as Matty walked to his dad's closet and opened it. From where I stood, I could see that the safe was still closed. Mike pulled his camera back out and took a couple of pictures.

"Can you open it up for me?" Mike asked.

Matty knelt in front of the safe. He spun the dial a few times then popped it open. Mike leaned in to take a few more pictures, then he nodded at Matty. Matty reached in and pulled out a stack of papers.

"Everything there that you expect?" Mike asked.

Matty sat on the foot of the bed and flipped through the papers. "Yeah, I think so. I don't really know everything he kept in here, but here's the will—" He pulled out a stapled bundle of papers and set it next to him on the bed. "And here's the life insurance paperwork." He laid the single sheet of paper on top of the will. "Do you need to look through these?" He held the other papers out to Mike.

"No, just wanted to make sure nothing was missing." Mike glanced around the room. "Speaking of missing, do you see anything that's not where it's supposed to be?"

Matty looked around. "No, I don't think so."

"Okay, well, if you notice anything, just give me a call, okay?" Mike reached into his breast pocket and pulled out a business card that he handed to Matty. "One for you, too." Mike passed another one to me.

I looked it over then put it in my pocket with my phone. I saw Matty put his on top of his dad's will and life insurance policy.

"Unless there's anything either of you want to ask me…" Mike looked between the two of us.

I shook my head.

"Matt?" Mike asked.

Matty looked up as though he'd gotten lost in thought. "What? No."

"All right then, I'll be on my way. If either of you think of anything else—" Mike was interrupted by a loud rap on the front door before it swung open.

One of the paramedics stuck his head in. "Hey, uh, Mike, we're about wrapped up out here. Does he want to—"

Mike nodded, understanding what he was being asked. He turned to look at Matty. "Matt, would you like to see the body before they take it away?"

I saw Matty's face go pale. He sat frozen for several seconds.

"There's nothing—no visible—" Mike stumbled over his words.

"Yes," Matty croaked, standing. "I'd like to see him."

The paramedic pushed the door farther open and stepped back outside. Mike went out first, then Matty, then me. The stretcher was on the front walk, a body bag containing Mr. Cardosi's ample form strapped on top of it. I almost bumped into Matty when he hesitated on the front step. The paramedics were standing at a respectful distance, and Mike stepped onto the grass so Matty would have room to walk by. Several of the busybodies who populated the neighborhood were gathered in front of Mrs. Howard's house across the street, gawking.

"You can do it, Matty," I whispered.

He glanced over his shoulder at me, nodded, and gave me the slightest of smiles. He stepped down the two front stairs and strode down the sidewalk to the stretcher. He stopped about a yard away, took a deep breath, and walked the remaining steps forward. I stayed at the bottom of the steps, not wanting to crowd Matty. He looked at his father's face, the only part of him not zipped up in the body bag, for a few minutes then stepped back and nodded to the paramedics. They walked forward, zipped the bag up the rest of the way, and wheeled Mr. Cardosi to the ambulance. They slid the stretcher into the ambulance, closed the doors, got in, and drove away as we all watched in silence.

Mike shuffled his feet as Matty stood perfectly still on the sidewalk. Mike glanced at me then at Matty.

I walked forward and put my hand on Matty's shoulder. "Come on. Let's go inside."

Chapter 4

BEFORE WE COULD EVEN TURN AROUND to go into the house, the neighborhood busybody contingent flocked across the street, past Mike on his way to his car, and surrounded Matty and me.

"Matteo, what happened?" "Was your dad sick, Matty?" "Francesca, dear, how did you find him? You were just walking home?" "What a fortunate coincidence, you finding him! He could have been out there God knows how long if you hadn't happened along!" "What an unfortunate coincidence, what with your mother just passing!" "If you need any help going through his things, Matteo, I'd be happy to help. You know, I've lived just down the street there since your parents first moved in, back before you were even born."

The women's voice overlapped and merged as they

went on and on in their chattering and so-called condolences that all too frequently sounded more like thinly veiled insults and criticisms.

"Such a tragedy, losing both your parents. And you so young yet!" "You're all alone in the world now! Neither of your parents will be there to see you get married when you finally find the right girl!" "Oh, your children won't have any grandparents!"

At that point, I grabbed Matty's arm and pulled him through the crowd toward the front door of Mr. Cardosi's house.

"Didn't Mike want us to look through the house?" I asked loudly.

"I can help you!" one of the women called.

"No, no, we have it!" We were almost at the door.

"I know where everything belongs! I spent quite a bit of time with Gino!"

Matty and I whirled around. Matty had specifically said that his dad didn't really socialize, so I wanted to see who was claiming to be his close friend. It was Mrs. Collins, a widow who lived across the street and two houses down, directly across the street from my house. She was rather well known for her, well, let's just call them "exaggerations." I narrowed my eyes at her, telegraphing a "back off" message. She stopped in her tracks at the edge of the group of women. Without taking my eyes off her, I pushed Matty toward the front door. I backed through it after him then slammed it and locked it for good measure.

"Thanks for that," Matty said as I stalked to the back door to lock that too.

Satisfied that we would have no surprise or accidental visitors, I walked back to Matty. "They should be ashamed of themselves."

I glanced around and noticed the living room curtains were open. I didn't put it past a single one of those women to walk through the flower beds and stare in, so I pulled the curtains closed, glaring through the window at the lingering crowd before I did. I walked through the first floor and closed the rest of the curtains before circling back to Matty, who was still lurking in the entryway.

"That should keep them at least from being full-on Peeping Toms," I said.

Matty nodded and shoved his hands in his pockets as he looked around. "He's really gone, huh?"

The aggression I had felt toward the meddling neighbors vanished, and I was filled again with sympathy for Matty. I rubbed his upper arm with my hand. "I'm so sorry."

He was quiet, staring at his shoes, then he looked at me. "So you found him?"

I swallowed hard and stepped back, shoving my hands deep in my pockets. "Yeah," I said as I nodded.

"Did he look—? How did he—?"

"I thought he was asleep," I said softly, understanding what Matty was asking.

"And you didn't see any—"

"No."

Matty nodded and looked at the ceiling with a sigh. "Thank you."

"For what?" I scoffed. I'd found his father's dead body and called the police. That was nothing special. In fact, I wouldn't have blamed Matty if he'd been angry with me.

"Finding him, calling the police, saving me from the biddy brigade out there," he listed.

"I didn't do anything special."

"Who knows how long he would have been back there if you hadn't walked by?"

I shrugged. "I'm sure it wouldn't have been long."

"Doesn't matter," Matty said. "Any time is too long."

I nodded sympathetically. My mother had collapsed in public and been whisked straight to the hospital. I couldn't imagine how awful it would be to know that your loved one had been lying somewhere, dead, for an extended period of time.

Matty took another deep breath. "Should we look around? See if there's anything missing or out of place that Mike didn't notice?"

"We?" I asked, surprised. We'd been close growing

up, but I had barely seen Matty since high school. Even though I'd been thrust back into his life, I didn't expect him to want to share such a personal moment with me.

He shrugged. "I don't really want to be alone. And you've just been through the same thing. You're not going to be all nosey and stuff, asking me a bunch of intrusive questions about how I *feel* about everything."

Well, that was true. The first days after I'd been home, several of my mother's "friends" had come by, including some of the women from Mrs. D'Angelo's Ladies Auxiliary. They supposedly wanted to express their condolences, but they'd seemed more interested in poking around the house, making snide comments and asking not-so-subtly about what had gone wrong with my fiancé. The people who came by and just wanted to express their condolences and sit quietly with me, drinking a cup of coffee while I stared into space, were few and far between, but they were much more what I needed as I struggled to process everything.

"Okay then," I said. "Where do you want to start?"

"Living room?" Matty suggested.

That seemed like as good a place as any, so we walked back to the room where we'd sat and waited for Mike what seemed like ages ago, even though it had only been an hour. We worked our way through the house, one room at a time. Matty looked around in each, surveying the contents. He told me stories about the objects in each room—souvenirs they'd picked up on vacation, the lamp he'd broken when he threw a baseball through the open window while playing catch with his dad, knickknacks that his grandparents had brought over from the old country, trinkets that had belonged to his mother. I already knew a lot of the stories from growing up with Matty, but I let him share them anyway. I knew how much he needed to talk about his dad without any pressure from me.

We finished without finding anything that looked unusual and returned to the living room.

"You want a cup of coffee?" Matty asked. "I know it's getting late, but I think my dad keeps some decaf. Although I feel a little inadequate making it for the coffee queen here."

I laughed a little. "Whatever you have will be fine." Yeah, I'd been around coffee my entire life and could tell a good cup from a bad cup by the look and the smell, but that didn't mean I didn't have manners. Besides, decaf or no, I knew I wouldn't be getting much sleep that night.

"All right," Matty said as we headed toward the kitchen. He reached to open the coffeepot to put in the filter and grounds but stopped suddenly.

"What is it?" I asked.

"I didn't notice before—the coffeepot's half full. It

looks like Dad was only on his first cup." He pulled out the coffeepot and held it up for me to see.

Sure enough, it was only partially empty. Matty paused, staring at the coffeepot. The visual evidence of his dad's interrupted morning must have brought his grief back to the forefront. Not that I could blame him. He looked at it for a few more seconds then poured the coffee down the sink. He rinsed out the pot and started a fresh batch.

We sat in silence at the kitchen table, each of us lost in our thoughts of our own parent's recent passing. With a lot of people, that kind of silence might have been awkward, but with Matty, it felt completely comfortable. When the coffee was ready, Matty poured us each a cup and brought them back to the table.

"Sorry, no fancy designs," he said with a sad smile.

"It tastes just as good without them," I said before taking a sip. It did not taste good. Clearly Mr. Cardosi hadn't spent any more on his coffee than he'd absolutely had to. It was so bad, I actually wondered if there might be something wrong with the coffeemaker. I set my cup on the table. I'd had a lot of bad coffee in my life, and swallowed some of them down just to be polite, but I wasn't sure I could manage it with this one.

Matty put his cup down at the same time as I did. We sat for a moment, each staring at our cups.

"We can just throw it out if you want," he said.

I couldn't stop the laugh from bursting through my lips. Clearly Matty thought the coffee was just as bad as I did. "That might be a good idea," I said.

Matty took my mug and his cup over to the sink. He poured them both out then grabbed the pot from the coffeemaker and poured that coffee down the drain as well. He rinsed them all out and left them in the sink. "Sorry about that."

"I don't think anything you did caused that," I replied, the bitter taste lingering in my mouth.

He smiled slightly as he stared out the kitchen window. After a few minutes, he took a deep breath, exhaled sharply, and turned to look at me. "I guess it's time to go home then."

"I guess so. Is there anything else I can do for you? Anything you need?"

"I don't know. I don't think so. Not now."

"Okay then," I said, getting up. I walked over to him and gave him a quick hug. "If you think of anything, let me know. You know where to find me."

"Thanks," he said.

"Seriously, Matty, I know I didn't want to ask anybody for anything those first few days, but I needed the help. There's a lot to take care of. Just ask."

He smiled sadly. "You know, you're the only person who still calls me Matty."

"You're the only person who still calls me Franny."

"What do people call you now, Franny?" he asked.

"Fran, Francesca." I shrugged. "Mostly Francesca in New York, mostly Fran here. Just depends on who's doing the calling."

"I see," he said.

"Everyone calls you Matt now, huh?"

"Yup... but you can still call me Matty if you want."

I smiled. "We'll see. We're not five years old anymore. But you're welcome to keep calling me Franny."

"Will do, *Franny*," he replied.

I chuckled softly. "I guess I'd better get going then."

"All right. I'll see you."

"See you."

Matty walked me to the door. I headed off to my house and my bed, which I knew I wouldn't be able to fall asleep in because of thoughts of my mother and Mr. Cardosi.

Chapter 5

I TRIED to help Matty as much as I could over the next few days. He took some time off work to deal with his dad's estate and funeral arrangements, and I cut back on my hours at the café. I still went in every day, just not for the full fourteen hours it was open. Since I'd just been through everything Matty was dealing with, I was able to suggest some things (go ahead and file for the life insurance so you can use the money for the funeral), warn him about others (the funeral home will charge you for those "refreshments" they so casually offer), and help him with the rest (how about the café provides the refreshments—my coffee will be better than the funeral home's any day).

It helped that Matty and I had been friends for most of our lives. I was able to pick out meaningful pictures of

Mr. Cardosi to display at the funeral home, particularly ones with Matty and the late Mrs. Cardosi or ones from special times they'd shared. I helped Matty go through some of his dad's things, even pulling out some mementos of Matty's mom that he'd never known existed.

As much as I wanted to help my friend in his time of need, part of the reason I felt so strongly that I needed to help Matty was because I'd been the one who found his dad's body. Sure, he had repeatedly expressed his gratitude to me for finding his dad and all, but that didn't make me feel much better about it. I felt somehow responsible for what had happened, so I wanted to do as much as I could to help out. I wouldn't say that I didn't enjoy spending so much time with Matty again though.

It took several days for the autopsy to be completed, and we obviously couldn't have the funeral until after it was done, so Mr. Cardosi wasn't buried until a week and a half after he'd died. I was glad for Matty when the medical examiner's office finally released the body. I knew it was wearing on Matty for things to take that long. I saw it in his eyes and the way he carried himself. He didn't magically stop being sad after the funeral, but at least he was finally able to get back to his normal routine and not spend all day, every day, thinking about his dad's death.

After we both went back to our jobs, we didn't see

each other as much. In fact, I'd only seen him once since the funeral, when he showed up in the café one day shortly after the lunch rush ended. We didn't offer a lot of food, just some pastries and sandwiches, but that didn't stop the tourists from flocking in to get something to take back to the beach.

Sammy, Becky, and I were all working. Becky was in the back washing coffee cups, Sammy was wiping down the counters, and I was making some fresh mozzarella-tomato-basil sandwiches to go in the refrigerator case. I heard the door jingle open but didn't look up from what I was doing, since Sammy was closer to the register.

Until I heard her whisper, "It's Matt!"

I looked over my shoulder. Sure enough, it was Matty. I was surprised to see him because, even though he lived in Cape Bay, he actually worked a couple of towns over. If we saw him at the café, it was usually first thing in the morning or just before close. I was surprised by how happy I was to see him. I'd enjoyed spending time with him, but I didn't realize how much I'd missed him until he walked in.

"Hello!" Sammy said in a singsong tone. "What can I get for you today?"

"I got it," I said, wiping my hands on my apron. "Can you finish up the sandwiches?"

"Sure thing," she replied, moving over to my station. "Nice to see you, Matt!"

Sammy's cheerfulness and friendliness were part of what made her such a great employee. We had customers who I swore came in just because they liked to talk to her. We also had customers who I thought came in just because Sammy wasn't bad to look at. She had a round cherub face to go with her blond angel hair and soft curves that I'd heard made men think about cuddling up with her on cold winter nights. But she, of course, had been seeing the same guy for almost ten years. He lived with his mother and said he couldn't possibly get married and leave her because it would break her heart. Why he wasn't as concerned about Sammy's heart, I didn't know. In any case, the men who came in to flirt with her didn't seem to bother Sammy.

I smiled at Matty. "Caffè mocha?" I confirmed, already starting the drink.

"Yeah," he answered simply.

I looked at him as I pulled the espresso. Something didn't seem right, and it wasn't that he was reaching for his wallet. "Put that away, Matty. It's on me."

He didn't argue, just shrugged and shoved his wallet back in his pocket. Something was definitely bothering him.

"Go ahead, sit down," I said. "I'll bring it over in just a minute."

Matty nodded and walked over to sit at a corner table. I made a second drink, that one for myself, while I worked on creating a sunrise in the foam of Matty's drink. It had been one of my favorite patterns in the weeks after my mother passed away. It reminded me that no matter how bad any given day was, there was always another day coming, and life went on. I finished it just in time to pour the milk on my own drink. Since it was just for me, I wasn't going to bother creating something terribly intricate, but sometimes I seemed physically incapable of not putting *some* kind of design in a latte. I poured in a quick rosetta.

I pulled off my apron and picked up the two cups and saucers to take over to Matty's table. "I'm going to take a quick break," I told Sammy as I walked past her.

"Sounds good!" she chirped.

I heard the smile in her voice. Since Mr. Cardosi's funeral, I'd actually cut back on my hours, and Sammy was happy about it. She'd been genuinely concerned about me working so much—that cheerfulness and friendliness wasn't just an act. As much as I hated to admit it, I was happier too now that I was working closer to forty hours each week instead of one hundred.

I set the cups on Matty's table, careful to make sure his was positioned properly. "Mind if I join you?"

"No, actually, that's why I'm here," he replied.

"We haven't seen each other much since the funeral."

"Yeah, I know, I've been catching up at work. They

didn't mind me being gone for two weeks, but that doesn't mean the paperwork didn't pile up my desk." Matty worked as a project manager at a telecom engineering company. He'd told me the engineers who worked under him could manage pretty well without him, but he still had to sign off on everything they did. If something on the project went wrong, he was the one who would get fired, not them.

"I can imagine." I knew how bad it used to get when I'd take just a couple of days off at my job in New York. I couldn't imagine how long it would take to get caught up after being out for two whole weeks.

Matty looked at the design in his coffee. "Sunrise?"

"Yup," I responded. "New beginnings, new life. It's always darkest before the sunrise—"

"It's always darkest before the dawn," Matty corrected.

"Same thing." I took a sip of my coffee. It was much better than that bitter brew we'd had the night Mr. Cardosi had died. Not that I was patting myself on the back—just about anything would have been better than that foul concoction.

"I almost hate to drink it," Matty said. "I don't want to mess it up."

"But the coffee's the best part!" I retorted. "It's the whole point! The cappuccino art is just there to enhance the experience. We eat—and drink—with our eyes first, you know."

My grandfather's motto had been: "Make your food delicious, and make it beautiful." He would never tolerate me serving a sloppy mess of food or drink to a customer, and he'd insisted I make it again and again until I got it right.

"You're the designer," Matty said as he raised the cup to his lips. His eyes rolled back a little as he tasted it. "God, this is amazing! You seriously make the best coffee I've ever tasted. I don't know how you do it."

"Amaro family secret." I smiled, taking another sip. We really did make some amazing coffee. Well, I guess *I* made amazing coffee, since I was the only Amaro left. "Here, have a cupcake."

I gave him one of the chocolate cupcakes from behind the counter. We didn't exclusively sell Italian drinks and desserts. After all, customers were crazy about cupcakes, and I made sure we stocked at least four flavors a day.

"This is heaven," Matty said. "I always get the chocolate when I come here. How did you know?"

"You can't go wrong with chocolate." I had one myself. They were dark chocolate, with the most delicious peanut butter filling that our bakers made to perfection.

We enjoyed our coffee and cupcakes for a few more

minutes before Matty pulled out a file folder. He drummed his fingers on it. "I guess I should tell you why I'm here."

"I thought it was for the pleasant company and the delicious coffee," I joked.

"I wish that's what it was. Mike called me this morning and asked me to come down to the police station. The medical examiner finished up the report on my dad's autopsy, and Mike wanted to give me the results." He was silent for what seemed like a very long time.

"And?" I asked, deciding that it was up to me to break the silence.

Matty pushed the folder toward me.

"What's this?" I asked.

"That's the autopsy report."

"You want me to read it?" I whispered.

He opened his mouth then closed it again and just nodded. From the look on his face, I wasn't sure he could have spoken if he'd wanted to.

My stomach clenched as I opened the folder. A picture of Mr. Cardosi was on the top, stapled to a report bearing the words "Autopsy Report: Office of the Medical Examiner of the Commonwealth of Mass-achusetts" across the top. I looked at Matty. His face was drawn. I resisted the urge to reach across the table and take the hand he rested there.

I looked back down and read the report. There was a lot of medical jargon and terminology I didn't really understand. It went through the physical examination and findings in detail, including specific information about Mr. Cardosi's health prior to his passing. I kept reading, absorbing what I could. No tumors, no significant narrowing of the arteries, no brain abnormalities, no blood clots, some mild arthritis. It appeared that for an older man, Mr. Cardosi had been in excellent health. Then I saw what must have caused that look on Matty's face.

Significant presence of potassium cyanide in blood, tissues, and digestive system... consistent with intentional poisoning... until further investigation can be completed, the medical examiner's office determines the cause of death to be homicide.

"Dear God," I whispered. I looked at it again, certain I had misunderstood, but I hadn't. It almost looked as if the words "cyanide," "poison," and "homicide" were in bigger, bolder print than the surrounding text, but when I looked closely, I could tell they weren't —it was just the horror of them that made them seem that way. "Poison?" I looked at Matty. "Poison?" I said louder, as the weight of it came down on me.

I must have said it louder than I thought because I heard a clatter from the backroom and saw the few lingering afternoon customers look at me.

I gave them all a smile and a little wave. "Sorry!" I

hoped they would all just think I was talking about Poison the band, not poison the killer. "Matty, what—? Who—?" I couldn't get words out of my mouth. I had so many questions. I couldn't comprehend what I was reading.

"I don't know," Matty said. "They don't know. Mike said they'll do an investigation, but—"

"But what?" I asked.

"But with the amount of cyanide in his system, death would have been nearly instantaneous."

I looked at Matty, trying to process what he was saying. "Do they think someone injected him? Like some lunatic ran up while he was sitting on the back patio and stabbed him with it?"

Matty shook his head. "He ingested it."

"What? Like a cyanide capsule? Like spies use to kill themselves if they're captured by the enemy?"

"No. More like a food… or a drink."

Then it dawned on me. *Ingested. Nearly instantaneous.* "The coffee!" I gasped.

Matty nodded, covering his face with his hands. I couldn't believe it. Someone had snuck cyanide into Mr. Cardosi's coffee to murder him. Then another thought occurred to me.

"The autopsy report said homicide."

Matty nodded.

"But they don't think he could have——" I wasn't sure how to even say the rest. "Done it to himself?"

Matty dragged his hands down his face. After a minute, he said, "No. I asked Mike the same thing. He said that since there was no note and no indication that he might have been considering it, and he still had most of a pot of coffee inside, they're going to investigate it as a murder. I mean, why would you make a whole pot of coffee if you just needed one cup to kill yourself, right?"

I nodded. It didn't make sense. Not unless you added the poison to the pot itself, thinking you might need more than one cup, but even then, why not just add more poison to the one cup? Then I had another terrible thought. "Matty?"

"Yeah, Franny?"

"What if the whole coffeepot was poisoned? We drank out of that coffee pot."

Matty held up a hand and shook his head. "I thought of that. Mike said pouring it out and rinsing it before we made another pot would probably have gotten rid of all the poison. And that we'd be long since dead if it didn't."

That was a relief. Although I felt bad being relieved about anything at a time like this.

Matty continued. "I'm going to meet Mike over at Dad's house later this afternoon so he can take the coffeepot into evidence. He said there's a good chance they won't find anything, especially because we used it afterward, but they'll give it a shot."

I took another sip of my coffee. "You don't think that's why the coffee tasted so bad, do you? Did Mike say what cyanide tastes like?"

"Bitter almonds, apparently. But I've had coffee at my dad's before. It was always pretty bad. I don't know if it was the coffeemaker or the kind he bought, but I don't think there was any way to redeem that stuff."

I nodded thoughtfully. The best technique can't save a bad brewer and bad beans. I glanced at the autopsy report again. It was so hard to believe. Even when Mike had been asking us a million questions and taking pictures of the house, I didn't ever really think something criminal had taken place. A heart attack or stroke just seemed like the most obvious culprits. And it had turned out to be a human culprit instead.

Matty looked at the wrought-iron clock on the wall. "I better get going if I'm going to be on time to meet Mike." He drained his coffee cup and set it back on the saucer. "Thanks for the coffee. Are you sure I can't pay you for it?"

"Absolutely not." I closed the folder and slid it back across the table to Matty. "Thank you for letting me know about the autopsy."

"I needed to talk to someone about it, and I knew you wouldn't say anything incredibly insensitive." He shook his head. "You wouldn't believe some of the stuff I've heard."

"Oh, I think I would. People have said some pretty awful stuff to me too. It's like they don't even think about what it sounds like to the person they're talking to."

Matty picked up the folder and tapped it on the table. "Well, I'm sure once word about this gets out, there'll be a whole new round of gossip."

"I'm sure there will." Cape Bay was a small town and news, especially sordid news, traveled fast in any small town.

Matty stood to leave. "Thanks again for the coffee."

"No problem," I replied, standing also. I picked up our empty cups to take into the back to be washed. "Let me know if you hear anything else."

"Will do. See you later."

I gestured good-bye with one of the cups as he left, then I went back to work behind the counter.

Chapter 6

I WORKED until close that night. I'd found that I preferred to come in around lunchtime and work through the afternoon. I'd always been a bit of a night owl, so even if I got off work in the early afternoon, I'd end up staying up way too late. Then I'd be dragging when I opened the café at six. Sammy was a morning person, though, so it worked out for her to handle the morning shift.

Right after Matty left, we got busy again as all the tourists came in off the beach and wanted to get something to eat or drink. One of the restaurants down the street had live music every night, so the evening crowd always had an atmosphere of gearing up for a party.

The customers kept my mind off Matty and the medical examiner's findings while I was at work, but once I got home and curled up on the couch with a book and a glass of red wine, my mind wandered back to our conversation. I was still in shock over what the autopsy report had said. The idea that someone had come into Mr. Cardosi's house and put cyanide in his coffee was just unfathomable. Who was it? Why would they do such a thing? It must have been someone Mr. Cardosi knew if he let them get that close to him. But Matty had said that his dad didn't have any real friends. On the other hand, Mrs. Collins had been pretty eager to get into the house. Maybe she wanted to see if she'd left any evidence behind? Maybe to dump and wash the contaminated coffee pot? It was a viable theory.

I stopped myself. It was not a viable theory. It was ridiculous. And besides, what business was it of mine? I was a former public relations manager turned café owner and artisan barista, not a detective. Sure, I'd read a mystery novel or two (or twenty), but it wasn't as though I was a professional or someone with any kind of background that would allow me to speculate on someone's motives. Besides, the police were investigating. I went back to reading my book.

On my second glass of wine, I started thinking that since I'd been the first one at the scene—I was thinking of it as "the scene" now—maybe I did have some qualification to do a little investigating. After all, I'd been the only one to see it as it originally was. I may have noticed something that no one else did. And the police didn't know about Mrs. Collins. They hadn't been there when the crowd spoke to Matty and me. Maybe I should just tell the police about it. But what if Mrs. Collins really was just a friend of Mr. Cardosi and had been making a genuine offer to help us? Or even just a meddling old woman? She didn't deserve to be investigated by the police for that. Maybe tomorrow before work I could just go over and have a neighborly little chat with her. I wondered if she was still awake.

I got up off the couch and crept across the living room to peep out the blinds. Mrs. Collins's house was dark. Of course it was. It was after ten, and all the old folks on our street went to bed by nine. I went back to the couch and curled back up with my book and my wine. I tried to think over what else I had seen that day that Mike might not have noticed. I remembered that the front door had been unlocked when Matty and I went in. I was supposed to tell Mike about it, but it had completely slipped my mind, and Matty's too, I guessed. That was another clue.

A clue. I scoffed at myself. Now I really was being ridiculous, thinking about clues and suspects. Even so, I got up and found a notepad by the phone to make some notes on. Notes of things I had to remember to mention to the police, I told myself, *not* notes about what investigating I was going to do. Although it wouldn't hurt to at least check a few things before I went to the police with them. I didn't want to bother Mike with a bunch of details that seemed relevant to me when he probably had much more important leads to chase.

I wrote down odd things I remembered—Mrs. Collins, the door—then I thought that it might be good for me to write down everything exactly as I remembered it before my memory faded. It had already been weeks since the murder, and even though I thought I remembered everything clearly, I'd probably forgotten more details than I realized. I thought I remembered something about that from my college psychology class —something about how memories fade and get altered. That was why I needed to write everything down *now*.

I flipped to a fresh page and wrote down absolutely everything I could remember about that day, starting from my walk home. I read something once about how you can remember more if you tie it to sense memories, so I wrote down the color of the sky, the temperature, how windy it was, what the grass had smelled like— every sight, sound, or smell I could remember. Then I thought about how Mike had asked about the last time I saw Mr. Cardosi, so I flipped to another page and wrote down everything I remembered about every encounter I'd had with him since I got back to town.

By the time I was finished, it was well after midnight and I was itching to talk to Matty to see if he remembered something that I'd forgotten. I could ask him more about some of what he'd said to Mike, specifically what he'd said about Mr. Cardosi's enemies being more in his head than in real life. Apparently at least one of those enemies was in real life. It was way too late to call, so I pulled out my cell phone and sent Matty a text asking if he wanted to meet for breakfast. Getting up that early would be rough, but I wanted to talk to Matty as soon as possible.

I went upstairs to my old childhood bedroom and got ready to go to sleep. I plugged my phone into the wall next to the bed and made sure the volume was turned all the way up. I wanted to make sure I heard it if Matty texted me back, so I put the phone right next to my head. I thought it would be impossible to fall asleep with all of the thoughts whirling through my head, but it seemed like only a few seconds later, Matty was texting me at six in the morning.

I jumped out of bed with more energy than I remembered having in the morning since high school and got dressed as quickly as I could. I took the long way to the café, out along the street instead of cutting through the neighbors' backyards. I hadn't taken the shortcut since the day Mr. Cardosi died, and I wasn't sure I'd be up to it again for a long time. Part of me thought I should always take it in case someone else was dead in their backyard, waiting to be discovered by a passerby, but the more logical part of me prevailed. Either that or I gave in to the fear that I actually would find another body. I guess it just depended on how I looked at it.

I got to the café before Matty, so I hurried in behind the counter to fix our drinks. Matty always—*always*, like, since high school—got a caffè mocha, so I didn't have to wait for him to arrive to find out what he wanted.

"Uh, Francesca?" Sammy asked as I grabbed cups and saucers.

"Yeah?"

"You know it's six thirty in the morning, right?"

"Oh, yeah, I know," I said.

"Are you feeling okay?"

"Yeah, why?"

Sammy just looked at me for a second. "Because it's six thirty in the morning and you're *here* and you're *perky*."

"Oh, I'm just meeting Matty for breakfast."

"Matt Cardosi?" Sammy asked.

"Yep." I had my milk steaming and was ready to pull the espresso.

"Didn't you have coffee with him yesterday afternoon? Francesca Amaro, do you have something to tell me?"

I wrinkled my forehead. What? How did she know about Matty's dad? Was it all over town already? Had we been talking that loudly yesterday? Then I noticed the look on her face and realized that wasn't what she'd meant at all. "Oh no, nothing like that. It's—it's actually something about his dad."

Before I could say anything else, Sammy leaned toward me. "Oh my gosh, have you heard? Karen Maynard, who works over at the police department, was in here when I opened up because she likes to get a cup of coffee before she goes and works out. She told me they think Mr. Cardosi was *murdered*!"

I was surprised. I had never known Sammy to be much of a gossip, but then again, we didn't really get much murder-level gossip in Cape Bay. The grapevine usually only discussed who took whose seat at a luncheon or who skipped the knitting club the night they were making sweaters for teddy bears to give to Sherpa children in Nepal.

"Oh, of course you know. You're good friends with Matt." Sammy stopped for a second. "He *did* tell you, right? I'm not breaking this news to you now, am I?"

"No, you're not," I said, perhaps a little curtly.

The bell on the door jingled before Sammy could say anything else. It was Matty.

"Good morning!" I called. "What do you want for breakfast? We have fruit bowls, parfaits, muffins, cupcakes... come look in the case and see what looks good." I poured the milk in Matty's coffee as I talked. I had decided on a butterfly to continue the theme of rebirth and renewal.

"You're going to let me pay today, right?" Matty said as he walked over. He looked handsome, dressed for work in gray pants and a crisp white dress shirt.

"Nope," I answered. "I asked you to meet me, so it's on me."

"You don't have to do that, Franny."

"Of course I do." I put his finished coffee aside and started working on mine.

"How are the snickerdoodle cupcakes?" Matty asked, inspecting the contents of the display case.

"You want a cupcake for breakfast?" I asked.

"Hey, you offered!"

"They're amazing!" Sammy interjected. "The cinnamon buttercream icing is to die for. Francesca made the cupcakes last night before she left, and you know how good her baking is."

"That I do," Matty replied as Sammy handed a wax paper-wrapped cupcake across the counter.

"Drinks are almost ready," I told him. "Make yourself comfortable, and I'll be right over."

Today, Matty chose a comfortable armchair in what my mother had called the "Chatty Cathy Corner." It was the corner with the most comfortable chairs where, during the school year, the stay-at-home moms would settle in for the better part of the school day. When I was growing up, Cathy Sampson had been one of the most dedicated sit-and-talkers, and so that section of the café was named. It didn't help that Cathy had been known to make snide comments about my mother being a single parent when she wasn't quite out of earshot. My mother would just smile sweetly through clenched teeth then go in the backroom and mutter to my grandmother about it.

I finished off my coffee, pouring a leaf into the foam. Another simple design but still beautiful. I carried our two cups of coffee over to the table between the chairs Matty had selected. His cupcake was sitting on the table, still wrapped up. I guessed he was waiting for me to get there with the coffee.

"What are you going to eat?" Matty asked.

"Oh, I completely forgot!" That happened sometimes when I was focused on coffee. I went back and grabbed a parfait out of the case and a spoon from the container on the counter. I made my way back over to the Chatty Cathy Corner and sat in one of the armchairs.

Matty unwrapped his cupcake and took a bite. "Oh, it's delicious, Franny!"

"Thank you." I smiled, taking a spoonful of my parfait. "How's the coffee?"

Matty looked at it. "I like the butterfly." He took a sip. "Excellent."

"Good. Sometimes I'm not so sure this early in the morning."

"I don't think you've made a bad cup of coffee in your life."

I thought for a moment. "No, I did once when I was nine."

Matty laughed and almost spit his coffee at me. "I'm not even sure that's true," he said when he'd recovered. We each ate a little bit more of our breakfast, then Matty leaned back in his chair. "So what's up? What did you want to talk about so badly that you texted me at one in the morning?"

I took a deep breath. "I was doing some thinking last night. About your dad. And how he died."

Matty nodded, looking as though he wasn't quite sure what to expect me to say next.

"And I want to ask you a few questions."

Chapter 7

"YOU WANT to ask me a few questions," Matty repeated. "About my dad?"

I swallowed hard. "Yeah, I mean, I was thinking last night—"

The look on Matty's face stopped me mid-sentence. His eyebrows were raised, and he was looking at me as if antlers were growing out of my head.

After several seconds of silence, Matty spoke. "You were thinking?"

"Um, yeah. It's just..." I took a deep breath. "Last night, I remembered that we never told Mike that the door was unlocked. And then there was the thing with Mrs. Collins..." I hesitated again.

Matty wasn't quite looking at me as though I was crazy anymore. That was a good thing.

"And I realized there might be more that we forgot to tell him. Or that we didn't realize at the time might be important, and now that we know he was—how he died —they might be important. And I just thought it might be good for us to go over things."

Matty just looked at me.

"You know, if you want to." I tried to read his expression, but I couldn't. I didn't know if he would be mad at me for wanting to investigate his dad's murder or interested in working with me. I suddenly felt that this may have been a very bad idea.

After what seemed like an eternity, Matty shrugged. "Can't hurt."

Relief flooded me, and I smiled. "Great!"

"So what did you want to know?"

"Well, I've already written down everything I remember from that day. I know Mike asked you this that day, but what I really want to know is, now that we know your dad was—I mean, how he died—I was wondering if you can think of anyone who might have wanted to hurt your dad."

Matty sighed and adjusted his position in his chair. "You're looking for suspects, huh?"

"Uh, I, uh, um—"

A half smile crept across Matty's face. "You can say yes. I'm not the police. I don't care who finds out who murdered my dad, as long as someone does and the guy

—or girl, I guess—goes to jail. If you asking some questions gets things done faster, ask away."

I exhaled the breath I hadn't realized I was holding and smiled. "So can you think of anyone?"

Matty tipped his head toward the ceiling in thought. He let out a long breath. "Well, you know how Dad was."

I noticed that he'd gotten used to using the past tense in reference to his dad. It was an inevitable part of the grieving process, an important part actually, but in a way, it was still sad, as if he was finally giving up his dad.

"He thought everybody was out to get him." Matty laughed softly. "I guess there actually was at least one person who was." He shook his head. "Anyway, the conspiracies against him were *mostly* all in his head, but that didn't mean he didn't make enemies. It was almost a talent of his. I've never met anybody who could hold a grudge like him—and against so many people too. You know how there's that new haircut place down the street?" He pointed down Main Street toward the beach.

I nodded. It wasn't really new, but it was new to us. It had probably been there about ten years or so.

"Half the men in town go there now. Not because they prefer it to my dad's place but because he banned them. If somebody said they didn't like their haircut, banned. If they complained about having to wait, banned. If they didn't tip enough, banned. Half the time, they didn't even know until they showed up for their next haircut and he started waving his comb at them, telling them to get out and they weren't welcome. I think some of the guys don't even know *why* they were banned." He chuckled. "You know, I think one time he actually kicked out the wrong guy. It was the guy's brother or something. He kicked him out then realized later it was the wrong guy, but he'd never admit he was wrong about something like that, so both brothers were banned."

"That's pretty hardcore," I said.

"Yeah, Dad didn't back down." His face lit up, and he leaned across the table toward me. His eyes were sparkling. "One time, and I shouldn't laugh about this, but"—he laughed—"right in the middle of his haircut, some guy said something bad about the Sox—this was back before they'd won the World Series—he said something about they sucked and they'd never win and the Yankees were so much better. Dad just took his clippers and shaved right down the middle of the guy's head. I guess he wasn't looking in the mirror, so Dad kept going and shaved the guy's whole damn head before he realized what was going on. Oh my God, the guy stormed out, swearing at my dad. When Dad came home and told me about it, he didn't even care that the guy didn't pay—he was just so happy about shaving his head."

I giggled as I pictured the scene. My grandparents

had emphasized customer service, so I couldn't imagine treating a customer like that, but it was funny to think about. I was enjoying the story so much I almost forgot that I was supposed to be looking for suspects. "Was there anybody your dad had been feuding with recently?"

Matty leaned back again and crossed his arms thoughtfully. I took a drink of my coffee while I waited.

Finally he sighed. "He'd been complaining a lot about the cell phone store across the street from the shop. He thought the signs in the windows were tacky and the guy who runs it was a jerk. He really hated when they had somebody out front dancing around in one of those giant squishy cell phone costumes." Matty chuckled. "That drove him nuts. I remember him yelling that you didn't see him having someone dress up as a giant pair of scissors and dance around outside the barbershop. 'If you need someone to dance around dressed up like what you sell, you must not be a very good salesman!'"

"Do you know if they ever spoke? Or did your dad just complain about him?" I asked.

"Oh, they had words," Matty replied. "You think my dad would pass up that opportunity? I know Dad went in there at least once because he was telling me about the cheesy cell phone cases the guy was selling. It annoyed the hell out of Dad for some reason. I mean, he didn't need to go in there and look at them. He didn't even have a cell phone that one of those cases would fit. I guess the guy just got under his skin for some reason. Dad yelled at him plenty from across the street, and the guy yelled back. I've seen him out there a couple times. He doesn't seem like the nicest guy anyway. Kind of a jerk. Really arrogant. I'm not surprised Dad couldn't stand him."

"Was it personal?"

Matty scoffed. "Everything was personal with Dad."

"Do you think it was personal for the other guy?"

He shrugged. "Hard to know. I mean, like I said, he seems like a jerk, but I kind of think he was just playing with Dad, antagonizing him because it was fun for him to see Dad get so angry. I don't know if he actually disliked Dad though. Especially enough to kill him." He stopped and drummed his fingers on the table. "Of course, until we got that autopsy report, I didn't think anyone disliked Dad enough to kill him." He took a deep breath. "But can you imagine being mad enough about getting blacklisted from a barbershop to kill somebody? What else could it have been? It's not like it was random."

"Well, I guess Cell Phone Guy is a place to start," I said. "Your dad didn't keep a list of who he banned, did he?"

Matty laughed. "With my dad's memory for imaginary offenses, he didn't need to keep a list. I swear he could remember—in detail!—people who pissed him off before I was born. He once told me a story about a guy who cut him off in traffic in *1976*!"

"So I'll start with Cell Phone Guy and work my way back. Did he happen to give you the name and contact information of the guy from 1976?"

Matty grinned. "No, but if that guy came back to kill him after all these years, he even beats my dad at holding a grudge!"

I laughed with Matty. I certainly hoped for the sake of everyone involved that neither the police nor I had to go that far back through Mr. Cardosi's history to find out who killed him.

"So you have any more questions?" Matty asked after we stopped laughing.

I thought back over my notes from the night before. For some reason, I hadn't thought to bring my notepad with me. I'd either have to go home to get it before I went to talk to Cell Phone Guy or run by the drugstore and pick up a new one. A new one would probably be good. The one at home was a giant yellow legal pad— not very subtle for toting around town.

"I don't think so," I said, unable to think of anything else I needed to ask him.

He glanced at the clock on the wall and groaned.

"Looks like I have to get going anyway. Thank you for breakfast."

"No problem at all," I replied. "Someone's got to eat all this stuff."

"Oh, I don't think you'll have a problem with that," Matty said, patting his stomach. "You know your baking is out of this world."

I waved dismissively even though I knew my baking really was good. A little humility never hurt anyone. Matty stood to leave, and I was surprisingly sad that he had to go. I knew we couldn't linger here all day, but I enjoyed talking to him and wasn't quite ready for it to end. I stood and gave him a hug. A piece of his hair fell down over his forehead, and I reflexively pushed it back before realizing that that was something of an intimate gesture. Matty didn't seem to notice or mind though.

"Guess I need to see about getting that cut, huh?" he said, sounding a little sad. "I'll probably be joining everyone from my dad's blacklist down the street."

"The barbershop's still open though, isn't it?" I asked. Mr. Cardosi had two part-time barbers who worked with him, old-timers like him, and they'd been working since his death. As far as I knew, Matty didn't have any plans to close the shop, at least not until his dad's estate was fully settled and he knew what he was dealing with.

"Yeah, but Dad's the only one who ever cut my hair,

and I don't think I could stand going in there and having someone else do it. It'll be weird enough going to a stranger, but I think it'll be easier."

I nodded sympathetically. I knew from experience that every day brought new reminders of a parent's passing, and in the most unexpected of places.

"Anyway," Matty said, shaking his head and shaking that piece of hair back onto his forehead. This time he shoved it back. "Anyway, I've got to get going if I'm going to make it to work on time."

We said good-bye, and he left, waving at me before he let the door close behind him. I gathered up our dishes and took them to the backroom to be washed.

"You guys have a nice chat?" Sammy asked.

"Yup," I said, not really feeling the need to elaborate.

"He doing okay?"

I looked at her. She looked as though she was back to regular good-hearted, compassionate Sammy instead of the gossipy Sammy from earlier.

"Yeah, he's doing okay," I said.

"Are *you* okay?" she asked.

I was a little surprised, and it must have shown on my face.

"It's just—with you losing your mom so recently and all, and then finding Mr. Cardosi's body, and you being so close to Matt—" She shrugged. "I just wanted to make sure you're doing okay. I don't ask enough. Some days coffee is all we talk about."

I stared at her for a minute then pulled her into a hug. I was actually moved by her concern for me. "Thank you."

Sammy rubbed my back vigorously. "That's what friends are for."

Friends. Somehow I hadn't actually thought of Sammy as my friend until that moment. She was my mom's friend if anything, but mostly just a coworker. But Sammy really had been there for me as a friend since I'd been back in town. Everything she'd done to help me get back into the swing of things at the café and to get everything for my mother in order had been the actions of a friend, not just a coworker or an employee. I hugged her a little tighter before we let go.

"Well, thank you for being my friend," I said.

Her big blue eyes smiled back at me. "I'm happy to do it. So are you going back home or are you sticking around for a while? I'm sure you can find something to do around here, but Becky and I have everything nailed down on our own if you want to go home and get a nap or something. I know this is still early for you." She grinned. My night-owl habits were no secret to her.

I looked around the café, which was still mostly empty. I knew the drugstore wouldn't open for at least a half hour yet and the cell phone shop would be closed for an hour or two after that, so I had some time to kill. It didn't look as though my coffee-making skills would be in much demand for the next little while. I had plenty to think about after my late night and my talk with Matty, though, so it might be good for me to get out of my home-and-café rut and go do something else for a little while.

"You know what?" I said to Sammy with a gleam in my eye. "I think I might go for a little walk on the beach."

Sammy smiled. I knew she was happy to hear that I was doing something for myself for a change. "I think that's an excellent idea."

Chapter 8

THE MORNING WAS STILL COOL as I stepped out of the café and headed toward the beach. I breathed the salt air deep into my lungs. Even though I'd grown up there and preferred to take my vacations in the mountains, far away from the seaside, I understood why people came. There was something restorative about the sea breezes. Standing at the edge of the world, the water swirling around your feet and inching you deeper into the sand, while staring off at the expanse of the ocean is grounding. Some people said it made them feel small, but it didn't do that for me. It made me feel a part of something big.

I pulled the legs of my jeans up toward my knee. One advantage of the skin-tight cigarette-style jeans that were in style was that they had a lot of stretch. I kicked off my shoes and carried them as I crossed the dune and stepped onto the sand. I smiled at the feeling of fine grains between my toes. I couldn't believe I'd been home for so long and hadn't come down to the beach.

I walked to the water's edge and let the waves wash over my feet. They were cold, but I held my ground. The water was always cold there—not like some of the beaches farther south that my college friends had visited for spring break. Those had always felt like bathwater to me.

I pulled my feet out of the sand and walked a little farther so that the water came up around my calves when the waves came in. I was one of the few people out there at that in-between hour. The people who came out to watch the sunrise had gone home, and the families wanting to play on the beach wouldn't be out for a while yet. It was just me, some seashell searchers, and a few fishermen reclining on chairs, their lines cast deep into the water. It was the most peaceful I'd felt in a long time.

I stood in the water for a while until the incoming tide threatened to soak my pants. I walked back a few yards and sat in the sand. I could always brush off my pants later or, if that proved too difficult, walk home and change. I watched the ocean change colors as the sun inched up in the sky. When the first tourists appeared on the beach, the family patriarchs weighed down with beach chairs and coolers and umbrellas and sand toys and more beach paraphernalia that I didn't know how they managed to carry, I decided it was time to head back to town and my investigation.

I made my way up off the beach and rinsed my feet at the spigot on the other side of the dune. When I felt as though I was sufficiently de-beached, I pulled the legs of my jeans back down and slid my shoes back on my feet. I walked up to the drugstore to get a less obtrusive notebook. I found a little spiral-bound one like Mike's. I figured if it was small and portable enough for him, it was small and portable enough for me. I picked up a two-pack of pens too. Purchases in hand, I headed back out on the street. I checked the time. The cell phone shop was probably open, so I walked up in that direction. When I came to the block where the barbershop and the cell phone store were, I stopped and stood at the corner for a few minutes.

Matty and Mr. Cardosi were right—the signs on the front of the store were incredibly tacky. They were bright yellow and red, with giant print and lots of exclamation points. "Cell Phone Accessories!!!" they screamed. "Lowest prices in town!!!!!" "Styles You Can't Find Anywhere Else!!!!" It was pretty obnoxious.

I decided to pretend I was in the market for a new cell phone case. I figured it was better not to start asking questions right away. Let him think I was just some random person coming in to look around and chit-chat a bit.

I walked down the street slowly, looking in all the shops as though I was just out doing some window shopping. I got up to the barbershop then looked across the street at the cell phone store. I made a beeline across the street, thinking that if anyone saw me, they'd assume I just really wanted a new cell phone case. I pushed open the door to the sound of a loud, annoying electronic jangle. Rock music played over the speaker system. Not exactly what I thought of when I thought about customer-friendly music, but if it worked for them, who was I to judge?

"I'll be out in a sec!" a voice called from the back.

I looked around at the displays. I had to hand it to Mr. Cardosi—he hadn't been wrong. A lot of the cases were pretty tacky. They looked like something only a teenager would buy. And a teenager with poor taste at that.

"What's up?" the owner of the voice said as he emerged from the back.

What's up? Who greets a customer with "What's up?" But instead of asking him what was wrong with him, I turned toward him with a smile. "Hi!"

When he actually looked at me, he grinned. "Well, hello there! Haven't seen you around here before!"

I shrugged. "Kinda new in town." That wasn't really a lie. I had only come back recently.

"Oh well, let me be the first to welcome you," he said, strolling up to me.

"I'm not *that* new." If he thought I'd just gotten there that week, my plan wouldn't work.

"One of the first then." He smirked.

I put on the most genuine smile I could. "Well, thank you."

He stepped around me and leaned against the display so he was looking at me straight on. He gave off a major sleazy salesman vibe while at the same time being completely unprofessional. His blond hair was slicked back with way more gel than was necessary, and he had a permanent smirk. His teeth were way too white in his darkly tanned face, and his clothes screamed former prep school boy.

"So where'd you move here from..." He implicitly invited me to give him my name.

"Francesca. And New York. I moved here from New York." I extended my hand to shake.

"Well, hello, *Francesca*," he said, taking my hand. His hand was clammy, and he held on much longer than he needed to.

After what I felt was a sufficiently polite amount of time, I withdrew my hand and tried to subtly wipe his sweat off on my jeans.

"I'm Chris. Chris Tompson. New York, eh?" he went on. "What brought you to sleepy Cape Bay from the big city?"

I tried to think fast. If I didn't tell him I ran Antonia's and he found out later, he'd know I'd been playing him. But if I told him, he might figure out that I wasn't all that new in town. Best to just sidestep the issue and hope it didn't come back to bite me. Once I got the information I needed, it wouldn't much matter if he knew I'd stretched the truth.

"Slower pace of life." I smiled. "You know, New York is so busy and hectic. I just wanted to be able to kick back and relax a little. Not stress so much. You hear so many stories about people who work hard their whole lives and by the time they finally get to retire, they're too old to appreciate it. So I thought I'd go ahead and enjoy the good life while I could!" That might have been a longer speech than I really needed to make, but my new buddy Chris didn't seem to notice.

"Well, we're definitely glad to have you. Are you liking it so far?"

"Yeah!" I nodded. "It's really cute here!"

"Great! That's great! How's your cell phone working here? You know, different phones work differently in different areas. A lot of people think they need a new carrier when they go to a new area, but sometimes all it takes is a new phone. Then you don't have to worry about a new billing system or anything. I have some right over here if you want to take a look. I sell phones for all the major carriers, and I can get you set up right here, right now if you want."

He led me over to the display case under the register. He had about three mid-range phones for each carrier, and not even the phone most people would actually want.

"I don't know," I said reluctantly. "My phone works pretty well. I think I just want a new case for it." I pulled my phone out of my pocket. It had an understated black case that blended in with the phone. It suited me and my style, but for the sake of my investigation, I would get one of the monstrosities Chris was peddling.

He took the phone from my hand and turned it back and forth. He looked almost as disgusted by my black case as I was by his multi-colored ones. "A case like this does *not* suit a pretty girl like you. Let me show you some that you'll like better."

That I'll like better? I scoffed to myself. *Because I didn't pick that one out in the first place or anything.* But I smiled. "Sure!"

He led me to a wall full of hot pink cell phone cases decorated with flowers and hearts and glitter. They made me gag a little. I was a thirty-four-year-old woman, not a twelve-year-old girl.

"See, aren't these more your style?" he asked.

I smiled tightly. "Yeah, they're much cheerier." At least that was true.

We looked through the cases for a few minutes, him explaining the relative merits of each of them to me. Like the phones, the cases weren't the top of the line, and I knew they wouldn't do much to protect my phone from drops and spills as he said they would. I eventually picked out a case with a large-scale floral print that I could claim vaguely reminded me of a Pucci print. As we went over to the register, I started to worry that I'd dealt with Chris's slime and the ugly phone cases without finding a way to work Mr. Cardosi into the conversation.

Chris insisted on putting the new case on my phone for me. "I can get rid of this old one for you," he said, pulling it across the counter toward himself.

I had paid a pretty penny for that case, and I didn't doubt for a second that he would try to resell it online. "Oh no, I'll keep it. You know, in case I break this one somehow." I giggled for good measure. "I'm such a klutz sometimes!"

"Customer's always right," he said, not really sounding like he meant it.

I took my bag with the new case's packaging in it and turned toward the door. The barbershop was directly in my line of sight, and I saw how to bring Mr. Cardosi up. "Oh!" I said, turning back around.

Chris was right in my face, and he didn't seem to

have noticed that I had started speaking. "So, Francesca, since you're new in town, maybe I could take you out sometime and show you around. You know, show you the good places to eat, the best place to get a cup of coffee, where the movie theatre is…"

As if I didn't know the best place to get a cup of coffee. "Um, I don't know." He was uncomfortably close, and I stepped backward. "You know, I'm still just getting settled here and—"

He moved in closer again. "That's exactly why you should let me take you out. I can help you get acquainted with the town!"

"Um, I don't—I don't—" I glanced out the front window at the barbershop. Distraction would be my technique. "Hey, isn't that the shop where the barber who just died worked?"

Chris looked across the street. I used the opportunity to step away again.

"Yeah, that's the place." He laughed.

"What's so funny?" I asked.

"He was just a grouchy old man. I mean, I'm not saying he had it coming, but as angry as that man was, I'm not surprised he pissed someone off enough to murder him."

That was a nauseating statement, especially since Chris was laughing as he said it, but the fact that he knew Mr. Cardosi had been murdered meant that I really needed to ask some more questions.

"He was murdered?" I gasped.

"Oh yeah, you didn't hear?" He sounded excited. "It's all over town. But I guess since you're new here…"

"Do they know who did it?"

"No, not yet," he said. "But it could be anybody. Seriously, dude was *angry*. He was always yelling about something or other. I'd see him outside his store screaming at his customers, telling them to never come back. Now me, I want to make my customers feel special so they want to come back." He gave me a slimy smile, as if he needed to make it more clear that he was coming on to me. When I didn't react, he went back to talking about Mr. Cardosi.

"He came in here once, like a month ago, to buy a phone. The one he had was so old, it still had an *antenna*. I mean, come on, the thing was from, like, the nineties! Anyway, he was in here looking at the new touch screens, and forget apps, he couldn't even make a phone call with one! He kept asking where the keypad was and how he was supposed to dial anybody. It made him *so* angry, but it was so funny! He just kept poking at it, and every time he'd get close to getting it to do what he wanted, he'd end up hitting the home button or the power button or the volume, then he'd freak out even more. Dude finally just threw the phone on the counter and stormed out.

'I'm taking my business elsewhere!'" Chris said in an impression of Mr. Cardosi.

That was the second Mr. Cardosi impression I'd heard that morning, and I preferred Matty's. Matty's was affectionate. Chris's was just... *rude*.

"I laughed about it for *days!*" he added.

He was still laughing about it. I knew Mr. Cardosi's fits could be comical, but it seemed wrong to laugh about it now that he was dead. Even if I would have considered going out with Chris before, which I wouldn't have, I really wouldn't now. Chris's diatribe had put a bad taste in my mouth, but it had given me the tidbit that Mr. Cardosi had been looking for a new, more modern phone. Maybe that was something useful.

"Well, that's certainly interesting," I said tersely. I was more than ready to get out of there. I looked at my phone briefly. "Oh, look at the time! I really need to get going!" I made for the door.

"What about that date?" Chris asked as I hurried past him.

"I don't think it's going to work out," I said, nearly out the door.

"But why not?" Chris called.

"Oh, just, um..." I glanced around the street. "You're not really my type." I took off down the sidewalk.

Chapter 9

I HURRIED down the sidewalk and turned the corner at the end of the block. I didn't know if Chris was watching me walk away—I wasn't about to turn around and look back—but if he was, I wanted to be out of his view as soon as possible. I paused just around the corner to see if I could hear footsteps following me. I couldn't, but I didn't know how likely it was that I would actually be able to hear someone behind me. People always could in the movies, but this was real life, not the latest blockbuster thriller.

I walked for a few more blocks, turning at every corner just in case someone was tailing me. I figured if I was going to investigate Mr. Cardosi's death, I may as well have fun with it. When I arrived at one of the town parks, I made my way to a bench and sat down to text

Matty. I assumed he was at work, but I thought I could go ahead and see if he wanted to get together that evening to discuss the case a little more.

I leaned back against the bench to relax while I waited for his response. I wasn't sure if he would be able to respond quickly or not, or if I even merited an immediate response in his book. I gazed around the park. It was one of those cute old parks with a collection of concrete chess tables. My grandfather used to take me there when I was growing up to play chess, but he'd made me practice at home for a long time before he'd let me go to the park and play with his buddies. A scattering of older men were at the chess tables, paired up in competition. A few of them seemed especially serious about it, hitting their chess timers between each move, but most of them were playing more leisurely, seemingly more interested in debating world events than in defeating their opponents.

Hardly a minute later, my phone buzzed. I was pleasantly surprised that Matty had gotten back to me so quickly. He agreed to have a late dinner with me that night after I closed the café. That reminded me I needed to get to work soon. I glanced at the time. I still had a little while. I considered lingering in the park for a while, but then it occurred to me that I also wanted to talk to Mrs. Collins and see if she had any other clues. If I left right away, I could make it back to my neighborhood to talk to her for a little while and still make it to work on time. I might be just a little late, but Sammy would forgive me.

I stood and headed to my street. It wasn't a long walk if you knew the back way. It was counterintuitive, but if I walked through the back of the park, went down the set of stairs in the side of the hill, and took the path around the little pond, I'd pop out just two streets down from my house. I moved quickly, waving at a few of the chess players I recognized as I passed. In no time at all, I was at Mrs. Collins's door.

She didn't have a bell, so I used the heavy, ornate door knocker. There was no answer for quite a while, and I couldn't hear any movement inside the house despite practically putting my ear right up against the door. I was just about to knock again when the door swung open.

Mrs. Collins stood there, her hair done up just so, her lips painted red, her blouse and slacks immaculately pressed. She would have fit in with the finest New York socialites, but that seemed typical of the older generation —they always wanted to look nice, even if they would just be sitting around the house all day. Sometimes I wished my generation had the same attitude, even if I did enjoy being comfortable. She made me feel woefully underdressed, despite the designer labels inside my jeans and black T-shirt. I might have fit in in a New York City office, but I would have looked positively slovenly next to the residents in the Cape Bay retirement home.

"Well, hello, Francesca dear!" Mrs. Collins said warmly, taking my hand in both of hers. "I've just put the kettle on if you'd like to come in for a cup of tea. I'm sorry, I don't keep coffee in the house—I know that's what you'd prefer."

I wondered if putting the kettle on for whoever was at the door was what had taken her so long to answer. I smiled at her warmly. "I'd love that, Mrs. Collins!"

"Well, come on in, dearie!" She stepped aside for me.

Like her, her house was impressively tidy and pulled together. "Neat as a pin," my grandmother would have said.

Mrs. Collins shut the door and shuffled past me down the hall. "If you don't mind, we'll sit in the kitchen. It's difficult for me to carry the tea set into the sitting room anymore."

"Of course!" I said politely.

We walked down the hall and into the brightly lit kitchen.

"Is there anything I can help you with?" I asked.

"No, no, dear, it'll just be a minute," she replied.

She certainly was fond of calling me "dear." As I sat at the table, it occurred to me that she hadn't yet inquired as to the reason for my visit. She must have just been so happy to have a visitor that she didn't care about the reason for their arrival. I watched her move around the kitchen, gathering tea cups and sugar and tea bags. She arranged it all neatly on a silver tea tray even though we would just be sitting at the table. When the kettle whistled, she added it to the tray and shuffled over to the table, dismissing my continued offers of assistance. She carefully poured tea for each of us and took a sip before speaking.

"So, Francesca, to what do I owe the pleasure of this visit?"

I decided to plead a need for commiseration. I sighed deeply. "Well, Mrs. Collins, you know, Mr. Cardosi's death has just been weighing on me. I know you said on the day he…" I paused for effect. "The day he passed away that you'd spent a lot of time with him, so I felt like you, of all people, would be able to chat with me about him."

"Oh yes, dear. So sad, isn't it? And him so young yet."

I hadn't really thought of Mr. Cardosi as *young*, but I supposed if you were pushing eighty, as Mrs. Collins was, Mr. Cardosi's late sixties did seem rather youthful.

I nodded. "You were close to him?" Chris the Cell Phone Guy had shared freely after just a simple question, and I hoped that technique would work similarly well with Mrs. Collins.

"I was! That's why it's been so hard for me. You know, so many of my friends are passing now. Your mother, then Gino Cardosi. And death comes in threes, you know. I just keep waiting for who will be next." She shook her head sadly.

I looked at her sympathetically. I wished she hadn't mentioned my mother, but I supposed it had been a bad couple of months for our block, and she was entitled to be sad about it too.

As I'd hoped, she continued talking after a brief pause. "You know, lately, I'd been going over in the evenings to help Gino practice courting a lady." The shock must have shown on my face because Mrs. Collins rushed to continue. "Oh no, no, no, dear. He wasn't courting *me*. It was someone else—he wouldn't tell me who. But he hadn't dated anyone since his Carolina—that was Matteo's mother—passed away twenty-five years ago, and he was dreadfully out of practice. We just went over basic things—pulling a chair out for a lady, helping her with her coat, how to not make a mess of himself when eating spaghetti Bolognese. I helped him pick out some outfits to wear out to dinner with her that made him look like the respectable businessman he was."

I got the feeling from the way Mrs. Collins was talking that she wished she really had been the one Mr. Cardosi was courting—if he was actually courting anyone at all. I reminded myself of Mrs. Collins's tendency to exaggerate and Matty's confidence that his dad was largely a loner. It seemed entirely possible that Mrs. Collins had invited herself over to Mr. Cardosi's with the intention of making him over as a suitor for herself, or some other watered-down version of what she had told me. But then something she said caught my attention.

"Apparently the lady he was seeing, despite being a more mature woman like myself, was quite technological. She wanted to be able to—oh, what is it you young people call that? When you type to each other on your phones?"

"Text?" I prompted.

"Yes! Text! Apparently she wanted to be able to text messages to Gino, but his cell phone didn't do that, and he wanted to get a new one that would let him do that. He went to that awful place across from his barbershop, but the young man who works there was quite rude to him. Gino didn't buy anything."

So maybe there was something to Mrs. Collins's story after all. I glanced at the clock on the wall and realized I needed to get to the coffee shop. I swallowed the rest of my tea. "Mrs. Collins, I've had such a lovely time with you, but I need to get to work. Thank you for the tea." I rose from my chair so she wouldn't be able to delay me by starting more stories.

She sighed and put everything back on the tea tray.

"Well, I do appreciate you coming, dear. You know you're welcome here any time. Watching you grow up was always such a joy. You know, Mr. Collins and I were never able to have children, so having you across the street was almost like having one of our own grandchildren there."

I stopped and looked at her. I had never known that she felt that way. I gave her a hug. "Thank you, Mrs. Collins. That's so sweet of you." When I pulled away, I thought I saw tears in her eyes. After being home for over a month, I was finally realizing how deep my roots ran in this town.

"Well, dear, it's the truth."

I smiled and noticed the tea tray on the table. "Let me carry that over to the sink for you." I put the rest of the dishes on the tray and carried it to the counter so she wouldn't have to. I gave her one more hug and hurried off to the café.

Chapter 10

"HAVE FUN AT THE BEACH?" Sammy asked as I walked into the backroom of the café. Her normally pale face was flushed bright red from working over steaming coffee all morning.

I smiled. "Yeah, it was nice! I got to get my feet wet, dig my toes in the sand, relax a little. I took off when the tourists started coming in."

It was a common sentiment in seaside towns: tourists leave the beach when the tide starts coming in; locals leave when the tourists start coming in. It wasn't that we didn't like the tourists—we really did. It was fun getting to meet new people all the time, and the boon to the local economy was great. By the end of the summer, though, we were ready to turn back into the sleepy town we were the other nine months of the year.

"I'm surprised there were any tourists left to go out to the beach—it seemed like they were all here," Sammy said.

"So it's been busy!"

Sammy turned from the dishes she was scrubbing, and I noticed her normally loose wisps of hair were plastered to her face. "Busy is an understatement."

I couldn't help but laugh at her deadpan delivery. I took my apron off its hook and dropped it over my head. I poked my head out into the café as I tied the apron's sash behind my back. Becky was wiping down the counter, her red curls a little extra frizzy from the heat and humidity. Several people were scattered among the tables and chairs, but it looked as if the rush had mostly died down.

"I can take care of that if you want to get out of here," I said, gesturing at Sammy's dishes.

"That's okay. I'm almost done." Sammy wasn't the type to leave a job unfinished, even if someone was offering to take it over for her.

I grabbed a rag and went out to the front to wipe down tables and straighten up. I could always find something to fiddle around with, whether it was cleaning things or moving things around or preparing food. Sammy finished the dishes and went home, and Amanda, another of our teenage part-timers, came in to relieve Becky. The afternoon just got slower. By mid-afternoon, we had taken care of everything that needed to be done and we didn't have a single customer, so I let Amanda go home after she promised to come back if things picked up and I needed her.

I stood behind the counter, glancing around the empty café. Days like this always made me nervous. They were few and far between, but they always made me worry that business was slowing down overall and soon we'd have to close. I knew it was ridiculous, especially as busy as Sammy said it had been during the morning, but I worried all the same.

I went in the back to get the notebook and pens I'd purchased and took them back to the front. I leaned over the counter and wrote down everything I'd learned that morning—everything I'd talked about with slimy Chris and old Mrs. Collins. I included my impressions about my conversations with each of them. I wanted to remember what I'd thought in the moment about Mrs. Collins's possible exaggerations and Chris's obnoxious offensiveness. With the small size of the notebook, I quickly filled up each page and found myself wishing I'd gotten a bigger notebook, even if it was somewhat less portable.

I finished my notes just as the late afternoon "rush" got started. Apparently everyone who was going to come in that day had come during the morning because, while I had to hustle, I never got to the point where I had to call Amanda back in. It quickly slowed back down, and I was left with a few pairs of customers lingering over their drinks. I felt a little bit guilty that things had been so hectic for Sammy but so easy for me. After the last of the customers left, I wiped everything down again and waited for closing time.

I was in the backroom five minutes before closing, rearranging items on the shelves, when I heard the jingle of the bell over the door. I walked out into the café, a little annoyed that I'd have to make someone a drink when everything was already clean and put away. At the same time, I recognized that was my fault for cleaning up early. A smile spread across my face when I saw Matty, still looking handsome in his work clothes.

"Hey!" I said cheerily.

"Hey yourself!" he replied. "You about ready to get something to eat?"

"Yeah, I just have to lock up." I glanced at the clock on the wall. There were still a couple of minutes left before the official closing time. To most people, that would be inconsequential, but I had spent so long working beside my grandparents and being told that you have to be open when you say you're going to be open, I wasn't sure if I would physically be able to turn the key in the lock before precisely closing time. I hesitated. "Well, in two minutes."

Matty looked at the clock and laughed. "Ghosts of

your grandparents keeping you from closing shop thirty seconds early?"

I shrugged with a smile. Even after spending most of the last fifteen years apart, he knew me too well. We stood and watched the clock tick down until the minute hand was precisely lined up with the twelve, then I walked over to the door and turned the lock.

I smiled at Matty. "Okay, now we can go."

He gestured at me. "Might want to take that apron off. Otherwise they might try to put you to work at dinner."

I rolled my eyes at his bad joke as I walked to the backroom and took off my apron. I grabbed my purse and headed for the door, turning lights out as I went. Matty followed me out and waited as I locked up.

"So what's for dinner?" I asked.

"I was thinking the little Mexican place down on the beach?" he suggested.

"Sounds good to me," I replied. "I could go for a margarita about now."

"No tequila shots?" Matty joked.

"I didn't say no tequila," I teased back. "I just said I wanted a margarita. We can work our way up to straight tequila."

Matty laughed as we walked down the sidewalk toward the beach. It was a warm night, with just the slightest breeze blowing out to the ocean. The sun was sinking below the horizon behind us as we approached the water.

"You want to sit outside?" Matty asked when we arrived at the restaurant with its deck that stretched out over the water.

"Definitely." The full moon would be rising momentarily, and there were few things I loved more than watching the moon reflected over the water.

Matty gave our request to the hostess, and she escorted us out onto the deck. Something about that evening must have made all the businesses on the beach slow, because we were the only ones out there, and the inside of the restaurant was sparsely populated. I tried to remember if there was a concert or something in a nearby town that was luring everyone away, but nothing came to mind. Matty pulled my chair out for me then went around to his side of the table as the waitress appeared, chips and salsa in hand, to take our drink orders.

"Margarita on the rocks, please," I told her.

Matty hesitated for a moment, giving me a look that I knew meant he was toying with the idea of jumping straight to tequila, but he ordered a beer instead. We studied our menus as the waitress disappeared to get our drinks.

"I don't know what I want," Matty muttered. "I want everything!"

"Hungry much?" I asked with a laugh.

"I haven't eaten since lunch." He groaned. "I'm starving!"

"Eat some chips!" I said, shoving the bowl across the table toward him.

Matty grabbed two and shoved them in his mouth.

"Charming," I said.

"I told you I'm hungry," Matty said around the chips.

I laughed at his obviously unnecessary crudeness. It was juvenile humor, but sometimes it's fun to be juvenile. The waitress reappeared with our drinks. That was one thing I liked about that place—they actually made your drinks and brought them out to you quickly. I couldn't stand it when you ordered a drink and for some reason it took twenty minutes to get to your table. I gave the waitress our orders then sipped our drinks as she left.

"So," I said, figuring we needed to get down to business. "I went and talked to Cell Phone Guy—his name is Chris Tompson—and Mrs. Collins today—"

Matty cut me off, reaching across the table. "Please, Franny, can we not talk about my dad just yet? Let's just sit and enjoy each other's company for a while, okay? We can talk about anything else."

I smiled. Matty and I hadn't just sat and talked in ages, certainly not since I'd been back in town.

"Sure," I said. Out of the corner of my eye, I saw the moon starting to peek up over the water. It sounded like a perfect way to spend the evening.

Chapter 11

WE LINGERED A WHILE OVER DINNER. I never did switch to tequila, but I did have more than one margarita. The moon was stunning over the water. It was large and full and made the night unusually bright. Matty and I chatted about our lives since high school and how we ended up back in Cape Bay.

Matty had gone away to college too, but he moved back right afterward because he didn't want to leave his dad all alone. He'd had a couple girlfriends, one of them pretty serious. She had wanted to get married, but Matty wasn't ready, and they broke up.

I filled him in on what had happened with my ex-fiancé. He'd heard about it, of course, because once my mother told one person that her daughter's engagement was off, the whole town knew—that was the way the rumor mill worked in a small town. I gave him the unex-aggerated version of the story, though, not the one that had been built up through retellings by people who weren't there and didn't actually know. The woman he'd left me for wasn't a model, I didn't catch them in bed together, I didn't throw all his belongings out the window. I told him the boring but true version—he left me, and my heart was broken.

We had long since finished eating and were nursing our third round of drinks when our conversation about our personal lives wound down.

Matty sighed. "I guess we should go ahead and talk about my dad." He gestured at the inside of the restaurant, where only a few customers were left and the wait-staff was wiping down tables. "They're going to want us out of here pretty soon."

I was enjoying my time with Matty so much, I had almost forgotten what had brought us out to dinner that night. I pulled my notebook out of my bag and flipped through the pages I'd filled at the café, refreshing my memory about my conversations.

"You took notes?" Matty asked wryly.

I glanced up, the very picture of seriousness. "Yes, yes, I did." I looked back down at my notes.

Matty chuckled and took a drink of his beer.

Satisfied I knew the points I wanted to cover, I flipped my notebook closed again. "Do you know anything about your dad shopping for a new cell phone?"

"No. Why?" Matty said slowly.

I gave him a brief rundown of my conversations with Chris the Cell Phone Guy and Mrs. Collins. That both of them mentioned Mr. Cardosi was looking for a new cell phone made me think there might actually be something to it. Matty listened thoughtfully.

After a long pause, he spoke. "The weekend before he died, he mentioned that he was going to Plymouth so he could go to one of those big box stores—I can't remember which one. I didn't understand what he needed to do out there, but I guess if he wanted a cell phone and didn't want to go to the cell phone shop— and you know he wouldn't go back there after he got into an argument with that guy—I guess he might have been going to get a cell phone." Matty looked thought- ful. "I wonder why he didn't tell me."

I shrugged, then something occurred to me. "If the thing Mrs. Collins said about your dad dating someone was true, maybe he was worried how you'd feel about it."

Matty played with his beer bottle. He sighed. "I just —Mom died so long ago. I would have been happy for him if he'd told me he found someone."

"You know how parents are. My mom talked about her 'friend' John for years, and every time I'd ask, she denied that there was anything between them. But the way she smiled when she talked about him said otherwise. They just want to protect us."

"I guess you're right," Matty said quietly. He shook his head. "I just wish I'd known."

We sat for a few minutes, both lost in our thoughts about our parents.

Finally Matty glanced up and gestured inside the restaurant with his beer bottle. "We should probably get going."

The other customers were gone, and the servers were hovering just inside, looking at us every once in a while as though they didn't want to pressure us too much even if they were ready to go home.

"Yeah, I guess we should."

Matty caught our waitress's eye, and she brought over the check. I reached for my purse, but before I could get my wallet out, Matty had slid his credit card into the folder and passed it back to the waitress.

"What was that?" I asked indignantly.

"Me paying for our dinner?" Matty answered.

"I can pay for myself. And if anyone's going to be paying for anyone, I should be paying for you because I'm the one who suggested dinner."

Matty shrugged. "Too late."

I looked at him through narrowed eyes. "Well, I'm paying next time."

He shrugged again, this time with a twinkle in his eye. "We'll see."

I had a feeling I'd have to fight to pay.

"You know, it's only fair that I pay," Matty said. "You've treated me at the café twice in the past two days."

"That's different."

"How?"

"It just is." I didn't really have a reason except that I ran the café and could give out free food and drinks to anyone at any time, but Matty was going out of his way to pay for my dinner.

Matty didn't bother arguing with me anymore. He just signed the check when the waitress brought it back. We left quickly so the staff could finish cleaning up and go home.

"Where's your car?" I asked as we started up the street toward the café. Matty's house was on the other side of town. It was a quick drive but far enough that I knew he wouldn't have walked to the café.

"I actually parked at my dad's house," he said. "I didn't see any reason to pay for parking when his place is just around the corner."

"Well, good," I replied cheerily. "I'll have company on my walk home."

Matty scoffed. "You think I'd let you walk home alone at this time of night?"

I looked at him, surprised by both what he said and how forcefully he said it. "You think I can't take care of myself? I lived in New York for twelve years! I think I can handle sleepy Cape Bay. It's not like this is a dangerous place!" Matty didn't say anything, and I realized what I had just said. "Oh... um, I mean, usually, um—"I couldn't believe how badly I'd stuck my foot in my mouth.

"It's okay," he offered. "I would have felt the same way before. I do have manners, you know." He chuckled softly.

"Thanks." I sighed, relieved that my gaffe hadn't upset Matty too much. "And sorry. I should have thought before I said that."

"It's okay." He rubbed the back of my shoulder. "Really."

We walked on in silence, enjoying each other's company and the peace of the night. After a few minutes, we turned onto our street—well, my street and Matty's old street.

"What are you going to do with your dad's house?" I asked.

"I don't know yet," Matty said. "It's paid for. I could sell it and put the money into my own place. Or I could take a cue from you and sell my place and move into his. It'd be nice to not have a mortgage."

"Hey! Then there'd be two young people on the street!"

Matty laughed. "That is true." We were walking up to his dad's house. "You want to come in and see if we can find anything about that cell phone? There wasn't one in his personal effects that they returned to me, so the old one or the new one's got to be inside somewhere, right?"

"Unless…" My newly discovered investigator's mind went off.

"Unless whoever killed him took it," Matty finished. "Either way, we should find out."

I agreed, and we headed into Mr. Cardosi's house to hunt for his cell phone or some evidence of it. Matty unlocked the door and flipped on the light. We stood in the foyer, taking in the space.

"Where do we start?" I asked after a minute.

"Anywhere we didn't already look." Matty looked around. "I'll start with the bedroom. Do you want to come with me or look somewhere else?"

I glanced around the entrance. "I'll start out here."

"All righty," Matty said and headed into Mr. Cardosi's bedroom.

A few jackets hung on hooks by the door, and a couple of shopping bags were on the floor beneath them. Wanting to start small, I stuck my hand in one of the jacket pockets and immediately closed it around a solid plastic rectangle. Not believing it could be that easy, I pulled my hand out slowly and turned the rectangle over. Sure enough, it was a brand-new smartphone. Not high-end but definitely a touch screen and definitely no antenna.

"Matty?" I called.

"Just a second, I'm just going through his nightstand."

"I found it."

There was a pause. "What?"

"I found it."

Another pause. Matty appeared in the bedroom door, an incredulous look on his face. "You found it? Already? What, was it in the first place you looked?"

I nodded, grinning. "Sure was!"

Matty took the two steps over to me with his hand out. I handed him the phone. He looked at it slowly.

"What do you know?" he said quietly. "He did buy one."

I wondered if it bothered him that his dad had bought a phone, supposedly so that he could text the woman he was dating, without breathing a word of it to Matty. He pushed the home button. Nothing happened. He pushed the power button. Nothing. He pushed it again, holding it down for several seconds. I saw his eyebrows go up, and he turned it around for me to see the screen light up.

"He always kept the old one off too," he said. "Said he wanted to make sure it was charged up in case he needed it in an emergency. I told him he could just charge it each night, but he thought that was ridiculous. 'Batteries should last longer than that!'" Matty slipped into his impression of his dad again, even shaking his fist for good measure. He chuckled softly as he thought about his dad.

I moved closer so we could look at the screen together. "Has he been texting anyone?" Since that was why he bought the phone, it seemed like the most obvious place to start.

Matty opened the text messaging app. It was empty.

"Call log?" I suggested.

Matty fumbled around briefly, trying to figure out how to see the call history. It was a different model phone from his, and it wasn't the most intuitive design. My phone was different too, so I wasn't any help. Finally he found it. All the calls were to one number. Matty read it out loud.

"Do you know whose number that is?" I asked.

"Nope."

"Let's call it!" I suggested.

He looked at the time on the phone then looked at me. "It's almost midnight."

"So that's a no?" I tried to look as serious as possible even though I obviously knew it was way too late to call.

Matty looked at me skeptically then laughed after he realized I was joking. I clearly wasn't doing a good job of looking serious.

"We'll call tomorrow," he said.

"Oh-kay," I said dramatically. I had gotten relatively little sleep the night before and was getting a little slap-happy.

Matty chuckled again. "I think you might need to get home and get to bed."

"Yeah, probably," I admitted.

Matty started to put the phone away.

"No, wait!" I put my hand on his arm to stop him. My investigator brain had kicked in again. I reached for my purse, which I had dropped on the floor when we came in. "I want to copy that number and the call times down."

I pulled out my notebook and wrote it all down as Matty held the phone patiently, rubbing his finger on the screen every few seconds to keep it from going to sleep. There were only a few calls, so it didn't take long to get it all.

"Okay, thanks," I said, slapping the notebook closed and stuffing it back in my bag.

"Can I take you home now?" Matty asked.

"It's just two doors down. I think I'll be okay."

Matty just looked at me.

"Okay!" I said, giving in. "Are you trying to make me feel helpless or something today?"

"I'm *trying* to be a gentleman," Matty replied, shepherding me out the door and locking it behind us.

"Well, I can't really argue with that, can I?" I was used to being independent, but it's not as if he was patting my head and telling me a pretty girl like me shouldn't be worrying her little head about something as big and complicated as a coffee shop. I just wasn't used to someone—a man especially—being so considerate. My ex-fiancé certainly hadn't been.

We cut across the neighbor's lawn on the way to my house on the other side. I unlocked my door then turned to look at Matty.

"Well, thanks for dinner," I said.

"It was my pleasure," Matty replied.

"You want to get together tomorrow and try to call that number?"

"Sure. Do you have to work?"

"Only a couple hours at close." The next day was Saturday which, weirdly, was one of our slowest days, at least during the summer. Since all the rentals rolled over on Saturdays, not many people had the opportunity to come in. The renters from the previous week were too busy packing up and heading out of town, and the next week's renters hadn't found us yet. As a result, we usually broke the day's shifts down so Sammy and I only had to worry about opening and closing, and some of the more established part-timers shared duty during the day.

"So maybe we can grab some lunch then see if we can figure out who my dad was calling?"

"Sounds good!" I replied.

We stood there, looking at each other awkwardly, for a few seconds, as if we were both waiting to see if the other had something more to say.

"Well, I guess I'll see you tomorrow," I said finally.

"Yeah." Matty stood there for a second then hugged me.

It was... strange. Hugging him wasn't unusual, but the nature of that hug seemed out of the ordinary. It seemed as though he held me maybe a little bit tighter and a little bit longer than normal. It wasn't bad, just... different. When he let me go, I opened the door and stepped inside. Matty gave me a little wave.

"Good night," he said before he headed back across the lawn to his car parked at his dad's.

"Good night." I watched him walk away then closed the door. I stood there for a minute and wondered if maybe there was something more to that hug than simple friendship.

Chapter 12

I KNEW I WAS TIRED, but I didn't feel like going to bed yet. I went into the kitchen and poured myself a glass of wine. The house was quiet. So very, very quiet. I wandered through the first floor, flipping lights on as I went. The lights made the stillness feel a little less ominous.

I opened the door to my grandparents' bedroom. I had never thought of my mother as a particularly sentimental person, but I supposed she had been since she'd never moved into their bedroom after they both passed away. She hadn't really cleaned it out. Their clothes were still hanging neatly in the closet, their knickknacks still arranged on the dresser.

I picked up a bottle of my grandmother's perfume and sprayed it in the air. Even after all these years, it still smelled just like her. My grandfather's cologne was the same way. I sat on the edge of their bed, closed my eyes, and breathed them in. On the one hand, it felt as if they had just died a minute ago, but on the other, I felt every one of the eleven years since their passing. They'd died within months of each other, my grandmother from a quick-moving pancreatic cancer and my grandfather from heart failure in his sleep. Losing them in such quick succession had been hard on my mother and me, but my grandfather hadn't been the same since my grandmother's passing, and we knew he was ready to be with her again.

I opened my eyes and looked around the room. Maybe I should move down there. Clean out their things, give it a fresh coat of paint. There was no sense in leaving it as a museum or treating the whole house as if it were frozen in time, a tomb for ghosts to lurk about in. I supposed that meant I'd need to go through my mother's things as well. Maybe I should go through the whole house. Spruce it up some, "young" it up, make it a place that a thirty-something single woman would live in. That sounded like a plan. Although the house still seemed dreadfully quiet. Maybe I needed a pet. A dog or a cat. Despite all of my grandfather's wonderful traits, he had adamantly refused to allow a pet in the house, no matter how much I'd begged and pleaded. But there was no reason I had to keep it "people only" anymore. If I wanted a pet, I could get a pet. It wasn't as though I had a job that kept me away for long hours each day—I could arrange my schedule at the café however I needed to so that I could come home to take care of Fido or Fluffy. That settled it. I was getting a pet. I would go to the shelter to find the perfect critter to love just as soon as I could.

I went upstairs and got ready for bed. I lay down and thought about what I would turn this room into when I moved downstairs into the master bedroom. Maybe an office. Or an exercise studio. I had my mother's old room to do something with, so I could make one room into an office and the other into an exercise studio. Or a guest room. I could make one of the rooms into a guest room. Sooner or later one of my friends from New York would want to come up and spend some time at the beach. I thought for a while about how I could redecorate and possibly renovate the house. I wasn't falling asleep. I let my mind wander, and it wasn't long before it drifted to my investigation of Mr. Cardosi's death.

I thought about that phone number. Which of us would call it—Matty or me? We shouldn't try to call from Mr. Cardosi's cell phone, should we? What if the person recognized his number? If it was the murderer, wouldn't that tip him off that we were on his trail? So we should call from a different number. One of our cell phones? What if that could be traced? What if the murderer just did an online search for the number and it turned up Matty's or my information?

I sat straight up in bed. If the murderer—or whoever the number belonged to, I was getting ahead of myself assuming it was the murderer's number—could find out online who called him, why couldn't I search for him? I got up and grabbed my laptop from my dresser. I was antsy for it to hurry up and turn on and for the browser to load. Slowness that normally didn't bother me was driving me nuts.

Finally, I got the browser loaded and the search engine pulled up. I typed in the number I had copied off the call log on Mr. Cardosi's phone. The number was for Mary Ellen's Souvenirs and Gifts, the local souvenir shop. It was just down the street from my café. When we were kids, Mary Ellen Chapman, the owner of the shop, was just about the only adult in town who we were allowed to call by her first name. She'd said it was silly for us to call her Mrs. Chapman when her first name was right on the front of the store. Of course, at our parents' insistence, we had to call her "Miss Mary Ellen," not just "Mary Ellen," but still, that made her instantly cool in our eyes. She was younger than our parents too—probably not as much as it seemed at the time because parents are decidedly ancient in their children's eyes—but her youth made her even cooler to us.

As far as I could remember, she had been married

once when she was young. Her husband had passed away, leaving her a chunk of money that was more than enough for her to move to Cape Bay, buy a house, and set up her souvenir shop. She didn't just sell kitschy Cape Bay memorabilia—she also sold a lot of handmade jewelry, clothing, and art from local artisans, including herself. She was a knitter and made sweaters that I swore were every bit as nice as the ones I could buy in a department store. Her shop was a surprisingly good place to go to get gifts for people.

I wondered whether Mary Ellen was the woman Mr. Cardosi had been seeing. I'd seen her around town since I'd been back, and while she was getting older, she still seemed youthful and spunky. She didn't really seem like the type who would be interested in Mr. Cardosi and all his grumpy argumentativeness, but what did I know? If he'd been spending time with Mrs. Collins to polish some of his rough edges, maybe he was a bigger softie than I'd thought. Mary Ellen was probably old enough that she could be considered "mature," as Mrs. Collins had referred to her, and she certainly seemed like she knew how to text. It was a possibility.

I put my laptop away and crawled back into bed. Instead of calling the number tomorrow, I'd suggest to Matty that we just go over to the souvenir shop and talk to Mary Ellen in person. I'd be able to get a better read on her if I could see her while we talked to her. I couldn't rule out the possibility that she was the murderer, as unlikely as it seemed. I drifted off to sleep as I planned out what I would say to her when we saw her.

I woke up late the next day—no surprise given that it had been after two when I'd finally fallen asleep. My text message alert finally roused me. I rolled over and looked at my phone. The message was from Matty.

What do you want for lunch?

Was it lunchtime already? I looked at the time. It was definitely pushing noon. I hadn't slept that late in ages.

I don't know, I texted back. *I need to get up and get a shower before we do anything.*

I had barely gotten out of bed when Matty's reply came in. He must have been waiting for my reply.

You're not up yet?? Lazy! You better hurry. My fingers are getting itchy to call this number!

I realized I hadn't told Matty what I'd discovered about the phone number last night.

Don't call it! I texted back. *I have something to tell you about it.*

Ok, but you better hurry…

Matty seemed as though he was in a playful mood. I hurried into the shower and heard another text come in. I thought about jumping out to see what it said, but I didn't really feel like cleaning up the water that would pour all over the bathroom floor in the process. Instead, I grabbed it as soon as I was done.

I'm going to head over. I'll be at my dad's whenever you're ready.

Matty's house was so close by, I needed to hurry if I didn't want him to be waiting forever. I reached into my closet, instinctively grabbing a black shirt. But I stopped myself. Black seemed so New York, and I wasn't in New York anymore. Black once in a while wasn't a bad thing, but I didn't need to wear it every day. I went across the hall to my mother's room. I was lucky that she had stayed stylish and my size. I pulled out a pretty corn-flower top I had always admired. I slid it over my head and looked at myself in the mirror. It suited me as it had my mother. It brought out the flecks of blue we both had in our eyes.

I finished getting ready and headed over to Mr. Cardosi's house. I rang the bell and looked around while I waited for Matty to open the door. The house was in decent shape—new paint, well maintained. The flower beds needed some attention, but I supposed that was up to Matty, or his real estate agent if he decided to sell the place. The door opened.

"Hey!" Matty said exuberantly. "You look nice! You're wearing a color!"

I glanced at my shirt. I wasn't sure if I was more surprised that he'd noticed that my shirt was blue or that

I usually wore black. "Thanks. You look nice too," I said, somewhat automatically.

"This?" He gestured at his T-shirt and shorts. "Your standards must have dropped since you left the city."

I laughed. Maybe his outfit wasn't the most stylish, but his hair looked good and I kind of liked his scruffy, unshaven weekend look.

"You ready to go?" Matty asked before I could say anything else.

"Sure, where are we going?"

"I have a craving for lobster rolls," he replied. "Sound good?"

My mouth started watering as soon as he said it. "Yes!" From the way Matty laughed at me, I probably sounded a little too enthusiastic.

"Well, let's go," he said, leading the way down the sidewalk.

There was only one place to go for lobster rolls in Cape Bay. Well, there was more than one place to go, but the locals knew only one place was worth going to. Sandy's Seafood Shack was pretty much the best place on the beach for any New England seafood—lobster rolls, fresh lobster, clam chowder in the winter. Some other places got by on the strength of the tourist trade and plenty kept lobster rolls on their menus just because they knew people would order it, but Sandy's was pretty much the be all, end all for those of us who lived there year-round.

Sandy's was way at the end of the beach, about a fifteen-minute walk from my house. One of my favorite things about Cape Bay, at least the part where I lived, was that I could pretty much walk anywhere. I had a driver's license and a car, but between growing up in Cape Bay, going to school in Boston, and living in New York for so long, walking everywhere was second nature to me. It felt weird to drive anywhere that took less than thirty minutes to walk to. On our walk, we chit-chatted about the neighborhood, how things had changed in town since we were kids, and our old friends from growing up. We were at Sandy's in practically no time.

Lots of people assumed that one of the married couple who opened Sandy's was actually named Sandy. Both of them were called that on a regular basis. Now that their kids ran the place, they also got called Sandy all the time by well-meaning tourists. Whenever some- body asked, "Are you Sandy?" whoever was being asked would just smile and say, "Sure am!" The name was actually a nickname for the owners' dog though. Her name had been Josie, but she liked to roll on the beach and get all sandy. Josie/Sandy had long since passed away and been replaced by other dogs, all of whom they continued to name Sandy. I think they were on Sandy Five by then.

As we settled into our lobster rolls, Matty asked me what I had wanted to tell him about the phone number we'd found.

I finished chewing and put my lobster roll down. "It's Mary Ellen's number."

Matty about choked. "What?"

"Mary Ellen Chapman," I clarified. "It's the souvenir shop's number."

"You think my dad was dating Mary Ellen?" Matty seemed more surprised than I'd expected.

"Well, I don't know if he was dating her, but that's whose number he was calling. I figured we could just go over there and talk to her instead of calling."

"Mary Ellen Chapman," Matty repeated, seemingly not hearing what I'd said. He shook his head slowly, and I thought I saw a bit of a smile on his face.

"Why do you seem so... I don't know, surprised? I mean, she's younger than your dad, but not that much. She was already running the souvenir shop when we were kids."

"No, I know," Matty said. "It's just—" He stopped talking and stared into space a little.

"It's just what?" I took a sip of my soda. Soda felt right with lobster rolls.

"It's just—" he repeated. "Well, I had a little bit of a crush on Mary Ellen growing up."

Chapter 13

IT WAS my turn to choke. I narrowly managed to avoid spitting soda all over Matty. "You what?" Somehow it seemed completely ludicrous to me that Matty had had a crush on Mary Ellen.

He shrugged, blushing a little. "You know, she was young and pretty and—what's so funny?"

I was giggling uncontrollably without really being sure why.

"Seriously, what's so funny?" Matty asked again, starting to giggle himself.

"I don't—I don't know!" I gasped through my giggles. "There's just something—something so funny about you having a crush on her and then your dad dating her twenty years later!" I was laughing so hard I was shaking the table.

"I don't know if you laughing so hard about it should make me feel bad or not." Matty laughed.

"It shouldn't make you feel any particular way. It's just—it struck me as funny." I was getting my giggles under control, taking big deep breaths to calm myself down.

I gradually managed to stop laughing, and we finished our lunch. We agreed to head over to the souvenir shop right afterward. I left the table to go wash my hands, and when I came back, Matty was standing by the table.

"Ready to go?" I asked.

"Ready to go," he replied.

We walked toward the front of the restaurant, where the cash register was.

"Did you grab the check from the table?" I asked him.

"Yup, and paid," he said, walking toward the door instead of the register.

"What!"

Matty grinned as he pushed the door open. "You got up. I paid. Too late again."

I glanced at the girl at the register, and she nodded and said, "Yup, he already paid."

I scowled at Matty as I walked through the door. "You were supposed to let me pay this time."

"That was something you decided," Matty said. "I never agreed to it."

"But it's not fair for you to always pay!"

"Fair only counts in horseshoes and—no, that's wrong," Matty said, interrupting himself. "The point is, I don't care. I invited you out to lunch. I paid. Simple as that."

"But I invited you last night and you paid!"

"Yeah, you're right," he said.

"So shouldn't I pay today?"

"Apparently not."

I glared at the back of his head as he walked down the sidewalk. Eventually he turned around and looked at me.

"You coming?" he asked.

"Are you going to let me pay next time?"

"Is that the only way you'll come with me?"

"Yes," I said.

"Then yes, you can pay next time." He muttered something else as I walked toward him.

"What was that?" I asked.

"What was what?" He had an innocent look that gave away how guilty he was.

"What did you say after you said I could pay next time?"

He threw his arm around my shoulders and leaned

his head toward me. "I *definitely* didn't say that there was no way you were paying."

He had a big grin. I knew I wouldn't win that battle, at least not that day, so I just shook my head.

It was about a ten-minute walk to Mary Ellen's store. It was a relatively warm day but not too humid, so the walk wasn't bad.

"So how are we going to do this?" I asked when we got to the block with Mary Ellen's store.

"You're the investigator," Matty said.

"I'm not an investigator," I scoffed.

"You're the one who's been doing the investigating?" Matty corrected, a question in his voice, seemingly unsure how I wanted to categorize my inquiries. "Seems like you've done well so far with Cell Phone Guy and Mrs. Collins, so I don't see why you shouldn't take the lead here too."

It made me nervous, but his confidence in me felt good. I thought about how to approach Mary Ellen as we got closer. With Chris the Cell Phone Guy and Mrs. Collins, I'd kept my cards pretty close to my chest, but I felt as though it might be better to be a little more open with Mary Ellen. We got to the store, and Matty opened the door for me, jingling the bell above the door. Mary Ellen appeared from the back as we stepped inside.

"Hello!" she called before she had quite seen us. She

gasped when she did. "Fran! Matt! What brings the two of you in today?"

I saw Matt look at me, so I smiled and stepped forward. "Hi, Mary Ellen!" I did my best to sound light-hearted and happy. "How are you today?"

"I'm good, I'm good," she replied.

She really did look good for her age. If I didn't know better, I would have thought she were ten years younger than she really was. Her clothes were still fashionable, and she either had amazing genes or she dyed her hair to keep it a warm chestnut. She stood behind the counter, looking completely comfortable in her skin.

"How are you?" she asked.

"I'm good," I said, smiling. I walked over to her, Matty close behind me. "I'm wondering if you could help us with something."

She wrinkled her forehead and frowned slightly. "I'd be happy to, if I can."

"Matty—"I needed to stop calling him Matty, at least when I was talking to other people. People had to think I sounded eight years old when I called him that when everybody else just called him Matt. "*Matt* and I were taking care of some of his dad's things the other day, and we found his cell phone. We noticed there were quite a few calls to your number."

She blushed and looked at the counter. She took a deep breath, and when she looked back up, tears were welling up in her eyes. "Gino—your dad," she said, looking at Matty—*Matt*. "Your dad and I had been spending some time together before he passed away."

"You were dating?" I prompted.

She looked back down. "Well, I wouldn't say—I suppose—it was casual. I was—I was also seeing another man." Her voice got very quiet as she said the last part.

My independent spirit reared up, not wanting Mary Ellen to feel bad for dating two men at once. As long as she wasn't cheating on one or the other, there was nothing to be ashamed of.

"Were you exclusive with either of them?" I asked. "I mean, did either of them think you were?"

"Oh, heavens no!" she said quickly. "No, no, I would never do that. See one man behind another's back, I mean. I suppose I would be exclusive with a gentleman under some circumstances, but I haven't since my husband passed. I haven't felt like I wanted to tie myself down that way again. No, they knew about each other. They despised each other, but they knew about each other."

I nodded sympathetically. I understood her wanting to maintain her freedom, and I wanted her to feel as though she could continue to confide in me. I glanced at Matt, who was making himself busy inspecting some magnets emblazoned with "Cape Bay." My ears had latched onto Mary Ellen's comment that Mr. Cardosi and her other suitor had despised each other. It seemed like the right moment to bring the conversation around to Mr. Cardosi's cause of death.

I lowered my voice and leaned across the counter toward Mary Ellen. "Have you heard that Mr. Car—that Gino was murdered?" I used his first name to make her feel as if she was speaking to a peer. It seemed like something the good cop in a good cop/bad cop scene might do.

The blush that had covered Mary Ellen's face disappeared, and she went ghostly white. "He—he was—" She mouthed the final word then covered her face with her hands. Apparently she hadn't known.

When she removed her hands, tears were spilling down her cheeks. I felt bad. I could have found a more delicate way to break it to her if I'd realized she hadn't heard yet.

"I'm so sorry to be the one to tell you," I said quite sincerely.

"No, no. No." She turned slightly away from me as she tried to gather herself. "No. No, not at all. Don't feel bad, Fran. I'm glad you told me." She had regained her voice, but tears were still pouring down her cheeks. "What happened?"

"He was poisoned," I said reluctantly. Playing detective had suddenly lost some of its allure.

Mary Ellen gasped. "Oh, good heavens!"

I saw Matt poke his head around a display of earrings then disappear again when he saw Mary Ellen's tears.

"Mary Ellen, since you were a friend of his, I was wondering if you might know of anyone who had a grudge against him, someone who might have wanted to —to hurt him."

She choked back a sob. "No, not a soul. Gino was such a kind man. I-I know he could be abrasive and he rubbed some people the wrong way, but his heart was good. I can't imagine anyone wanting to harm him."

I nodded agreeably and waited until Mary Ellen seemed a bit calmer to ask my next question. "You mentioned you were seeing someone else? What was his name, if you don't mind my asking?"

"His name?" she repeated. Then I saw understanding dawn on her face. "Oh, you don't think Karl —!" She seemed to visibly crumple.

I reached across the counter and rested my hand on hers. She grasped onto it and held it tight.

"Mary Ellen, I'm sorry to even suggest such a thing, and it's not that I even think he may have done it. It's just—Matt's been my friend my whole life, and I'm doing everything I can to give him peace about what happened to his father. I'm trying to talk to everyone I can to see if they can give us any idea who would have done this. If I could just talk to this—this Karl, you said his name was? Since he knew Gino, even though he didn't like him, maybe he could give us a little more insight into his life. I guess Gino wanted to protect Matt from the news that he was dating, so we're discovering this whole other part of his life Matt knew nothing about. We just want to understand him better." I hoped Mary Ellen wouldn't pick up on my somewhat fuzzy, meandering logic.

Mary Ellen straightened her spine and cleared her throat. "His name is Karl Richards. Karl with a K. He's fairly new in town. He works at Paul Hamilton's electrical shop."

"Thank you," I said, squeezing her hand quickly before letting go.

She sniffled, pulled a tissue from underneath the counter, and dabbed at her nose and eyes with it. "I just can't believe someone would do something like that to Gino." She looked past me and out into the store. "Matt? Are you still here?"

Matt appeared from behind some postcards. "Yep, still here." He came toward the counter.

"Matt, Fran here just told me that your father—" She fought back a sob. "That your father was murdered. You can't believe how sorry I am. Gino was just such a wonderful man, and he loved you so much. He talked about you all the time and the important work you did. Fran said that you didn't know he was dating. I'm sure that was just because he didn't want you to think he was trying to replace your mother. I never knew her—I moved to town after she'd passed—but I understand that she was lovely, and I know your father still loved her very much. We would often talk about our late spouses and how different our lives had been since their passing. You know, you're what kept your father going all those years. He loved you more than anything."

Matt was speechless. I didn't think Mr. Cardosi had ever been openly affectionate with Matt, and that was likely the first time he'd ever heard such an enthusiastic expression of his father's love for him.

I saw Matt's Adam's apple bob as he swallowed hard.

"Thank you—" He stopped to clear his throat. "Thank you, uh, Mary Ellen. That means a lot." He raised his hand to his face, probably to wipe away a tear.

I rubbed his shoulder, and he gave me a weak smile of appreciation.

"Do you want to go?" I asked softly. I wasn't sure if Matt would cry in front of me, but I was certain he didn't want to do it in front of Mary Ellen. If we got outside, it would be easier for him to brush it off as the wind blowing something into his eye.

"Yeah," he said quickly.

I turned back to Mary Ellen. "Thank you for your help, Mary Ellen. I know Matt and I both appreciate it."

"Of course, dears. Come back any time. And Matt?

If you ever want to talk about your father with someone who cared for him also, please feel free to come by or call me." She handed him a business card with her cell phone number on the bottom. "I also text, if you prefer that. It's something I was trying to teach your father to do, but Gino was rather set in his ways."

"Yeah, he was," Matt said with a chuckle as he put the business card in his wallet. "And thank you again."

We left the shop and walked slowly toward the beach. I didn't say anything, leaving Matt with his thoughts of his father for the moment. We sat on a bench facing the water. I inhaled the salt air, enjoying the feeling of the breeze trying to pull my hair out of its loose chignon.

"So do you think this other guy Mary Ellen was seeing may have killed my dad?" Matt asked after a while.

"I don't know, but I want to talk to him. She said he works for Paul Hamilton, so I may have to go by there, at least to see what he looks like."

Matt nodded but didn't say anything. His elbows rested on his knees, hands folded, as he stared at the ocean.

"You okay?" I asked.

He nodded again. "Yeah, just hearing Mary Ellen say all that about how much my dad loved me and my mom—you know, that was stuff he never said to me. He wasn't affectionate like that. I guess he thought he had to be a manly man for me. I could have used that growing up—hearing he loved me. I was never sure if he really loved me or just tolerated having me around."

I didn't really know what to say. My mother and grandparents had always been warm and affectionate, giving lots of hugs and kisses and "I love you"s. But I was a girl. Maybe that was the difference. I rubbed his forearm, and he reached across with his other hand and squeezed mine. We stared at the crashing waves, each of us lost in our thoughts.

Chapter 14

I DIDN'T PURSUE the investigation much more that weekend. I needed to think about how I was going to handle the next step. Since this Karl Richards fellow was new in town, I couldn't rely on my prior knowledge as I had with Mary Ellen. I'd have to do some genuine sleuthing this time. I knew where he worked, but the store was closed on the weekends, so I couldn't go over and poke around until Monday. Monday was when I would see Sammy again and could bring up Karl without seeming overly curious. Matt was the only one who knew I was investigating his father's death, and it seemed best that I keep it that way, at least for the time being. So I lay low.

Matt and I went back to our respective houses after we left the beach on Saturday. Finding the owner of the phone number his dad had been calling had been our only purpose for getting together. It wasn't as if we were dating or doing anything that required spending much time together. And I was absolutely not going to let him pay for a third meal in a row, so not eating together was an easy way to avoid that debate. I spent the rest of Saturday and most of the day Sunday going through my grandparents' things in an effort to start my revamp of the house.

I started in their bedroom partly because that was the room I wanted to move into and partly because they'd been gone long enough that I didn't think it would be as painful to sort out their belongings as it would be my mother's. It was one thing to go into her room to borrow a shirt or some shoes, but to decide which items to throw out or donate to charity? That seemed nearly impossible. Her room still smelled like her. Most of her life had been spent sleeping in that bed and spraying her perfume between those walls. There was even still a stain on the carpet from where she'd spilled nail polish as a teenager. I had every intention of going through her room eventually, but for now, it seemed unbearable.

I started out with the plan to keep one box each of my grandmother's and grandfather's possessions, but as soon as I ran into joint belongings, like the sampler my grandmother had stitched with their names and wedding date, I decided on three boxes—one for her, one for him, and one for them together. Then I made a separate box for items I might want to use to decorate. I'd already decided that I'd never want to or be able to stop feeling their presence and that of my mother in the house, so I wanted to fill a whole wall in the living room with mementos—pictures, samplers, shelves with some particular favorite trinkets. My four-box system resulted in me keeping a bit more than I had planned, but my Donate and Trash piles were substantial enough that I didn't judge myself too harshly.

Monday rolled around, and I headed into the café for my shift, reminding myself that I needed to find a way to casually bring Karl Richards up to Sammy before she left. I needed to do it in a way that didn't seem too suspicious. It was a gorgeous day, sunny and not too hot, so the café wasn't very busy. During the summer, rainy days mid- to late-week were the ones that got us really busy. By then, each week's tourists had gotten comfortable enough with the town to know where they could go to escape the weather and their families at the same time.

"Hey! How was your weekend?" Sammy asked brightly as I came in.

"Pretty good, and yours?"

"It was good. My sister was in town with her kids, so I mostly hung out with them. Compared to where they live, this is the big city, so they had a pretty good time just wandering around town."

"I bet!" I laughed. Sammy's sister lived in the back woods of Maine with her lumberjack husband and their two kids. I couldn't imagine being that far away and out of touch with civilization.

Sammy and I worked for the next hour or so. I kept on the lookout for opportunities to ask her about Karl Richards, but we were both working pretty steadily, and I didn't get the chance until she was almost ready to leave. The café was quiet. No one was waiting for a drink, all the dishes had been washed, and all the counters were wiped down. Sammy was in the backroom folding some dish rags, so I walked in the back and helped her fold.

"Hey, do you know a guy named Karl Richards?" I asked, trying to sound as casual as I could. "I think he's new in town? I was talking to Mary Ellen over at the souvenir shop the other day, and she mentioned she was dating him. She said he comes in here sometimes, but I couldn't place him, so I thought I'd ask you." A little white lie surely couldn't hurt.

"Karl Richards," she repeated thoughtfully. "I think he works at the electronics shop, doesn't he?"

"Yeah, Mary Ellen mentioned something about that."

"I think he's been in here once or twice. Older guy, kind of nice-looking actually. He looks like he'd be the distinguished older agent in some spy thriller or something. That's about all I know about him. He doesn't say too much, kind of keeps to himself. That's probably why I think he looks like a spy." She giggled as she said it.

I folded some more towels. Quiet and nice-looking wasn't much to go on.

"Oh!" Sammy said after a minute. "He plays chess in the park a lot! I've seen him there on my way home from work."

That was something I could work with. My chess skills were rusty, but I'd be able to talk to him longer and get a better feel for the man from across the chess table than by trying to chat him up at work.

Sammy and I finished folding the towels, and she headed out for the day. The café stayed medium busy the rest of the day, enough so that I stayed on the move but didn't feel frantic or fall behind on keeping things neat. As I walked home that night after closing up, I noticed that it was already getting dark. It always seems unfair that the summer solstice is in June, when the summer months are only just starting. By the end of the summer, it would be dark out long before I closed the café for the night.

That night, as I continued going through my grandparents' things—there was a lot stuffed in that little bedroom!—I came up with my plan for how I would talk to Karl. In the back of my grandfather's closet was an old radio that hadn't worked for as long as I could remember. In the morning, I'd take that over to the electronics shop and talk to them about getting it fixed. Hopefully I'd run into Karl there and get a look at him. Then, later on, I'd just happen to run into him at the park and try to get myself into a game of chess with him. That would give me plenty of time to get him talking and ever-so-casually bring up Mr. Cardosi. With any luck, he'd slip up and give me some information I could use. It wasn't a foolproof plan—lots of hoping and trying and lucking into things—but it seemed as though it had a decent chance of working. I put the radio by the front door, set my alarm for earlier than I would have liked, and went to bed.

The next morning, bright and early, I headed over to the electronics shop, ancient radio in hand. The door announced my presence with the customary jingle, but no one came out to greet me. I walked in and rested my grandfather's radio on the counter while I waited. After a couple of minutes with no sign of life from the back, I leaned across the counter and looked around. I saw a bell tucked behind the register where it was virtually impossible for a customer to find it. I pulled it around toward me and tapped it rapidly three times.

From the back, I heard old men's voices, but I couldn't make out what they were saying. I could tell there were two of them though. I was getting ready to tap the bell again when an older man came out of the back. He had a thick shock of white hair carefully combed back, and he was wearing a neat black shirt tucked into his khaki pants. I noticed with pleasure that he was wearing a name tag with "Karl" printed on it. Sammy was right—he was pretty nice-looking for an older guy.

"Can I help you?" he asked. He didn't sound as though he particularly wanted to help me, but he didn't sound quite hostile about it either. It was the most neutral, perfunctory tone I could imagine. Certainly not the warm, inviting style of greeting my grandfather had drilled into me.

I smiled my biggest, friendliest smile. "Hi, um, Karl, is it?" I pretended I was just now reading his name tag. I thought I saw him give a brief nod, but it was clear that was all I would get. "I'm Francesca Amaro. I run Antonia's Italian Café down the way." I stuck out my hand.

He took it reluctantly and gave it one hesitant shake before letting go.

"Karl, my late grandfather—" I paused for effect, hoping my grandfather wouldn't mind too much my invoking his memory this way. "Had this old radio in the back of his closet. For the life of me, I can't get it to work, but I have such fond memories of listening to Red Sox games on it with him that I'd love to get it working again. Do you think you can help me?" I was banking on

Karl not having relocated to Cape Bay from New York or some other rival baseball team's territory. The one sentence he had uttered didn't sound particularly "Noo Yawk-y," so I thought I was safe.

He pulled the radio toward him and popped open the empty battery compartment. After closing it back up, he plugged the cord in under the counter. He punched a few buttons. As expected, nothing happened.

"We'll take a look." He scrawled out a ticket and handed it to me. He scribbled some more on another piece of paper and taped it onto the radio. He picked it up and turned to walk into the back.

Was that how they treated their customers?

"How much will it be?" I asked.

"Won't know until we figure out what's wrong," he said.

"Well, how will you contact me to let me know?"

"You said you work at Antonia's, right?"

"I own it, yes."

"We'll call you there," he said, not unkindly but not exactly warmly either.

I opened my mouth to say something else, but I couldn't quite figure out what that should be. "Well, thank you!" I gave him a big smile. If he couldn't be polite, at least I could be. "I'll look forward to hearing from you!"

He nodded and disappeared into the back. Mary

Ellen certainly had unusual taste in men. For such an exuberant woman, she seemed to like her men quiet and a little grumpy.

There was nothing else I could do there, so I took myself for a walk. Sammy had said that she often saw Karl playing chess at the park in the early afternoons. I wasn't sure what time he usually got there, but I guessed it might be after lunch, when I was supposed to be working. I pulled out my cell phone and called the café. Sammy answered on the second ring.

"Antonia's Italian Café, this is Samantha. How may I help you?" she singsonged.

"Hey, Sammy, it's Fran."

"Oh hey!" she said, much less formally. "What's up?"

"Do you think you could get somebody to cover for me if I took today off?"

Sammy only paused for a second. "Yeah, I'll call Rhonda and see if she can come in."

Rhonda was a little older than me, and she worked for us a few hours a week, mostly during the school year when her kids were out of the house. They were old enough now that she didn't have to be home with them all the time, but she still liked to keep an eye on them when she could.

"Okay, that's great," I said. "Tell her I'll put a little extra in her paycheck for the short notice."

"Oh, you know that'll get her in!" Sammy laughed.

I knew it would. Rhonda mainly worked to fund her occasional trips to Neiman Marcus. A couple hours' work at the café didn't go very far there, but I think she liked being able to buy something from the makeup counter and walk out with a Neiman Marcus bag for everyone to see.

I thanked Sammy and hung up, leaving myself a few hours to wander around town. It was actually fun. Thinking about that furry friend I wanted to get, I walked to the animal shelter across from the police station. I thought about popping in to see if Mike had made any progress on Mr. Cardosi's case, but I figured he didn't need to be bothered, and I didn't have any solid leads of my own yet that I wanted to share.

I walked into the animal shelter and smiled at the girl behind the desk.

"Hello!" I said. "I was wondering if you had any adoptable pets I could look at?"

"Of course!" she replied. "Are you looking for a dog or a cat?"

"I'm not sure yet." I shrugged. "I like both. It just depends on who I fall in love with."

"Not a problem. Everyone's through there," she said, gesturing to a door behind her. "Dogs are on the right, and cats are on the left. Let me know if you have any questions about any of the animals or if you find someone you want to adopt!" She was an exceptionally chipper young woman.

I went into the cat room first. It was much nicer than I remembered. About five kitties shared two large spaces with scratching posts and places to climb and even a few toys. I stopped at each enclosure. They were adorable, but none of them really called out to me.

I went over to the dog space next. It was also much fancier than it had been. That was actually nice to see. I always felt bad for dogs locked in cages that seemed both sterile and filthy at the same time. If the dogs had still been kept that way, I might have adopted them all just out of pity. They all seemed comfortable and happy, but none of them quite made me feel like they were My Dog.

I walked back out into the lobby.

"Find anybody you liked?" she asked.

"No, not today," I said, shaking my head. "But I'll be back."

"That's great!" she replied. "We'll look forward to seeing you!"

I walked outside. I was near the park, so I walked in that direction. I could see the chess tables from the road, so I would be able to see if Karl was there without seeming as though I was spying or lurking. Only two men were sitting at the tables, and neither one was Karl. I would have to wait to see if he'd show up later.

It was still on the early side, so I ate beach food and strolled around some streets I hadn't been on since my return. I went past my old best friend's house—her family had moved to California when we were in high school. We'd exchanged letters then emails on and off ever since. The new owners had repainted the house and completely changed the front garden, so I had to look at the house number to make sure I was looking at the right place. It reminded me that I should email her—I hadn't told her about my mother's death yet, let alone Mr. Cardosi's. She had also played with Matt when we were kids, and she still asked about him every once in a while.

When I felt as though I'd wandered around long enough that Karl might be at the park, I turned back in that direction. I was on the back side of the park, so I had to go around the pond and up the hill stairs to get to the chess tables. The stairs were at an angle, so I couldn't see anything at the top of them until I came up over the hill. As I crested the hill and came around the corner, I smiled. Karl was sitting at one of the chess tables, all by himself.

Chapter 15

I STROLLED up to him as casually as I could, trying to look as though I was just wandering through the park before I came across my new acquaintance.

"Karl?" I said as I got close.

He looked at me. I could tell he couldn't quite place me at first, but after a few seconds, I saw recognition dawn on his face.

"Francesca. You brought in your grandfather's radio." He still had that very neutral tone.

"Do you mind if I join you?" I asked, smiling and slipping into the seat across from him without waiting for an answer. He had the chess pieces already laid out. "My grandfather used to bring me here to play chess with his buddies when I was a kid. It's been a long time, but I think I can still hold my own if you want to play a game."

He didn't say anything, just nodded and moved his pawn.

We were mostly quiet during the game. That had been my grandfather's style of play also. Whenever I started to be too much of a chatterbox, he would stop playing and lean back with his arms crossed until I noticed and stopped talking. It had taken a while, but I eventually learned my lesson.

I kept up with Karl pretty well for a while, but it was quickly evident that he was a much better player and much more practiced. I managed to work my way out of a check once, but only a couple of moves after that, he called checkmate. I stared at the board in complete surprise. I thought I'd at least had it under control—the checkmate took me completely off guard. I looked at him with my mouth open. I was surprised to see a bit of a smile on his face, the first hint of emotion I had seen from him. He reached his hand across the table for me to shake.

"I didn't even see that coming," I said as we shook hands.

"I think your grandfather would be proud if that's how you play when you've been away from the game for a while. I thought I had you a couple times, but you made good moves to get out of it."

"Thank you," I said. That really felt like a genuine compliment. "So you're new in town, right?"

He seemed to give me a suspicious look as we went about setting the pieces back up. "I am."

"What brought you to Cape Bay?" I felt as though he wasn't eager to answer the question, so I kept talking in an effort to set him at ease. "Friends? Family? Just looking to retire by the sea?"

He continued eyeing me, but at least he answered. "Retirement. The beach seemed like a good place to start this part of my life."

"Well, that's nice!" I said cheerily, trying to keep the conversation going. "Do you have any grandkids that'll be coming to visit you? I can imagine Grandpa living by the beach would be quite a draw!"

"No kids, no grandkids," he said briefly.

"Oh well, at least you don't have to worry about them tracking sand all over your house then!" I was trying to keep the conversation going even though I felt as if I was sinking. "How long have you been in town?"

"Few months."

"Oh, just in time for the summer tourist season! Well, after Labor Day, things will calm down quite a bit. We get tourists all year 'round, but summer is naturally the busiest." I glanced at him. He didn't have much of a reaction, so I kept going. "This summer has been especially crazy for me. I grew up here, but I was living in

New York until a couple of months ago. My mom—I don't know if you got to meet her—her name was Carmella? She ran Antonia's?"

He didn't really give any indication as to whether he had met her or not.

I went on. "She passed away a couple months ago, and I moved back to run the café. Then just a few weeks ago, my neighbor Gino Cardosi—he was the town barber?—*he* died." Still no reaction. I decided to go for broke. I leaned in. "And there's a rumor that he was *murdered*. Can you believe it? A murder in Cape Bay? It's been a crazy summer!"

I leaned back and watched his face. I saw something flicker across it, but I wasn't sure what it was. What was clear was that he was frowning more than he had been, and he was picking up the chess pieces instead of putting them down.

"I didn't realize the time. I have to go," he said brusquely and without looking at his watch. He put the pieces all back into their spaces in the case and closed it. "Nice playing with you."

He walked away before I had a chance to fully process what was going on. I had obviously hit a nerve with my comments about Mr. Cardosi. I sat at the table, completely stunned. Who acted like that? And how guilty did it make him look? Very guilty, in my opinion.

I looked around to see if any of the other chess

players had noticed Karl's peculiar behavior. It didn't seem that anyone had. They were all going about their games, oblivious to what had just happened at my table. I stood slowly and walked through the park, still baffled by the turn of events. Confused as I was, I knew I wanted to go home and get online to see what I could find out about Karl Richards.

I walked quickly through the park, down the stairs, and around the pond. I arrived back at my house and headed straight up the stairs to my room to get my laptop. As usual, it took forever to boot up, but once it did, Karl spelling his name with a K instantly made my investigation easier.

Six months ago, Karl Richards, age 61, had been released from prison after completing a twenty-year sentence for multiple counts of robbery.

I leaned back in my chair and stared at the computer. There was no way that was right. But right there in front of my disbelieving eyes was his mug shot. He was younger in the picture, with fewer lines on his face and much darker hair, but his hair was just as thick and still combed back in the same style. Besides, the caption laid it out for me:

Karl Richards, now age 61, as he looked upon his sentencing

I read the accompanying article that had been published after his release. Conveniently for me, it gave a detailed overview of his case for people who didn't know about or remember his crimes. Apparently Karl had spent years breaking into the homes of the rich residents of Boston, picking their safes, and stealing their highest-priced valuables. Detectives were stuck for over a decade as the robberies continued. The jewels never showed up in local pawn shops or at any traceable auctions, foreign or domestic, despite the astronomically high prices they would bring. The police came to the conclusion that they had been sold directly to overseas buyers who had the wisdom not to resell them. But the robberies continued. No matter how sophisticated a security system someone installed, Karl, or the Filigree Filcher as the media took to calling him before they knew his identity, managed to get past it.

Homeowners and the police tried everything from stakeouts to booby traps. The Filigree Filcher didn't seem to have any kind of pattern, rhyme, or reason to his thefts. The police couldn't determine any connection between the victims beyond their wealth and exquisite taste in jewelry. He'd go quiet for so long that everyone assumed that he must have died, moved away, or been arrested for an unrelated crime. Then he'd pop back up, stealing something more glamorous and expensive than anything he'd stolen before and from a house with an even more elaborate security system.

It wasn't until a good fifteen years into his thievery that a homeowner managed to rig up a night vision camera system that got a picture of the Filigree Filcher in action without him realizing. They plastered his image all over the news and newspapers, and it only took a few days for someone to identify the man in the picture as mild-mannered Karl Richards, who worked as an electrical engineer for a popular stereo maker.

When the police searched his home, they were shocked to find every single piece of jewelry that had been stolen over the years packed into shoe boxes and tucked away into his closet. He hadn't sold, given away, or otherwise divested himself of anything he had taken. The mountain of evidence against him was insurmountable. Despite that, he refused to plead guilty and was convicted of every last charge at trial. He declined to ever give a reason for his crimes. Because of the sheer number of thefts and the hundreds of millions of dollars the jewelry added up to, he was sentenced to twenty years in prison. He'd had opportunities to get out on parole, and he had declined all of them. He didn't leave prison until he had served every last day of his sentence.

Even after reading the whole article, and several others I found online, I still couldn't quite believe it. "Retirement" indeed! He'd moved to Cape Bay because he was too well-known to go back to Boston! I wondered if he was still up to his crimes. Not that we had the kind of fabulously wealthy people with extravagant jewelry that Boston had. And I hadn't heard of any robberies.

News like that traveled fast in our small town. Whether or not that was what he was up to, though, what I knew was that I was looking at a known criminal who had a clear motive to murder Mr. Cardosi—they were both dating the same woman. *And* they'd openly despised each other.

Then I thought of something else. What if Mr. Cardosi had done the same Internet search I had? He hadn't been a very technologically savvy guy, but I'd seen a computer in his house and it wasn't really that hard to do a search. That lent a whole new element of intrigue to the case. If Mr. Cardosi had known about Karl's criminal history and threatened to tell Mary Ellen about it if Karl didn't back off, then Karl would have not one but two motives for murder.

For the first time since I'd started looking into Mr. Cardosi's death, I had a murder suspect.

Chapter 16

MY MIND WAS SWIRLING with my discovery. I wondered if the police knew, if they'd gotten this far in their investigation. I debated calling Mike right away to share what I'd learned, but I decided I should fill Matt in first. He was at work, of course, and this wasn't the kind of information I could give by text or over the phone, so I'd have to wait until he got home. I grabbed my cell phone to send him a text.

I found out something kind of big. Can we get together tonight?

I went back to my computer and looked at Karl's mug shot again. Murder was a far cry from robbery, but I imagined that twenty years in prison could change a man. Still, was that the face of a man who would kill another man? Could the man who had complimented my chess game have murdered my neighbor? That was where the evidence was pointing, and a good investigator couldn't ignore the evidence.

My text message alert sounded. I went back over and picked up my phone.

Sure. Want to get dinner too?

Dinner sounded good, but only if I was paying. I texted him back to say so. His reply came in quickly.

Yeah, we'll see about that. ;)

A winky face! What did a winky face mean? Was it just a casual, joking reference to our ongoing debate on who was paying, or was he flirting with me? I wasn't sure and I didn't necessarily think it required a reply, so I left it alone.

I picked up the little notebook I'd been keeping my notes in. It was almost full. I needed to buy another one, but for now, I'd just go back to my legal pad. I flipped through the pages until I got to a blank one. There, I wrote down every detail of my two interactions with Karl Richards and a summary of what I'd found online, complete with the URLs of the articles I'd consulted.

By the time I was done, it was late afternoon, so I didn't have long to wait before Matt got off work. I went downstairs and worked through some more of my grandparents' things. I was making good progress. I'd completely finished both of their closets when I heard my text message alert. I was concerned that Matt might be cancelling our dinner, and I was surprised to see that it was already past five. I must have gotten way more involved in sorting and categorizing than I'd realized.

Heading your way. Hope you're hungry.

I put a last couple of things in boxes then headed upstairs to check my hair and makeup. It wasn't that I wanted to make sure I looked good for Matt. It had just been a fairly long day, and I was certain that I looked like a mess. But I didn't look as bad as I thought. I tucked a few hairs back in place, touched up my makeup, and decided I was satisfied.

The doorbell conveniently rang at that moment. I ran downstairs, checked the peephole to make sure it was Matt, and pulled the door open. He was grinning and holding a pizza.

"Hungry?" he asked as he stepped past me.

I just stood there gawking at him and the food that he'd paid for. "You sneak!" I fully realized that was such a weak insult it didn't even deserve to be called one.

"I thought it would be easier if we just ate in," he called over his shoulder as he walked toward the kitchen.

"But I was supposed to pay for dinner tonight!" I shut the door and followed him.

"Oh yeah!" he said innocently. "I completely forgot!"

"You lie!"

He shrugged. "Yeah, maybe." He put the pizza on the counter. "What goes with pizza? Red or white? What do you have?"

"I have red," I said, stalking across the kitchen to the wine rack.

I pulled out a bottle I thought would go well with pizza and slapped it into his hand. I pulled open the drawer where I kept the corkscrew and handed it to him. Matt opened the bottle as I got two glasses. He filled them generously and handed me one. I wasn't actually mad at him for buying dinner yet again, but I didn't want to take advantage of him.

"I got margherita. I hope that's okay. I figured it was simple and classic enough I couldn't really go wrong."

Margherita was fine by me. As far as I was concerned, simple and classic was the only way to go with pizza. We sat and ate at the kitchen table, sipping our wine between bites.

"So what was it you wanted to tell me?" Matt asked when we were finished.

I took a deep breath and anxiously played with the stem of my wine glass. This was big news, and I wasn't quite sure how to tell him.

"Franny?" he said after I had remained silent for a good minute or two.

"I managed to talk to Karl Richards—that guy who was also dating Mary Ellen. He was kind of weird, especially when I mentioned your dad's murder. He basically just got up and walked away. So I looked him up online."

"And?" Matt prompted when I fell silent again.

I took another deep breath. "And it turns out he's a convicted felon. Robbery, but he spent twenty years in jail. I-I think he might have killed your dad."

Matt looked at me in silence. I couldn't tell what he was thinking. When I noticed the way he was working his jaw, though, I had a pretty good idea.

"You think he killed my dad over Mary Ellen?" he asked after a moment.

"That, and I think it's possible that your dad found out about Karl's criminal record and tried to use it to pressure him to break up with her."

"You have evidence of that?" he asked.

"No," I admitted. "But I think it's something the police need to be aware of. I thought I'd go talk to Mike about it tomorrow."

Matt nodded. "I think that's a good idea. They should look into it as soon as possible. If he killed my dad, I want him in jail, not out walking the streets."

"I'll go first thing in the morning," I assured him. "Do you want to come with me?"

"No, I'll let you handle it. I—" He seemed to be looking for the right words, maybe to say that he wanted to think about the circumstances of his father's death as little as possible. He shook his head slightly. "I'll let you handle it."

We talked for a little while longer, some about his dad and some about other things. I told him about my plan to sort through all of my mother's and grandparents' things and redecorate the house in more my style. He suggested that I work on his dad's house when I was done at mine. He was making a good effort to keep up the conversation, but I could tell his mind was elsewhere. Eventually he admitted it and said he should probably just go home so he could be alone with his thoughts.

"Are you sure you'll be okay?" I asked as I walked him to the door.

"Yeah. I just need to go home and chill out and get some rest."

I eyed him warily. "You're not going to do anything stupid, are you?" Matt had never been the violent type, but he'd never before dealt with the possibility of knowing the identity of the man who had killed his father.

"No! No," Matt scoffed. "That's for the police to handle." He rubbed his face. "I just need to go home and turn on the ball game or something and chill out. No offense." He put a hand on my shoulder.

"None taken. We all need personal time."

He pulled me into a hug. "Thank you for looking into this. I know the police are too, but I know it's personal for you. It makes it a little easier knowing someone who cares so much is on it."

"Of course, Matty," I said. "You know I'll do anything I can to help get this all wrapped up for you.

You shouldn't have to deal with your father's murder being unsolved for one second longer than you have to."

"Thank you." He rubbed his hands up and down my back. He finally let me go and headed out to his car.

I went straight upstairs to review my notes again before bed. I had a big day coming up, and I wanted make sure I was ready.

I woke up excited and raring to go. I wanted to look professional, like someone whose opinion a police officer would take seriously, so I pulled out one of the outfits I used to wear to make presentations to clients in New York and put that on. I styled my hair a little more than I'd been doing to go to work at the café. All in all, I thought it came together nicely. I got my notes together and made sure they were in order so I could refer to them quickly if Mike had any questions. I gave myself one last glance in the mirror and headed for the police station.

"Is Mike Stanton in?" I asked the woman at the front desk.

She looked at me over her glasses. "Who can I tell him is here?"

I gave her a big, professional smile. "Francesca Amaro."

She looked at me again then pulled off her glasses. "Fran? It's me, Margaret. Margaret Robbins. From high school."

I stared at her. The name sounded familiar, but the face didn't register.

"Cheerleading squad?" she prompted.

All of a sudden, it clicked. I could see her in my mind's eye in a short cheerleading skirt with her long hair pulled up into a high ponytail. "Margaret! I'm so sorry! I've just been running into so many people I haven't seen in years, and it's taking a while to place everyone."

"Oh no, I understand. I didn't recognize you until you said your name." She paused. "I'm very sorry about your mother. And you found Gino Cardosi's body, didn't you? Is that what you're here to talk to Mike about? Let me call him for you." She picked up her desk phone and punched a few buttons.

I remembered something else about her as she murmured into the phone—it had always been hard to get a word in edgewise when talking to her.

She hung up and smiled at me. "If you want to have a seat over there, Mike will be out in just a minute."

I thanked her and sat in one of the ancient pleather chairs lining the walls of the lobby. I took a deep breath. I was actually getting a little nervous. I felt good about my theory—it was solid—but I wasn't sure how Mike would feel about me doing my own investigating. I didn't want him to feel as though I was invading his turf, but I'd felt strongly that I needed to help Matt. I had a duty to him as his friend and to his father as the one who found his body.

Mike stepped into the lobby and glanced around the room for me. He gave me a tight smile when he saw me. "Fran? If you'd like to come with me?"

He held open the door that he had just come through. I felt unnervingly as though he were calling me back to be questioned instead of me coming to give him information. I walked through the door, and he led me to a small, windowless room that I suspected they used for interrogations. It didn't lessen the weird feeling I had in the pit of my stomach.

"Have a seat," Mike said, gesturing at the lone metal chair in the room.

I sat and put my notes on the table. I noticed that my hands were shaking. I'd never been in the interrogation room of a police station before. The atmosphere must be getting to me.

Mike perched on the edge of the table. "So what can I help you with today, Fran?"

This was a different Mike from the one I'd seen in the initial stages of the investigation. That Mike had been warm and jovial, the guy I grew up with. This Mike was stern and terse. I had a feeling that if this were a good cop/bad cop situation, I would be dealing with the bad cop. I had to look up to talk to him and couldn't help but wonder if that was an intentional power move, like when a talk show host's chair is ever-so-subtly raised six inches above his guests. Even though I was there of my own volition, it all made me nervous.

I inhaled deeply and spread my hands on the table to steady them. "Well, Mike, I'm here because—" I took another deep breath and looked him dead in the eye. "I'm here because I know who killed Gino Cardosi."

Chapter 17

MIKE RAISED his eyebrows and was silent for a moment longer than I was comfortable with. "You know who killed Gino Cardosi," he finally said slowly.

I nodded. "Yes, I do."

Mike looked at me silently for longer than I would have liked. "And who is that?"

"Karl Richards. You might not know him. He's new in town, but I did some investigating, and I'm confident that he did it."

"You are," Mike said, more as a statement than a question. The way he kept using that flat tone of voice was making me nervous.

"Yes." I flipped through a couple of pages of my notes, looking for the one that had my findings about Karl. "See, he and Mr. Cardosi were both dating Mary

Ellen Chapman, which in and of itself isn't necessarily a huge motive for murder, but I did some research online…" I hesitated when Mike stood and started walking back and forth on the other side of the room, his arms crossed. I wasn't sure what that was about, so I just kept going. "And I found out that he has a criminal record. A major one. Six months ago—"

Mike spun around and slammed his hands on the table. "Do you think I don't know that?" He sounded really pretty angry.

"Um, I don't—I didn't think—"

"You didn't think what?"

"I didn't think you knew the thing about Mary Ellen. I only found out because Matt and I went looking for Mr. Cardosi's cell phone because Chris at the cell phone shop told me Mr. Cardosi was looking for a new one, and when Matt and I found it, there were just a bunch of calls to Mary Ellen's number—" I was rambling, but Mike was making me nervous.

"Have you ever heard of phone records, Fran?" Mike asked, sounding exasperated.

"Yes." Of course I had. That was what the phone company sent me every month with my cell phone bill— a complete record of everyone I'd called. *Oh.*

"We're the police. The first thing we do when we have a murder victim is pull his phone records. We don't have to go looking for his cell phone. The phone company knows all that. Hell, the phone company can give us the contents of all his text messages. Sent *and* received."

I was starting to feel a little bad. As soon as Mike said it, it made perfect sense that they had pulled Mr. Cardosi's phone records and knew everyone he'd talked to. But the thing about Karl Richards—that had to be new information, right? Against my better judgement, I said it. "But Karl Richards—?"

He rubbed his face. I got the sense he couldn't believe he was having this conversation.

"Karl Richards just finished serving twenty years in prison. You think he's going to kill somebody so he can get himself sent right back?"

"You think he's not?" I asked, a little indignant. He couldn't just blow off my theory because he thought Karl would abide by the law so he could avoid prison. Prison hadn't seemed to scare him very much over the fifteen years he was stealing jewelry and hoarding the evidence. "You don't think Mr. Cardosi could have found out about Karl's criminal record and threatened to out him to Mary Ellen? You don't think Karl could have killed him to stop him?"

"No, I don't," Mike said firmly.

"And why not?" I asked.

"Because he was at his doctor's office in Boston when Gino Cardosi was killed."

Oh. Well, that changed things. I went from feeling a little bad to a lot bad. And like maybe my detective skills weren't as good as I thought they were. The metal chair I was sitting in suddenly felt very cold and hard. I tried to think of where I had gone wrong, what lead I'd failed to track down. Apparently I'd forgotten to check Karl's alibi, but it had seemed like such a slam dunk!

"You can't go poking your nose in police business," Mike said, interrupting my thoughts. "There's a reason why we don't just leave it to civilians to solve crimes. Hell, there's a reason we don't just let rookies investigate crimes on their own! It's hard. It takes training. A lot can go wrong, and you can ruin someone's life by accusing them of a crime. It's not something to be taken lightly!"

I couldn't remember ever seeing Mike so worked up, except maybe on the football field in high school. It made me realize why police interrogations worked so well. Normal Mike was a pleasant enough guy, but this version of him was a little scary. If I'd committed a crime, I'd be shaking in my boots from watching him pace around and rant and rave.

He took a deep breath, as if he was trying to calm himself down. "Look, I know you were just trying to help Matt figure out what happened to his dad, but you can't just go messing in people's lives. Do you know how freaked out Karl was after you talked to him? He thought you were going to tell the whole town that he was a convicted jewel thief. He thought he would have to pick up and move again to get away from the rumors. He's an old man, Fran, and he's paid his debt to society. It's not up to you to make him continue paying."

I barely heard the rest of what Mike said after he mentioned that Karl had been freaked out after I'd talked to him. *How did he know that?* I held up my hand to stop him. "How did you know I talked to Karl?"

Mike sighed. "He came in here and told me."

I was confused. "He just walked in here and told you that? Why?"

"Like I said, because he was worried."

"So he just came in here and confessed that he was a jewel thief and said he was worried that I was going to drive him out of town?"

Mike looked at me as if I wasn't getting something obvious. "I'd already questioned him, Francesca."

He'd used my full name. That was bad.

"When I identified him as a suspect, I pulled his criminal record," Mike said. "I interviewed him and asked him about it. Then when you showed up, talking to him about the Cardosi case, he got worried and came in to talk to me. He moved here to start a new life where people didn't know his name and his face, and you took that from him. You think something like that will stay a secret for long in Cape Bay? And what do you think Mary Ellen'll do when she finds out? You think she'll just be cool with it? God, Fran, you've got to just leave it alone from here on out, okay? No more investigating, no more slinking around asking people questions. You've got to cool it, okay?"

I nodded. I was embarrassed to say the least. I thought I'd been slick enough that Karl hadn't realized I suspected him of anything, but apparently I was wrong. I'd accidentally tipped him off to my sleuthing, which wasn't exactly a brilliant investigative technique, and possibly ruined his newfound anonymity and romantic relationship. I hadn't set out to ruin anybody's life—at least, no one other than the person who'd killed Mr. Cardosi—but apparently I'd done that, or nearly done it anyway. "I'm sorry, Mike."

"I'm not the one you owe an apology," he said curtly.

I nodded. I did owe Karl an apology. I might not be able to fix what I'd done, but I could at least let him know I was sorry.

Mike stood there for another minute or so before he asked me if there was anything else I wanted to share with him.

"No," I said quietly. "There's nothing else."

"Do you need a minute, or are you ready to go?"

Apparently I was more visibly shaken up than I realized. "I'm ready to go." I gathered up my papers.

Mike put his hand on the doorknob then looked back at me. "Just so you know, I'm not mad at you. Like I said,

I know you were just trying to help Matt, and I know it's personal for you because you found the body. And that's on top of you already having a rough summer. Just try to chill out a little, okay?"

I nodded as I picked up my notes and walked to the door. Mike patted my back as we went out.

"I'll see you around," he said as he bid me good-bye in the lobby.

"See you," I replied.

I walked outside and stood on the sidewalk, facing the park. I could go straight across the park toward home, where I could crawl back into bed or curl up on the couch to watch some crappy daytime TV court shows. Or I could turn left and go to the café to bury myself in work for a while. But I turned right to go down the street to Paul Hamilton's electronics shop. I wanted to apologize.

Chapter 18

AFTER MY FIRST VISIT, I knew not to expect anyone at the electronics shop to appear immediately upon my arrival, but it still took so long that I was hunting for the bell before Karl came out to greet me. He didn't exactly look excited to have a customer in the first place, but his face got even more miserable-looking when he saw me.

"If you're here about your radio, it'll be ready tomorrow," he said by way of greeting.

"That's actually not why I'm here, but thank you." I had butterflies in my stomach. I always got nervous when I had to admit to screwing up or doing something wrong, but when I had to admit to a man that I had thought he was a murderer and had even gone to the police to tell them, I was extra nervous.

He just stared at me. I guessed if I wasn't there about

my grandfather's radio, he wasn't interested in finding out what I did want. Not that I blamed him, under the circumstances. I tried to smile. We were standing barely a couple of feet apart with only the counter between us. I wasn't sure if anyone was in the back, but I thought I heard some shuffling. Assuming that whoever was back there didn't know about Karl's history, I didn't want to negate my apology by filling them in.

"Karl, I understand that I owe you an apology," I said quietly.

He gave no indication that he'd heard me but none that he hadn't either.

"I made some assumptions and leapt to some conclusions and came up with something that was totally wrong. I should have stayed out of it and let the police do their job. I'm sorry," I said.

He stared at me for a few seconds then gave me the slightest of nods. "Thank you." We looked at each other for a few more seconds. "Is there anything else?"

"No," I replied. "That's all."

"We'll call you when your radio's done," he said and turned to go into the back.

He was a strange man for sure, but I didn't fault him for not wanting to hang around talking to me. I waited until he had disappeared, just to make sure he wasn't going to suddenly turn around and come back, then left to go home. I could have gone to work, but I needed to think. I tucked my papers under my arm and shoved my hands in my pockets as I walked toward the park and its shortcut to my house.

It had been, by pretty much every imaginable measure, a pretty awful summer. First my fiancé had left me, then my mother passed away, then Mr. Cardosi was murdered, then I accused an innocent man of the crime. At least only one of those things was my fault. The rest of it was just the universe trying to mess with me. What doesn't kill you makes you stronger, right? That was what my mother would have said anyway. So far the only good that had come out of the past few months was getting to quit my job and escape the New York City rat race. That, and getting to reconnect with Matt. Spending time with Matt again was like getting transported back in time to my high school days, but without all the awkwardness that came with being in high school. Being with him now was just fun. I was my adult self, with all of my knowledge and confidence, but without all the awkwardness that usually came with dating someone new. Not that Matt and I were dating. We just didn't have any getting-to-know-you discomfort when we hung out.

Being so off-balance from all the changes in my personal life had to be how I'd gone so wrong with the whole Karl debacle. Everything I'd relied on for so many years had been completely upended. I'd latched on to my investigation of Mr. Cardosi's murder as something to give me purpose and direction, but work could give me that. Redecorating my house could give me that. My friends—Matt and Sammy—could give me that. My new pet could give me that, as soon as I found him. I didn't need to be an amateur detective to have purpose, especially since I was apparently pretty terrible at it. My work, my house, my friends, and my pet would be my focus. That was what I would do with myself and my time.

I was in the park, walking past the chess tables. A dog ran along by the tree line. It stood out to me because stray dogs weren't common in Cape Bay. I thought he must have gotten off his leash or escaped his yard. He didn't have a collar, but I remembered one time when I was a kid and my best friend and I were walking her dog. He had managed to slip completely out of his collar and left us standing with an empty collar hanging from the leash. I wondered if this dog had done the same thing. He didn't seem particularly interested in or afraid of me. He just ran along, roughly keeping pace with me as I walked fairly quickly through the park. Eventually, though, he turned off and ran down the hill ahead of me, as if he'd suddenly realized he had somewhere to be.

It must not have been too far away, though, because as I got toward the stairs, I heard him barking. The closer I got, the louder and more frantic it got. I usually almost ran down the stairs, but when I reached the top, I realized the dog was right at the bottom, barking furiously. I hesitated, resting my hand on the railing. Just as I decided not to show the strange dog any fear and lifted my foot to take the first step, I felt something sweep my feet out from under me.

I yelped as my face flew down toward the steep concrete stairs. My papers went flying, and I barely stopped myself from tumbling down the stairs head over heels. If my hand hadn't already been on the railing, I wouldn't have been able to stop myself. Sharp pain shot up my right leg as I twisted on it in an attempt to regain my footing. The dog flew up the stairs past me, still barking loudly. My arm wrenched as my body rotated toward the top of the stairs. I saw feet clad in men's shoes disappearing back toward the chess tables, assisted by the cane I instinctively knew had been used to trip me. The dog perched on the top stair, barking at the fleeing feet.

I struggled to my feet to follow the tripper and his cane, but as soon as I put weight on my leg, it gave out beneath me. With the amount of pain I felt, there was no way I was walking anywhere. I wiggled around so that I was sitting on one of the steps, my hurt leg stretched out in front of me. I tensed up when the dog came down the couple of stairs to where I was sitting. When he immediately shoved his wet nose into my palm, I calmed down, though. He was a friendly dog. His mouth was shaped as if he were smiling. Medium-sized with scruffy gray and brown fur, he looked like a stray. I wondered where he had come from.

It occurred to me, if not for his barking, I would have been going a lot faster and not holding onto the stair railing when I was tripped. He wasn't just friendly —he was *my* friend. I scratched his head in thanks.

As soon as I did, as if that indicated to him that I was okay, he ran back up the stairs and barked again. I turned as best I could to look up toward where he was standing, but he disappeared from my view and his barking faded. I sighed. Maybe he wasn't my friend after all. I was glancing around at my notes scattered all over the ground and trying to figure out how I'd get myself up or down the stairs when I heard his barking get louder again. I looked back up to see the dog return. He scampered down the stairs, bumped his nose against me, then took off back up the stairs, barking furiously. The barking got fainter then louder as he repeated his run-away-and-come-back pattern. I wondered if it was possible that he was trying to get help. That seemed like an out-there idea and I hadn't exactly had the best track record with crazy ideas lately, but what else could he be doing, running back and forth like that?

I couldn't just sit there and wait, even if he was trying to help me. I glanced up and down the stairs. I had definitely landed closer to the top than the bottom. I pushed my right heel into one of the steps below me. Pain shot back up my leg. Definitely my knee hurt. I tested my left leg. That one had been spared. I braced my palms against the step above me and pushed up with my arms and my left leg. I only had a few steps to get up. As long as I didn't put any pressure on my right leg, I was okay. I worked my way up the stairs as the dog continued to race back and forth. I crested the stairs and scooted off to the edge of the sidewalk.

The dog raced back again and sat on the pavement next to me. He kept barking, so loud it hurt my ears a little, and I had to lean away. Even so, I couldn't help but reach out to scratch my new buddy's chest.

"Franny, is that you? Are you okay?"

I looked up, shocked to hear Matt's voice. "Yeah, I just had a little tumble."

Matt hurried over and crouched down beside me.

"What are you doing here?" I asked. At that time of day, I expected him to be at work.

"Looking for you. What happened? Did you trip over your feet or something?"

"More like I was tripped."

Matt looked startled. "You were *what*?"

I sighed. "I was walking home from the police station, and someone with a cane tripped me when I got to the stairs. If it wasn't for this guy, I would have gone down a lot harder." I gestured toward the dog.

"Are you hurt?" he asked, looking me up and down and seeming to focus on the awkward way I was holding my leg.

"I twisted my knee. I can't really put weight on it."

"God, Franny, we need to get you to a doctor. Come on, let me help you up."

Matt stood and reached down to help me to my feet. Well, to my foot, since the left one was the only one doing me much good at the moment. He stood on my right side and wrapped his arm around my waist.

"We'll get you out to the street, then I'll run and get my car, okay?" he asked.

"Okay," I replied. We started limping along. "Wait! We need to bring the dog!"

Matt looked back at the mutt still sitting on the ground where I'd been.

"Are you sure he doesn't belong to someone?" he asked me.

"No, but he doesn't have a collar. He saved me. The least we can do is help him find his owner if he has one."

"All right." Matt shrugged. He patted his leg with his free hand. "Come on, boy!"

The dog popped up and trotted over to us, following along as we limped out to the street.

Chapter 19

"CAN we drop the dog off at my house?" I asked as Matt pulled his car away from the curb. "He can't stay in the car while we're at the urgent care."

Matt looked skeptical. "Are you sure you want to drop some strange dog off in your house then leave it for a few hours?"

"Well, what do you suggest?" I asked.

"For you to worry more about your leg and less about the dog. How's it doing there? Does it have enough support?" Matt had put his briefcase and a balled-up sweatshirt under my heel to keep my leg straight and propped up.

"It's okay," I replied. "I'm sure it can wait a while if you think it would be better to run to a store and pick up some food and a crate for him."

"That's not exactly what I meant," Matt said. "You know he probably belongs to someone, right?"

I wanted to think that he didn't actually. He was friendly and comfortable with people, but he was on the thin side, as though he hadn't been getting enough to eat lately.

"Yes," I said reluctantly. "But don't you think they'd want him to be safe and well taken care of until they can be reunited?"

Matt rolled his eyes. "Don't you think they're more likely to look for him at the shelter than in your house?"

As much as I didn't want to admit it, I knew he was right. "I guess so."

"Besides, they'll be able to get him all checked out and dewormed or whatever." Matt pulled the car into the animal shelter's parking lot.

"Okay." I sighed as he got out of the car. "But make sure you give them my name! I want that dog if no one comes for him!"

"Yes, ma'am." Matt opened the back door to let the dog out.

The little mutt obediently followed him into the shelter as if it was the most normal thing in the world and he'd known Matt for years.

"Bye, Latte!" I called softly, waving. I'd already started thinking of the dog as Latte because his fur was the exact shade of a perfectly mixed latte. I really hoped he'd come home with me someday soon.

I wiggled around to get my phone out of my pocket while I waited for Matt to come back out. I had four texts and two missed calls from Matt. I'd completely forgotten that I'd put my phone on silent when I went into the police station. I turned the volume back up and had just opened the Internet browser when Matt came back out of the shelter. A big smile broke across my face when I saw Latte tripping along beside him.

Matt opened the car's rear door and guided Latte in with a new bright-blue leash. Matt tossed a baggie of dog food in behind him.

"What happened?" I asked, trying to restrain my glee as Matt got back in the car.

He sighed. "If someone finds a lost dog, they encourage them to keep it. She said it's better for the dogs. She scanned him for a microchip, which he didn't have, took a picture for their website, and gave me enough food to get him through until we can get to the store. I guess you get to take him home after all."

I clapped and squealed as if I was eight years old. I twisted around as best I could to look at Latte without hurting my leg. "Do you want to come home with me, Latte? Would you like that? I have to go to the doctor for a little bit, but when I come home, we can snuggle on the couch and—"

"Wait, did you already name the dog?" Matt interrupted.

"Well, I couldn't just keep calling him 'the dog'! Especially not if he's coming home with me!"

Matt just shook his head. He drove us over to my house to drop Latte off.

"Put him in the upstairs bathroom—it's bigger than the downstairs one," I said. We'd decided that locking Latte in a bathroom would be the best bet for the time being so he wouldn't get overwhelmed by a big new house and go crazy. "And don't forget to give him a big bowl of food and water. He looks hungry, don't you, Latte?" I scratched his chin one more time before Matt got him out of the car.

When Matt came out, he drove me to the doctor, who said I had definitely sprained my knee and would have to wear a brace for a few weeks until it healed. Elevate, rest, cold compresses, and painkillers.

"Do you have anyone at home to help you out around the house until you're back on your feet?" the doctor asked.

Before I could say I didn't but that I would be fine on my own, Matt interrupted. "I can take care of her."

I looked at him, surprised. "You don't have to do that."

He shrugged. "I don't mind."

We picked up some burgers and fries on the way

back to my house—after I'd called Sammy to tell her what had happened, of course. With all the excitement, I'd completely forgotten that I hadn't eaten until suddenly I was starving. I tried to get Matt to let me pay, but he just refused to take my credit card with him when he went inside. I surreptitiously stuffed fries in my mouth as he drove, and Matt pretended he didn't notice.

When we got to the house, Matt got my crutches out of the backseat and helped me navigate my way inside, then he went upstairs to let Latte out of the bathroom. Latte raced down the stairs and ran around the house until he found me in the kitchen. He jumped up and licked my face. I knew I should stop him from putting his paws on the table to reach me, but it was so sweet that he was so excited to see me that I figured I'd let him do it just this once.

When Matt and I finished eating, he helped me into the living room and got my leg propped up with some pillows on the couch. Latte jumped up with me at first, but that was a little uncomfortable, so he ended up lying on the floor beside me. Matt sat in my grandfather's old recliner.

"You know, we should probably call the police if someone deliberately tripped you down the stairs," he said.

"Yeah." I thought for a minute. "Who in town walks with a cane? Or maybe a limp?"

"Other than you?" Matt asked.

"I use crutches, thank you very much."

Matt chuckled. "A lot of people use a cane. Half of this street uses a cane." Matt studied my face. "This is getting dangerous, Franny. Don't you think it's a little suspicious that as soon as you leave the police station after telling the cops about this Karl guy, you get tripped down the stairs?" Realization dawned across Matt's face. "Wait, does Karl walk with a cane?"

I hadn't told Matt yet about my meeting with Mike. He didn't know that Karl was *not* the man who had killed his father.

"Um, no," I said.

"Franny?" I could hear in Matt's voice that he knew I wasn't telling him something.

"Karl's not the one who killed your dad. Mike already talked to him, and he was at the doctor's in Boston during the murder. I don't know who did it, but apparently someone thinks I do, and they're trying to stop me."

Matt stared at me for a minute, then he stood and walked across the room. He pulled his phone out of his pocket and dialed a number.

"Matty? Who are you calling? Matty?"

He didn't answer, but whoever he was calling did. "Hi, it's Matt Cardosi. How're you doing today?... good, good. Look, the reason I'm calling—somebody tripped

Franny at the stairs in the park today and she messed up her knee pretty good. I don't know if this is related to what happened to my dad, but we need to file a police report either way... yeah... yeah... okay... yeah... okay, see you in a few minutes... thanks, Mike. Bye." Matt turned around and looked at me. "Franny, I know you feel strongly about finding whoever killed my dad, and obviously I do too, but not at the expense of your life! You could've broken your neck falling down those stairs! Mike'll be here in a few minutes to take a report. Will you just take a step back and let the police handle this?"

"Matty, whoever it was pushed me down the stairs! He may not have been trying to kill me, but he was trying to hurt me. Even if I am a terrible detective, I can't just sit here and accept it."

"I'm not saying let it go—I'm saying let the police do their jobs. You don't need to be the one who solves this."

Yes, I do. No matter what Matt said, someone had come after me. I couldn't just take that lying down. Well, figuratively anyway. For at least the next few days, I would be taking pretty much everything lying down since I couldn't put any weight on my leg. But I couldn't tell Matt that. Not right now anyway. Not until he'd calmed down a little.

"Okay," I said with a small smile. "I'll lay off. But if someone tries to come after me again, you better believe I'm taking them down!"

"Just smack 'em with your crutches." He gestured at Latte. "Or sic your vicious dog on him."

I looked at Latte on the floor next to the couch. He had fallen asleep and rolled over with his paws in the air. Vicious dog indeed.

Chapter 20

I SPENT most of the next few days on the couch. As the doctor had predicted, the day after my fall was worse than the day I actually got hurt. My knee was swollen and painful, and it hurt even worse when I so much as tried to get up to go to the bathroom. Keeping it elevated really did make a difference.

Matt took a few days off work to help me out and take care of Latte. I slowly gave up on trying to pay for the food that he either bought or brought over to cook. It was just too hard with my leg. Once I got back on my feet and was able to sneak over to restaurant cashiers, I'd start trying again.

Matt and I put together some Found Dog posters, and Matt drove us around town to hang them up. I got more and more used to having Latte around, and I hated to think about someone calling to say he belonged to them. I considered putting the wrong phone number on the signs but figured Matt would catch me. It was probably a good thing that I couldn't really get around too well, because otherwise I would have been seriously tempted to sneak around town and tear down all the signs.

Sammy held down the fort at the café. It would be a few weeks before I was really able to work normally. I called her every day to check on things, but she seemed to be doing well on her own. She mobilized our battery of part-timers to work the middle of the day and came in herself for open and close. I was glad my mother had trained her so well.

Still, I was itching to get back to my investigation. Every time Matt took me out, I kept my eyes peeled for men with canes. Whenever I saw someone, I'd make a note on my phone about who it was or what they looked like. I tried to pay particular attention to shoes and canes, since that was what I saw the day I fell, but it was hard to see those things when we were driving by. What I'd seen as I tried to catch my balance hadn't been that detailed anyway—just heavy black shoes and a brown wood cane with a black rubber bottom. Not exactly a unique or unusual combination. When Matt asked what I kept doing on my phone, I told him it was ideas for the café. I felt bad about lying to him, but I knew he'd have thoughts on the matter if I told him the truth. I didn't think he really believed me anyway.

My biggest problem was that I had so many names and descriptions of possible murder/tripping suspects and no way to narrow the list down. The only way I could think of to home in on the culprit was to figure out who had a connection to Mr. Cardosi. To do that, I needed Matt. But Matt didn't want me pursuing the investigation anymore. I had to figure out a way to get him to support my sleuthing. I probably spent as much time thinking about that as I did actually thinking about the case.

We were sitting in my living room one night as we'd gotten in the habit of doing—him in my grandfather's chair, me on the couch with my leg propped up, Latte curled up on the floor next to me. It had been several days since my accident and several days since Matt and I had last discussed my investigation. It had also been several days since I'd heard anything from Mike about my assailant. I was beyond antsy.

As the TV show we were watching went to commercial, I heaved a big sigh. It seemed like an effective but subtle way to get Matt's attention without seeming as though that was what I was trying to do.

He sat up in his chair. "Are you okay? Is your leg okay? Do you need anything?" He had been that concerned and considerate since I got hurt.

"Yeah, I'm fine." I sighed.

"Then what's with the huffing and puffing?"

"It's just kind of frustrating that it's been almost a week and we haven't heard anything from Mike yet about who pushed me down the stairs."

"Investigations take time. Just think how I feel not knowing anything about who killed my dad."

"I know, I know." *If you'd just help me narrow down my suspects, maybe we wouldn't have to wait for Mike.* But I couldn't say that out loud. Instead I said, "I just keep seeing men with canes while we're out, and I can't help but think that one of them is the one who tripped me. Some of them I know, some of them I don't, but one of them was perfectly willing to kill me and may very well have killed your dad. How am I supposed to go about my life knowing that he could be planning to try to kill me again?"

"You want to start your investigation again, don't you?" I took a breath to answer him, but he barely paused before going on. "That's what you've been doing on your phone, isn't it? Taking notes about potential suspects?"

I nodded. Matt exhaled sharply but didn't say anything. The show we were watching came back on, but neither of us really paid any attention.

After a few minutes, Matt spoke. "Who do you have in mind?"

My heart pounded. I couldn't believe he was actually asking. This was such a good sign! "I only know a few of them."

"Who are they? Tell me the ones you know, and we can figure out the ones you don't know later."

I took a deep breath. "The ones I know: Don Sampson, Jack Newman, Paul Hamilton, Pete D'Angelo, Steve Baker, and Bill Stanton."

"How many do you have on your list that you don't know?"

"It's hard to say. If I didn't recognize them from day to day, I might have written them down twice or even more."

"Your best guess."

I picked up my phone and opened up the notepad app. I scanned my list and counted the descriptions I had entered. "About five. Maybe seven."

Matt nodded. He glanced out the window. "It's getting late."

My heart fell. I was sure he'd just been humoring me and was now going to make his escape.

"I don't think a lot of cane-users will be out walking around at this time of night. How about tomorrow we go drive around for a while and see who we can see? I've been around more the past few years, plus I know a lot of people from the barbershop, so I'll probably recognize some people you don't know." He took a deep breath. "Sound like a plan?"

I tried to hold back my smile, but I didn't think I did a very good job. "Sounds like a plan."

"And what's your plan for once we have a complete list?"

"Then I need your help to figure out who had a connection to your dad."

Matt nodded. "You had this planned, didn't you? From the time you brought it up, your goal was to get me to help you figure out who else might be a suspect then narrow down the list based on who had a connection to my dad."

"Not quite," I said coyly.

"No?" he asked, a half smile creeping across his lips.

"I wanted your help with the connection to your dad. Helping me identify additional suspects is just a bonus." I was still trying hard not to smile too much, but Matt laughed out loud. I hadn't heard him laugh that loud or hard since I'd been back in town.

"Oh well, as long as you were only trying to use me a little bit!"

I giggled. "I wasn't trying to use you at all! I was trying to help you, and I just needed your help to do it!" I knew my logic wasn't quite sound, but we were both laughing so hard, I didn't think it mattered. It felt really good to just be happy with him.

Our laughter woke Latte. He stood and nudged my hand with his nose, then turned to stare at the door. For some reason, even though Matt was always the one to take Latte out, the dog still always came to me. It was as if he knew he was *my* dog, even when he had a helper in his care.

"Oh, come on, boy." Matt stood and patted his leg for Latte to follow him.

They went outside for a few minutes.

"Is there anything you need before I leave?" Matt asked when they came back in.

"No, I think I'm good," I replied, glancing around. My crutches were within reach, all the dishes had been put away, and there was nothing on the floor for me to trip over when I hobbled to bed. Latte and I had been sleeping in my grandparents' old bedroom so I didn't have to deal with the stairs.

"Well then, I'll see you tomorrow." He looked kind of awkward standing in the doorway, but I wasn't sure what to do or say to make him feel more comfortable.

I just nodded and smiled. "I'll see you tomorrow."

He went to the door. "You'll call if you need anything, right?"

He'd been staying at his dad's house so that he'd be close if I needed anything during the night. I'd been wondering if he was seriously considering selling his place and moving in next door, but I hadn't found the opportunity to ask yet, and I was a little afraid it would sound as if I was coming on to him. I liked the idea of him living so close by and didn't want to scare him off.

"Yes, I'll call," I assured him.

He said good night and headed home before I headed to bed with Latte trailing behind me.

Chapter 21

MATT CAME over in the morning to make us breakfast before we headed out on our mission. I hovered on my crutches in front of the coffee machine to make cappuccinos for us. It wasn't easy, but I couldn't very well let Matt do it when I was the one who ran a coffee shop. Matt made us pancakes. Apparently they were one of the few things Mr. Cardosi could make, so Matt ate them a lot growing up.

"It seems appropriate to eat them on the day we find my dad's killer," he declared.

"That seems optimistic." I only had a rough list, that we both knew was incomplete, of suspects, and we still had to figure out who on that list had a strong connection to Mr. Cardosi. Plus, I'd been wrong once already, and that made me trigger shy.

"I have to be optimistic." Matt shrugged. "I'm tired of waiting."

I understood the feeling, even if I wasn't as confident as he was that we would figure it out today. Even if we did, I wouldn't get my hopes up that we were right. If we found someone, they would just be a suspect, nothing more. I wasn't calling anyone else a murderer without some concrete proof.

After breakfast, Matt and I got in the car and drove around town. It was a beautiful day and still early, so lots of old folks were out taking their "morning constitutionals." I added a few more names to my list based on people Matt knew that I didn't or just didn't recognize. It simultaneously felt as if we were inching closer to finding the killer and moving further away. I knew that each name I added to the list might be the killer's, but also that if it wasn't, I was just making it harder to actually identify him. Still, I added them and tried to keep my spirits up.

As usual, a group of men was playing chess in the park. Matt and I recognized several of the men, but a few were unfamiliar, and two of them had canes. I considered chess players to be strong potential targets as I could easily have walked past them that day in the park without noticing if one of them was watching me. Playing chess with the men seemed like a good way to get information about the ones we didn't recognize without seeming strangely curious.

Matt parked out on the street and helped me climb out. Moving was getting easier as I got used to balancing my weight on only one leg, but I still got wobbly easily. He let Latte out of the backseat, because of course we'd brought him with us, and we headed over to the chess tables. Matt and I played each other the first game. He was terrible, and I made sure everyone knew.

"You're hopeless, Matt!" I said loudly. I heard a few of the men chuckle, and I looked around at them. "Do any of you want to play me? I can't handle winning that easily again!"

One able-bodied man stood. "I'll play you." He made his way to my table.

I didn't recognize him, but I figured it might still be a chance to learn some names. Matt walked over to the man's former partner, who I noticed with glee had a cane propped against his chair.

"Mind if I join you?" Matt asked the man.

"Not if you're as bad as she says." The man laughed.

Matt and I played a few games, moving to different partners each time. We easily got the names of all of the men with canes. Around lunch, we decided to head out to get something to eat. We went to Sandy's Seafood Shack again, because the lobster rolls were calling my name and they had a nice covered porch we could eat on with Latte.

"Do you want to keep driving around?" Matt asked as we ate.

"Maybe just a little, but I feel like we've found pretty much everyone we're going to find, you know? At this point, we've identified everyone who's out and about, so unless the Tripper is in hiding somewhere, we should have already gotten him."

"I need to go by the barbershop to pick up the mail. I was thinking I'd get as many of my dad's papers as I can, and we can start going through them. He kept track of all of his customers, so maybe we can find something there."

"Sounds like a plan," I replied.

We finished our delicious, buttery lobster and got back in the car. At the barbershop, I waited outside while Matt went in to get the papers. Getting in and out was too hard for me to bother with when Matt would only take a few minutes to get everything he needed. He came back with more than I was expecting—a big box full of stuff. He put it in the trunk and got back in the car.

"Did you take every piece of paper in the store?" I asked.

"No, just what was on my dad's desk."

"*All that* was on his desk?"

"It was pretty covered."'

We set up shop with the papers at my kitchen table. It gave us plenty of space, and I could prop my leg up on one of the unused chairs. We started by sorting through the paperwork, arranging it all into piles based on category—ledgers, records, mail, things that should really have been thrown away a long time ago—then went through each pile, highlighting our Cane Walkers' names as we found them. It was a tedious process, and I didn't feel like we were actually making much progress. Almost every Cane Walker had gotten his hair cut at the barbershop, so it seemed like Mr. Cardosi had some level of connection to all of them.

Matt made us spaghetti Bolognese for dinner. He moved most of the papers off the table so that we had room to eat and didn't have to worry about splashing sauce on anything. We were both getting discouraged that we hadn't yet found a smoking gun, or empty cyanide caplet as the case may be, but neither of us wanted to admit it. I especially felt that Matt would be disappointed if we didn't at least find a new lead.

Matt cleared the table and washed the dishes as I continued through the paperwork.

"You know, I think my dad kept some of his records at the house," he said when he was done putting the dishes away. "Do you care if I run over there and see what I can find?"

"No, no, go. We should look at every available shred of evidence." I was glad he'd thought of more papers. We were getting toward the end of what we had, and I was a little anxious.

Matt brought my phone over to me in case I needed to call him. He let Latte out real quick, then he headed over to his dad's house. I kept flipping through papers. The mail pile was the only one I could reach, and it was phenomenally boring and useless. It seemed as if Mr. Cardosi had never thrown away a single credit card application or advertisement for business cards. Still, I had to look through everything. The one thing I needed might very well be hidden among all the junk mail.

My phone's text message alert sounded. It was from Matt.

Ran into Paul Hamilton. Started talking about Dad. Said they used to have coffee together, so I invited him in for a cup. Will be back in 30 minutes or so.

Paul Hamilton, the one who Karl worked for at the electronics shop, wasn't the most pleasant person, so I wouldn't complain about Matt not inviting him back to my house instead.

I continued flipping through the mail, finally landing on a section that seemed to be personal correspondence. I wasn't expecting to find anything useful, but it had to be more interesting than the junk I'd been looking at. It was mostly letters from Mr. Cardosi's old military buddies and a few letters from family back in Italy. I skimmed each one then set it aside in a separate pile. They seemed like mementos that Matt might want.

I picked up one that looked as if it had been scribbled more quickly than the others. The writing was large and messy and missing the customary "Dear Gino" at the top. The contents were different too. No reminiscences of youthful exploits or updates on shared acquaintances. No, this one was angry. Aggressive.

Stay out of it, Cardosi! My finances are none of your business!

Directly beneath it was a response Mr. Cardosi had apparently written but never sent.

Paul, It is my business when you're using my name as part of your scheme. I'm not letting this go.

I looked at the paper, trying to figure out what it meant. Both notes seemed angry, but I wasn't sure if they were evidence. I flipped through the rest of the pile quickly to see if there were any more notes like them. There was nothing. I crossed my arms and stared at the kitchen wall. When I glanced back at the papers on the table, my eyes fell directly on Mr. Cardosi's note, and the very first word he had written. *Paul.*

Paul Hamilton walked with a cane. He said he used to have coffee with Mr. Cardosi. He was having coffee with Matt now. The cyanide that had killed Mr. Cardosi had been in a cup of coffee.

My blood ran cold. I grabbed my phone and dialed

Matt. There was no answer. I had to get over there *now*. My crutches were across the room. I struggled up from my seat and hopped over to my crutches. I shoved them under my arms. Just before I started hobbling out of the house, I had the clarity of thought to put in a call to the police. I didn't know what I was walking into and didn't want to be trapped with a murderer with no help on the way. I dialed 9-1-1, pressed the phone between my ear and my shoulder, then started limping across the room. Walking on crutches was hard enough, but doing it while keeping my ear glued to my shoulder was next to impossible. I was inching my way down the front walk when the dispatcher answered.

"I need help. I need police *now*," I said into the phone.

"What address?" she asked.

I spouted off Mr. Cardosi's address, listened for her confirmation that she had heard it, then I let the phone drop to the ground. I could move faster without it. The distance from my house to Mr. Cardosi's seemed exponentially longer than it ever had. When I was a kid, I could run from door to door in less than thirty seconds. This would take me several minutes, minutes I didn't know that I had.

Latte seemed to know something was going on. He ran back and forth beside me, barking loudly the way he had the day I'd found him. When I turned onto Mr.

Cardosi's walk, he went ballistic, running up to the door and punctuating his barking with long, loud howls. It was as if he knew the man who had tripped me was inside.

When I was just over an arm's length from the door, I lunged for it, turning the doorknob and pushing it open. Latte rushed past me and into the kitchen. I lost my balance and fell facefirst into the foyer.

"Matty, don't drink that!" I screamed.

I heard nothing from the kitchen. I was too late. I crawled, dragging myself into the house with just my arms.

"Franny?"

I looked up to see Matt in the kitchen doorway. I dropped my head to the floor in relief. He was alive.

He rushed over to me. "What are you doing?"

Matt started to help me up when I saw Paul Hamilton step out of the kitchen.

"I should have pushed you," he sneered.

Matt looked between Paul and me. "What? What's going on here?"

"Paul killed your father! I found letters between them! He was going to kill you too!"

"Franny, that's—" Matt stopped when he saw Paul moving across the living room, a look of pure hatred on his face.

Latte circled Paul, barking at ear-piercing volume.

"Damn dog!" Paul spat.

I screamed when I saw him lift his cane and strike Latte. Latte yelped and ran past me out of the house. I heard him barking and howling on the lawn. Paul moved closer. I wasn't sure what he was going to do. Matt was definitely bigger and stronger than him, but if the man would poison someone with cyanide, I wasn't sure I would put a poison-tipped cane past him either.

He swung the cane at Matt, and it came in too low for Matt to grab, smacking his shin. He grunted at the pain. Paul swung the cane again, striking my hand as I tried to catch it. Through Latte's howls, I heard sirens in the distance. We only had to hold Paul off for a few more minutes before the police arrived. Paul lifted the cane again as Matt moved to grab it from him. Before he could, Paul brought the cane down on the back of my head. I saw stars and, through them, the flashing red-and-blue lights of police cars.

Chapter 22

NEEDLESS TO SAY, Paul was arrested. When the police tested the coffee Matt had made for Paul and himself, they'd found enough cyanide to kill not just one but several men. Paul was charged with Mr. Cardosi's murder, attempted murder and assault for his attack on Matt, and assault for his multiple attacks on me. Just for those charges, he should be in jail longer than Karl had been, and for a man Paul's age, that was at least a life sentence.

It turned out Mike had suspected Paul for quite a while, but he hadn't been able to find any direct evidence to use to get an arrest warrant. Walking into a vicious cane-based assault on two people was more than enough to put him in jail while they investigated his motive for murder.

The police went through Mr. Cardosi's paperwork and found bills for clipper repairs that Paul had supposedly done for him. But Matt was able to show invoices and shipping documents that proved that Mr. Cardosi had always sent his clippers back to the manufacturer when they needed repair. According to Matt, he only trusted the people who had made them in the first place to fix them right.

When the police dug into Paul's books, they found that he had been recording electronics repairs for businesses all over town, repairs not a single one of them had ever ordered. When Karl started working for him, not knowing that the unpaid invoices were fake, he sent the ones with Mr. Cardosi's name on them over to him. Mr. Cardosi put two and two together and figured out that Paul was running an elaborate money-laundering scheme. He threatened to turn Paul in unless Paul did so himself. Apparently the money laundering didn't bother Mr. Cardosi as much as Paul using Mr. Cardosi's name on the fake invoices.

The reason for the money-laundering scheme was every bit as crazy as the scheme itself, probably even more so. It had started with illegal betting on horse races. Paul was good at gambling—shockingly good— but that wasn't enough for him. He wanted to bet on the long shots. He started paying jockeys and trainers to fix the races. That had led to even bigger paydays and ultimately to the laundering scheme that was his downfall. It was pretty dramatic stuff for a sleepy little town like Cape Bay.

It seemed as though it took my leg forever to heal. According to the doctors, my fall into the Cardosi house's foyer had set me back a good week or two. Still, I finally got back on my feet (literally) and went back to work at the café. It was nice to get back into a routine again. I spent my time working, playing with Latte, and redecorating my house.

In a weird twist of fate, it turned out that Latte had actually briefly belonged to Paul—that was why he barked so much whenever Paul was around. Latte, whose previous name was Barkley, had belonged to a family that moved overseas for the father's job. They weren't able to take the dog with them, so they gave him to their neighbor Paul, who apparently seemed like a nice enough man. But Paul hit Barkley with his cane every time he did something remotely impish or dog-like. Paul quickly got tired of him, took him to the park, and let him go. Apparently Barkley disliked living with Paul enough that he never tried to go back. I felt as though Latte deserved a fresh start after his rough time with Paul and decided to keep him. I liked the name Latte much better than Barkley anyway.

Matt and I had been spending a lot of time together. I guess you could call it dating. We had dinner a couple of nights a week after I closed up the café and spent the day together at least once on the weekends. It was casual, but a lot of fun. And I had even managed to pay a time or two. It took me slipping the waiter my credit card on the way in, but I'd done it.

I was in the café late one quiet afternoon when Matt came in with a big smile.

"Hey! How are you?" I greeted him.

"I'm great!" He came around the counter to give me a hug.

I had to just lean into him because my gloved hands were all wet and slimy from the mozzarella I was making. "What's got you in such a good mood?"

"I sold the house!"

That was news that required a real hug. I peeled off my gloves and threw my arms around his neck. "Congratulations, neighbor!" I was excited. Matt had finally decided to sell his house and move into his dad's. It wasn't solely because of my presence two doors down, but I liked to think that I was at least part of his motivation. "This requires a celebratory coffee!"

I closed the lid on the mozzarella and put it aside before I turned to the espresso machine to steam the milk for our drinks.

"So I was thinking," he said, going back around the counter so he could face me as I worked. "I have to invest most of the profit from the sale of the house to avoid paying half of it in taxes, but there's a good bit of it I can keep."

"That's awesome!" I said, pulling the espresso. "Are you going to buy yourself something nice? A new car maybe?"

"Actually, I was thinking of taking a little trip. Maybe someplace exotic, like the Caribbean or Europe. Maybe even Italy."

"Oh, Italy! I'd love to go to Italy! I've always dreamed of seeing the place my grandparents came from." I poured the milk into the cup. It was silly, but I was making a smiley face. It was a simple, happy design for a happy day.

Matt smiled. "I had a feeling you might say that."

"So you just thought you'd try to make me jealous? Is that it?" I joked as I worked on the second cup, this one for me.

"Well, no. More like I thought you could come with me."

I looked at him, completely surprised. I had not expected him to say *that*.

"Yes? No? Only if I put us up in four-star hotels?"

"Um, yes, I mean, if you're sure. I don't want to take advantage—" I was stumbling over my words and had let the espresso sit too long to boot. It would be way too bitter to drink, so I dumped it and started over.

"You're not taking advantage. I want to do it. To

thank you for everything you've done the past few months."

"Well, I didn't do all that much." This time I managed to add the milk to the espresso in time. I poured in a heart because it was simple and the cup was just for me.

"You were there when I needed you. That's all you needed to do."

"And I get to go to Italy as a reward?" I handed his cup to him across the counter.

"Yup." He looked at his cup then back at me with a smile and raised eyebrows. "A heart? You tryin' to tell me something, Franny?"

I looked at the cup in front of me. It was the smiley face I'd made for Matt. I was so flustered I'd given him the wrong one! "No, I meant to give you this one." I tried to hand the smiley face cup to him.

"Too late." He took a sip.

The bell over the door jingled, and a delivery man walked in with a large bouquet of red roses. "Francesca Amaro?" He came toward me.

"That's me," I said, glancing at Matt. He had an innocent expression that I didn't believe for a second. I signed for the delivery and set the roses on the counter. I pulled the card out and read it.

To Francesca. The beauty of these roses pales in comparison to yours. Signed, Your Secret Admirer.

"Really?" I asked, looking at Matt. "'Your Secret Admirer'? You invite me to go to Italy with you, but think you have to be coy with the flowers?"

"I didn't send them," Matt said.

"Sure, you didn't," I retorted.

"No, really. I would have sent you lilies. I know you like them better."

That was true. I did like lilies better. I looked in confusion at the card. "Then who sent them?"

"Damned if I know." Matt smiled. "But I'm the one going to Italy with you." He drank the rest of his coffee. "I've got to go. I have a travel agent to see." He leaned across the counter and kissed my cheek.

My heart fluttered a little. I would be happy to go to Italy with Matt.

"I'll see you later, okay?" he said.

"Okay." I smiled and watched as he left.

My life had changed a lot in the past few months, but it was all working out. I was home in Cape Bay where I belonged, doing what I loved, and planning a trip to Italy with the boy next door. Life was good. Very good.

Recipe 1: Dark Chocolate Cupcakes with Peanut Butter Filling

Makes 24 cupcakes

Ingredients:
- ¾ cup + 2 tbsp cocoa powder
- ½ cup boiling water
- 1 ¾ cup all-purpose flour
- 1 cup buttermilk
- 1 ¼ tsp baking soda
- ¼ baking powder
- ¼ tsp salt
- 1 ½ sticks + 3 tbsp unsalted butter, softened
- 1 ½ cups granulated sugar
- 2 large eggs, room temperature
- 1 tsp pure vanilla extract
- 1 cup creamy peanut butter

- 2/3 cup confectioners' sugar
- 1 cup heavy cream
- 8 ounces semi-sweet chocolate, chopped

Preheat oven to 350F. Line 24 muffin cups with paper liners. In a medium bowl, add cocoa powder and boiling water. Whisk into a smooth paste, then whisk in buttermilk until combined.

In another medium bowl, sift flour together with baking soda, baking powder and salt.

In a large bowl, beat 1 ½ sticks of butter with the granulated sugar with an electric beater for 3 minutes, or until light and fluffy. Beat in eggs and vanilla, then the dry ingredients in two batches.

Spoon batter into lined paper cups. Fill two-thirds. Bake for 20 minutes or until cupcakes are springy. Let cool in pan for 5 minutes, then transfer to wire racks to cool.

For filling:

In a medium bowl, beat peanut butter with 3 tablespoons of butter until creamy. Sift confectioners' sugar and beat together until light and fluffy, about 2 minutes. Spoon all of the peanut butter into a pastry bag with a ¼ star tip. Plunge tip in from the top of each cupcake to about ¾ -inch deep. Squeeze pastry bag to fill cupcake, withdrawing it slowly. Repeat for all the cupcakes.

For icing:

In a small saucepan, bring the heavy cream to a simmer. Add the semi-sweet chocolate to the cream. Let stand for 5 minutes, then whisk the melted chocolate into the cream until smooth. Let the chocolate icing stand until slightly cooled and thickened, about 15 minutes. Dip the top of each cupcake, letting excess drip back. Dip again and transfer them to racks. Using the remaining peanut butter filling into the pastry bag, pipe tiny rosettes on the top of the cupcakes.

Recipe 2: Snickerdoodle Cupcakes

Makes 24 cupcakes

Ingredients:
- 2 2/3 cups all-purpose flour
- 3 tsp baking powder
- 2 tsp ground cinnamon
- ½ tsp salt
- ¾ cup shortening
- 1 2/3 cups granulated sugar
- 5 large eggs
- 2 ½ tsp vanilla extract
- 1 ¼ cups milk
- 1 cup unsalted butter, softened
- 2 ½ cups powdered sugar
- 2 tsp vanilla extract

- 1 tbsp heavy whipping cream
- cinnamon-sugar (to sprinkle on top)

Preheat oven to 350F. Line 24 muffin cups with paper liners. Set aside.

In a medium bowl, mix flour, baking powder, 1 tsp of ground cinnamon and salt.

In a large bowl, beat shortening with mixer on medium speed for 30 seconds. Gradually add sugar. Add eggs, one at a time, beating well after each addition. Beat in vanilla extract.

Slowly add flour mixture and milk until just combined, being careful not to overmix.

Pour batter into liners, about ¾ full. Bake for 18-20 minutes or until toothpick inserted into center comes out clean. Let cool before frosting.

For frosting:

Mix butter on medium speed with an electric mixer for 30 second until smooth and creamy. Add powdered sugar, heavy whipping cream, ground cinnamon and vanilla extract. Increase to high speed and beat for 3 minutes. Add more cream if needed for spreading consistency.

Frost cupcakes with a piping bag or knife. Sprinkle cinnamon-sugar on top.

Book 2: Tea, Tiramisu, and Tough Guys

Chapter 1

MAKING the perfect cup of tea at my café was a completely new challenge for me. I studied the information about temperatures and steeping methods on the laptop in front of me, but it was contradictory and frustrating. I wanted straightforward, black-and-white information, and that was anything but.

Coffee was an art, too, but it had always come easily to me because it was in my blood. Tea was foreign, not something Italians were known for.

Why was I researching tea? The week before, a lovely older British couple had come into the café and ordered a "cuppa tea" for each of them.

"We've heard such good things about this place!" the woman exclaimed as I made their drinks.

"Really? From whom?" I asked with a smile. I

wanted to thank the kind local-business owner and be sure to mention the source to my own customers. We Cape Bayers all made it a point to recommend each other's businesses to tourists. The more great places people found in town, the more likely they were to come back, and the better off our little town was.

"Oh, everyone!" she gushed, her light-blue eyes sparkling.

I got the feeling she was a very enthusiastic person in general.

"Everyone says you just have the best drinks and baked goods on the coast!" She leaned across the counter and lowered her voice conspiratorially. "I know you specialize in coffee, but I'm sure you make a wonderful cup of tea as well."

I certainly hoped so. I'd spent the better part of my thirty-four years perfecting my coffee-making technique, having started as soon as I was tall enough to see over the counter while standing on a stool. I had never really contemplated tea-making technique, always just pouring hot water from the espresso machine over a tea bag and handing the whole thing to the customer. I wasn't sure whether or not that constituted a wonderful cup of tea.

"If you'd like to find a table, I'll bring your drinks around to you," I told her.

For the most part, I preferred to serve my customers at their tables. I feel that makes for a more personal experience. It's the same reason we use cups and saucers unless the customer specifically requests a to-go cup—to make the customer feel at home in our little café—at home, but with better coffee.

The woman and her husband sat down at one of the little tables along the exposed brick wall, and I brought their tea over to them. I set the cups down with a smile and walked back around the counter to watch them surreptitiously from behind the espresso machine. I know Brits are picky about their tea, so I wanted to see their reactions as they took their first sips. Antonia's Italian Café might have been known for our artisan cappuccinos and coffee drinks, but that doesn't mean I don't care about my customers' experience with other drinks.

I could tell they were trying to be polite, but they couldn't disguise the displeased looks on their faces as the tea touched their tongues. I waited until they each took another sip, in case my interpretation of their faces was wrong, but when they did raise the cups to their lips again, I saw the same look of dismay in their eyes. I had a feeling when they put the cups down that they wouldn't be picking them back up again.

I debated whether to go over and ask them about it or to stand my ground and see if they picked the cups back up. I ended up hesitating only a minute. I'm not the type to beat around the bush. I took a deep breath as I approached their table.

"Is the tea not good?" I asked.

The couple exchanged a look as the husband exhaled. The woman looked slightly embarrassed.

"Well, dear." She glanced at her husband again and sighed. "I'm sorry, it's not." She hesitated for a moment. "But we're British, and we're very particular about our tea. I'm sure it's perfectly fine for an American palate."

An American palate. I wasn't sure if that was an extremely politely phrased insult or just a statement of fact. Or perhaps the tea was really that bad, but she was trying to find something she could say that wasn't completely awful.

I stood for a moment, trying to figure out what to do or say. I would give them their money back, of course, but other than that, I wasn't sure.

"I'm so sorry," I said. The perfectionist in me kicked in. "What can I do to make it better?"

"Oh, dear, you needn't worry about it. Another drink will certainly suffice. What would you recommend?"

"Well, cappuccino—I know I make a good one of those—but it's important to me to learn how to make better tea. For the next time you come in," I finished with a smile.

The woman glanced at her husband again, and he gave a little nod. I was beginning to wonder if he ever spoke.

"It *is* more complicated than it seems at first glance, dear," she said hesitantly.

"If you're willing to teach me, I'm willing to learn."

"Pull up a chair and join us, then."

"Sammy, can you run the front for me for a few minutes?" I called into the café's back room as I pulled a chair over to the table where the Brits were sitting. The chair's style didn't match that of the table, but that was okay because none of the chairs did. The entire café was furnished with estate-sale and antique-store finds my grandmother had picked up when her namesake café first opened. Despite none of the furniture actually matching, it all came together to give the café a warm, cozy feel.

"Sure thing!" Sammy called from the back. Her blond head bobbed over the display case as she came around toward the front. The face of my trusty second-in-command was flushed from working over steaming-hot drinks in the middle of the steaming-hot summer. She flashed a brilliant smile at me and busied herself with wiping down the counter.

"By the way," I said, taking my seat at the table, "I'm Francesca Amaro. I own the café." That felt weird to say, but it was true. I'd inherited it outright when my mother passed away at the beginning of the summer.

"It's a pleasure to meet you, Francesca! I'm Rose Howard, and this is my husband Edward." She then started in on what she called the basics of good tea making. For the better part of an hour, she went over tea varieties, water temperatures, brands, and steeping procedures. After only a few minutes, I went to the back to grab a notepad and pen to take notes on all she was telling me. Good tea making was every bit as complicated as good coffee making, and I'd had no idea.

And that was what led me to research the intricacies of tea brewing, leaning on the front counter with the laptop set up in front of me, a tea-aficionado message board pulled up on the screen, trying to make sense of the conflicting information in front of me.

Earl Grey tea should never *be brewed above two hundred degrees!*

Earl Grey tea should never be brewed a degree below a full boil!

Steep for at least three minutes!

Steep exactly two and a half minutes!

This all made my brain hurt. But I was determined to become as good at making tea as I was at making coffee.

Rose Howard had coached me through the rest of her vacation, declaring the last cup I served her before she left town "perfectly acceptable." Comparing that to "perfectly fine *for an American palate*," I thought that was an acceptable outcome, for less than a week of practice. But I wanted to see my customers' eyes widen with pleasure when they tasted my tea, the way they did when they tasted my coffee. I was also determined to learn to create pretty pictures in my tea cups the way I could with a latte, but taste came first. Pretty could come later.

"How's it going?" Sammy asked, emerging from the back room, where she'd been sorting through our newest supply delivery and coming up behind me to peep over my shoulder at the screen. She had been keeping close tabs on my quest to conquer the world of tea.

"Oh, it's so confusing!" I groaned. I turned my head toward the ceiling and rubbed my eyes with the heels of my hands. Sammy chuckled as she patted me on the back.

"Coffee would be just as confusing if you hadn't been learning it since you were a baby."

"I don't know about that," I replied.

Sammy chuckled again. "Oh, trust me. When I started working here with your mom, I could barely understand instant coffee. Coffee is plenty confusing. Do you know how long it took me to understand the difference between a café au lait and a caffè latte? They're both coffee and milk! Their names both *mean* coffee and milk!"

"You know the difference now, don't you?" I asked, momentarily concerned.

"A latte's the one with regular coffee and milk, and the café au lait's the one with espresso."

I think my heart actually stopped for a second at hearing her get them exactly wrong. Had she been serving customers the wrong drinks the whole time? I spun and looked at her, only to be greeted by a wide smile and a twinkle in her blue eyes.

"Oh, you know I'm kidding!" she laughed.

I eyed her suspiciously.

"Latte is espresso, café au lait is coffee. You don't think someone would have complained in all this time if I was doing them wrong? You think your *mother* would have let me get away with that?" She reached out and gave me a big hug. "Franny, you know me better than that!"

She was right, as usual. I'd only been working with her since moving back to town after my mother's death, but I'd known her for years as she worked with my mother. She was always trustworthy and reliable and right about anything that mattered. There was no way she didn't know the difference between a latte and an au lait. Still, she'd nearly given me a heart attack there for a minute.

"Yeah, I guess I do. I just get a little touchy about the café."

Sammy laughed her melodic laugh. "I can tell!" She patted me on the back and went back to work, arranging the contents of our delivery.

"Did my tea come in?" I called back to her, remembering that my order of an assortment of high-end loose teas was due any day.

"I haven't seen it yet," she called back, "but I have a couple more boxes to go. I'll let you know if I see it."

I sighed, blowing a loose strand of my black hair out of my face. I was really anxious to get the new tea varieties and start playing with them, but I resigned myself to the fact that I might just have to wait another day.

"What are you huffing and puffing about?" I heard a teasing voice ask in conjunction with the ringing of the bell over the door.

I looked up to see Matt Cardosi, my longtime friend and neighbor and maybe soon-to-be boyfriend, walking into the café.

"Matty!" I exclaimed, reverting to my childhood nickname for him, something I did a little too often in public. I hurried around the counter to give him a hug.

"Hi, Matt," Sammy called from the back room.

"Hey, Sammy," he replied.

"What are you doing here?" I asked. Matt worked a couple towns over, so we didn't often see him at the café in the middle of the day.

He shrugged. "I needed to run by the barbershop and check on some things, so I thought I'd take the afternoon off."

Matt had inherited ownership of the town barbershop after his father was murdered a few weeks earlier, and he was still trying to get it all under control. He glanced around the room. "Flowers haven't died yet, huh?" he said, his eyes settling on a bouquet of roses in a vase on the counter.

"Nope," I replied, stepping over to stroke one of the blossoms. "It's impressive." The flowers had been delivered a week and a half earlier and were only then starting to show signs of wilting. I needed to make a note of the florist who delivered them so I could be sure to always order from them. Maybe I could start having fresh flower arrangements in the café. I would have to make sure whatever I used didn't have a strong scent that interfered with the coffee, though.

"Did you ever figure out who they were from?" Sammy asked, coming out of the back room, carrying a box.

"Nope. Just 'your secret admirer.'" I plucked the note from where it nestled among the roses and read it over again.

To Francesca. The beauty of these roses pales in comparison to yours. Signed, Your Secret Admirer.

I had assumed they were from Matt when they first arrived since we'd had a bit of a flirtation going on over the past few weeks, but he'd denied it at the time and seemed a little curmudgeonly about them ever since.

Aside from Matt, the only person I could think might have sent them was Chris Tompson, the sleazeball who ran a little cell-phone shop in town. I'd had some brief dealings with him a few weeks before, ending with him offering to take me out and show me around town. I'd turned him down, but I wouldn't have put it past him to keep trying.

The possibility that they could have been from a customer had also crossed my mind. No one took credit for them, though a smattering of customers complimented them. I'd kept on the lookout for anyone who seemed overly interested in them, to get a clue as to who my admirer was, but no one seemed like a contender. I wasn't sure if I liked the idea that I had a secret admirer or thought it was a bit creepy. In any case, the flowers were pretty.

"Well, here's something to keep you busy until you figure it out," Sammy said, closing the distance between us and hefting the large box into my arms. The top was partially open where she'd checked the contents, and the unmistakable aroma of tea wafted out.

"My teas!" I exclaimed, as excited as a kid on Christmas. Matt and Sammy chuckled.

"Well, now I know what to get you for your birthday," Matt said.

I maneuvered the box onto the counter and began pulling boxes and jars and tins of tea out of it.

"How much did you order?" Matt asked, surprised.

"Just a little," I replied.

"That's just a little, huh?"

I nodded. It wasn't just a little. It was a lot. I'd gone a little overboard. But Mrs. Howard had emphasized how different brands and varieties of tea could vary dramatically in how they tasted and behaved when brewed. She gave me the names of her favorites, of course, but encouraged me to try an assortment to determine what I liked best. That was all the push I'd needed to order almost every option from our supplier's catalog.

"Fran's a little excited about this tea thing," Sammy stage-whispered to Matt.

"I see that."

"I can hear you!" I interjected.

They both laughed.

The bell over the door jingled again, and all three of us turned to see who it was.

Chapter 2

"FRANCESCA!" Mrs. D'Angelo exclaimed, bursting into the café.

I held back a groan and caught Sammy suppressing a giggle as Mrs. D'Angelo surged past her. Mrs. D'Angelo was a lovely woman but exuberant, to say the least. About once a week, she came into the café like a whirling dervish, completely unconcerned with who was there and what they were doing, to share some usually inconsequential bit of news, primarily with me, for some reason.

Sammy had said Mrs. D'Angelo used to do the same thing to my mother, so maybe that was just something else I had inherited along with the café. Maybe she expected me to pass on the news to my customers as I served them.

"Oh, Francesca! Samantha! Matteo!" she cried. She dug the red-painted nails of one talon-like hand into my shoulder, turning me away from the counter and toward her. She hugged me briefly and forcefully, then turned and extended her free arm out toward Sammy and Matteo, motioning for them to come closer while keeping a tight grip on me. They each stepped toward us, but I noticed they were careful to stay out of the reach of Mrs. D'Angelo's grasping arms.

"Oh, my dears, have you heard the news?" she asked. "It's just awful, just—" She gasped as though overcome by whatever terrible thing she had to tell us. "Just awful!" In my experience, "just awful" to Mrs. D'Angelo wasn't much of a concern to the rest of us. So far, that summer, "just awful" had been a body board— later found propped up against a lifeguard stand—going missing from one of the beach rental houses, the daughter of someone I didn't know losing her job out of state, and some teenagers breaking into the local high school to fill the principal's office with balloons as a prank.

"What hap—?" Matt started to ask, not realizing that Mrs. D'Angelo didn't really allow much of an opportunity to get a word in during one of her procla-mations.

"There's been a murder!"

All traces of amusement vanished from Sammy's face at the same time Matt went pale. Only a short time had passed since his father's murder. The culprit had been put in jail, thanks to my own personal investigation and Matt's help, but I hadn't expected another murder so soon, either. Then again, nobody ever really expects murder, especially not in a safe town such as ours.

None of us spoke for a moment as we tried to process Mrs. D'Angelo's news.

"Another one?" I finally managed to ask.

"Yes!" Mrs. D'Angelo's voice was breathy. "Can you believe it? In our dear Cape Bay! Two murders in as many months! Good heavens, what is this world coming to? Things weren't this way when I was a girl!" She pulled me into another hard, furious hug.

"W-what happened?" I stuttered.

"He was stabbed! Stabbed to death! Right in the chest! They found him this morning in the parking lot of Todd's gym. He was there all night! Can you believe it? It's so awful!"

For once, she was right about it being awful. I was curious, though, why she had just referred to the place as "Todd's gym". I didn't know this Todd that everyone else seemed to. I considered that I might need to work on getting out of the coffee shop a little more to reacquaint myself with the town after my long absence. There were too many people and businesses I wasn't familiar with after having spent most of the past fifteen years living out of town.

"Who was it?" Sammy asked softly, having finally found her voice.

"Little Joey Davis! Oh, his poor mother! Poor Denise! She must be just devastated! Devastated!"

Joey Davis, Joey Davis. I ran the name through my head, trying to determine if it was someone I knew. The name sounded vaguely familiar, as though it belonged to someone who may have been a few years behind me in school, but I couldn't be sure.

"What time is it?" Mrs. D'Angelo asked, finally letting go of my shoulder to glance at her watch.

I rubbed the place where her fingers had been, expecting a mark there the next day.

"I need to go. The Ladies' Auxiliary will want to take meals to little Joey's mother, and I'll need to coordinate that." She looked pointedly at me and Sammy, whose eyes were filling up with tears. "The two of you are welcome to participate if you can make the time. Just let me know!" And with that, she bustled back past Matt and out the door.

Matt sneezed, probably from the overwhelming cloud of heavy floral perfume lingering behind.

I immediately went to Sammy, whose tears were

threatening to spill over, and wrapped her in my arms. She held on tightly for a few seconds before letting go.

"Thank you," she whispered, wiping at her eyes.

"Did you know Joey?" I asked.

"Joe," she corrected. "He hasn't gone by Joey since he was little. Mrs. D'Angelo probably just calls him that still because his dad's name is Joe, too." She took a deep breath. "I went to school with him. He was my age."

Sammy was twenty-seven, so it made sense that his name only sounded vaguely familiar to me. I didn't know him, but I could have seen him or his dad around town even if I didn't know who they were. Cape Bay wasn't so big that residents weren't at least passingly acquainted with each other.

"We weren't close or anything, but we'd chat when he came in," Sammy went on. "He'd been having a hard time lately. He lost his job, had to move in with his parents—"

The bell over the door jingled as a customer came in, clearly a tourist, based on his loud Hawaiian shirt and the camera draped prominently around his neck. I found it strange that people didn't know they were dressed like a stereotype.

"Can you take this one?" Sammy asked quietly. "I just need a minute."

"Of course, of course, go, go!" I waved her off

toward the back room, and she hurried away. "Hi," I said brightly, turning to the customer. "I'll be right with you." I headed around the counter to the register, where I could punch in his drink. "Matt, can you—" I started, motioning toward the pile of teas littering the counter.

"I got it," he said and started to put everything back in the box.

"What can I get for you, sir?" I asked the customer.

"I've heard you make a pretty good latte," the man drawled in a southern accent.

"That I do," I said with a smile.

"Then I'd like one of those, please, ma'am."

I told him the price, and he paid for the drink.

"If you'd like to take a seat over there, I'll have that right out to you," I said, handing him his change.

The man walked over to one of the tables as I pulled the espresso for his drink. After all the time I'd spent studying tea that afternoon, doing something I was comfortable with felt good. When the espresso was ready and the milk fully steamed, I poured in my design—a beach scene, complete with palm tree—to suit my customer's vacation style. My grandparents had perfected our family's method of brewing coffee, but I had elevated the drinks with my artistic creations.

I took the drink out to the man's table and set it down, the design facing him.

"Well, look at that!" he exclaimed. "If that's not the

prettiest cup of coffee I've ever been served. You don't mind if I take a picture of it, do you?" He gestured at the camera around his neck.

"Not at all," I replied. "Please let me know if it doesn't taste every bit as good as it looks. I'll be right over there." I gestured toward the armchair Matt had parked himself in after he finished boxing up my tea order.

"Will do. Thank you, ma'am."

"Thank *you*, sir."

I headed over to the armchair next to Matt. The customer's back was toward me, so I couldn't see his reaction when he put his camera away and took his first sip, but he didn't immediately turn around to find me, so I figured that was a positive indication regarding the coffee's taste.

"So," I said to get the conversation started.

"So," Matt parroted.

I wasn't quite sure where to take the conversation next. "You okay?" I asked.

Matt sighed. "Yeah, just…" He paused for a moment to collect his thoughts, then took a deep breath. "Yeah, I'm fine. I'll be fine."

"Did you know Joe?" While I had moved to New York City after college, Matt had come back home. He knew a lot more of what had gone on in town over the past several years than I did. I was slowly catching up, but there was still a lot I needed him to fill me in on.

He shrugged. "Not really. Not too well. We'd say hello, but we weren't buddies or anything."

I nodded.

"Like Sammy said, he was a good bit younger than you and me, so we didn't really run in the same crowd." He chuckled. "Well, from what I know of Joe, we wouldn't really have run in the same crowd if we were the same age."

I raised my eyebrows, silently asking him what crowd Joe ran with.

Another shrug. "You know, just—"

I looked at him. I didn't know.

He sighed. "Sammy would know better since she went to school with him, but I kind of remember him being a big-shot athlete in high school. Baseball, and I think he might have boxed, too. I'm not really sure. My dad was the one who kept up with all that."

That was it? Just that Joe was an athlete? Matt hadn't been athletic back in school, but I didn't think that was enough to warrant the "different crowd" comment.

"I didn't think you hated athletes that much," I said. "Weren't you friends with some of the guys on the hockey team?"

Matt shifted uncomfortably in his chair. He had more to say. I could tell.

"Well—" He exhaled sharply and lowered his voice even though I had only the one tourist sitting in the café. "He was supposed to have a full ride to college for baseball, but he got caught with drugs or something and lost the scholarship. Things kind of went downhill for him after that."

Then I understood. Matt had always been a pretty straight-and-narrow kind of guy. He wouldn't have hung around with a guy who was into drugs.

The tourist stood up and glanced around. I hopped up out of my chair.

"How was the latte?" I asked, moving toward him.

"Best I've had in a long while," he responded with a smile. He held up the cup and saucer that had held his drink. "Where can I put this?"

"You can just leave it on the table, or I can take it from you. You definitely don't have to bus your own table." I stepped closer to him, took the dishes from him, and placed them behind the counter.

"Well, thank you, ma'am." He glanced around the nearly empty café. "Things always this slow in here?"

"No," I exclaimed with a laugh. "You came in at the slowest time on the slowest day of the week! Give it a day or two, and we'll be packed. Every week, there's a couple of days before the new batch of tourists finds us. We're busy in the mornings and evenings, no matter what. It's just the midday that takes a hit."

"Well, I'll be back for another one of those lattes before I leave town even if I have to fight a crowd!"

"We'll look forward to seeing you," I replied with a smile.

He turned to go, and I took his dishes into the back-room to be washed. Sammy was still there, leaning against the desk.

"How are you doing?" I asked.

She took a deep shaky breath. "I'm okay. I'm just kind of shaken up. I'm not sure why. I guess—just—you know…" She trailed off and took another deep breath.

"I know," I said. "If you want to go on home, it's fine with me. I'll be fine here alone, and if I'm not, I can call in one of the girls."

A couple high schoolers worked with us part time, in addition to a couple older women who helped out from time to time. At least one of them would almost defi-nitely be available to come in and help me on short notice.

"No, I'll be okay." She stood up.

"Sammy?" I said, a warning tone in my voice. I knew she wouldn't want to leave me alone, but I also knew Joe's death was hitting her harder than she wanted to admit.

She sighed. "Are you sure?"

"I'm sure."

"Okay." She reached around her back and untied

her apron, then pulled it over her head, her blond pony-tail momentarily flipping up over her head. "Thanks, Fran," she said. She gave me a quick hug, grabbed her purse, and headed out the back door.

"I sent her home," I announced to Matt as I walked back into the main part of the café.

"That's probably good." He stood from his chair and stretched. "She looked kind of shaken up."

"Yeah, I figured it would be better for her." I leaned my hip against the counter. Even though I didn't know Joe Davis, Mrs. D'Angelo's announcement still bothered me. My entire life, Cape Bay had been a safe place, the kind of place where people barely locked their doors, especially during the off-season. We were a little more careful when tourists packed our streets. I found it troubling to think about having another murder in town. I was guessing it had at least doubled our usual murder rate.

"So where's this gym where Joe was found? And what's it called?" I asked Matt.

"Todd's gym? It's out on the edge of town. Near the marina."

I was happy to hear it was as far away as anything still in Cape Bay could be. "But what's it called?"

"Todd's gym," Matt repeated.

"I don't know who Todd is, and I don't care that it's the gym he goes to. I just want to know the name of it,"

I exclaimed, getting a little exasperated by how hard it was to get Matt to give me a straight answer.

"Franny"—he looked me in the eye—"the name of the gym is Todd's Gym. Todd owns it, and he named it after himself. And, yes, you do know him. It's Todd Caruthers."

Chapter 3

"TODD *CARUTHERS*?" I repeated.

Matt nodded. "You remember him, right?"

I certainly did remember him. Todd Caruthers had gone to school with Matt and me, graduating the same year we did. He was, in my eyes—and the eyes of most of the female population of our school—the be-all and end-all of high-school boys. He was tall, tan, and blond, with male-model-turned-movie-star good looks.

He was a three-sport varsity athlete, covering pretty much every variation of the all-American boy you could ask for—quarterback on the football team, star of the basketball team, and home run–hitting pitcher on the baseball team. He was the consummate athlete and the consummate jock, and I adored him. But there wasn't a chance a guy like that would give a shy, quiet girl like me the time of day. He was always dating one pretty cheer-leader or another. Once in a while, he'd mix it up and go out with a girl on the field-hockey team, but the girls like me who were on the debate team and school newspaper never stood a chance. I pined away for him from a distance all through high school. So, yes, I remembered Todd Caruthers quite well.

I spared Matt my reminiscences of adolescent angst and limited my response to a simple, "Yes."

Matt could barely conceal his snort. "I bet you do."

Though he was looking down at the floor, I saw crin-kles at the corners of his eyes. "What's that supposed to mean?" I exclaimed.

Matt shrugged and glanced up at me before quickly looking away again. "Just, uh, just that, well, I seem to recall you had a bit of a thing for him back in high school."

"What!" I screeched.

That made Matt laugh outright. "What? You thought it was a secret?"

I could feel blood rush to my face. "Yes, well, I mean, um—" I sputtered.

"Oh, come on, Franny! You went to every football, basketball, and baseball game he played in. *Even the away games.* You don't even like sports."

"I do so! I like the Red Sox and the Patriots!"

"That's because you're from Massachusetts. You

practically have to swear on a Bible that you like the Pats and the Sox before they'll give you a driver's license," he joked. "I bet you can't even name the starting center fielder for the Sox this year."

I tried to think of every baseball player I'd ever heard of in hopes of getting incredibly lucky and blurting out the right name. *Babe Ruth? Joe DiMaggio? Mickey Mantle?* I was reasonably certain none of them had played in my lifetime, but I wouldn't bet on it.

Apparently my silence and wrinkled forehead were enough to convince Matt I had no idea.

"Yeah, I thought so," he said.

"I can't believe you knew." I hid my face in my hands.

"It's not like you were the only one. I think every girl got all drooly when he walked by. I never really thought anything of it." He shrugged.

I still felt embarrassed. As a teenager, I had put a lot of time and effort into making my interest in Todd or any other boy seem as inconsequential and nonchalant as possible. To hear, even fifteen years later, that it had been as plain as the nose on my face to everyone around me was completely mortifying—especially when the guy I was currently interested in was the one telling me.

"So," I said, deciding to move the conversation forward. "Todd owns a gym now?"

"Yup. Todd's Gym, like I said. The name's supposed

to make it easy for you to know who owns it," he said with a smirk.

I gave him a dirty look in response. "What kind of gym is it? Like treadmills and weights or boxing or what?" When the tourist season died down, I would have some time to take an exercise class or two. I was hoping for some kind of yoga or spinning, but Cape Bay is a small town, and I knew my options might be limited.

"Lot of stuff. It's a big place. Two stories. Big concrete square." Matt gestured with his hands to indicate the large squareness of the building. "It's the only place in town, so I think he tried to cater to everyone."

"I might have to go check it out."

"Check it out or check *him* out?" Matt asked. I couldn't tell by his tone or his expression whether he was joking.

"The gym," I said out loud. I kept the rest to myself: *Jocks don't usually hold up over the years.*

Matt eyed me, looking somewhat suspicious, but really, what did it matter? Even if I was going over to check Todd out, he probably wouldn't even remember me. I had been completely inconsequential in his high-school experience. Besides, Matt and I had never discussed what was going on between us. A lot of dinners, a good bit of flirtation, and a few kisses on the cheek were as far as anything had gone. I was free to check out another man if I wanted to.

The bell over the door jingled, and a family of five walked in, all sunburned and sandy from their day on the beach.

Matt glanced over his shoulder at them. "You got this?" he asked.

I nodded. He was kind to check, even though I was pretty sure he couldn't figure out our espresso machine if his life depended on it.

"I'm going to go then," he said. "Let me know if you want to get dinner later, okay?"

"I have to go home and let Latte out. If you want to go out after that…"

"Sounds good. I'll see you." He rapped twice on the counter with his knuckles and waved before heading out the door.

"Hi, can I help you?" I asked, turning to the family of tourists. Out of the corner of my eye, I saw Matt hold the door open for another group headed into the café.

The rest of the day went pretty much like that—a steady stream of customers, one after the other—never more than I could handle on my own but always enough to keep me busily going from one task to the next, making drinks, cleaning them up, serving food, or wiping down tables. By the end of the evening, I was more than ready to turn the Open sign around to Closed.

I finished cleaning up, made sure the refrigerated display case was fully stocked with parfaits and fruit cups for the morning breakfast crowd, and headed toward home. The sun had already set, and night was quickly falling, so I walked out along the street instead of taking the shortcut through my neighbors' backyards. I probably would have stayed under the streetlights no matter what, just so I could see where I was going, but the thought of a murderer roaming the streets was lurking in the back of my mind, which kept me to the well-travelled route.

My house was just a few blocks away, tucked down a side street. It was a Cape Cod–style house surrounded by other Cape Cod–style houses. My grandparents had bought it shortly after their arrival in the country and raised both my mother and me there. Matt's house, the one he had grown up in and recently inherited from his father, was two doors down from mine. We were, by far, the two youngest people on the street.

As soon as I slid my key into the lock on the door, I heard canine feet running down the stairs. A wet nose poked out the door the second I cracked it open. It had only been a few hours since I'd last been home to let him out—he was equally excited to see me whether I'd been gone five minutes or five hours. I grinned as the dog jumped up on me in a desperate effort to cover my face with his kisses. I'd only had Latte a few weeks, but I already couldn't imagine my life without him.

He was a stray that I'd assumed was a mixed-breed mutt until I took him in to see the veterinarian.

The doctor's face broke into a grin when he walked in the door. "A Berger Picard!" he exclaimed in a French accent. "I haven't seen one of these since I came to the United States!" He immediately started ruffling Latte's fur as though he was a long-lost friend.

When I expressed my surprise at the vet calling Latte a purebred, he told me that the scrappy, scruffy appearance of the Berger Picard often led people to believe that they were mixed-breed dogs.

"But I can assure you, this dog is a Berger Picard," he said. "My family has raised these dogs for generations. After the world wars, we helped to rebuild the breed!" He gave me a meaningful look. "The wars were very hard on the breeders. It is difficult to feed your dogs when you can barely feed yourself."

He offered me a breed DNA test if I wanted to verify his assertion, but since Latte hadn't come with any papers, I didn't see the point in spending the hundred dollars on it. If my vet, an expert in Berger Picards, said that that's what Latte was, I would believe him. I loved the little guy no matter what his genetic background was.

I was happy to know a little more about him, though. He was sweet and friendly and affectionate, just like the breed description, which I later looked up, had said he would be. Even his perfectly latte-colored fur was typical of the breed.

I scratched behind Latte's ears with both hands. "Have you been a good boy? Are you ready for some din-din?" My voice had a more "baby-talk tone" than I would comfortably admit.

I went to the kitchen and scooped out Latte's dinner, then ran upstairs to my bedroom to change. I had a plan to clean all my grandparents' possessions out of the master bedroom on the first floor and redesign it for me to move into, but I'd only gotten as far as cleaning out the fifty years' worth of accumulated belongings. Someday soon, I needed to get to the hardware store to look at some paint colors and the housewares store to get some curtains and linens. I just hadn't had the opportunity—something else to add to my list for when the season ended.

I pulled off the black shirt and pants I'd worn to work—remnants of my New York City wardrobe—and pulled on a pair of jeans and a light-blue T-shirt that felt much more appropriate for a casual Cape Bay dinner. Glancing in the mirror, I smoothed my hair and ran a finger under each eye to clean up the little bit of mascara that had migrated off my lashes during the day. By the time I got downstairs, Latte was prancing at the door, ready for his evening walk.

I'd been enjoying the twice-daily walks he made me

take. It felt good to get out and breathe the salt air as it blew in off the ocean. It wasn't as strong near my house as it was at the café, but I could feel it all the same. I felt as though I was home, safe and secure, the way I felt back when I was in high school and the world seemed like a much simpler place.

I didn't want to leave Latte home alone again so soon after getting home, so we stopped by Matt's house on our way. He answered the door, wearing jeans and an old T-shirt instead of the button-down and khakis he'd been wearing earlier. His dark hair was disheveled. I did think he looked pretty cute.

"You ready for dinner?" he asked. He noticed the dog standing by my side. "Latte coming with us?"

"That's actually what I wanted to ask. I feel bad leaving him home by himself. Would you want to go to Sandy's?" Sandy's Seafood Shack was the best place around for New England seafood, and since its namesake was the owner's former four-legged furry friend, they allowed dogs on the patio and would even bring them a bowl of water and complimentary snack. I'd never thought I'd be one of those people who take their dog out to eat with them, but well, there I was.

"Sure," Matt replied. "You ready to go?"

"Let me go get my purse, and I will be." I handed Latte's leash to Matt and jogged across the yard between Matt's house and mine. I unlocked the door, grabbed my purse from where I'd dropped it just inside, locked back up, and jogged back.

"You hungry or something? You were moving pretty quick there," Matt said with a laugh when I got back.

"Actually, I am!" I replied. The only thing I'd consumed since lunch was a single cappuccino, and it was nearly nine o'clock.

"Well then, let's go!"

Matt held Latte's leash as we walked toward Sandy's. One of the things I loved about living in a small town is that I could pretty much walk anywhere I needed to go. For the most part, the only time I got in the car was to go grocery shopping, and that happened only if I needed so much stuff I couldn't carry it all.

Sandy's wasn't busy. Another couple was eating inside, and a bunch of college kids were hanging around the bar. It was a pretty safe bet they were in town for summer jobs—lifeguards, waiters and waitresses, store clerks. A lot of businesses scaled up for the summer by hiring college students. I did find it strange while growing up that college kids wanted to come to sleepy Cape Bay to work for the summer, but I guess it's pretty appealing when you don't already live at the beach.

Matt and I stuffed ourselves on beer and lobster rolls while Latte munched on apples with peanut butter. When we couldn't eat any more, we headed back home. We went past his house to mine. Even when there weren't murderers on the prowl, he liked to walk me to my door. He claimed it was the gentlemanly thing to do, just like he claimed it was the gentlemanly thing to pay for my dinner almost every time we went out. I'd managed to sneak a few in here and there, but I thought it was a game for him to pay for both of our meals before I could object or pay myself.

We lingered at my door for a few minutes while I finished filling Matt in on my newest thoughts on tea preparation. I knew he wasn't exactly interested, but I appreciated him humoring me.

"And then I should be able to try to make tea-latte art," I said as I wrapped up my perhaps overly detailed explanation of how I was going to determine the perfect amount of milk to use in my tea drinks. In addition to my research into brewing techniques, I'd also been considering what tea-based drinks I wanted to add to the menu at Antonia's.

"Well, I'll be happy to serve as a taste tester for you when you need it," Matt replied.

I laughed and then yawned. "I'll keep that in mind. For now, I'd better worry about getting to bed."

Matt chuckled. "I'll see you tomorrow, then?"

"Yup, sounds good," I said, rocking on the balls of my feet.

"Okay." He handed me Latte's leash and started to

let his hand fall back to his side, but he stopped and tucked a loose strand of hair behind my ear instead.

I held my breath.

Matt pushed his hand into his pocket. "Good night, then."

"Good night," I replied.

Matt turned to head home. I sighed and went inside to sleep.

Chapter 4

I WOKE up in the morning with Todd Caruthers on my mind—nothing in particular, just vague thoughts about the murder, the gym, and Todd from back in high school. I checked the time on my bedside clock. I had plenty of time if I wanted to check out Todd's Gym before I headed in to the café—to see if they offered any classes I was interested in, of course. Seeing how well Todd had held up—or hadn't—would just be a side benefit.

After showering, I pulled on a T-shirt and shorts, seeing no sense in getting more dressed up when I'd just have to change into work clothes in a few hours. I fed Latte and then took him for a quick walk around the block. I would have taken him to the gym with me, but I doubted they let nonservice dogs in.

"I'll be back to play with you before work, okay?" I said, ruffling Latte's ears in my hands as I got ready to walk out the door. "You're a good boy! Yes, you are!" I had somehow become a dog person when I wasn't paying attention.

Todd's Gym was just far enough away that I debated actually getting in my car and driving over there, but the weather was perfect, so I decided to walk. I followed the road I lived on out to Main Street, which followed the beach. It was late enough in the morning that the tourists had already started to fill up the beach, so I stuck to the road. I could only see the ocean through occasional breaks in the businesses lining the beach, but I could hear it and smell it, and that was enough to make the walk pleasant.

After almost half an hour, I came upon a large concrete structure my grandmother would certainly have called a monstrosity. Emblazoned across the structure in giant yellow letters was TODD'S GYM in all caps. The name definitely couldn't have been easily missed.

I walked up to the heavy glass double doors and pulled one open and was greeted by a rush of air conditioning. Just the entryway by itself was huge. I could've done cartwheels if I wanted to. The floor below my feet was a shiny black tile, and the ceiling had to be at least twenty feet above me. From where I stood upon walking in, I could see the entrance to a basketball court on my right and a room full of exercise equipment on my left. Beyond the basketball court was a metal staircase leading up to the second floor. I couldn't be sure, but I thought I detected the scent of chlorine coming from somewhere in the building.

Directly in front of me was a large reception desk with a perky-looking blond girl sitting behind it. I guessed she was about nineteen years old. Her ponytail was as high as it could possibly have been without actually being on top of her head. She had a fairly deep tan that I couldn't quite pin down as being from the sun or a bottle. She was wearing layered hot-pink and black tank tops and, presumably, skin-tight yoga pants. All that, combined with her full face of makeup, made me feel as though I was woefully underdressed and a little bit old.

"Hi! Can I help you?" she chirped.

"Um, yeah, I was wondering what kind of classes you offer?" I was still looking around the massive space, not quite paying attention to the girl.

"That's great. We have some brochures right here. Is there a certain kind of class you're looking for?" She stood up and began pulling shiny sheets of paper from a plastic rack on the counter. "We have all the usuals, of course: Pilates, yoga, *hot yoga*"—she raised her eyebrows as she mentioned hot yoga, clearly suggesting that class was one of their most enticing—"spinning, aerobics, dance fitness… water aerobics if that's more your style."

I groaned internally at that perky, fit young woman thinking that water aerobics might be the most physical activity I could handle. I took the brochures and started glancing through them. Apparently, I would have plenty of options when I had the time. I was about to ask her about their membership plans when a man came out of the back and leaned over the counter to talk to Perky Girl.

"Karli, were there any calls for me while I was gone?" he asked.

"Just one." She picked up a slip of paper from the desk and handed it to him. "Oh, this woman was asking about our classes."

I looked up into a stunning pair of deep-blue eyes. Todd Caruthers. Despite my expectation that Todd, as a former high-school athlete, would have gotten soft and maybe developed a paunch, he was every bit as handsome as he had been back in high school, maybe even more so.

"Franny? Francesca!" he exclaimed, as Karli took a phone call.

I caught my breath. *He remembers me?*

"Todd." I smiled.

He stepped around the curve of the desk and put his arms around me. His chest was every bit as muscular as I had imagined it to be in high school. He released me and stepped back. "I was wondering when I'd see you."

In a lower voice, he said, "Did you get my flowers? I wanted to come by the café to see if you liked them."

The flowers were from *Todd*? I was speechless. Why had Todd sent me flowers, and why on earth did he sign the card "your secret admirer"?

"I, um, yeah. Yes, I mean, yes, I did." I was so thrown that I could barely put a sentence together. "I didn't know they were from you."

He grinned, flashing shiny white teeth. "You didn't? I thought you'd seen me when I came in to Antonia's."

I thought back, trying to think of when I might have seen him or how I might have missed him. *How could I miss Todd coming into my café?*

"No—no, I didn't. I guess I've had a lot on my mind." That was the only reason I could think of that I hadn't noticed him. With my mother's death and Matt's father's death and my investigation into his murder and learning how to manage the café all over again, I probably couldn't have told you most of the people who came in, even the ones I'd known my whole life. Matt and Sammy were really the only people I'd managed to connect with, and circumstances had thrown me together with them more than I'd sought them out. I figured I should reach out to more of my friends when the busy season ended.

"Yeah, I can see that. Still, my feelings are a little hurt!" He reached out and swatted me playfully on the arm. "You don't even notice your old friend, Todd?" His eye twitched in a wink.

My old friend? That's not exactly how I would have described our relationship. I almost wondered if he'd confused me with someone else, but he used my name, so he must have remembered who I was.

"Why didn't you sign the card?" I asked, trying to get away from the awkward question of why I hadn't noticed him.

"Oh, well, I wanted to play it cool. You've had a lot going on, and I didn't want to make anything complicated. But I thought you might like some flowers. Every girl likes flowers, right?"

I smiled. "Flowers are always good. And the ones you sent were beautiful. And still alive, surprisingly."

He smiled, a gleaming, sparkling smile that made me weak in the knees. "Great. I'm glad you liked them." He lowered his voice again and leaned in toward me. "How are you doing? Since your mother…?"

I was surprised by his compassionate question. He'd been such an arrogant jock in high school and hadn't seemed all that much different so far in our conversation, but maybe there was more to him after all.

"It's been rough. But I'm doing okay. It was a lot of change all at once."

Todd nodded. "And Matt?"

I was even more shocked. He was interested enough

to ask not only about me but about Matt also? He really must have changed.

"He's getting there. Both of our parents' deaths were sudden, but emotionally, I think they were very different. An aneurysm, like my mother had, is so different from murder."

Todd nodded thoughtfully, but I realized with a sinking feeling what I'd said. I had mentioned murder when there had just been one in Todd's parking lot.

"I bet," he said sympathetically. He shook his head. "You know, I just keep thinking about Joe's parents— how they must be feeling right now. Did you know Joe? Did you hear—?"

I nodded. "Yes. Well, yes, I heard, but no, I didn't know him. Was he a friend of yours?"

Todd glanced around, checking on what Karli was up to at the desk, then took my elbow again and led me toward a door that led off the main lobby. I hesitated a moment, not sure where he was taking me. He typed a combination into a keypad on the door and swung it open, revealing a normal-looking office. I decided it was safe to follow him in, and he shut the door behind us.

"Take a seat." He gestured at one of the guest chairs sitting in front of the desk. He walked around it and settled in on a large leather chair on the other side. I picked the chair closest to the window and sat down. Todd rubbed his face with his hands.

"I'm lucky they let us open today," he said. "They had the parking lot all blocked off with crime-scene tape all day yesterday. I guess I'm lucky they found Joe first thing in the morning so they could get all their investigating over with in one day."

I was surprised by how mercenary his comments sounded, but I supposed it was reasonable to feel that way when your business and your livelihood were being affected.

He must have seen something in my face or realized how his comments could be interpreted because he quickly added, "A lot of people depend on me for their income, you know."

"Did they need to search inside the gym?" I asked. When Matt's dad had died, the police didn't realize it was murder until after the autopsy, so they didn't start out the investigation the same way they would have, had they known. I was curious about what they'd done when the cause of death was more obviously foul play.

"They did a basic search," he said. "Confiscated some trash bags and laundry. I had to go out and buy a bunch of new towels so people would have some to use in the showers and in the pool. They didn't dust for fingerprints or anything, though. Out in the parking lot though, man, I think they picked up every last rock that was out there. Cleanest the parking lot's ever been."

"Did they have to question people?" I asked.

He groaned and leaned back in his chair. "Every last person who works here! And now, they're working through all my members. I'll be lucky if they don't scare half of them off."

"Do you know if they have any leads yet? Any suspects?" I felt as though I was interrogating Todd, but I found it more than a little unnerving to think of a murderer wandering around town.

He looked me dead in the eye as he replied. "They have at least one."

"They do?" I asked. "Who?"

"Me."

Chapter 5

"WHAT?" I shrieked, a little more loudly than I meant to. How on earth could they think Todd killed someone?

I realized in the next second that I'd spent precisely five minutes with him in the last fifteen years, which wasn't exactly enough to make a well-grounded character judgment. Still, he didn't seem like the kind of guy who would kill someone. He wasn't acting the way I imagined a murderer would act—he was calm, relaxed, flirty even!

"They questioned me for hours yesterday."

"It's your gym. Are you sure it's not just standard procedure? You know, to make sure they know about anything that could have led to... to the murder?" Even though Todd obviously knew what had happened just outside his office window, I still felt awkward saying "murder" in front of him. It wasn't something people got much practice discussing in polite conversation.

He shook his head. "Not with the questions they asked me." At first, he didn't elaborate, and even though I wanted to know, I didn't want to ask. Then he exhaled sharply and leaned forward, resting his elbows on his desk. He covered his face with his hands.

I sat still, not knowing what to do. Should I reach out and comfort him? Sit quietly until he gathered himself? Leave him in peace?

Before I could decide, he dropped his hands and looked at me, shaking his head. "You wouldn't even believe, Fran. Where was I every second of the day he died? Could anyone verify what I did? How well did I know Joe? For how long? How are the gym's finances? Did I have any kind of grudge against Joe? Could I tell them again where I was at nine o'clock? Who was working that day? Did I know if anyone had any issues with Joe? When was the last time I saw him? When did I expect to see him? How long has the gym been open? And it was like that, too—one question after another, on all different subjects, bouncing around from one thing to the next. I know they were trying to get me to slip up, but there was nothing to slip up about! And do you know how hard it is to remember exactly what you were doing at seven-fifty-five last night? And not to forget anything? I swear, I had to account for every breath I took."

He sounded frustrated and angry and, I think, even a little bit scared, not that I could blame him. Someone had been murdered in his parking lot, and he'd been interrogated—intensely, it sounded like. But the way he talked about it convinced me even more that he was innocent. Those questions the police had asked were designed to trip up someone who was lying. He didn't sound as though he'd had any problem keeping his story straight, and that had to count for something.

He leaned so far back in his chair that I thought he might fall over, and he let out a long, deep breath, his eyes fixed on the ceiling. "I don't know, Fran. I just don't even know."

I said the only thing I could think of. "I'm so sorry this is happening to you, Todd."

"Thank you," he said, leaning forward again. "And I'm sorry I dumped on you like that. I don't really know where all that came from. I guess I just had to get it off my chest. I don't have that many people I can talk to. Everyone here is my employee or my customer." He waved his hand expansively to indicate the gym. "I'm not going to tell my mom her son is a murder suspect. I live alone. You just happened to be in the right place at the right time. Not exactly a great way to say hello to an old friend, huh?"

There was that "friend" thing again. Did he just remember it differently than I did? Was I the one remembering it all wrong? Did he just consider everyone a friend? And why was I complaining about Todd Caruthers considering me a friend? Wouldn't I have died for that back in high school?

I chose to smile. "I'm glad I could be here when you needed me."

Todd flashed back his toothy white grin. His teeth practically glowed against his tanned skin. "So am I."

I felt warmth spread across my chest when he smiled at me like that. It made me feel like the homecoming queen.

"Now," Todd slapped his hand on the desk. "I know you didn't come here to listen to me go on about the cops asking me a million questions. What brought you out today?"

I tried to remember. Between getting lost in Todd's deep blue eyes and hearing about the murder, I'd virtually forgotten why I came. After an almost embarrassingly long pause, I noticed the same plastic display that had been on the reception desk sitting behind Todd.

"I wanted to see what kind of classes you have," I said. "What was her name—Karli?—she filled me in on all the different classes you offer, got me some brochures. I think she actually would have broken into a demonstration if you hadn't walked up when you did." I laughed so he knew I was kidding.

He laughed too. "Yeah, Karli's got some energy. She's great to have at the front desk. She really gets people in, makes them feel welcome, gets them raring to go." He paused and looked toward the papers in my lap. "Which brochures did she give you?" he asked.

I handed them over to him. He murmured as he flipped through.

"Yoga, Pilates, aerobics, dance, spin. Good stuff. We also have ballet barre and boot-camp classes you might like." He piled two more brochures onto my stack.

"I'm impressed how many different classes you have," I commented. "Honestly, I didn't expect there to be so many options in Cape Bay. We're not really known for being cutting edge here."

"Classes are one of my prime focuses," Todd said. "They're just the best way to get people in and get them moving. So many people come in, play around on the treadmill, get bored, and go home. Classes really get people engaged, get their blood flowing, keep them coming back. I actually pay a lot of attention to what they're doing in New York and LA. That's where the really exciting stuff comes from. I mean, who would have thought back when we were kids that stationary bikes would be the coolest workout on the planet? You can't see the trend until it hits, but when it hits, I want to be there. I want people to know that Todd's Gym is every bit as good as some fancy gym in the city."

I had never heard anyone speak so passionately about exercise classes. Well, some of the public relations girls I'd known back in New York talked about their spin classes with near-religious fervor, but Todd was different. He wasn't just obsessed with one particular class but with *classes* as a whole. I imagined his obsession was a little like the way I used to sound when I'd go on and on about coffee back before everyone and their brother was an "expert" on the subject. I'd always found that kind of passion deeply appealing in a person, even when I didn't understand the subject of their passion. I thought perhaps Todd and I could end up as real friends.

"That's awesome," I said. "I always liked trying different classes when I was back in the city. Some of them were just weird, but some of them were really amazing. I'd work out parts of my body I didn't even know I could work out!"

"See? That's what I love. People getting to do new things, move new ways. Not everyone is going to like every class, but just getting them to try it is a win. Man, I love that stuff!" He had a grin plastered on his face from ear to ear. "Hey, you know what else you should take?" He turned in his chair and pulled another brochure out of the rack to hand to me. "Kickboxing! Have you ever taken it? There are actually a lot of women who are really into it."

"Actually, I have," I replied. It hadn't been my thing. I could handle the kicks in a dance aerobics class or in a boot camp, but those were always air kicks. Kickboxing wanted you to kick something, even if it was just a punching bag. I didn't have that much aggression in me. "I didn't really like it."

"Oh, no?" The smile left Todd's face. Then he said, "Joe was a kickboxer."

"Professional?" I asked.

"Technically, yeah. He competed in the professional fights and got prize money, but he didn't make a living off of it. He was trying, though. He lost his job a few months back, so he was putting a lot more time into training. He was good. He had potential. He was getting a little old, but he was tough."

"Old? Wasn't he in his twenties?"

Todd chuckled. "Twenty-seven, yeah. Makes you feel *really* old, hearing that, doesn't it?"

I nodded. No wonder Karli had mentioned water aerobics to me.

"Me too," he continued. "Late twenties isn't old to be a fighter, but it's old to still be coming up. Most of the guys who are going to make something of themselves are going to start being known in their early twenties. It's just a couple of years, but it's enough to make a difference. Of course, a lot of them are going into MMA now."

"MMA?" I asked.

"Mixed Martial Arts. It's where you mix different styles of fighting instead of just following the rules of just one."

"Oh, that's the one where they look like they're trying to kill each other!" I had seen it on TV in the background at bars. It looked violent and bloody—also not my thing.

"Yeah, I guess it could look like that," Todd replied with a smile.

"Did Joe do MMA?"

"He was experimenting with it. He didn't have a background in any of the standard martial arts like a lot of these guys, so that put him behind, too. Poor kid. Couldn't catch a break."

I got the sense that Todd had a soft spot for Joe. "Did you know him well?" I asked.

"Yeah," he said. "He was a friend."

"I'm so sorry. This must be really hard for you."

"Thanks. It's tough. Between him being a friend and the impact on the gym's business and then waiting for the cops to break down my door and arrest me..." He exhaled. "Yeah, it's tough."

I instinctively reached my hand out across the desk toward him. He took it and squeezed. We sat there for a moment until I realized I was basically holding hands with Todd Caruthers. Even though it gave me a thrill, as soon as I was aware of it, I felt uncomfortable and pulled my hand away. I gave Todd a smile to make up for it.

"If there's anything I can do," I said, "please, let me know."

"Thank you, I will."

Just then, the phone on Todd's desk rang.

"Hang on, just a second, will you?" he said before picking it up. "Hello?" A pause. "Really?" He sighed. "Yeah, okay... Yeah... Tell them I'll be out in just a minute... okay... yeah... yeah... okay... bye." He put the phone down in its cradle and his head down in his hands.

"Everything okay?" I asked, knowing it wasn't.

"The cops are here. They want to talk to me."

"Again?"

"Again." He closed his eyes and took a deep breath. "Well, I guess we'll have to pick this up again later. Maybe I'll come by the coffee shop sometime? Assuming I'm not in jail."

"You won't be in jail!" I retorted, based solely on my own observances and not the years of police work and training that the detectives would be relying on.

"Let's hope," he replied, rising from the desk. He handed me the pile of brochures still sitting in front of him, and I added it to the kickboxing one in my hand.

He walked around the desk and gave me a hug as though it was no big deal. I hugged him back because he was Todd Caruthers and my teenage self would have killed me if I didn't. "Thanks, Fran," he said, stepping away from me and toward the door. "You're a good friend." He pulled open the door, and I saw a small cluster of blue uniforms and black suits in the lobby.

"Come by the café sometime, and I'll buy you a cup of coffee," I said quietly as I walked past him.

"Thanks, I will," he replied. Then he addressed the police waiting for him. "Officers," he said. "If you'd like to come in…"

As they started to move into his office, I thought it would be a tight squeeze to fit all those broad shoulders inside Todd's office. It wasn't a particularly small room, but none of them were particularly small men either.

"Hello, Fran," one of the officers said.

I turned around and scanned their faces until I landed on the one who had spoken. Mike Stanton had been a classmate of mine and worked for the police department. Because the police department was small, he worked as a patrolman or a detective as necessary. Based on his black suit, I guessed he was a detective on that case. He'd been the detective on Matt's dad's murder case as well. I wondered if he was becoming Cape Bay's murder expert. I didn't think having a murder expert on the police force was something Cape Bay should necessarily be proud of.

"Hi, Mike," I said with a smile.

"You here catching up with an old friend?" he asked. There was that "friend" thing again. He sounded suspicious. Of course, the murder scene at the gym was the second he'd found me at or near, so I supposed that made sense. At least I hadn't been the one to find Joe's body.

I glanced back at Todd, who was still holding the door open, waiting for Mike to follow the rest of the officers. Todd gave me a grim smile.

"Yup," I said. I waved my hand around the large, open space. "And I wanted to see the gym. I didn't even know it was here until a couple of days ago."

Mike nodded. "Well, I'm sure I'll see you around." He didn't exactly sound pleased about that.

"See you!" I made it a point to sound as cheery as possible. I liked Mike. He was a good guy. My new knack for hanging around murder scenes just complicated that.

He nodded and stepped into Todd's office. I thought I saw a worried expression on Todd's face as he let the door close behind Mike. I hoped the conversation would go better than I knew he feared.

I caught Karli's eye as I turned to leave the gym. Her big blue eyes looked even bigger. She looked scared. If I were nineteen, my boss suspected of committing a murder, the victim of which was found practically where I parked my car every day, I would've been terrified. I felt a surge of sympathy for the girl.

"It'll be okay," I called softly to her.

She nodded but grabbed a tissue and turned her chair around to face away from the door.

I certainly hoped it would be okay.

Chapter 6

I HAD dinner with Matt that night. We went to a little authentic Italian restaurant in the next town. I'm generally suspicious of Italian places that claim to be authentic because most of the time, what they really mean is that they are authentic what-people-think-is-Italian. They are almost never right, partly because Italy is a big country with lots of different styles of food. The food in the north is, in a lot of ways, more like the food of Austria or France than it is like the food in Sicily. One size does not fit all. And a chef who is good at cooking one style isn't necessarily good at cooking another.

Osteria di Monica, though, was probably the most authentic I'd ever been to. My family had been eating there my entire life. The original owners had come over from Italy around the same time as my grandparents, after the war, and cooked exactly the same in the restaurant as they had back home. When their son was old enough, he went to culinary school. His parents were less than pleased with some of the "Italian" cooking methods he picked up there and sent him back to Venice, where they had emigrated from, for two years to learn how to cook proper Venetian food.

Presently, his son, the original owners' grandson, was now getting his full-immersion lesson in Italian cooking on his own two-year trip to Venice. He was due back in a little over six months, and the rumor was that he might be bringing a girl with him—a Venetian girl he'd met at the restaurant where he worked. The family could not have been more excited at the prospect of marrying off their boy and getting a new, properly-trained chef at the same time.

Matt and I studied our menus. We'd each been there easily over a hundred times, but they kept the menu seasonal, aside from a few staples, so we always wanted to look it over before deciding. We decided on carpaccio for an appetizer, then Matt ordered polenta with shrimp, and I chose risotto nero—a creamy rice dish colored black by cuttlefish ink. It wasn't an Americanized dish, that's for sure, and I'd certainly gotten some weird looks from people who found its color unusual and off-putting.

"So what's going on with you?" Matt asked after we ordered.

I looked at him curiously. "You know everything that's going on with me," I said. "I saw you yesterday."

"That's not what I mean," he replied. "What's going on? Why are you upset?"

I hadn't realized it was so obvious. I hesitated.

"Whatever it is, you can tell me, Franny."

I let out a long sigh. "I went over to Todd's Gym today."

"Hmm." Matt leaned back in his chair and crossed his arms over his chest. That seemed a strange reaction. I didn't know what else to do, so I went on.

"I just wanted to see what kind of classes they have."

"They have a website, you know."

I couldn't tell if he was being critical or factual. I didn't usually have so much trouble getting a read on Matt and wondered if he was upset about something too.

"I didn't think of that," I said honestly. "I guess I thought it would be too small and rinky-dink for that."

"No, he's pretty sophisticated about it."

"I noticed," I replied. "I know you said it was a big concrete square, but I didn't expect it to be that nice inside. And huge. It's huge!"

"Yeah, he went all out with that place," he replied with a chuckle. His posture seemed to relax. "Is that what bothered you? That you went over there and the place was nice?"

"No." For some reason, my worry felt personal, and even though I was close to Matt, I was conflicted about telling him what was on my mind.

"Then what?"

I blurted it out. "They suspect Todd of Joe's murder."

Matt paused as he appeared to think this over. Then: "And it bothers you that he's a suspect or that he may be a murderer?"

The difference between the two options was almost insignificant, but I understood what he was really asking —did I think Todd was guilty or innocent? I didn't have a doubt in my mind.

"Todd didn't kill Joe."

"I wasn't saying he did," Matt replied. "I just wanted to understand what was bothering you." I could see the sincerity in his face.

"I know. I just… It's been a long day. I didn't go out there expecting to see Todd, and then there he was, just out of the blue. I didn't even think he'd remember me, but he did. And he was so thoughtful, asking about how I was doing since my mom passed away—and you! He asked about how you've been doing since your dad's murder."

"Todd Caruthers asked about me?" Matt asked.

"Yes!" I replied. "He seemed different from the way

he was back in high school. He was polite and thoughtful. I was really surprised."

Matt considered that information, though he seemed not to believe me. "So you don't think he's a murderer because he was nice to you, a pretty girl." Matt's tone was so flat and even that it took me a second to realize what he'd said.

"You think I'm pretty?" I asked with a smile. He'd mentioned it in such an offhand way, I almost laughed.

"Of course I do." He scoffed. "And I'm sure Todd does, too. He has eyes, doesn't he?"

Stunning blue ones. "Yes, I seem to recall eyes."

"Well then, he's seen you, and he knows you're pretty. And guys tend to be nice to pretty girls." He was an odd combination of flirty and combative—calling me pretty one second and dismissing Todd the next. He really was in a strange mood.

The waitress brought our appetizer, and I took the opportunity to change the subject.

"So, how's work?" I asked as we cut into the thin slices of beef.

"It's good."

"Just 'it's good'?" I laughed.

"Oh, you know. Same old, same old."

"Any new and interesting projects?"

"Actually, there is one. There's a big private university down in Virginia that wants to completely revamp their network—everything from how the school's network connects to the Internet all the way to how students and staff access the network. It's huge—a million moving parts. We just signed the contract with them this morning, and it'll probably be a year before we make any physical changes on the campus and another two or three years after that before we're done."

"Wow," I said. It was a simplistic response, but only because I could only barely understand what Matt did for a living. I knew he was a project manager for telecom engineering. I knew that, in addition to projects, he also managed several engineers. I knew they were all good at their jobs and fairly self-sufficient, but Matt's job was the one on the line if they ever screwed up. He worked on several projects at a time and was one of his firm's top engineers, getting sent out across the country to work on their highest-priority jobs.

"Yeah, I have to fly down early next week to meet with them and have the project kickoff meeting."

"You're going out of town?" Because of his father's death, Matt had taken some time off from travelling for work and hadn't been out of town since we'd reconnected. We had spent so much time together over the past few weeks that I wasn't sure what I would do on my own. I was glad I would have Latte to keep me company.

"Yup," he confirmed. "It's been kind of nice sleeping

in my own bed the past few weeks. It's going to be kind of strange getting back out on the road again."

I had never traveled for work like Matt did—just some conferences here and there when I worked in public relations back in the city. I couldn't imagine what it was like to spend so much time on the road.

"I don't know how you do it," I said. "I don't think I could."

"You get used to it," he replied with a shrug. "I get to see a lot of parts of the country I probably wouldn't otherwise."

"I feel like I would get bored spending all that time in hotel rooms."

"I usually get to sightsee a little. There are only so many hours of the day you can be in meetings. I mean, when else are you going to find yourself in a position to go to the Zippo lighter museum?"

"There's a Zippo lighter museum?"

"Yup, right there at the factory. It's actually a pretty cool place." He paused and smiled. "And I never would have gotten to see it if I wasn't bored and alone on the road."

I had to laugh. He had a point there.

"What else have you seen?"

"You want weird, quirky stuff or the serious museums and national landmarks?"

"Oh, definitely the quirky stuff. You can go to an art

museum just about anywhere. I want the one-of-a-kind stuff."

He thought for a moment. "Um, lots of presidential birthplaces, but those are on the more serious side. The world's largest teapot. A life-size chocolate moose. The most historic alley in Delaware."

I interrupted him. "Wait, what happened there? What makes it so historic?"

He fought back a smile. "The riverboats offloaded at one end of the alley, and the stagecoaches picked up at the other end. Lots of important figures in history walked along that alley to get from the riverboats to the stagecoaches."

I looked at him for a few seconds, judging how serious he was being. The tale sounded like something he could very well be making up.

"How do you know it's so historic?" I asked.

"The plaque they had posted there told me."

I burst out laughing and had to cover my mouth with my hand to stop myself from disturbing the whole restaurant. There was something extremely entertaining to me about the idea that a state had gone to the trouble to erect a plaque to commemorate where some historical figures had once walked.

Matt was trying to restrain his laughter as well. I wasn't sure whether he thought the alley was as funny as I did or my laughter was making him laugh along. Either way, the two of us were cracking up when the waitress brought over our meals and set them in front of us.

Matt's polenta was thick and creamy, with a generous helping of shrimp piled on top. My risotto was black as night, with chunks of cuttlefish mixed into it. We both calmed our laughter down enough to start eating, although I convinced Matt to continue his stories about interesting places he had visited in his travels around the country. I even got to hear all about a museum he visited that was devoted entirely to art and artifacts related to death and mourning. It was an unusual premise for a museum to be built on, but according to what Matt said, it was a really nice museum and an interesting place. I told him I'd take his word for it.

We decided to split a dessert since neither of us was very hungry after our full meals. Any other time, we probably would have skipped it, but Osteria di Monica has the most delicious desserts. We ordered the tiramisu because, in my opinion, it's the best of all. Setting aside all the rest of the food, I would go there just for that.

When it arrived, I sat and looked at it for a moment, admiring its beauty and anticipating all the flavors.

"What are you waiting for?" Matt asked, his fork poised over the dish.

"Nothing," I said and plunged my own fork in. The tiramisu was every bit as delicious as I had expected—maybe even more. I sometimes wondered if it was possible to remember something that good accurately or if you always convinced yourself that you were remembering it through rose-colored glasses. There weren't many things that were better than I remembered, but this always seemed to be one of them. Either that or it actually got better every time.

"Oh my God, Franny," Matt said.

I momentarily wondered if he'd forgotten that I wasn't the one who made the dessert.

"This is so good! You know, you should serve tiramisu at the café. It's Italian and has a lot of coffee in it, just like you." His eye gleamed as he said it. "You're a great baker. I bet you could make something every bit as good as this, if not better."

"I don't know about that," I said, taking another bite. It really was exquisite. The flavors were perfectly balanced, and the texture was everything I would want it to be. Putting something together that well took skill and practice, even with a no-bake recipe. Still, his comment gave me an idea.

"How was it?" the waitress asked, coming by a few minutes later to drop off the check.

"Amazing!" I answered.

"The best thing I've ever eaten," Matt said. Then to me: "No offense, Fran."

"None taken," I replied sincerely.

"Great!" the waitress chirped. "Is there anything else I can get you?"

"Actually, would it be possible for us to speak to the chef?" I asked.

"Sure!" she replied. "I'll go get him." She laid the bill down on the table. "And I'll take that whenever you're ready."

Matt grabbed the check before I could even make a move for it. I gave him a dirty look.

The chef, the son of the original owners, came out moments later. He was a tall man with dark hair and olive skin.

"Matteo! Francesca! How are my two favorite customers?" He was exaggerating, of course. I was reasonably certain he greeted all regulars that way.

We exchanged pleasantries, and I asked how his son Stefano was doing in Italy. He gushed about how much Stefano was learning and how much they were looking forward to his return. The young lady that Stefano was expected to bring back with him received a fair bit of enthusiasm as well.

"How was everything?" Alberto asked when we were all caught up. "Did everything taste good?"

"Everything was delicious," I said. "That's actually sort of what I wanted to talk to you about. Is your mom still making the tiramisu?"

"She is, yes, with my wife helping also. Was there a

problem with it?"

"No, no, no! Not at all. It was amazing!" I said hurriedly. His face was covered with curiosity, so I just went ahead and asked my next question. "You know I'm running Antonia's now, right?"

"Of course." He was still baffled.

"What would you think of selling your tiramisu in my café? It's so good—I know people would buy it, and I bet you would get new customers out of it, too."

I could tell he had never thought about selling his food off-site. But dessert—tiramisu especially—was a different animal than risotto. It could be made ahead of time. It could keep for several hours or even days.

"We could start small," I told him, sensing his indecision. "Maybe five or ten pieces? You set the price, and we can split the profits—fifty-fifty, sixty-forty, whatever you want. Monica's doing the work of making it. I just have to put it in my display case, and it'll sell itself."

Alberto crossed his arms across his chest as he thought over my offer.

"Let me talk to my mother. And my wife. We'll see what they think, if they want to make more each day. If they say yes, then it's a deal."

"Great!" I replied. "I hope it works out. And if it doesn't, no hard feelings. I'll be back here to eat every week anyway."

He laughed. "Oh, I know you will!"

Matt and I expressed our thanks for the exceptional meal and said our goodbyes as Alberto went back to the kitchen.

"I didn't see that coming," Matt said. "When did you decide you were going to ask him that?"

"When you suggested I sell tiramisu at Antonia's."

"I suggested you make it. You're an amazing baker."

"Well, thank you." I smiled. "But Monica's been perfecting her tiramisu recipe for years. It's the best I've ever tasted. Why try to improve upon perfection?"

"Your coffee's pretty perfect, and you're always trying to improve on that."

"That's because it's *mine*. You should always try to improve on yourself. But I don't have to be the best at everything. I'm perfectly happy letting Monica be the best at tiramisu."

"Well, I'm glad I gave you the idea," Matt replied with a smile.

I laughed at his effort to take credit for something he could barely argue he had suggested. "Thank you for that," I said through my laughter.

After Matt finished paying, we walked out to his car. He usually drove when we went places because he liked to drive about as much as I didn't. I was excited about the possibility of selling Monica's tiramisu in my café, but once we were in the darkness of the car, with only the road ahead of me to focus on, my mind drifted back to my morning visit to Todd's Gym and the revelation that he was a suspect in Joe's murder. That did bother me, mostly because I didn't think he'd done it. I realized that if I was able to find out who had killed Matt's dad, maybe I could use those same investigative skills to help Todd by finding out who had really killed Joe.

Chapter 7

"YOU DOING ALL RIGHT OVER THERE?" Matt asked after a few minutes.

"Hmm?" I responded. His question had barely penetrated my thoughts.

"I asked if you're all right over there. You've been awfully quiet since we got in the car."

"Oh. Yeah." I stared out the window. Based on Matt's reaction earlier when I brought up the subject of Todd, I wasn't sure I wanted to mention him again, especially not my idea of helping him.

"Thinking about Joe's murder again?"

I looked over at Matt in surprise. I hadn't expected him to guess what was going on in my head. "Yes," I admitted. "It just bothers me that the police seem to have jumped on him so readily without doing much investigating."

"I'm sure they have their reasons."

"I know. I just—" I stopped and sighed. I wasn't the kind of person who doubted the police, since I generally assumed they knew what they were doing. Still, Todd being a suspect didn't sit right with me. He didn't *feel* like someone who could commit murder, and I was fairly certain that wasn't just because I thought he was good looking. He didn't talk like a murderer or act like a murderer. He talked and acted like a guy who was freaked out about being a murder suspect and having his livelihood on the line due to a murder having taken place in his business's parking lot. "I just don't think he did it," I said finally.

Matt was quiet. I worried that he was upset with me.

After a few minutes, he said quietly, "You know, you're the one who found out who killed my dad. You did a good job with that—finding evidence, figuring out what you needed to investigate next. As long as you don't get in the way of the police investigation, maybe it wouldn't hurt to do it again. Even if you don't figure out who else might have done it, you might be able to find enough evidence to know whether or not it was Todd." He glanced away from the road and over at me, then back at the road. He shrugged. "You know, if you wanted to."

I couldn't believe Matt had come to the same conclusion I had. Not only that—he was actually suggesting it.

"You really think it's a good idea?" I asked.

"Only if it's something you feel like you want to do. I'm not saying you have to or that Todd's life is in your hands or anything. I'm sure the police will figure it out sooner or later. But if it makes you feel better to look into it on your own, I don't see what it could hurt."

"I was actually thinking the same thing," I said.

"You were?" He sounded surprised.

"Yeah, I mean, if I did it once, I can do it again, right? And now I actually have some practice with it. I think I could do it. I think I could help Todd."

"I could help you if you want," Matt offered.

"Really?" I asked. "You would do that for me?" I hadn't expected that. Matt had been a huge help to me in solving his father's murder, and I couldn't have done it without him, but I hadn't anticipated him offering to help me investigate a murder that had nothing to do with him.

"Sure. I don't want you running around, chasing a murderer on your own—you could get hurt again."

He had a point. My last investigation had proven dangerous, and I still had twinges of pain every once in a while. That didn't stop me from wanting to do it again, though.

"Thank you!" I replied with a smile. I wanted to

throw my arms around him and give him a big hug, but I didn't think that was a wise move while he was driving. I realized I would have to save it for later. For the moment, I focused on plotting out how I was going to get started.

"I think I'll go see Todd again," I said.

"You will?" Matt asked, sounding surprised again.

I wondered if that was just a result of him being focused on driving.

"Yes, I think I will. When we talked this morning, it was just chitchat, catching up on what was going on. I don't know what kind of evidence the police have against him or anything. I won't know what to look for if I don't know what evidence they have already."

Matt didn't say anything. My mind was whirling, so I kept talking. Thinking out loud would at least keep Matt in the loop on where my brain was going.

"I almost think he's not actually a suspect—that the police are just doing their job and questioning him thoroughly because the body was found in his parking lot—and he just thinks he is. It makes sense that the police would need to talk to him a lot. It doesn't necessarily mean he's a suspect, right?"

Matt stayed quiet.

"Matt?"

"Yeah."

I couldn't tell if that was a statement or a question,

whether he was agreeing with me or hadn't been listening, so I repeated myself. "The police questioning Todd a lot doesn't necessarily mean he's a suspect, right? They may just be covering their bases?"

"I don't know. I'm not a cop."

I heaved a sigh. "Well, I know that. I'm just asking your opinion."

"I think it looks suspicious," he said. "And he said that they consider him a suspect. I don't know why he would think that if he's not. But it's always possible that he's wrong. Or they're wrong. Every cop show I've ever seen goes through a list of suspects before they catch the guy who did it."

It was a levelheaded response, weighing the possibilities. I would have liked his reply better if he'd come down solidly on the side of Todd probably not actually being a suspect, but I had to respect his honesty and logical approach. Besides, it would be good for our investigation, for him to have such a reasoned approach to balance my more instinctual one.

"I guess you're right," I admitted. "But that still means I need to figure out what the evidence is so I know how to prove that he's innocent."

"Or guilty," Matt added. "He could be guilty."

I looked at him, but I couldn't read his expression in the darkness of the car. "He could be," I agreed. "I don't think he is, but he could be." As much as I wanted to prove that Todd was not the murderer, finding out who really killed Joe was more important. Letting a murderer walk the streets was unacceptable.

We were almost home by then, just crossing into Cape Bay. Todd's Gym was on our left as we drove in, its bright yellow sign gleaming in the night. Light poured out of the large front entryway, and the parking lot was lit up as bright as day.

"Are they still open?" I asked Matt.

"Yup," he replied. "Twenty-four hours."

"Really? A twenty-four-hour gym in Cape Bay? How did I not know about this? Does it have enough business to support it?"

"I guess so. I think he gets people from some of the neighboring towns and some shift workers. And I think the fighting is at night."

"The fighting?" I gasped.

"I mean boxing. Kickboxing, MMA, whatever they do there."

"Oh," I breathed with relief. "I thought you meant fight-club kind of fighting!"

Matt laughed. "No, but have you seen that MMA stuff? It's not far off."

"Mm-hmm," I murmured, nodding even though he couldn't see me. There was a thought playing at the back of my mind. I knew it was important, but I couldn't quite catch it. And then I did. "Wait, is the parking lot always that bright, or is it just because of Joe?"

"It's always that bright," Matt replied.

"So whoever killed him did it in a brightly lit parking lot, and then he was right there where anybody could see him until the morning. That's weird, isn't it?"

"All murder is weird in a way, isn't it?"

"I guess so," I said. Still, the murder having taken place in such a brightly lit place seemed strange to me, and I realized that, in addition to finding any evidence against Todd, I also had to discover more about the murder itself—all I knew was that Joe had been stabbed to death. I needed to know who found him and when he was last seen and probably a lot more that I hadn't thought about yet. So many thoughts were racing through my head that I was getting antsy to get home and start writing them down so I wouldn't forget anything. Fortunately, Matt was turning the car onto our street.

He parked in his driveway. "I'll walk you home," he said. We cut across our neighbor's yard, and Matt waited until I had unlocked the door and Latte had shot out between us before he hugged me good night.

"Don't spend too much time thinking about this Todd thing, okay?" he said.

"I won't," I replied. I planned to think about it a good bit before I went to sleep, but "too much" was a relative concept, and I didn't feel as though the thinking I had planned quite qualified.

Matt waved and headed back across the grass toward his house.

"Come here, Latte!" I called. He ran past me into the house and danced around my feet as I locked up, waiting for me to pet him. I knelt down and rubbed his ears vigorously for a minute, and then we headed upstairs.

I picked up a yellow legal pad from my dresser, flipped to a blank page, and sat down with it on the edge of my bed. I jotted down a series of notes about what I wanted to know:

What evidence do they have against Todd?

Who found Joe's body?

Where in the parking lot was it found?

Who last saw him?

Did anyone have a grudge against Joe?

And so on and so on. Every question that crossed my mind, I added to the list. I had almost a full page by the time I was finished, from the biggest, broadest, most general questions—*Who killed Joe?*—down to the most detailed—*Where did the murderer get the weapon?* I didn't know how I was going to get answers to all of them or even if I would, but I felt my list was enough to guide me as I got started.

I glanced at the clock. Between closing the café,

having dinner with Matt, and making my list of questions, time flew until it was well after midnight. I needed to get to bed if I was going to get up and go back to the gym in the morning to try talking to Todd. I quickly changed my clothes and got ready for bed and then snuggled between my sheets with Latte, as usual, curled up at my feet. I fell asleep almost immediately.

Chapter 8

I WOKE up in the morning with Latte nudging me for his breakfast and morning walk. He was hungry, and I had slept later than usual. I stumbled downstairs and fed him and then went back upstairs to get dressed while he ate.

I needed to go straight to work after visiting Todd, so I put my work clothes on—black pants and a black top, despite the heat—and put my hair up in a ponytail. Latte was waiting for me at the bottom of the stairs when I came back down. I hooked his leash on, and we headed outside.

Our morning walk is usually the longest. I usually come home from the café a couple of times throughout the day for a few minutes to take him out and play, and then we take a walk around the block every evening. In the morning, though, sometimes we'll walk all the way out to the beach so Latte can play in the waves for a few minutes. On our good days, we'll go a couple of miles, walking all around town. That day, though, we didn't go that far, and I promised him we'd go out longer when I got home that night. Once Latte was all taken care of and safely back in the house, I walked to Todd's Gym.

I mentally reviewed the notes I'd made the night before as I walked, preparing myself to see Todd. The legal pad was tucked away in my purse, which was rather large. Every so often, I try to downsize and carry fewer items, but that only ever lasts a week or two before I find myself back to using the bigger bag.

I just found it so much more convenient to be able to carry around tissues and pain killers and extra makeup and pens and whatever else I might need with me at all times. Back in my stiletto-wearing New York City days, I'd even been known to carry an extra pair of shoes in my purse for when the heels started to kill my feet. Being back home in Cape Bay and working on my feet in the café all day had reminded me of the pleasure of flats and relegated my stilettos to the back of my closet. The large purse was still convenient for when I needed to tote around a legal pad, though.

I arrived at Todd's Gym and was again impressed by its size. One wouldn't realize, without standing right there by it, how incredibly large it was. The parking lot was fuller than I'd expected it to be in the middle of a weekday. I looked around before I went through the big glass doors into the foyer, trying to guess where in the parking lot Joe had been found. Nothing I could see seemed to indicate where that might have been, so I went on inside.

Perky, blond Karli was sitting at the reception desk again, her hair still in that impossibly high ponytail. I wondered how her scalp didn't hurt.

She waved, apparently recognizing me from the day before. "Hi! Welcome back! How are you today?"

"I'm good." I smiled, approaching the desk and reaching my hand across it. "You're Karli, right? I'm Fran."

"Hi, Fran!" she replied, taking my hand and shaking hesitantly. I got the feeling she didn't do much hand-shaking at her age or in her job.

"Is Todd in?" It hadn't occurred to me until that very moment that I probably should have called before I came over in case he was out or busy.

Karli opened her mouth to say something, glanced at Todd's office door, and then closed it again. "Yes," she said after a few more seconds. "But he's with the police."

"The police?" I repeated, a little louder than I meant to.

Karli nodded furiously.

"Again?"

She nodded again.

"How long have they been in there?"

She glanced at the clock on her computer screen. "An hour, maybe?" she said softly, almost as though afraid they would hear her across the huge foyer, through the door, and over whatever conversation they were having.

"Wow." I glanced over at the door. He must be a serious suspect if they were back yet again and talking to him for such a long time. But they hadn't arrested him or even taken him down to the police station, so maybe it wasn't that bad after all. "How long were they here yesterday?"

She shrugged. "I'm not sure. A while."

That wasn't particularly helpful. I looked toward the door again and wondered if waiting was worthwhile. I figured the morning would be wasted if I didn't get to talk to Todd, but I'd be kicking myself if I found out the police left only a few minutes after I did. I sighed and drummed my fingers on the counter. I looked back at Karli. "Think I should wait?"

Before she could say anything, a lock clicked, and Todd's office door swung open. I turned, and Mike was the first one out the door. We made eye contact briefly before I looked away. Mike said nothing, just continuing out the front door with his fellow officers trailing behind him, one dressed in a suit like Mike's, the other two in uniform. Todd appeared in the doorway after them, haggard and exhausted. He looked over toward the reception desk and caught sight of me.

He pushed a smile onto his face and started across the lobby toward me.

"Hey, Franny," he called, his cheerful demeanor the polar opposite of what it had been moments earlier as the police left his office. "You here to sign up for some classes?"

"Nope, I'm here to see you," I replied.

"Really?" I saw his smile switch from the fake business-owner one it had been to a genuine one. "To what do I owe the pleasure?"

"Could we talk in your office?" I asked.

"Sure thing!" He looked past me. "Karli, hold my calls, please."

"Okay!" she chirped.

I wondered how many calls he got but then considered that he probably had a fair number of suppliers and support people calling him, not to mention clients who were wondering whether the gym was open and safe after what had happened to Joe.

In Todd's office, I took the same seat I'd had the day before, and he again sat in his chair on the other side of the desk.

"So, what's up, Franny?" he asked.

I noticed he always called me "Franny," which I'd

gone by in high school. I supposed that wasn't very different from my tendency to call Matt "Matty."

"The police were here again," I stated.

He sighed and sank into his chair. I caught a glimpse of the worn-down expression he'd had on his face earlier. "Yep, they were back," he sighed, staring down at the desk.

"Third time?"

"Yep."

"Are you still a suspect?"

"More than ever, I think."

"Why?" I asked. The question burst through my lips before I had a chance to stop it. I hadn't meant to ask that way.

Todd looked up at me with an expression that was equal parts confused and surprised.

"Sorry, that came out wrong." I took a deep breath. "Todd, I want to help you. I don't quite know why it is, but I don't think you're a murderer."

"Maybe because I'm not?" he interjected.

I smiled. "That could be one reason. But if you really didn't do it, there has to be some kind of evidence, some proof that you didn't. Or, failing that, that someone else did. And I want to find it. I want to find it to get you off the hook and get justice for Joe and Joe's family. But I need your help to do that. Before I can do anything else, I need to know what they have against you." I almost got out my notepad but feared he would feel as though I was interrogating him. I decided I would just talk to him and write down my notes as soon as I got outside.

Todd stared at me critically, as if trying to see whether or not I was lying. He either gave up or decided I was telling the truth because he exhaled and shook his head. "Not much," he said. "Circumstantial. They have more evidence of where I *wasn't* and what I *wasn't* doing than what I was."

"What *weren't* you doing?" I asked.

"Most importantly to them, I wasn't doing anything I can prove. And I wasn't doing it with anyone who can tell them that I was doing it."

Though it might have been awkward, I had to ask the obvious question. "Were you doing it with someone who *can't* tell them? Or doesn't want to? Because maybe it was something she wasn't supposed to be doing?"

Todd looked at me incredulously, apparently not believing I was asking him what he thought I was asking. I deliberately kept an innocent look on my face. Todd finally laughed, hard and loud. "No," he said, regaining his composure. "I was home alone, watching TV. Probably the most normal thing I could do, but it's the most suspicious to the cops."

"Is that the only reason they suspect you, or is there something else?"

He took a deep breath. "It's my gym, and he was killed here and found here."

That reminded me. "Oh yeah, he was found in the parking lot, right? Where in the parking lot? I drove by last night with Matt, and the place was lit up like it was daytime."

"Yeah, that was to make it safe since it's open twenty-four hours." He scoffed. "So much for that."

I waited a moment to see if he was going to answer my question and then, when it was apparent he wasn't, I reminded him of my question. "Where in the parking lot was he found?"

"The side lot. There aren't as many lights there. I didn't think there needed to be, with how bright the front and back lots were. Who knows if that would have made a difference, though? If somebody wanted him dead, some lights weren't necessarily going to stop them."

"Do you think someone wanted him dead?" I asked. Somehow, that question hadn't occurred to me before. It wasn't even on my legal-pad list.

"Cape Bay's not exactly a hotbed of crime," he said dryly.

"True," I replied. "So do you know anybody who had it in for him?"

"No. Not really. I mean, the fighters tend to all leave it in the ring. They beat the crap out of each other, and then it's over. They walk away, and they're done. All that aggression stays in the ring."

"He was stabbed anyway, wasn't he?" I figured a kickboxing grudge would've been settled by more kickboxing.

"With a piece of glass." Todd scoffed.

"Really?"

"Yeah, trust me, I got the third degree from the cops on that one, too. I can't keep the kids from coming out here and drinking beer and leaving their bottles in the parking lot to get broken. I have a million lights out there. I don't know what else they want me to do."

"How does a piece of glass give you a wound deep enough to kill you?" I asked. It was a gruesome question, but I had to know.

"Apparently, it punctured his heart or something. Cops said it was either an accident or the guy knew what he was doing. They grilled me on how much I knew about anatomy, whether I'd taken any biology classes in college or anything."

"And did you?"

"What? You think I did it?" He sounded a little defensive.

I realized I might have been getting a little too aggressive in my questioning. "No, of course not! I just want to know what they know. Really, I want to help you, Todd."

"Of course I did," he said, giving in. "I was an exer-cise-science major. We took practically as much anatomy as the pre-med majors."

"I have a few more questions if that's okay."

"Go ahead. I'd rather talk to you than the cops again." Based on how unhappy he sounded about talking to me anymore, he must have been really unen-thusiastic about talking to the police.

"Who found Joe's body?" I asked.

"Cleaning crew. They come in overnight when things are slower and leave around five in the morning. That's when they found him."

"Was he here before that?"

"Yeah, he was with his trainer."

"Was he here every Monday?"

"Every Monday." I was starting to detect some hostility in Todd's voice. I didn't blame him, though— he'd been through a lot the past few days.

"What about security cameras?" I asked. A big, fancy place like Todd's Gym seemed like it should be wired up with security cameras covering every inch. In fact, I was pretty sure I'd seen the cameras, both in the parking lot and inside the gym. I couldn't imagine the police hadn't already asked the question, but if they had, they would have made an arrest by now, and we wouldn't have been sitting there discussing it.

"Don't ask." Todd shook his head.

"That makes it sound like I do need to ask."

"They're not working."

I raised an eyebrow, realizing why he didn't want me to ask.

"It's something with the software," he continued. "I don't really get it. My IT guy explained it, but all I really got was that there's a problem with the software. They're supposed to be motion activated so we don't use a ton of storage space or something, but something about the calibration or the servers or something… I don't know. The guy's been working on it for like a month and keeps saying he's got it figured out, but apparently not."

I understood why that made the police suspicious. A big fancy security system like that conveniently not working—no wonder Todd was a suspect. At least he had the IT guy to vouch for him that the system had been down for a while.

"Is there anything else you can tell me? Anything that can point me to who else might have done it?"

"I don't know, Franny." He shook his head. "Joe was a friend of mine. I want his killer in jail. I don't know who it was, but it wasn't me. That's all I know. That's all I can tell you."

"Well, thanks," I said. "I'll get out of your hair now." I scooted to the front of my chair, ready to get up.

Todd sighed. "I'm sorry if I've been kind of a jerk. It's just been a rough week."

"It's no problem," I said with a smile.

Todd stood up and came around the desk to give me a hug good-bye. I was impressed again with how strong his arms were. He opened the door to let me out. "Come by anytime," he said. "Or maybe we could get dinner sometime."

"That'd be fun!" I said. I waved good-bye and went outside. Some benches were in front of the gym, and I sat down on one to think about what Todd had told me and to write everything down.

The gym was Todd's, he knew Joe, he knew there were broken beer bottles in the parking lot, he had a knowledge of anatomy, and he didn't have an alibi. I understood why the police suspected him. If I was going to prove that Todd hadn't done it—and I still believed he was innocent—I had my work cut out for me. I was going to have to find more suspects.

Chapter 9

I WAS at the café with Sammy that afternoon, finally getting the chance to go through my box of tea. I had ordered everything from our supplier that I'd ever heard of before, everything that looked interesting, and everything the supplier's website recommended, based on other people's purchases.

Even though I was the one who had placed the order, I was surprised by the sheer number of boxes and tins I was pulling out of the shipping box. Earl Grey, Darjeeling, English breakfast, Irish breakfast, Scottish breakfast, black, green, white, oolong, rooibos, chai, chamomile, peppermint, herbal. I had loose leaf, square teabags, round teabags, pyramid teabags. I even had silk sachets of tea that I fully recognized were in no way practical for use in the café.

The table in the back room was completely covered when I heard the jingle of the bell over the front door. I angled my head so I could see who it was and how many there were so I would know if Sammy needed my help out front. The visitor was just Mike, so I went back to my teas.

I decided to organize them by how the tea was contained—loose versus types of teabag. I wanted to compare how the flavors of one tea were different in each form. What I'd seen online basically told me that loose leaves would give the best flavor, then the pyramids, then the flat teabags, but I wanted to see for myself. I also had to figure out which was the most practical for use in the café.

I could hear Mike and Sammy talking out front and Sammy making his drink. No matter what I was doing in the back room—sorting through shipments, paying bills, balancing the books—I always liked to keep an ear out for what was going on in the main part of the café. I could tell how things were going by the clink of cups and saucers, the hissing of the espresso machine, the murmur of conversation, and the jingle of the bell on the door.

Sammy had more than once been impressed with how I'd popped out of the back exactly when she needed an extra pair of hands. That was a skill I'd picked up when I used to do my homework in the back while my mother or grandparents worked out front. Mike and

Sammy were just bantering happily, so I knew everything was under control.

I separated the Earl Grey teas into a different pile. It wasn't possible to find all the different forms of tea from one brand, but Earl Grey was common enough that I was able to get all of them from just two. I even got the loose tea from both brands so I could compare them.

I had brought a couple French presses from home so I could prepare the loose teas simultaneously without mixing the flavors of the different brands. I pulled them out of my massive purse and found a space for them on the tea-covered desk. I pulled out the teaspoons I had packed in my bag and was getting ready to measure some tea into each French press to start my first test when I heard a rap on the doorframe.

"Franny? Can I talk to you for a minute?"

I looked up to see Mike standing in the doorway and immediately felt a wave of dread wash over me.

I forced myself to sound cheery. "Hey Mike, sure. Come on in!" There was always a chance Mike could be there on a social call. I pushed a rolling chair toward him.

Mike came in and sat down. I took another chair, trying not to look nervous.

"What's up?" I asked.

"Just wanted to come by and say hello, see how you're doing," he replied.

"I'm doing pretty well. And yourself?" I tried to disguise my suspicion with politeness. The last time I'd been in a small room with Detective Mike Stanton, he hadn't been too happy with me.

"I'm all right. Got another murder case."

"I heard." So the conversation was going where I'd thought.

"So I guess you also heard the victim was found in the parking lot of Todd's Gym?"

"I did." I thought it best to keep my answers brief at that point.

"I couldn't help but notice you've been over at the gym the last couple of times I've been there to talk to Todd. Any reason that is?"

I was glad he didn't have his notebook out, scribbling down notes about our conversation. "Yesterday, I was over there to find out about what classes they offered. I'd like to take a couple when the busy season is over."

"You could have checked their website, you know," Mike replied.

Again with the website! Weren't people these days always complaining about how no one ever wanted to talk face-to-face anymore?

"Matt said the same thing," I said, figuring Mike didn't want to hear all that.

"Matt's a smart man."

"I honestly didn't think they would have a website." I

decided to give Mike more of an explanation. "Especially not one with that information. It's Cape Bay. We're not usually that sophisticated."

Mike chuckled. "I'll give you that. But, Fran, I have to ask, I saw you coming out of Todd Caruthers' office. I can't believe he meets individually with everyone who comes in to see what classes his gym offers—behind closed doors in his office, no less."

"Just what are you insinuating?" I asked, incredulously, my voice rising a little further than I probably should have let it.

"I'm not insinuating anything. I'm just saying—it seems like you were there for more than information on classes."

"That's why I went there," I said. "I talked to the girl at the desk—"

"Karli," Mike prompted.

"Karli," I repeated after him. "I talked to Karli, and she gave me a bunch of brochures, and as I was talking to her, Todd came up to the desk. I hadn't seen him since high school. We started talking. It was no big deal."

"And how did you end up back in his office?"

"Am I being interrogated?" I asked, suddenly wondering if, despite the lack of a notebook, there really was something more to this conversation than a friendly chat.

Mike held up both hands in a gesture of surrender.

"No, no, no. Sorry. I get a little too used to asking people questions, and I forget that's not how normal people talk. My wife always gives me grief about it. Tells me I'm interrogating her when she's just trying to tell me about her day at work."

I knew his wife—she'd gone to high school with all of us—and I could just picture her going off on Mike about something like that. "Well, I guess if it's the same treatment you give Sandra, I can't complain about it too much." I laughed.

Mike chuckled along with me. "A'right," he said after a few moments. "So, I'm not going to grill you on how exactly you ended up back in Todd's office because it's probably—hopefully—none of my business, but I will say that I want you to be careful. I don't know who killed Joe Davis, but I know someone's not telling me the truth. I'm going to find out what happened, and I don't want you getting caught in the middle of it when it all goes down. And if you're thinking about undertaking another independent investigation like you did with Gino Cardosi, I'm going to go ahead and advise you against it."

I opened my mouth to protest, but Mike held up a hand to stop me.

"I know you solved the case, but you put yourself and other people in danger doing it. I don't want that happening again. You need to stay out of it. Do you understand?" Mike's tone had changed from friendly and amenable to stern and police-like.

"Okay," I said, simply. Whether I agreed with him or not, there was no use arguing.

"Okay!" he replied, accepting my answer and slapping his hands on his knees. "Now, I think Sammy probably has some coffee ready for me."

Sammy came through the door holding a to-go coffee cup with a protective cardboard sleeve wrapped around it. I wondered how much of our conversation she had heard and if she'd been listening at the door. "Here you go. One large coffee, black."

"Mike, I think Sammy had your coffee ready before you even made it back here. It's plain black coffee," I exclaimed.

Sammy shrugged. "I made a fresh pot. The other one was getting kind of old."

Most of our customers ordered lattes and cappuccinos, so it wasn't uncommon to find ourselves having to make a pot for just one customer.

Mike smiled. "Sammy takes care of me."

I almost pointed out that Sammy's job was to take care of the customers, but I was only tempted because I was a little annoyed at Mike wanting me to lay off my investigation. At the same time, I knew he was only doing his job, just like Sammy, so it didn't seem quite fair to snip at him about it.

Sammy handed the paper cup to Mike as the bell jingled to announce another customer coming through the door. "Gotta go!" She hurried off.

Mike winced as he took a sip of his coffee. "Hot!" he muttered. He shook his head a little bit then looked up at me. "So are we clear?"

I smiled and gave him a quick nod. "We're clear," I chirped.

We were perfectly clear—I fully understood that Mike didn't want me to continue investigating Joe's murder. Whether he understood that I was still going to do it, I didn't know.

"All right, then." He stood. "It was good to see you."

"You too," I replied genuinely. "Say hello to Sandra for me."

"I will." He tipped his coffee cup to me. "I'll see you around." He paused. "Well, as long as 'around' isn't Todd's Gym." He chuckled, and I wasn't sure if that was because he was confident that he wouldn't see me or that he would. "Enjoy your day!" Mike walked back out into the front of the café. "Bye, Sam," he called to Sammy.

"Bye, Mike," she replied, working over another customer's drink.

Relieved that my conversation with Mike was over, I turned back to my tea, trying to remember exactly what I had been doing when he'd interrupted me.

Chapter 10

I HAD JUST PICKED up my teaspoon to measure out some tea for my testing when I heard another customer come in. I paused and listened to hear if Sammy would need me. She was speaking to someone, but I couldn't tell what she was saying. Then, she popped her head through the doorway.

"Someone's here to see you," she said.

"Who is it?" I wasn't expecting anyone and didn't know who might have been there that Sammy wouldn't have just sent back.

"You'll see," she said, a smile gracing her cherubic face. She disappeared from the doorway, apparently confident I would be following.

I put my teaspoon down among my piles of tea and headed out front.

There, looking nervous and proud, was Monica Basso, the namesake of Osteria di Monica. As always, she had her wire-rimmed glasses perched on her nose, and her kind blue eyes sparkled behind them. Though I had never seen it down, I knew her silvery-gray hair was rather long, based on the thickness of the bun she always had it wrapped in. She was wearing one of her standard floral-print dresses with modest high heels. I had no idea how she managed shoes like that at her age. I spotted a fairly substantial rolling cooler just behind her.

"Francesca!" she said excitedly, her face lighting up when she saw me.

"Monica!" Even though she was older than my mother had been, and my family was very strict about being respectful to my elders, I had always called her by her first name. I wasn't sure how that had come about or how I'd gotten away with it. "You came to see me?"

"*Sì*, Francesca, I did." Monica had been born in Italy and still occasionally lapsed into Italian here and there.

"What can I help you with?" I asked.

"Here, this is for you." She grasped the cooler by its handle and pulled it toward me.

"What is it?" I had an inkling of what it might have been but didn't want to get my hopes up too much, in case I was wrong.

"Tiramisu!" she declared.

I was right. "Really?" I squealed. A couple of

customers glanced my way, but I didn't care. Maybe I could sell them some tiramisu! I knelt down and opened the cooler. It was full to the brim with neatly sliced pieces of tiramisu, each in an individual plastic container. By a quick count, I guessed there must have been about two dozen slices inside.

I looked up at Monica, a big grin on my face. "So you decided to do it?"

"Of course! Your grandmother and I talked about doing this years ago, and we never did. When Alberto told me you wanted to sell my tiramisu, how could I say no?"

I stood up and hugged her. "Oh, thank you so much. I'm so excited!"

Monica laughed good-naturedly. "There's no need to thank me, Francesca. You're the one selling my desserts!"

"But they're such good desserts. It's an honor to be able to sell them here." I caught Sammy eyeing the cooler from across the counter. I hadn't told her about my proposal to Alberto the night before, partly because I didn't expect Monica to be so quick to take me up on it. "Monica brought us some of her tiramisu to sell," I told her.

"Ohh," Sammy replied, drawing the word out. "Well, that's not going to be good for my waistline."

"Would you mind stocking the refrigerated display with these while I go talk to Monica in the back for a few minutes?" I pulled the cooler around to the back side of the counter for Sammy and then led Monica into the back room to work out the details of the agreement.

"So how much do you want to sell them for?" I asked. "The same price as the restaurant? More?"

"How about the same price? It's a fair price there. It's a fair price here."

"Okay, good." I smiled. "And how do you want to split the profits? I told Alberto we could do whatever you wanted."

"We'll split them evenly, of course," she replied.

"Are you sure? You're doing the hard work of making them. I'm just putting them in the case to sell."

"Evenly," she affirmed. "It's only fair."

I would have been happy to give her more money, but wasn't going to argue with her over it. I knew I'd never win. "Should we draw up a contract?" I asked, moving to sit down at the computer.

"Of course not!" Monica scoffed. "I don't need a contract with you."

"Are you sure?" I asked. I had lived in the big city long enough to expect to need a contract for any business deal. The small-town way of verbal agreements seemed foreign to me.

"A handshake," she replied firmly, "although I have known your family long enough to take you at your word."

She reached out her hand, and I took it.

"Thank you, Monica," I said.

"I already told you, I am the one grateful to you for giving me the opportunity to share my food with more people."

We went back out front, and Sammy wheeled the cooler around the counter for Monica to take with her.

"Should I bring more tomorrow?" Monica asked.

I nearly choked. "Tomorrow?" I looked over at the case, chock full of tiramisu. Our standard refrigerated offerings were relegated to a small section in one corner. I was grateful we had another case to store our other products in. As much as he loved Monica's tiramisu, Matt would have never forgiven me if I didn't have chocolate cupcakes on hand. I didn't see how we would possibly need another delivery of tiramisu the next day.

"Tomorrow's Friday," she said matter-of-factly as though that would make me understand. "I take the weekends off. I won't be able to bring you any more until Monday."

That made a little more sense, but I had asked Alberto for only five or ten pieces. I had no idea how long selling five would take, let alone twenty-five. I also worried about needing to throw some out if they didn't sell as well as I expected them to. I didn't want to have even more, that I might not be able to sell.

"Monica, I don't know if I can sell that many."

"Oh, don't worry, dear. I'm sure you will. And if you don't, you just take them home and give them to your friends and don't worry about paying me for them."

"Monica—" I started.

"I don't want to hear anything else about it! I'll see you tomorrow." She reached for the cooler, but Sammy swatted her hand away.

"I'll take it out for you," Sammy said. She and Monica headed out to Monica's car. I glanced around the café to make sure everyone was taken care of and then went into the back room to grab the chalkboards we used to advertise specials. One was small and counter-sized while the other was a full-size sandwich board for out front on the sidewalk. I laid the small one on the counter and took the other one out front. Monica was just pulling away from the curb. I handed Sammy a pack of multicolored chalk.

"We've got some tiramisu to sell. Time for you to work your magic," I said.

Sammy had impeccable handwriting and impressive artistic skill. Whatever she would create would be way more visually appealing than whatever my efforts would produce. It wasn't just that I wanted to make sure we sold the tiramisu—I also had a compulsion to make sure everything I presented in relation to the café, from the drinks and food to the way it was decorated, was nice to look at.

"I'll do my best," she replied sunnily, taking the chalk. She slid out a blue piece and immediately started drawing on the large slate.

Before she had even finished writing the first word, I could tell the board was going to be beautiful. I left her to it and went inside to tend the counter, where I was surprised to see a customer waiting even though I'd only been outside for a minute.

"Can I help you?" I asked.

"Could I have a piece of tiramisu?" the woman asked. "It's my absolute favorite."

"Coming right up," I replied.

I removed the dessert from the container it had been delivered in and arranged it on a plate with a little paper doily before handing it to the woman, who was practically drooling by the time I put it in her hand. I could only hope that others would also be tempted by the tiramisu in the display.

Chapter 11

I COULDN'T BELIEVE how quickly we sold them. By the time Monica came with another, even bigger delivery the next day, we had almost completely sold through the first batch. I didn't know whether to credit Sammy's exquisitely drawn signs—complete with beautifully drawn slices of tiramisu—or the sheer deliciousness of Monica's desserts or downright luck, but I was astounded.

"I told you," Monica said when I told her. Her blue eyes were twinkling with pleasure behind her glasses.

"I just—I can't believe it!" I said. "I never dreamed we would sell that much. People bought multiples at a time."

"What can I say? People like good food," she replied.

I certainly had to agree. "Are you going to be able to

keep up with making all the extras?" I asked, concerned that making twenty or more extra pieces of tiramisu a day would be too much for her. She wasn't as young as she used to be.

"Oh, *sì*, of course, Francesca. It's not difficult to make a little more for you. I just put out extra pans."

I laughed at what I knew was an oversimplification. My grandparents' attitude had been much the same, though—a little bit of extra cooking, baking, or whatever was no worry when one was already doing it. Even though I knew she had to multiply the recipe many times over, my grandmother had always insisted that all she had to do to make an extra lasagna for the family down the street with the new baby or for the new teacher in town or for the widower who came into the café every day for a mozzarella-tomato-basil sandwich—or all three!—was to lay out an extra pan. I always wanted to point out that she still had to make the extra noodles and sauce and prepare the extra meat and cheese, but I knew she would have none of it. I had gotten the sense that the attitude of a little hospitality never being any trouble was something engrained in my grandparents and in Monica years before, back when they were in the old country.

"Well, I'm glad you're doing it, Monica," I said. "And I'm always sure to tell everyone who buys a slice about your restaurant."

"*Grazie mille*, Francesca. It's good for us to all work together."

I helped Monica load her coolers back into the car and set to work storing away the masses of tiramisu in my possession. Knowing that I had to make the second batch last through the weekend and that there wasn't any more room in the front display anyway, I stored some in the back room's refrigerator. I decided I would only put out a certain number each day, and when they were gone, they were gone. It was more important to me that we have some available every day than that we sell through them as quickly as possible. I wanted people to know that Antonia's had a steady stream of tiramisu coming in.

Satisfied that I had everything arranged satisfactorily, I went back out to the front. Sammy had taken the day off to go to the memorial service Joe's family was having for him, so I was working alongside Becky, one of the high schoolers who helped us out part-time. Her curly red hair was pulled and looped into a small ponytail at the back of her head, but fuzzy ringlets had escaped and were curled all around her face. I realized that constantly working over steaming-hot beverages wasn't the best way for her to keep her unruly locks in check.

She was preparing a drink for someone when another customer came in. She glanced up at the door.

"I got it," I said, crossing behind her toward the

register. "Can I help you?" I asked the customer. He looked familiar, more familiar than one of the tourists who made multiple visits during their weeks of vacation but less familiar than a local. I struggled to place where I might know him from.

"I'd like a latte, please," he said in a thick Southern accent that just made me feel even more as though I knew him from somewhere.

"Anything else?"

"I'll take a piece of that tiramisu you got over there," he replied.

I was grateful Monica had brought so much to get us through the weekend. "You'll enjoy it. We just started carrying it. It's from a local restaurant called Osteria di Monica."

"If the tiramisu's good, I'll have to try that place out before I leave town."

"Oh, it is." I told him the price for the two items.

"It's busier in here than the last time I was in," he said as he handed me his credit card. "You got that shipment of tea all straightened out yet?"

I finally remembered who he was. He was the gentleman who had been in earlier in the week—the day Mrs. D'Angelo broke the news to Sammy, Matt, and me about Joe Davis's murder.

"I knew I recognized you!" I said with a smile. "I'm still working on the tea. I want to make sure I have my technique all sorted out before I put the new stuff on the menu. I'm hoping to have at least a couple tea drinks on the menu sometime next week."

I had pretty much come to the conclusion that I would never have time to sample the teas while I was at the café, so I'd taken the whole box home with me the night before and had spent the evening experimenting with different brewing temperatures and steeping times. I felt I had made pretty good progress.

"Well, I'll have to come back and try one," the man said.

"Are you in town that long?" I asked, somewhat surprised. Most people only spent a week in town before heading back to wherever they came from. I was certain the man had said he was just visiting, but maybe I'd misunderstood.

"I'm spending some time traveling all along the New England coast this summer," he said. "I'm sure I'll find myself back here soon enough."

"We'll look forward to seeing you. If you want to go grab a seat, I'll have this right out to you." I had been preparing his drink as we spoke and was ready to pour the milk into the espresso, a task I liked to be able to focus on. I also felt I had a reputation to live up to for that customer, especially since I seemed to remember having created a fairly intricate design in his foam the last time he was in.

I briefly considered pouring in a design based on a piece of tiramisu, but I had never practiced and wasn't sure it would come out as perfect as I wanted it. I decided on a self-referential design I usually only used for myself or Sammy when I was in a silly mood—a coffee cup with a few wisps of steam coming out, as though it contained its own fresh hot coffee. I poured the design in and held back a smile as I looked at the finished product. The man seemed the type that would appreciate the joke. I quickly arranged a piece of tiramisu on a plate and carried the drink and dessert over to the table where the man was seated.

"Here you go," I said, setting both dishes down so he could see my handiwork. To my delight, he chuckled when he saw the design in the latte.

"You definitely don't get a plain rosetta here, do you?" he laughed.

"Not if I'm working," I replied.

Sammy could hold her own with the standard designs, although she was better with a pen or a piece of chalk. Becky and the other kids who worked with us pretty much stuck with rosettas, leaves, and hearts.

"I'm Francesca, by the way," I said to him. "Or Fran. I'm the owner."

"It's a pleasure to meet you, Fran," he replied, reaching up to shake my hand. "I'm Jack." He paused and glanced around. "If you're Fran, I'm curious—who is Antonia? I assume you didn't just pick that name out of the blue."

"She was my grandmother. She and my grandfather opened this café almost seventy years ago after they moved here from Italy."

"And it's been in the family ever since?" he asked.

"It's been in the family ever since," I confirmed. "After my grandparents passed away, my mother took it over, and after she passed away earlier this summer, I took it on."

"I'm sorry to hear about your mother," he said, sounding surprisingly sincere for someone who had never known her. I guessed that was a by-product of his Southern charm.

"Thank you," I said. "The next time you come in, feel free to ask for me if I'm not out front. I'm not always here, but I am most afternoons."

"I'll do that," he said with a smile. "If only to see what design you'll come up with next."

"I'll take that as a challenge," I replied. As I walked away from his table, I told myself I'd have to spare some time from my tea experimentation to practice pouring a tiramisu design into a latte.

Chapter 12

MATT and I had planned to have dinner that night. As a way to avoid our constant debate over who was paying, he had offered to cook. It seemed to me a sneaky way to pay without being obvious about it, but I let it go. At least he was letting me bring the wine.

I arrived at his door a little while after closing up the café, a bottle of red in my hand and Latte at my feet. I was glad Matt didn't mind me bringing the pooch over. Thinking that he was all alone at my house while I was enjoying a pleasant meal just down the street would have made me sad.

As soon as Matt opened the door, tomato-stained wooden spoon in hand, the smell of Bolognese sauce poured out of the house, and my mouth started watering.

"It smells delicious, Matty," I exclaimed.

"Good," he replied with a smile, reaching out with his non-spoon-holding hand to hug me. "It should be ready in just a few minutes. I just have to throw the spaghetti in."

"Is there anything I can do to help?" I asked, stepping inside. Latte trotted past me and into the kitchen, where he knew Matt would have laid down a bowl of water and a rawhide for him.

"Open the wine."

We went back into the kitchen, and Matt handed me a corkscrew. It was one of the old-fashioned ones with no bells or whistles—just a twisted piece of metal that would shred a piece of cork if not used properly. Fortunately, I'd had some practice and was able to remove the cork in one try. Matt already had two wine glasses sitting on the table, so I poured the wine into them and sat down in one of the chairs.

"So how's everything going?" I asked. We hadn't seen each other since our dinner at Osteria di Monica a few days earlier, and as quickly as new projects came up for him at work and old ones were put on hold, I figured he would have something new to tell me.

"Pretty good," he replied. "One of our big customers had an agreement fall through with a service provider yesterday, so we're scrambling to find them a new one. They're working on some really exciting stuff, and the other company chickened out, putting the whole project back to square one. Everything had been going really well with them, too."

I wasn't really sure what any of that meant, but it sounded important and mattered to Matt, so I did my best to follow along.

"Fortunately, we have plenty of contacts within the industry, so I don't think it'll take us long to find them a new partner. I actually think the new deal we're working on might turn out even better for them than the old one." Matt pulled a pan of garlic bread out of the oven and set it on a trivet next to the stove.

"Do you need help with that?" I asked.

"The project? I don't think you—"

"The garlic bread."

Matt laughed. "No, I got it. I was confused there for a minute about what contacts you had with Internet service providers. I guess you could have some from when you were in New York, though."

Actually, I did. However, they were all public-relations and marketing people—probably not the sort that could help him with his client's project.

Matt transferred the garlic bread to a plate and brought it to the table.

"Eat up," he said. "It's the best when it's still hot." To prove his point, he grabbed a piece off the top and shoved it in his mouth. "Careful, it's hot," he said around the bread he was holding delicately between his teeth to keep it from burning his lips.

"I think I'll wait a couple minutes," I said. "Might be safer."

"Suit yourself," he replied, but I noticed he still hadn't actually bitten into it.

I watched him as he moved around the kitchen for a few minutes, draining the spaghetti and mixing it with the sauce just enough to give it a good coating. He transferred the rest of the Bolognese into a bowl so we could each add however much we wanted to our individual plates.

"You know, you don't have to get all those dishes dirty," I said as he poured the spaghetti into another bowl to bring to the table. "I'm not above getting my food straight from the pot."

"What kind of host would I be if I did that?" he asked.

"Apparently the same kind I am," I retorted.

Matt laughed. "I'm just trying to make it nice for you. The meal's not fancy, so I may as well make the presentation look good."

I couldn't fault him for that, since it was a variation of my own approach to food.

He finally got everything ready and sat down across from me at the table. He took a long drink of his wine. "That's good wine," he announced. "I should have tried some earlier—I could have been on my second glass by now."

The wine was indeed really good. I'd been lucky enough to find it relatively inexpensively at a store nearby when they were cycling their inventory. I poured a little more into each of our glasses as Matt scooped spaghetti onto our plates.

"No sense in letting the glasses get low," I said with a smile.

"Did you just bring one bottle?"

"Yeah, but I have more at home."

"Good." Matt laughed. "I don't have to go to work tomorrow, so I don't have to hold back."

I laughed along with him as we dug into our meals. We had a long, rambling, pleasant conversation as we ate, one of those conversations where people talk about everything and nothing—his work, my work, TV shows we both liked, people from high school we both knew. I told him all about Monica's tiramisu and how well it was selling and gave him excruciating details about my experimentations with tea. The one thing we didn't talk about was the thing everybody else in town was talking about—Joe Davis's murder. It just didn't come up. Until I brought it up.

"I went to see Todd the other day," I said as Matt put the dishes in the dishwasher. I'd offered to do it and had even started, but he insisted on taking care of it, so I was leaning against the counter and sipping my wine as he worked.

He paused for a second, I thought, just before he asked, "You did, did you?"

"Yeah," I replied. "I really wanted to find out more about the murder and why the police suspected him."

"Hmm." He kept loading the dishwasher.

I wondered if I should tell him more about my visit to Todd.

"What did you find out?" he asked finally, saving me from needing to decide.

"They really don't have much on him," I said. "It's not even circumstantial. He was home alone watching TV. They think he must have done it just because it happened at his gym and he doesn't have an alibi."

"Or maybe they think he did it because he did it."

I looked at him in surprise. "You think he did it?"

Matt sighed. "I don't think he didn't do it."

"But why?"

"Because the police think he did it. Or he may have done it. They think it enough to investigate him. And because I'm not one of the cops investigating the case, I don't have the evidence that they have to know whether or not there's more that points to Todd. I don't assume blindly that he didn't do it because he doesn't *seem* like a murderer. Most murderers don't seem like murderers, Franny. That's how they manage to kill people. If everyone who was a murderer seemed like one, they wouldn't get the chance to murder anyone because no one would get near them."

I didn't know what to say. I didn't know where this was coming from. "I thought you were on my side," I said.

"I *am* on your side, Franny. I'm not on Todd's side."

I opened my mouth to protest, but Matt cut me off.

"I'm not against Todd either. Not unless he killed Joe. I'm against the murderer, whoever that is. Because I don't know who did it. And neither do you. Neither of us knows because neither of us were there and neither of us are the police."

"Matt, that's not fair," I managed to get out.

"What's not fair? That I won't let you keep going around, swearing up and down that Todd is innocent when you don't actually know? You haven't lived here since high school. You don't know how things have changed or what people have gotten into. You assume that Todd is the same guy you idolized back in high school, but you didn't even know him back then. Not really."

"No, Matt," I said angrily. "What's not fair is that you let me think that you were going to help me prove that Todd was innocent when this is how you really felt all along. You led me on. You let me think that we were a team. And you know what? I may not have known Todd

353

that well back in high school, but I did know you pretty well, and I know you didn't like him. You didn't like anyone who was athletic, just because you weren't athletic. And now that we're all grown up, you're still carrying the same grudge. It's ridiculous, Matt! He's made a success of himself being an athlete, and you've made a success of yourself not being an athlete. It doesn't have to be one way or the other. Everyone can be happy doing what they're good at. Todd being a good athlete doesn't mean you can't be good at something else."

"Maybe you should tell him that, Franny. He's the one who's an arrogant jerk. He acts like he owns the world just because he has a big concrete block with his name on it. It's not that special. It's just a gym. I could go open one tomorrow that would be just as good as his because it's a *gym*. You put in some rooms with some mirrors, a few treadmills, some weights—boom! Matt's Gym! It's not that hard."

"You don't even go to the gym!" I shot back. "I have been to plenty of them, and plenty of them are not good. They have teachers who don't know what they're doing or machines that don't work right. It's not that easy. Todd has classes—good classes!—and lots of them. In Cape Bay, that's practically unheard of. It's a great gym—a beautiful place. Have you even been in there to see what it's like?"

"No," Matt admitted.

"See? You don't even know what it's like. How can you judge it if you've never been inside?"

Matt was quiet.

"You can judge it because Todd owns it—is that it?"

Matt still didn't say anything. He just leaned on the edge of the sink and stared out the window above it.

"That's it, isn't it?" I gave him a chance to answer, but he didn't. "Matt, you can't judge the place just because Todd owns it, and you can't hate Todd just because you did back in high school. It's not fair to him, and it doesn't do you any good either. How does it benefit you to dislike him so much? It doesn't. You need to let it go."

I was getting frustrated with Matt's continued silence. I didn't know whether he was doing it to make a point or to annoy me. Or maybe he'd just run out of things to say. I stared at the side of his head, trying to read what I could see of his expression. I got nothing. He didn't look angry or upset or sad or happy or any other emotion I could discern.

"Matt," I said finally.

He heaved a big sigh. "It seems like you've already made up your mind, Franny. I don't know if there's anything I can say at this point to convince you that Todd may have done it." I opened my mouth, but Matt, still staring out the window, held up his hand. "Not that he did it—just that he may have done it. Just that you should keep an open mind."

"He didn't even have a motive to kill him."

"You don't know that," he said.

"Is there something you know that you're not telling me?"

"No, Fran." He finally turned and looked at me. "Look, I know you've sat and talked with him and he's done nothing to raise your suspicions, but he wouldn't exactly come right out and announce it if he had a motive, would he? Especially not to the pretty girl from high school who just came back to town."

"Stop saying that Todd thinks I'm pretty. He doesn't, okay?"

"What makes you so sure?"

"I'm not a pretty, blond, perky, cheerleader type. I'm a calm, boring, normal-looking brunette. I'm not his type."

"Don't sell yourself short, Franny," he said quietly.

"We're not talking about me anyway, Matt. We're talking about you and why you dislike Todd so much."

"I thought we were talking about whether Todd killed Joe Davis."

"He didn't."

"You think."

"No, I know," I said firmly.

He looked at me, his warm brown eyes meeting my

blue ones. I tried to keep my gaze strong and level, but I found that difficult when Matt was looking at me so intensely.

"Okay. You know." He paused and took a deep breath. "But I don't. I need some kind of evidence, some proof one way or the other. And until I get that, I can't say that I think Todd is innocent."

"Well, I do."

"That's fine," he said.

"And I'm going to keep looking for evidence that he didn't do it."

"Then I hope you won't fault me if I look for evidence that he did."

"You would work against me like that?" I asked, taken aback.

"It's not working against you, Franny. Wouldn't you rather have me look and find nothing than not look and find out later that there was something obvious that was missed because we weren't looking?"

"I would rather find the person who actually did it so I can prove it wasn't Todd."

"So would I. I would rather find out that it was someone I've never even seen before in my entire life. I don't want to think that anyone I know is capable of killing someone like that. But that doesn't mean I can just blindly rule out everyone I know."

I was at a loss for words. Part of me knew that Matt

was right—that all leads had to be chased even when I didn't like where they went. But another part of me deeply believed that Todd wasn't a murderer and that to investigate him would be a waste of time—time that I could better spend finding the actual murderer.

"I understand how you feel," I said finally. And I did understand. I didn't agree, but I understood. Also, I wasn't going to be able to change his mind—at least, not until I had proof of Todd's innocence—so I decided I would drop the subject. For the time being.

Chapter 13

LATER THAT NIGHT, I sat on my couch with Latte curled up beside me, his head resting on my legs. I idly scratched him between the ears with one hand while I flipped TV channels with the other. A glass of wine sat on the end table next to me, waiting for my remote-control hand to be freed up. Unfortunately, it was late enough at night that there wasn't much interesting on except reruns of ancient sitcoms and talk shows aimed more at the drunk-college-student demographic than the wine-sipping over-thirty adult women.

By the time I'd made my way through all the channels, the hour had rolled over, and all the shows had changed. I couldn't stand the thought of going through all hundred-some channels again, so I switched over to the network whose lineup consisted primarily of shows that had originally aired when my mother was growing up and left it there.

I didn't actually care that much what I watched as long as my ears weren't ringing with the silence of the house. My mind was mostly occupied by my previous conversation with Matt. Or had it been an argument? Either way, that was what was on my mind.

I had been shocked by his reaction when I'd said the police didn't have much evidence against Todd. I recalled that he might have suggested that that was how he felt the other night, but I'd been focused on my own agenda and didn't notice it. Whatever the case, we clearly felt differently about whether or not Todd killed Joe. That was frustrating.

I actually wondered how much of Matt's doubt was rooted in high-school insecurities. He had been popular enough in the school newspaper–yearbook–band kid crowd we both ran in back then. He was always friendly and good-natured, and more than a few of my friends thought he was pretty cute. I had grown up side-by-side with him though, and he was more like a brother to me back then than anything else. Whenever my friends would comment on his looks, I stayed out of the conversation.

Matt was never scrawny or out of shape—he could always hold his own in gym class—but he wasn't an athlete like three-sport-letterman Todd. He always seemed to have a bit of an inferiority complex about that, too—as if being a trumpet player was somehow less worthwhile than being a football player. I never understood it. Todd particularly seemed to rouse Matt's ire for some reason. Matt calling Todd an arrogant jerk was nothing new—I'd heard variations of the sentiment since high school.

Part of what I never understood about it was that Todd was a great athlete, but Matt was a great student. He was *so* smart. He used to build circuits in his spare time, just for fun. He majored in electrical engineering, and not at an easy school either—he went to the best engineering school on the East Coast and graduated with a four-point-oh grade point average! And Todd owned a gym, sure, but Matt had an important job. He supervised people. He managed multimillion dollar projects. How was that less impressive than owning a gym?

Latte shoved his nose under my hand, and I realized I'd stopped petting him. I glanced at the clock. If I was going to get any sleep, I needed to take him out one last time and get to bed.

"Come on, boy," I said, unfolding myself from the couch. I walked to the front door and opened it for him. He darted out and ran around in the shadows. When he was finished, he ran back inside and straight up the steps to the second floor. He knew our routine. I followed him up to get ready for bed.

I lay in bed for a while after I woke up late the next morning. Latte was still asleep next to me, his head resting on the pillow as if he was a person. I loved when he did that. It cracked me up. We stayed that way for a few more minutes until my phone beeped, alerting me to a text message and waking up Latte. He rolled over onto his belly and looked around, trying to figure out what the noise was and where it had come from. He must have decided that, whatever it had been, it wasn't a threat, and laid his head down between his paws.

I rolled over and picked my phone up from the nightstand where I had it plugged in.

The text was from Matt. *Found something out about Joe. Want to meet for lunch?*

I thought for a minute about what Matt might have learned and whether it was something I would actually want to know. Ultimately, whether it was good news or bad news for Todd, I knew I needed to hear it and sooner rather than later. Delaying the inevitable wouldn't do anyone any good.

I texted Matt back. *Sure, 1 hr?*

One good thing about Matt living two houses down was that when we decided to go out and do something, we didn't have to go through the endless back-and-forth of "Where do you want to eat?" "I don't care—where do you want to eat?" "I could go anywhere, but Mexican sounds good." "Really? I was thinking sushi sounded good." Back in New York, with its thousands of restaurants, that conversation could take longer than the eventual meal. In Cape Bay with Matt though, we could hash that all out in person, which involved less typing and waiting.

Matt texted me back quickly. *Come over whenever you're ready.*

As soon as I got out of bed, Latte perked up, jumped off my bed, and pranced around the room, eager to get his breakfast and start the day. I laughed at his enthusiasm, wishing it was that easy for me to jump out of bed, raring to go. We made our way through our morning routine—breakfast for Latte, a quick shower and clean clothes for me—and then I took Latte on a walk around the block before giving him a treat to remember me by and heading down to Matt's house.

"Where do you want to eat?" Matt asked as we headed down the sidewalk toward Main Street.

One of the many things I loved about living in a small town was that we could just start heading toward the one street where everything was located and decide on the way where exactly we were going.

"I don't care—where do you want to eat?" I replied, holding up my end of the predictable conversation.

"I could really just go for a lobster roll and some

fries," Matt said, giving voice to a craving I didn't even know I had until I heard him say it.

"Sandy's it is!" I said.

As we headed toward our favorite seafood joint, we avoided the two most obvious topics of conversation—Joe Davis's murder and our heated debate from the night before. We had ended the night on relatively good terms, agreeing to disagree, but there was still a little bit of tension between us. Instead, as we walked, we talked about the weather and how the summer tourist season was going. Even when we got to Sandy's, we talked about anything but Joe.

Even though I knew Matt had information I wanted —or needed—to hear, I was the one who had brought the case up the night before, which had ruined the evening, so I wasn't going to do it again. I would let Matt bring it up whenever he saw fit. Since whatever he'd found out about Joe was the whole pretext for our lunch, I knew he would get around to it sooner or later. I just had to bide my time even if I was incredibly impatient.

He finally brought it up after our food arrived.

"So, about Joe," he said just as I took a big bite of my lobster roll. I suspected he did it on purpose so I couldn't make much of a reply.

"Mm-hmm?" I mumbled through closed lips and a mouthful of buttery chopped lobster.

"I found out that he was three months behind on his gym-membership fees."

I swallowed my food and washed it down with a sip of my soda before responding. "So?" I asked.

"So, it's a possible point of contention between Joe and Todd."

I tried to keep from glaring at him. "I'm sure plenty of people are behind on their membership fees."

"Yes, but plenty of people aren't dead. Only Joe is."

"And so you think Todd killed him over three months of fees?"

"I didn't say that. I'm just telling you because it's a piece of information that I thought was relevant," he said calmly.

"And how did you get this piece of information?" I asked, his controlled demeanor only riling me up more. "Did you already know last night and just not mention it for some reason, or did you go out first thing in the morning to dig it up?" Both options annoyed me—that he'd been hiding something or that he was going out of his way to find information that could make Todd look bad.

"I didn't dig anything up. I woke up early this morning and went to the grocery store to pick up some stuff. While I was there, I ran into a guy I know who trained with Joe at Todd's Gym, and he told me that Joe was having money troubles and that he was behind on his gym dues. I figured it's something the police know, so I thought you'd want to know, too."

I studied his face carefully and ultimately chose to believe that he was being honest about his reasons for telling me. Matt had never been the type that would lie about anything, even things that seemed inconsequential, so I had no reason to doubt him. Besides, he was right—if the police knew, I needed to know too. As much as I hated that he was right, I was glad at the same time. And even though I knew Matt thought the overdue gym fees were a potential motive for Todd, the fact that Joe was having money issues gave me another idea.

"You know, if Joe owed Todd money, I bet he owed other people money, too."

"It's possible." Matt picked up his lobster roll and took a bite out of it.

"I don't think it's just possible," I replied. "I think it's likely. I mean, how much are gym fees? Fifty dollars a month?"

"Probably a little more since he was doing his kickboxing training there and all."

I hadn't thought of that. That would have increased the cost. "Still," I said. "Even if it doubled the price, that's only three hundred dollars over three months. If money was that tight, he'd have to be cutting corners somewhere else, wouldn't he?"

"I guess so. Didn't Sammy say he had moved in with his parents?"

"Yeah, but that doesn't mean he didn't have other bills he may have been skimping on."

"True, but if you think not paying a bill is enough reason to kill someone, that doesn't rule Todd out."

"We're guessing that Joe only owed him about three hundred dollars, right?" I waited for Matt's response, which was just a nod. "That's not much off the bottom line," I finished.

Matt shrugged and picked up some fries. "Depends how tight his profit margins are." He pushed the fries into his mouth.

"Todd's Gym didn't look like the kind of place that was three hundred dollars away from shutting down." I took a bite of my own lobster roll while I waited for Matt to finish chewing and swallowing.

He had a lot of fries in his mouth, so it took him a minute. Finally, he said, "Looks can be deceiving. I've worked on projects with companies that were throwing cocktail parties right up until they closed their doors. Of course, I think some of those shut down *because* of the cocktail parties, but that's beside the point. The point is that you can't necessarily tell how strong a company's finances are by the way they look or act. Plenty of people would rather go down in a blaze of glory than let on beforehand that they were in trouble."

"I guess you're right," I conceded. "But if the gym was in that much trouble, why wouldn't Todd have told me that when I was talking to him?"

Matt looked at me with his eyebrows raised. He didn't even have to say anything. I knew what he was thinking.

"Because I'm a pretty girl?"

"Well, that, yeah. But it's also not like you guys have been close over the years. You just came back into town —have you even seen Todd in the past fifteen years?"

I shook my head.

"Not a lot of people are going to confess to someone they haven't seen in over a decade that their big, flashy business is in trouble."

Despite his subtle dig at Todd's Gym, I had to admit he had a point. "Could you stop being right? It's getting annoying."

Matt laughed, covering his mouth to keep from spitting half-chewed lobster all over the table. That in turn made me laugh, and just like that, all the tension between us was gone.

"I'll try," Matt said. "But I've had a lot of practice at it, so it'll be a hard habit to break."

I giggled again and took another sip of my soda. "You're too much, Matty."

"Ah, you like it."

I did like it, and I was surprised to realize I was going

to miss him when he was out of town the next week. Since we'd reconnected, we'd seen each other almost every day, if only because we lived so close. But I knew what I was going to do with the time that he was away. I was going to go talk to Todd again and see if I could find out the state of the gym's finances and whether Joe's three months of delinquent payments could really be hurting them—or, at the very least, see if I could tell whether he was hiding anything from me.

Chapter 14

AFTER LUNCH ON SATURDAY, Matt had some work stuff to take care of before he left for Virginia, so we walked back to our street. Matt went to his house to hole up with his laptop and send a million or so e-mails so everyone would know who was responsible for which aspect of what project. I didn't have to be at the café until late afternoon, so I went down to my house to get Latte and go for a walk.

He bounced around on the end of his bright-blue leash as we walked back in the direction I had just come from with Matt. I felt like going down to the beach even though I knew it would be packed with families of tourists. I just wanted to walk down the boardwalk and listen to the sound of the waves even if they were punctuated by the shouts of playing children.

The beach was packed, since all the timeshares and rentals turned over on Saturdays. Everyone wanted to get one last day on the sand before they headed home. Mother Nature had kindly given them a beautiful, sunny day by which to remember Cape Bay, and it seemed that almost no one had decided to stay in.

Latte was popular on the boardwalk, and he loved the attention he got from all the dog lovers. We could barely walk five feet without someone stopping to pet him or a toddler pointing out the "doggie woof woof." The walk wasn't exactly relaxing, but at least it served to get my mind off of Joe Davis's murder.

When we'd walked the entire length of the boardwalk, we turned around and made our way back the way we'd come, again stopped by excited tourists, some of whom had just seen us on our way down the beach. Even though it was on the hot side of warm out, I didn't quite feel like going home yet, so we took the long way, making our way through town to the park. The typical gaggle of old men was collected around the concrete chess tables, ostensibly competing, but more likely spending most of their time socializing.

We gradually made our way across the park and down a set of stairs that led to a pond. I noticed a crumpled piece of paper in the corner of one of the steps. Annoyed with whatever litterbug had left it there, I picked up the garbage and carried it to the nearest trash can. We continued through the back of the park and onto my street. When we got to the sidewalk in front of my house, I let Latte off his leash. I pulled out the tennis ball that I'd shoved in my pocket on the way out of the house and threw it as far as I could down the side of the house and into the backyard.

The backyards all along our street were nice and deep, with a natural fence along the back formed by a row of hedges and a thicket of trees. If I stood at the front of the yard and threw as hard as I could, Latte could get a good run in on the way to the ball and back. I threw the ball and let him chase it several times until he eventually let me know he had had enough exercise by lying down at my feet with the tennis ball in his mouth instead of dropping it as he did when he wanted to keep playing.

"Okay," I said, leaning down and holding out my hand for him to drop the drool-covered tennis ball into it. I held it gingerly between my thumb and forefinger, trying to get as little dog slobber on my hands as possible. Latte waited patiently as I unlocked the front door, but I could tell he was ready to get inside, get a drink of water, and relax on my bed in the air conditioning. I, meanwhile, had to change and get to work.

When I arrived, the café was completely slammed. Becky was working the register, calling out one drink after the next for Sammy to prepare. Sammy was making multiple drinks at a time, expertly pulling espresso and steaming milk in quick succession to prepare each customer's order. Becky herself handled the orders of food or plain coffee, quickly grabbing each component and passing them to the customer before taking the next order.

I grabbed my apron off its hook and slid it over my head. "I got the next one," I called as I tied the strings behind my back. I saw Sammy glance up in relief as Becky called out the next order.

"One cappuccino, one latte, one mocha," she announced.

"One cappuccino, one latte, one mocha," I confirmed as I lined up the cups and started the espresso.

"I also asked for two cupcakes and a cup of black coffee," the woman on the other side of the register said huffily.

"Yes, ma'am, I'm getting those now," Becky replied as she darted behind me and Sammy to the coffee pot. I was impressed with how well she handled the woman's rudeness, letting it roll off her back as though it was nothing. I wasn't sure I would have been that composed about it back when I was her age. I probably would have gotten anxious and wondered what I had done wrong.

Becky handed the woman the plain coffee and two cupcakes. "We'll bring the other drinks over to you as soon as they're ready," she said with a smile. She looked over the woman's shoulder at the next customer. "May I help you, sir?" she asked.

The woman reluctantly stepped aside, seeming annoyed that she hadn't managed to fluster Becky. She stood across the espresso machine from me, craning her neck to try to see what I was doing. I flashed her a smile and kept working. I knew I didn't have the time to linger over something intricate and I didn't particularly want to give any ammunition to the demanding woman staring me down, so I poured in designs that were quick but beautiful—swans encircled by hearts, tulips beside roset-tas, a spiral of hearts.

Sammy came back from delivering a tray of drinks just as Becky called out the next order.

"Two lattes!"

"Two lattes!" Sammy echoed. She grabbed two cups and saucers and started preparing the drinks.

I looked up at the woman in front of me. "If you'd like to take a seat, I'll bring these over to you." I carefully arranged the three cups on a tray.

"All the tables are taken," she huffed.

"I think there are some chairs open in the corner," I replied, keeping the smile on my face. "Or there are a couple of tables outside."

The woman made annoyed little noises as she glanced around the coffee shop. I didn't know what she wanted me to do—she was already holding a cup of coffee and two cupcakes in her hands. There was no way she could hold more. And with an order of four coffees, I knew she had to be there with other people who must be somewhere nearby. She either finally spotted them or finally decided I didn't require any further supervision because she tromped off across the café to a table with three people and an empty chair just as I picked up the tray.

I walked over and dropped off the drinks, making it a point to smile brightly as I did so. My grandparents never would have tolerated me being anything but unfailingly polite to a customer, no matter how abrasive she was. I made it back to the counter just as Becky called out the next order.

We continued like that for the next hour or so until the traffic in the café died down.

"Why didn't you call me to come in?" I asked Sammy as we wiped all traces of the rush from the counters. Becky was busy gathering up dishes left on the tables and carrying them back to be washed.

"It just got busy all of a sudden. Everything was calm and quiet, and then it was like somebody rang a bell or something, and the whole beach decided to come in. You know how it is when it's a nice day and then it starts pouring rain and everyone runs in from the beach? It was like that, except with not a cloud in the sky."

"Well, you know you can call me in if I'm not here, anytime you need me."

"Of course," she replied.

We worked on cleaning up for a few more minutes until Becky finished clearing the dishes and disappeared into the back to wash them. It wasn't that I didn't want her to hear what I wanted to ask Sammy, but I wanted to be sensitive to Sammy's feelings.

"How was Joe's funeral?" I asked.

She sighed. "It was rough," she said. "You know, he'd had such a hard time lately, but it seemed like he was finally getting back on his feet. Or at least getting his act together. I didn't know this, but his parents were paying for him to take some computer classes at the community college so he'd have better skills to get a job." She sniffed and grabbed a napkin from her counter to dab her eyes. "Melissa was there with Emmy—that was really hard."

"Who are Melissa and Emmy?" I asked, thinking Joe perhaps had younger sisters or they were friends of Sammy who had been close to Joe.

"Melissa is his ex-girlfriend. And Emmy is their daughter."

"Oh." That was the only thing I could think to say. Among all the people I'd talked to about Joe, no one had ever mentioned a daughter. I wondered if she was something he kept quiet. "I had no idea."

"It's weird, but somehow it made it worse that you could tell Emmy had no idea what was going on. She was sitting up there in the front row with Melissa and Joe's parents, and every few minutes, she'd turn around to make faces at everyone. Melissa had to keep sitting her back down and telling her to be quiet, but it was like she could see how sad everyone was and just wanted to cheer them up. Gosh, Joe was so proud of her, too. He'd show me pictures every time he came in and just go on and on about all the new things she was doing."

So much for the secret-child thing. Still, I wondered if that might be a lead. If the spouse was always the first suspect when someone was murdered, didn't it stand to reason that the ex-girlfriend and mother of the victim's child would be a prime suspect?

"It just killed him that he couldn't pay child support after he lost his job." Sammy's eyes got big, and her hand flew to her mouth when she realized what she'd said. "Oh! I didn't... I didn't mean—" She grabbed another napkin and held it to her face. I reached out my hand and rubbed her shoulder.

"It's okay. I know it's just an expression."

"An awful expression!"

"Unfortunate," I said.

I hesitated, wanting to ask her something, but I didn't know how to phrase it without sounding as though I was suggesting, well, exactly what I was suggesting. In the end, I decided to just go for it. "Sammy, you don't think Melissa…" I trailed off and let her fill in the rest of the sentence.

She took a few seconds to put together what I was asking, but understanding finally appeared on her face. "Oh my gosh, no! Melissa would never… No! No, I can't even imagine. Melissa wouldn't do that."

"Okay," I said quickly, ready to move the conversation in a different direction. If Sammy didn't think Melissa could have done it, I wasn't going to push her. "I'm just grasping at straws. It's creepy knowing there's a murderer on the loose."

"I know," Sammy sniffled. "It's so scary thinking that it might have been random. Is there someone out there just looking for people walking alone to stab?" She shuddered. "I don't even like to think about it."

I thought her statement might have been inspired by more than just idle fear. "Are you worried that something might happen to you coming to and from here?" It was getting dark early enough that whether Sammy opened or closed the café, she was walking in the dark. Even if she drove in, she'd still have to come in from the parking lot on her own, and a parking lot was where Joe was murdered.

Sammy hesitated, but I could see the look on her face and guess what was coming. "I know it's stupid, but—"

"It's not stupid," I said, interrupting her. I looked at Becky in the back room. She was only sixteen and just a little tiny wisp of a thing. She and the other part-timers normally worked during daylight hours, just because that's when we needed the most help, but occasionally they helped open or close. I would feel awful if anything happened to them. "I'll call Mike and see if he knows anybody who could help make sure you get to and from work safely."

A big smile came across her face. "Thanks, Fran. Like I said, I feel silly, but I just keep waiting for some guy to come out of the shadows and get me."

"Don't worry about it," I replied. "I don't know what Mike will say or how long it will take to get something figured out, but I want you guys to be safe. But that reminds me—isn't it time for you to go home? You've been here all day."

Sammy glanced at the big wrought-iron clock on the wall. "Yeah, I guess it is time for me to get out of here." She slung the rag she'd been wiping the counters with over her shoulder. "I guess I'll see you tomorrow?"

"Yup, see you tomorrow."

Sammy went in the back, took her apron off, and dropped her rag in the basket we had for laundry. She grabbed her purse and turned around to wave to Becky and me. "Bye, guys!"

I waved and said goodbye, and Becky lifted a soapy

gloved hand in Sammy's direction. I walked over to the door to the back room.

"What time did you come in?" I asked Becky.

"Noon."

"Why don't you head home when you're done?" I was putting myself at risk if things got busy again, but she'd already worked plenty of hours, and my talk with Sammy had me thinking it was best for her to get home before dark.

"Okay, cool!" She smiled, so excited that I got the feeling she had plans for the evening.

I went back out to the front to finish cleaning up the few remaining signs of our hectic hour. Everything was neat and orderly by the time Becky stuck her head out from the back.

"I'm all finished. Are you sure there isn't anything else you want me to do before I go?"

"Nope. Go. Enjoy your Saturday night."

"Awesome, thank you!" She was so happy she was practically jumping up and down. She pulled off her apron, hung it on the hook, and then disappeared out the back door so quickly I thought she was worried I would change my mind if she waited another second.

I checked behind her to make sure the back door was closed and locked, and I crossed my fingers and hoped we wouldn't have another wave of customers.

Chapter 15

A SLOW BUT steady stream of people came in, keeping me busy enough that I wasn't bored but not so busy that things got out of hand. It was getting close to closing time, and only a couple of customers were left sitting and chatting in the big armchairs when the bell over the door jingled and I looked up to see Todd.

"Hi," I said cheerfully. I liked seeing a friendly face after a fairly busy day, and I had questions to ask him anyway.

"Hi, yourself," he replied. He glanced around the café as he walked up to the counter, where I was standing. "I thought you said the roses I sent you were still alive. Or did you take them home to enjoy them there?"

"They finally died," I said. "I actually just threw them out yesterday." They'd lived a good life, and I probably would have kept them a little longer if I actually had taken them home, but I didn't think wilting flowers really made customers feel as though we were a clean, well-run establishment. "They were beautiful while they lasted, though," I assured him.

"Well, I guess I'll just have to see about getting you some new ones, then," he said and winked at me. I didn't know what to make of the wink, so I ignored it.

"I actually did want to know what florist you got them from. They were so beautiful and they lasted for so long, I was thinking it might be nice to have them in the café more often."

"Are you trying to tell me that you don't want me to send you more flowers?" he asked, leaning across the counter toward me.

"Well, I don't want you to feel like you're responsible for making sure we always have fresh ones!" I laughed, avoiding the question I knew he was actually asking.

He chuckled and ran his fingers through his thick blond hair, almost as if he was deliberately trying to draw my attention to it.

"So can I get you anything?" I asked.

"I would love one of your amazing lattes."

"Coming right up." I started preparing his drink. "Can I get you anything else? Something to eat, maybe?"

He leaned back to look at the display case with its

assortment of heavy, rich baked goods and shook his head. "Nah, it's not my cheat day. The latte will already be more than I should have."

I always thought of cheat days as being associated with diet-conscious fashionistas, but I understood how that approach to eating could be something they shared with athletic, exercise-junkie types like Todd. Somehow, I thought Todd's cheat-day foods were more substantial than the cocktails the girls in New York splurged on.

I finished pouring a daisy into Todd's coffee and started working on one for myself. "Do you mind if I join you for just a minute?" I asked. "I had something I wanted to ask you about."

"Not at all," he replied, his broad smile revealing his gleaming white teeth.

"Let me just make my drink real quick, and I'll bring them around." I saw him reach for his wallet. "You don't owe me anything," I said, waving him off. "It's on the house."

He smiled that brilliant smile at me. "Thanks, Franny."

He went and sat down at one of the tables while I finished preparing my drink. I poured a many-leaved tulip into my cup and then took both drinks over to the table. I set Todd's down carefully in front of him so the daisy was facing the right way, and I took the seat opposite him, angling my chair so I could see any customers walking in or out of the door.

"So you said you wanted to talk to me?" Todd leaned toward me across the table.

"Yeah," I said distractedly as I watched to make sure a customer walking toward the counter didn't need me for anything. When she turned around after grabbing a napkin, I directed my attention back to Todd. "I wanted to ask you something about Joe."

"Oh." Todd leaned back in his chair. He sighed. "What do you want to know?"

"Well, I heard that Joe was three months behind in his membership dues."

His eyes narrowed. "Where did you hear that?"

"It doesn't matter where I heard it—" I started to say before Todd cut me off.

"No, I want to know. If someone's sharing confidential information about my members, I want to know."

I sighed. "I heard it from Matt. But he heard it from someone who trained with Joe at the gym. It wasn't a staff member or anything like that."

"Are you sure?"

"I'm as sure as I can be. I don't think Matt would go to the trouble of making up something like that."

"Okay." Todd crossed his arms against his muscular chest.

"So I take it it's true? Joe was behind on his dues?"

"Yeah."

"Was that something that concerned you?"

"You mean was I worried about him not being able to pay or was I worried about missing out on the money?"

"Either," I replied. "Both."

"Yeah, I mean, I was worried about him being out of work and living with his parents, but I wasn't worried about the money. One guy's not going to break me."

"You weren't worried about setting a precedent or anything?"

He looked at me curiously. "No."

"Why'd you let him get away with it? Not paying and still coming to the gym, I mean. Why'd you let him work out if he wasn't paying you?"

"You ask a lot of questions."

"I'm trying to help you, Todd," I replied. "When Matt came to me and told me about how far behind Joe was, he thought it was a possible motive. If I'm going to help you, I need to know why you let him keep working out."

"He still doesn't like me, huh?" He scoffed.

"Who?" I asked. "Matt?" I hesitated, searching for the best thing to say. I was surprised Todd knew of Matt's distaste for him, although I realized at the same time that I shouldn't have been. They'd lived in the same small town for most of their lives. Of course Todd would have noticed Matt didn't like him. "No, when he told me, it was for the same reason I'm asking you now—so we could eliminate it as a possibility. We need to rule everything out so we know when we find the real murderer and the real motive. If we have two people with two good motives, it doesn't help us. Especially not if one of those people is you."

Todd clenched his jaw a couple times, apparently thinking over what I had said. Finally, he gave in. "He was my friend. And he was having a hard time. I'm not going to screw over my friend just because he's having a hard time. Especially not when I don't need the money. Besides, kickboxing was Joe's way out. If I took that away from him, he'd be stuck in his parents' house forever."

"Hmm," I murmured. I took a sip of my coffee as I mulled over what Todd had said. I believed him, of course, about not being concerned about Joe's debt because he was a friend. He said it far too casually for it to be a cover-up of some sort. I was more perplexed by Todd saying that kickboxing was Joe's only road to get his life back in order. I knew he'd said before that Joe had promise, but he'd also said Joe was getting too old to be coming up in the sport and he didn't have the skills that some of the other guys had. I hadn't taken that to mean that he had a promising future in the sport. But Todd was talking about how kickboxing was Joe's only hope. And that, after Sammy had told me that Joe had been taking night classes to help him get a job.

"When I talked to you the other day, I thought you made it sound like he wasn't good enough to make a living off of kickboxing," I said finally.

"Did I?"

I waited for him to go on, but he didn't. "Yes, you did."

He shrugged and shook his head the slightest bit. "It's been a crazy week. I can't remember what I say from one day to the next."

"Oh well." I decided to laugh it off. It wasn't going to do any good to press Todd on which he really meant. Either he had been telling the truth then and being generous to the memory of a dead man now, or something, possibly grief, had led him to undersell Joe's skill when he first talked to me. I didn't think I was going to get him to admit to either option.

However, I was a little surprised that Todd thought the best way for Joe—a young out-of-work father rapidly coming up on thirty—to make a living was to literally fight for it. A nice, calm office job seemed like a much better—and safer—bet to me.

It was getting close to closing time when we finished our coffee. The other customers had gone, and no one else had come in, so it was just the two of us in the café when I picked up our cups and saucers to take to the sink in the back. Mine was light, but his was heavy. I glanced down and saw he'd taken maybe one sip as the daisy I'd crafted with the milk was barely distorted. I had to admit I was a little disappointed he hadn't drunk any more of it, but I was even more worried that something had been wrong with it.

"Was there something wrong with the coffee?"

"What?" Todd looked up from his phone, which he'd pulled out of his pocket.

"The coffee. Was there something wrong with it? You hardly drank any of it."

"Oh. No. Just gotta watch what I eat," he said.

When paying customers said stuff like that, I usually just shrugged it off. I didn't understand why people would come in and pay good money for drinks they weren't actually going to consume, but as far as I'm concerned, the customer is always right, so I didn't let it bother me.

Somehow though, Todd's full cup did bother me because I'd given the drink away for free—almost as though I had given him a gift and he'd shrugged, said "Oh, that's nice," and never looked at it again.

I tried to push that out of my mind, though. As Todd had said, he'd had a crazy week, and I would be nuts to take it personally.

I had a few dishes to wash and a little bit of cleaning up to do before I could head out for the night. With

Sammy's worries about the safety of walking home alone in the dark ringing in my ears, I thought I would ask Todd if he could wait a few minutes and then walk me home or, I supposed, drive me if he'd brought his car.

I had just deposited the dirty dishes in the sink when I heard his voice behind me.

"Hey, Franny?"

I turned around to see him leaning into the doorway, his hands pressed into either side of the doorway, his cell phone clutched between his fingers.

"Yeah?" I asked.

"I'm going to get out of here, okay?"

"I was actually just about to ask if you could hang out for a few minutes until I get everything ready to lock up and then walk me home."

A look I couldn't quite define passed over his face, and for a second I thought he was going to agree. "I can't," he said. "I have to meet someone. You'll be okay getting home on your own?"

"Yeah, I'll be fine," I assured him. "Go. Don't let me keep you."

"Cool. Thanks for the coffee." He stepped all the way into the room and wrapped his arms around me in a quick hug. "I'll see you soon, a'right?"

"Okay," I said.

He strode across the café and out the door, setting the bell jingling as he flung it open.

I glanced at the clock, then went behind him and turned the lock in the door. As I walked back to take care of the dishes, I pulled my phone out of my pocket and sent Matt a text. *Any way you can spare a few minutes to come walk me home? Murder has me spooked.*

He texted me back shortly. *Sure thing. I'll be there in a few.*

I felt silly asking him to escort me like that, but I was glad I could rely on him.

I washed the few dirty dishes and was wiping down the tables when I heard a rap on the glass door. I almost jumped out of my skin, but when I looked, it was only Matt.

"I didn't mean to scare you like that," he said when I opened the door.

"It was that obvious?"

"You jumped about a mile high." He laughed. "I thought about just standing outside until you noticed me so I wouldn't startle you, but I thought that might be scarier."

"Please, do not ever do that. I would have a heart attack. You would have to break through the glass to come rescue me."

"I'd do it," he replied.

"Scare me like that or rescue me?"

"Rescue you. I don't want to have to do it, so I'll try not to ever scare you that bad."

"Thanks," I said. "But if you could try not to scare me at all, that would be even better."

Matt laughed. "I'll do my best." He looked around the café. "Are you ready to go, or is there something I can help you with?"

"I just have to wipe down the last of these tables, and then I'll be ready," I said. "Do you want a cup of coffee or anything?"

Matt wandered over to the display case. "No, no coffee," he said, peering inside. "I'd ask for a piece of tiramisu, but that might be hard to eat. Can I have a cupcake?"

"Chocolate?"

"Of course!"

"Help yourself." I ran my cloth over the last of the tables. Satisfied everything was cleaned to my standards, I headed for the back room to take off my apron and grab my purse.

"Oh my God, Franny." Matt groaned.

"Good?" I asked, poking my head out and seeing him go for a second bite of cupcake.

"I think it's the best you've ever made."

"You say that about everything I make."

"Then stop making such good food."

I laughed at him as I slid my purse over my shoulder. "Are you ready to go? Can you manage to eat and walk at the same time?"

"I'll try," he said. "If it turns out I can't, we can sit down on the curb until I'm done."

I laughed again. "Let's go," I said, shepherding him out the door and locking it behind us. "You can hold onto my elbow if you have to."

Matt chuckled, barely managing to keep the cupcake in his mouth, and we headed down the street toward home.

Chapter 16

"TODD CAME INTO THE CAFÉ TODAY," I said as we walked down the street.

Matt cocked his eyebrow at me but didn't say anything because his mouth was full of cupcake.

"I was going to ask him to walk me home, but he had to leave."

"Oh, so I was your second choice?" Matt asked after swallowing the bite he had in his mouth.

I looked up to study his face in the streetlight, but I couldn't quite tell whether he was just giving me a hard time. "I just knew you were working and didn't want to make you come all the way out when he was already there."

"I don't mind walking you home, especially if you don't feel safe walking alone."

"I know, I just—he was there. It made sense."

"He's a suspect in a murder case, Franny."

"That doesn't mean he's a murderer."

Matt gave me a "we've talked about this" look, so I knew Todd's innocence wasn't worth trying to go over any more.

"Anyway, while he was there, I asked him about Joe being behind in his dues."

"And?" he asked as he took another bite of his cupcake. He was practically inhaling it and only had a couple bites left. And it was not a small cupcake.

"And he says that he didn't care because Joe was his friend."

Matt almost spat the chocolate confection from his mouth. "I don't believe that," he said.

"What? Why not?"

"I just don't buy it." He shrugged.

"Tell me why. Do you not believe Todd would give his friend a pass on his dues? Or do you not think Todd could possibly have any friends?"

"I just don't think he's that generous."

"Because you don't like him."

"I didn't say that," he replied, shoving the last piece of cupcake in his mouth.

"You didn't have to."

We walked on quietly. I was feeling conflicted. I believed Todd, but Matt was my good friend and maybe more. However, that "maybe more" seemed to have gotten sidetracked with the news of Joe's murder. I think it was bothering both of us more than we liked to admit —Matt because it reminded him of his dad's murder and me because, well, why *wouldn't* a murder in my small hometown bother me? Whatever the exact reasons, I felt like we'd both been distracted the past few days.

"It's not that I don't like him," Matt said after a few minutes. "I just don't get why the guy would charge his friend for membership in the first place but not care that he can't pay. Why not just let your friend work out for free in the first place?"

"Maybe because all his friends would think they should get to work out for free and then he wouldn't make any money?"

"You give me free cupcakes."

"Yeah, but you don't come in *expecting* free cupcakes. You always offer to pay."

"I only do that to make you *think* I don't expect free cupcakes. I always expect free cupcakes. Free cupcakes, free coffee, free tiramisu. I expect it all to be free."

I looked over at him to see if he was serious. The twinkle in his eye and the upturned corner of his mouth told me he wasn't.

"My point is," I said, rolling my eyes, "that it makes sense to me he would charge everyone as a rule but give his friend a break when he needed it."

"I don't know. I just don't buy it. I just don't think you let people get away with not paying you the money you need to run a business."

"I don't think he's hurting for it."

"Why? Did you ask him about that too?"

"No. It was just the way he talked about it. Like he was really doing Joe a favor. Because he cared about him and he wanted to."

Matt give me a sidelong glance, which I chose to ignore. "You're too nice, you know that, Franny?"

"Yeah, I know. That's why I keep hanging out with you."

Matt looked at me curiously and then burst out laughing. "I guess I had that one coming, huh?"

"Yup, you did."

We walked along a little further then in a more comfortable silence.

"So should I plan to walk you home every night until Joe's killer is caught?" Matt asked as we walked up to my house.

"You could, but you leave for Virginia tomorrow, don't you? Might make it a little difficult."

"Oh, that's right!" Matt groaned. "I forgot about that. I guess I won't be doing the honors then, will I?"

"Guess not." I shrugged.

"You're not going to ask Todd to walk you home every night, are you?"

I thought about teasing him and saying yes, but I decided to go easy on him. "No, I actually promised Sammy I'd call Mike and see if he knows someone who could provide an escort. It's not so much that I'm worried about me walking alone as that I'd never be able to forgive myself if something happened to Sammy or Becky or any of the other girls. It's dark now when we open and when we close."

"Hard to believe it's that time of year already."

"I know. The season's flown by. It's hard to believe it's almost over."

"It's been a crazy summer."

"You can say that again," I agreed as I slid my key into the lock. Latte bolted down the stairs as soon as the sound reached his ears. I opened the door, and he flew out into the yard, running around Matt and me and shoving his wet nose into our hands.

"Looks like somebody's happy to see you," Matt said.

"Yeah, it's nice having somebody so excited to see me when I get home every day."

"Hey, maybe I should get a dog."

"You should. Latte could have a little friend to play with." Latte raced past us as I spoke and went straight back into the kitchen. I knew he would be sitting by his bowl with his little paw up in the air, waiting patiently for me to serve him his dinner. "Guess I better go take care of him," I said.

"Yeah, I should get home—I still have some stuff to take care of before I leave tomorrow."

"Will I see you before you leave, or should I say goodbye now?"

"You can always say goodbye now and then again tomorrow if we see each other."

I stepped toward him and put my arms up around his neck. "Have a safe trip, okay?"

"I'll try," he said, his arms wrapped around my back.

"Don't try," I admonished playfully. "Just do it."

"Yes, ma'am." He chuckled as he stepped off my front step. "If I don't see you tomorrow, I'll see you in a couple of days."

"Okay, see you then. Good night." I gave him a little wave as I stepped inside.

"'Night, Franny."

I shut the door and went to feed Latte, who was, as I'd predicted, patiently waiting for his supper. I fed him and let him out again and then headed upstairs to go to bed. It was early, but I was tired. As soon as I climbed into bed, Latte hopped up next to me, snuggling in close. I ran my fingers through his fur as I waited for sleep to come. It did not. Despite how tired I was, my mind was racing.

I thought about Matt and Todd and Joe and Melissa. I wanted to talk to Melissa, but I didn't know her last name or where she lived or anything about her except that she was Joe's ex-girlfriend and they had a daughter named Emmy. That was nothing—nowhere near enough information to find her. I couldn't even look her up online with that much information. Though Cape Bay was small, I figured at least ten or twenty Melissas lived there, and even if I could find them all, I didn't think they'd appreciate me showing up to talk to them.

I tried to think of some other way to track her down and realized I could always ask Sammy—I could tell her I wanted to send a sympathy card. But that would be dishonest, and I didn't want to deceive a friend like that. There was Mrs. D'Angelo. She knew everything about everyone in town. I was sure she didn't approve of Joe and Melissa having a baby without being married, but I didn't see why that would stop her from giving me some more information about Melissa.

That was the last thought I remembered before waking up to the sun shining in my face and Latte staring at me.

"Good morning," I told him. He gave me a good lick, running his tongue from my chin to my forehead. I pulled the sheet up to wipe away his slobber and gave his head a good scratch. "Should we go play in the park today?"

I didn't know how he could possibly understand me, but he jumped to his feet and stared at me, his tongue out, panting excitedly, the exact same way he did when we played fetch.

"I'll take that as a yes," I said. I got out of bed and went about getting both of us ready for a trip to the park.

Less than an hour later, we were in the park, getting ready for an intense game of fetch. We went to a corner of the park I didn't often go to, where there was a playground and a couple of fenced-in fields the rec leagues and kids in general used to play soccer or baseball.

A dog park was in the works for Cape Bay, but we didn't yet have one. We'd actually only gotten a leash law in the past five years or so. It had just never been an issue. People would go to the park to let their dogs run around and have fun without any issues. But someone had moved to town from somewhere that did have leash laws and had complained so vociferously about the lack of regulation that the town had no choice but to start requiring everyone to keep their dogs on leashes, even in the park.

Long-time residents then complained that there was nowhere for their dogs to run free, which led to the development of the dog park. It was supposed to have been built in the next year or so, but until then, residents had begun using the playing fields as a de facto dog park —they were fenced in, they had a gate, they had enough space for a dog to run, so they were perfect.

We had been playing fetch for several minutes when, instead of returning the ball to me, Latte shot past me with the ball and made a beeline for the gate.

"Latte, come here!" I called out, turning around to see what he was trying to get to. I hadn't realized that anyone had arrived to play at the playground, but Latte clearly had, and he apparently wanted them to join our game. A small child and a woman I assumed to be the child's mother were sitting on a bench keeping watch. The child had caught sight of Latte and was walking across the mulched playground toward the fields. Latte ran right up to the fence and dropped his ball in the gap between the gate and the fence. He lowered his nose to the ground and nudged the ball through.

The child at the playground seemed to understand Latte's invitation and took off running toward us. I couldn't quite tell, based on the child's chin-length brown hair or plain blue-and-white shorts and T-shirt, whether it was a boy or a girl, but whichever it was, it was excited to come play with Latte. The mother took a moment to realize her child had taken off, but when she did, she jumped up and started running across the playground.

"Doggie!" the little one squealed, moving faster than I thought a child that size could.

I was running, too. I wasn't worried about Latte hurting the child at all, both because of the fence separating them and because he was as sweet and docile as they come, but I was concerned that the child might get scared once he—or she—was up close and personal with Latte. I also didn't know how the mother would react with her child being so close to a strange dog.

"Latte! Sit!" I yelled. I felt that if he was sitting and responding to my commands, the mother would at least be able to see that he was a calm dog. Thankfully, Latte sat and even lifted one paw into his begging position. If I hadn't needed all my breath to propel my continued running, I would have breathed a sigh of relief.

The mother and I reached them at the same time.

"I am so sorry!" she panted, trying to catch her breath. She knelt down next to the child. "Don't run away like that. You can't try to play with doggies you don't know."

"It's okay," I assured her. "He wanted to play. He's really friendly. I think he saw your little one over there and thought they could be playmates."

"Doggie!" the child exclaimed, pointing at Latte. The child leaned into the mother and said something I couldn't hear.

"She wants to know if she can pet the dog," the mother said.

"Sure," I replied. "Let me just grab his leash." I jogged back over to where we'd been playing fetch and picked up the bright-blue leash. I went back to the gate, where Latte was still patiently waiting, paw in the air, for the tiny girl to pick up the ball and throw it for him. I hooked the leash onto Latte's collar and guided him back away from the inward-opening gate. "Sit, Latte," I instructed him, wanting to be sure that he behaved himself and didn't inadvertently scare the little girl. I wrapped the leash around my hand to keep him close then reached out and pulled the gate open. The little girl darted in, excited to get close to Latte.

"Emmy, stop. Wait!" the mother called out.

I couldn't believe what I'd just heard. "I'm sorry," I said. "Did you just call her Emmy?"

Chapter 17

"YES," the mother said, looking at me suspiciously. She grabbed Emmy's hand and pulled her back away from Latte and me.

"Doggie!" Emmy cried, pointing at Latte and straining from her mother's grasp.

"You're not Melissa, by any chance, are you?" I asked.

"Why?" She took a small step back, looking as though she was ready to run at a moment's notice.

"I'm friends with Samantha Eriksen. She works for me," I said. The woman seemed to relax, but only a little. "She told me about her friend Melissa and her daughter Emmy. If you're Melissa, I just wanted to introduce myself. And express my condolences. I'm Francesca Amaro. I run Antonia's Italian Café."

She became clearly more at ease, even letting Emmy, who had never stopped straining at her mother's hand, move toward Latte.

"Oh, you're Francesca? I knew your mom. She was wonderful. She loved Emmy to death." She stopped and blushed, realizing her unfortunate choice of words. "Oh my God, I'm so sorry," she muttered.

"It's okay," I said, marveling at how many casual death-related phrases there seemed to be and how that only became obvious when someone close passed away. "It's just a figure of speech."

"Still"—she held her free hand to her face, colored red with embarrassment—"I should know better."

"Really, it's okay. I know you didn't mean anything by it." I gave her a moment to compose herself. "So, you are Melissa?"

"Oh, yes. Sorry. Melissa Harris." She extended her hand for me to shake. "And you already know this is Emmy."

"Hi, Emmy," I said.

The little girl was ignoring us, making faces at Latte and laughing at his antics. My greeting did nothing to distract her.

"Emmy, say hello," Melissa said.

Emmy turned her big hazel eyes up to me. "Hello," she said in a clear little bell-like voice before turning her attention right back to Latte.

"Kids," Melissa said with a shrug.

I laughed. "Would she want to throw the ball for him?" I asked.

"Do you want to throw the ball for the doggie, Emmy?" Melissa asked, leaning down toward her.

"Yes!" she exclaimed.

I grabbed Latte's ball and closed the gate, latching it so it wouldn't swing back open, letting a dog or a child out. I unhooked Latte's leash from his collar and handed the ball to Emmy. She threw it as hard as she could, which wasn't really very hard, but Latte ran the five feet, picked it up, and ran it back to her, dropping it at her feet. She squealed with glee and threw it again. We watched them play for a few minutes, then Melissa stepped toward me.

"Did you know Joey?" she asked quietly. She had one arm folded across her chest as if to guard herself, and the other hand nervously played with her brown curls. Her blue eyes flitted to my face and then back away to where Emmy was playing with Latte.

"No, I didn't," I admitted. "His name was familiar, but he was a few years behind me in school, so I never really knew him. I was very sorry to hear, though."

"Thanks," she said quietly. "I was sorry about your mother."

"Thank you," I replied. We stood quietly for a

minute. I wanted to find a way to ask her about Joe, but I couldn't quite figure out how to bring it up. "How are you doing?" I asked.

She took a moment to answer, and I wasn't quite sure she had heard me. "I'm making it," she said finally.

"And Emmy?"

Melissa sighed. "She doesn't really understand. He didn't live with us, so she's used to him not being around, but she still wants to call him on the phone and talk to him."

I decided to just go for it and ask about the murder. "Do the police have any suspects?" I asked, trying my best to sound casual.

"I don't really know," she said. "They don't really tell us what's going on with the investigation. And they talk to his parents more than me. 'Baby mama' apparently doesn't count as next of kin." She scoffed a little as she said it, but I could tell the situation bothered her.

She fell quiet, and I struggled to think of a way to ask about her own potential motive when she handed it to me.

"Of course, they sure didn't hesitate to rake me over the coals about where I was that night and whether I was angry that he wasn't paying child support. I was down at the police station for four hours on Tuesday. I was supposed to be planning Joey's funeral and comforting our daughter, but I was holed up in an interrogation room, telling some cops my life story."

"You didn't do it, did you?" I asked, making sure my voice was jovial enough that she didn't think I was accusing her.

"No," she exclaimed. "I loved Joey. Always have. Ever since back in high school. He just needed to get his life together, get a job—grow up, you know? He loved Em, but I don't think he'd really realized he was a father yet, like, a father who had responsibilities and all. He still wanted to act like he was a single guy."

"You said he wasn't paying child support?" We both had our eyes fixed on Emmy and Latte still playing with the ball, so I felt that asking tough questions was a little easier.

"Not really. On and off, like he'd pay a month here or there, but it wasn't regular like it was supposed to be. He hadn't paid in a while, but a couple of days before he died, he came and gave me two thousand dollars. I was almost afraid to ask where he got it, but I needed it. Emmy needs new clothes—she's wearing hand-me-downs from my cousin's little boy half the time. She loves glitter and sparkles and girlie stuff, but all she has is plain shorts and T-shirts. I try to at least put ribbons in her hair so she looks like a girl, but she always pulls them out." She looked over at me. "You don't think it was wrong of me to take the money, do you?"

"No, not at all! You need that money for your little girl. I don't fault you at all." And I didn't. My mother had been a single parent, too. She'd been lucky enough to live with my grandparents and rely partly on them, but she still needed every penny she could get, to keep me clothed and fed. I didn't judge any single mother's efforts to care for her child.

She sighed and gave me a halfhearted smile. "I think he was gambling," she said.

"Like casinos?"

"Sports. That was his thing. He understood sports. He could have been a professional athlete, I think, if he'd made some different choices."

"Do you think his…" I paused, not wanting to say the word *murder*, "his death was related to the gambling?"

"I don't know," she said, her voice barely over a whisper. The subject seemed hard for her to talk about, but at the same time, she seemed to want to vent. She probably hadn't had much of a chance over the past week to really talk about her feelings. "There was a guy at the gym…" she started before trailing off.

"He was having a problem with someone?"

"I don't know. Joey would never admit that he was having a problem or that he couldn't handle something. I worried about him kickboxing, though."

"You were afraid he'd get hurt?"

She shrugged. "That, yeah. And it was so violent. I know it's all supposed to be very controlled and all, but some of the guys he fought were kind of scary. I mean, Joey knew it wasn't personal, but I didn't know about some of those guys. There was this one guy Joey fought a couple of months ago, and I don't know what happened, because I never really understood how the kickboxing worked, like how much they were supposed to beat each other up and when they stopped the fight and all, but Joey just beat the guy to a pulp—broke his nose and everything. It scared me that Joey could hurt someone like that, but the guy, he's just a thug. And he was mad at Joey for beating him up like that."

"Do you think he could have done something to… to hurt Joe?" It occurred to me that I might have another suspect.

"I don't know." Melissa's voice was breaking. "Maybe. I don't want to think about it, but I'm afraid he might have."

"Do you know his name?" I asked.

She shook her head. "No," she said, practically in a whisper. "Joey didn't talk about it very much. I only heard about it in the first place because I overheard him telling someone about it on the phone. When I asked, he refused to tell me anything except that he was fine and there was nothing for me to worry about. I hate to think

—" She cut herself off, apparently not wanting or finding herself able to say more.

I reached out and rubbed her arm to try to comfort her. She was practically a stranger, but I felt for her and what she was going through. She stared at Emmy and Latte, who were now chasing each other playfully in circles.

"It's good to see her having fun," she said softly. "She's been around a bunch of sad adults all week."

"Latte seems like he's having a lot of fun, too."

"His name's Latte?" Melissa asked with a smile.

"Yeah, I figured he was the right color."

"It's a great name," she said.

"Maybe we could get them together to play again sometime," I suggested. They really did seem to be having fun together. And even though I'd only known her for a little while, I felt I could be friends with Melissa.

"Yeah, that would be great!" A big smile spread across her face, and I could tell she genuinely liked the idea and wasn't just agreeing to it to appease me.

I glanced at the time on my phone and realized Latte and I had to get going so I could make it to work on time. Much to Emmy's dismay, I called Latte over and put his leash back on. I shoved the drool-coated tennis ball back in my pocket even though I knew I would regret that later. At least that was better than carrying it the whole way.

"Bye-bye, Emmy!" I said as Latte and I started toward the gate. A thought crossed my mind just before I walked out.

"Hey, Melissa," I called back to her. "Do you know Todd, the guy who owns the gym?"

Her previously bright face darkened. "Yes. Why?"

I realized I needed to be cautious. "I graduated high school with him. I know he owns the gym, so I thought I'd ask."

Melissa walked over to me and lowered her voice. "You know how I said I didn't really like Joey kickboxing?"

I nodded.

"Todd encouraged it. Todd filled Joey's head with the idea he could be really successful at it and make a living off of it. Joey would have quit a long time ago and focused on his night classes if Todd hadn't filled his head with all that nonsense. I told him right before he died— that night that he brought over the money—that I wanted him to stop, and I think he was going to. I think he was going to quit the night that he died. I don't know if he did or not, but I know Todd wouldn't have been happy about it. I don't know if Todd did something directly or indirectly to get Joey killed, but he wouldn't have been at that gym if Todd hadn't encouraged it. And if he hadn't been at the gym, he wouldn't have died. Maybe it's not fair, but I hold Todd responsible. I absolutely believe that if not for Todd, Joey would be here today."

I could tell by the fire in Melissa's face that she believed every word and believed so strongly I had to reevaluate my confidence in Todd's innocence.

Chapter 18

SAMMY WAS WORKING with Rhonda at the café when I got in. Rhonda was a housewife in her late thirties who worked with us a few hours a week, mostly so she could say she had a job and so she could have a little pocket money to finance an occasional trip to the Neiman Marcus up in Boston. Generally, she worked while her kids were in school, so we hadn't seen much of her over the summer, but her husband was on his annual golf trip, and her kids were at their grandma's for the week, so she was picking up some extra hours. I also suspected she had her eye on something that cost a little more than two hours of work could pay for.

"Hello, ladies!" I said as I slipped my apron over my head and tied it. "How's everything been today?"

"Slow!" they both replied.

"That bad, huh?"

Sundays were always slow. We got a rush first thing in the morning and then around lunch, but other than that, Sundays were like a faucet that was turned down to a drip.

"Yes," Sammy said emphatically. "We were just debating which one of us should go home. I said Rhonda should go home and enjoy her quiet house—"

"But I told her that Louboutins don't pay for themselves," Rhonda interrupted.

So I was right—she did have her eye on something. Still, I wrinkled my nose at her mention of Louboutins.

"Prada makes lovely shoes," I said. "They have some really great ones in their fall collection." Thanks to my mother and grandmother, I was an exclusive purchaser of Italian leather. Growing up, I'd heard them extoll the virtues of the grain, the finish, and the stitching on shoes and bags made in Italy. It was so ingrained in me, I'd never been tempted by the ubiquitous shoes made by Christian Louboutin while I lived in New York.

"But Prada doesn't have those red soles!" Rhonda moaned. Her eyes were obviously already envisioning what it would be like for everyone to see that flash of red when she crossed her legs.

"You know the red wears off, right?" I asked.

"Yeah, but you can get them repaired. I think they even sell paint kits for you to do it yourself."

"If I paid that much for a pair of shoes, I don't think I'd be taking a paintbrush to them. Pay a professional for that," Sammy said.

"Or just buy Prada. Or Fendi. Or Ferragamo," I suggested.

"Nope, gotta be the Louboutins," Rhonda said.

Apparently, there was just no beating the allure of the scarlet soles of those shoes. Even I had to admit they looked nice, even if I wasn't interested in owning a pair myself.

"How about you both stay," I said. "At least for a little bit. I need taste testers. I've figured out what kind of tea drinks I think I want to add to the menu, but I want someone else's opinion first, to make sure I'm not the only one who likes them."

"All right, let's go!" Rhonda said enthusiastically. I knew she was more excited about the extra money she'd get for sticking around than she was about trying the new drinks.

"Sammy?" I asked.

"I'm in."

I went into the back and unloaded the box of tea and supplies I'd brought with me, arranging everything in the order necessary to prepare the drinks. I grabbed one of the French presses and the tin of Earl Grey tea and took them out front.

"So what are we having?" Sammy asked. She and

Rhonda had gone around to the customer side of the counter, apparently looking forward to the experience of being waited on instead of doing the serving.

I measured out enough tea for three small drinks and dumped it into the center of the French press. I figured that if we were going to be sampling several drinks, we didn't need full-size helpings of each. I poured boiling water from the espresso machine into the press and closed the lid. After all my research and testing, I had come to the conclusion that black tea tasted best when the water was at a full boil when the steeping began. I glanced at the digital clock we used as a timer, to make sure I got the steeping time just right for my sample drinks.

"We are having a drink called a London Fog," I said finally as I started steaming the milk. I could practically steam milk in my sleep, so talking was easier while I did that.

"Sounds fancy!" Rhonda said, clearly enticed by the mention of the cosmopolitan city.

"What's in it?" Sammy asked, more practically.

"It's basically a latte, but with tea instead of coffee," I said, looking up from my steaming with a grin.

She laughed. "So you went with something comfortable."

"Of course!" I replied.

"So is it just tea and milk? Do we do tea latte art?"

"It is tea, steamed milk, vanilla, and sugar," I said, keeping my eye on the clock, not wanting to let the tea steep too long and get bitter. "I haven't really had success with the art. I don't think the tea's the right consistency. It doesn't have the crema like espresso does. I have a couple of ideas, though." I smiled at Sammy, guessing what her reaction would be.

"Of course you do," she said predictably. "I don't know what you'd do if you couldn't do something artistic with your drinks."

"That's because Francesca is very sophisticated," Rhonda interjected. She liked to call me by my full name because she thought it sounded more refined. "And the designs she puts into lattes makes the drinks look so sophisticated."

"Thank you, Rhonda," I said pointedly. "At least somebody appreciates me."

"Oh, stop!" Sammy laughed. "You know I think you do an amazing job."

"I just wanted to hear you say it," I replied.

Sammy rolled her eyes. "Isn't it time for you to do something else with that tea?" she asked.

It was. I slowly lowered the plunger in the French press, then turned the lid to open it. I filled each of the three cups I had laid out about a quarter of the way full and then added the milk. Sammy and Rhonda leaned across the counter, watching what I was doing. Sammy, in particular, was studying the process so she'd be able to recreate it later. When the cups were halfway full, I drizzled in some vanilla extract and then topped them off with a sprinkling of sugar before stirring it all together.

"Just enough so you can get the taste of the drink." I slid the cups over in front of them. "They'll be full when we serve them for real, of course."

I watched as Sammy lifted the cup to her nose and inhaled.

Apparently deciding she approved, she started to take a sip, but abruptly stopped before the cup touched her lips. She raised an eyebrow at me. "Aren't you going to try it?"

"What? You think I'm pranking you?" I laughed.

She kept her suspicious gaze on me until I relented, rolling my eyes. I picked up my cup and took a sip. It was as delicious as a drink that wasn't coffee could be. I nodded and put it down.

"Well?" Sammy asked.

"It's good," I said. "But I already know what I think. I want to know what you think."

Sammy and Rhonda finally tried their drinks. Sammy nodded approvingly, but Rhonda's eyes lit up.

"It's really good!" Rhonda exclaimed. She quickly downed the rest of the beverage.

Sammy sipped from her cup more slowly, savoring it.

Finally, she spoke up. "I like it. I think it will be good on the menu."

"Good!" I replied, happy that my first offering had met with their approval. "On to the next!"

After all my experimenting, I had settled on the London Fog, a chai latte, and a green-tea latte. For customers who didn't want a latte, we would also serve plain hot tea. I felt those choices would provide enough variety to cater to different tastes while not adding too much bulk to the menu. I didn't want to add a ton of new products—just enough to diversify a little bit.

We went through each of the drinks and sampled them. Sammy and Rhonda had their favorites and their less-than-favorites, but overall, they agreed the selection would work well on our menu and wouldn't be any harder to fix than the drinks we already sold, which was important to them being successful. If they were great but took forever to make or were so complicated we could never get them right, no one would order them more than once, and all my effort would be for nothing.

We had only a couple of customers during the whole time we were testing drinks, so I was finally able to convince Rhonda to go home when we were done. I reminded her of how luxurious a long, hot bubble bath in a quiet house would be, and she was more than happy to go. I used the excuse that the menu board was in Sammy's handwriting to convince her to climb up and update it with the new tea drinks. I did want the board to be consistent, and I also wanted to avoid having my atrocious handwriting up there.

"Latte and I ran into Melissa and Emmy today," I told her as she wrote.

"You did?" Her tone told me she was more focused on her writing than on what I was saying. "I didn't think you knew them."

"I didn't before today. Latte and Emmy started trying to play, and when I heard her name, I realized who she was."

"Did you mention you knew me?"

"Yeah, Melissa seemed a little creeped out until I told her. I figured I should mention it to you in case you ran into her and she said something."

"Yep." She was completely absorbed by drawing a picture of a steaming cup of tea. She drew one final wisp of steam then stepped back to look at her work. "What do you think?" she asked me.

"It's pretty perfect," I replied. I was constantly in awe of Sammy's artistic skill.

"Thanks!" she chirped happily. Apparently satisfied that it was indeed pretty perfect, she climbed up the stepladder to hang the board back up.

I stood back from the counter, watching to make sure it was straight.

"Good?" she asked.

"Good."

She climbed back down.

"Do you need me to hang around, or are you good on your own?" she asked.

"Why? Do you have big plans tonight?" I teased.

She shrugged, but the blush on her cheeks told me she did.

"Ooh-ooh-ooh," I sing-songed like a middle schooler. "Hot date with Jared?"

Jared was her boyfriend, who in my opinion, had more flaws than charms, but they'd been together practically forever even though he refused to propose. His mother needed him to take care of her, he insisted.

"It's our anniversary. He said he has a surprise for me," she admitted, her blush deepening.

"A sparkly surprise?"

"I don't know. I mean..." She paused and took a breath. She'd gotten her hopes up before, I knew, and she was obviously trying to contain them to prevent disappointment. Finally, she shrugged. "A girl can hope."

"Go, then!" I urged, shooing her off.

She took off her apron, getting ready to leave, then paused. "Have you called Mike yet? About some kind of security?" She was asking for my sake since I'd be the one closing up.

I shook my head. "No, not yet." I cast a glance

around the empty café. "But if it stays this busy, I may do it today."

"You should," Sammy said earnestly. "But, either way, be careful going home."

"I will," I assured her. "Now go. Get out. Go get all dolled up for your date. And have fun!" I was practically pushing her out the door, knowing she'd linger forever if I didn't.

"Okay." She laughed. "I'll see you tomorrow!"

"Bye!" I replied, waving her away. I watched her trip off down the sidewalk and then went back inside to find something in the vacant coffee shop to occupy myself with. It was only after she'd disappeared from view that I remembered wanting to ask her if she knew the name of the guy whose nose Joe had broken. I made a mental note to ask her the next day—about that and about her anniversary date.

Chapter 19

THE REST of that day was predictably slow, but the next day was surprisingly busy. We were never that busy on Mondays, but that day, we were slammed. Sammy actually called me to come in early because it was so hectic. I could pretend that word had gotten out about the new items on the menu and people were flocking in to get them, but it was far more likely that the weather was driving them in, actually. The day was gray and on the cool side, not exactly ideal beach weather.

The new drinks were as popular as anything else on the menu. Sammy had added them to the chalkboards out front and on the counter so people would notice we had them. Most of the people who came in were tourists and didn't know that the tea lattes were new, but a few locals came in and tried them over their regular drinks.

They all seemed pretty pleased with their orders, and I was glad I had chosen the ones I had. I made a mental note to e-mail Rose Howard, the Englishwoman who had given me the idea to enhance our tea offerings, to let her know we would be much better prepared the next time she came in.

Things were blessedly slowing down, though still busy, when Jack walked in, dressed as much like a stereotypical tourist as ever.

"Hi, Jack!" I called to him as I glanced up from my place behind the counter. "I got that tea added to the menu."

"I saw that," he replied in his thick Southern accent. "Which one do you recommend?"

"My favorite's the Earl Grey—the London Fog—but Rhonda has her own thoughts." I nodded at Rhonda standing at the cash register.

"Oh my God, the chai! It's amazing!" she gushed.

Jack laughed as he approached the register. "How about I try one of each?"

"You may as well get all three, then," Rhonda suggested. "Try the full range."

Jack laughed again, at her not-so-subtle attempt to upsell him. "Sure, why not?"

"Let me know what you think," I urged him.

"Don't worry, I will." He smiled.

Sammy and I set about preparing the drinks as

Rhonda took the next order.

I was a little disappointed that, after he finished his drinks, he left without telling me what he thought of them. I hoped he'd be back sometime so I could ask his opinion. He seemed like something of a connoisseur of coffee and cafés, so I figured that I could please anyone if I could please him.

"Wasn't he here last week?" Sammy asked quietly as he walked out the door. "The day they found Joe's body?"

"Yeah." I nodded as I worked on preparing a customer's drink.

"That's a long stay for a tourist."

I shrugged as I handed her a cup to take out to the table we'd been preparing drinks for. "He said he's spending the summer travelling along the New England coast. I guess he just liked us enough to stay for a while."

Sammy seemed to accept my answer and took the drinks out to the waiting customers. We worked on steadily for a couple more hours until Rhonda had to leave so she could get a shower and get ready to go out to dinner with a friend. Fortunately, traffic in and out of the café had slowed down even more, and Sammy and I were able to handle it with no problem. In fact, I was getting ready to send her home when the bell over the door jingled and a slightly overweight middle-aged man in a warm-up jacket came in. I felt he looked familiar—

an older version of someone I used to know—but I couldn't be sure whether he was actually someone I used to know or his father.

Sammy immediately greeted him warmly. "Hi, Coach Snyder!"

As soon as she said it, I remembered him. Steve Snyder had been the baseball coach and history teacher at Cape Bay High School for as long as I could remember. In a small town like ours, the varsity sports coaches were local celebrities. Everyone knew them and called them "Coach" whether they'd gone to the high school or not.

"Hi, Coach," I said.

"Hi, Sammy. Hi, Franny," Coach replied as he approached the counter. His tone was subdued, and I wondered if everything was okay. I was about to ask when Sammy spoke up.

"How's retirement treating you, Coach?"

"You know, it's not as easy as I thought it would be," he replied. "I'm used to spending summers writing football plays and checking in on my players, not piddling around, looking for things to do."

Sammy nodded sympathetically. "I can imagine that's difficult." She paused, tipped her head down, and leaned toward him. "And Joe. That must be hard for you, too."

Coach tensed as though someone had punched him.

He closed his eyes and swallowed hard. When he finally opened his eyes, he nodded. "Yes," he said hoarsely. "I don't… Joe was a good kid. Back when I coached him, I thought he had a good chance to make it as a ballplayer. I still can't believe—" He broke off and shook his head. "He was a good kid."

Sammy and I waited quietly while he composed himself. A week wasn't much time to process a sudden death. Sammy still had her moments when she had to pause and take a deep breath, and Melissa had certainly still been deeply emotional. My heart went out to him.

"Well," he said finally. "I didn't come here to make two young ladies feel sorry for an old man. I came here to get something to eat. Let me get a…" He took a moment to scan the menu, rubbing his hand absently as he scanned its offerings. "I'll take a tea and a tiramisu."

"What kind of tea would you like?" Sammy asked.

Coach stared at her blankly.

"We have Earl Grey, chai, and—"

"I just want a regular iced tea," Coach interrupted.

Sammy looked at me.

"I'll take care of it," I said quickly. I hadn't planned for anyone ordering iced tea, although I should have. For the moment, I decided to just make a strong Earl Grey tea and pour it over ice. If it tasted good, that's what I would plan on doing every day. At least we could make iced tea ahead of time and serve it throughout the day.

My plan seemed to work out well enough. Coach did declare the beverage "different," but that was to be expected since Earl Grey isn't typically used for iced tea. Still, he drank it all down without complaint, and I considered it a success. In the hope that the tea would be good, I'd used my large, fifty-ounce French press to make the tea, so I poured it out into a pitcher and put it into the refrigerated case to chill.

"Sammy?" I gave her a charming smile.

"Yes?" she replied, knowing I was about to ask her to do something.

"Could you add *iced* tea to the menu for me?"

She laughed brightly at my second request for an update in as many days. Before that, I didn't think she'd had to make any changes to it in months, perhaps longer. "Of course, Franny. I'd be happy to," she said, her tone making it clear that she had seen my question coming.

She went and got her chalk and added the words "iced tea" to the menu.

"If you keep adding stuff, we're going to have to get another board," she commented as she drew. She was filling in an empty space at the bottom of the board with a remarkably lifelike picture of a glass of iced tea.

"Stop acting like you wouldn't love having more space to draw," I retorted.

"You got me." She added a small spot of white chalk to one of the ice cubes and declared her work finished.

A customer who had been lingering in an armchair got up and left, leaving Sammy and me alone in the café for the first time all afternoon.

"So, how was your anniversary surprise?" I asked as soon as the door closed behind the woman.

Sammy's previously cheery countenance turned to a scowl. "Go-karts. My big surprise was go-karts."

"For your anniversary?"

"Yup. And surprise, surprise, heels aren't the best footwear for driving them."

I nodded, seeing how that would be a problem.

"Jared had fun anyway." She shrugged.

"So no sparkly jewelry?"

"No sparkly jewelry."

I decided to abandon being a neutral observer. "Why are you still with him?" I asked.

Sammy turned her big blue eyes to mine. "Because I love him."

I returned her gaze for a moment, gauging her sincerity. "Well, I can't argue with that," I said finally.

We spent the next several minutes cleaning up everything we'd failed to attend to during the rush. It wasn't that things were dirty or messy—the health inspector still would have passed us easily—but they weren't quite up to our standards.

I was putting some clean towels away in a cabinet in the back room when I turned suddenly and smacked my nose on the cabinet's open door. It hurt, but it also reminded me of something I wanted to ask Sammy.

Holding a paper towel to the nick on my nose, I went out front to where Sammy was scrubbing down the counter.

"Are you okay?" she asked.

"Yeah, just hit my nose on the cabinet door."

Sammy shook her head.

"But, speaking of noses, do you know anything about Joe Davis breaking some guy's nose in a kickboxing match a couple of months back?"

"Not a thing," she said, giving the counter one last swipe with her rag. "Do you need anything else before I get out of here?" She had opened the café that morning, as she did most mornings, and had by then put in more than her time for the day.

I looked over at the clock. "Actually, could you hang out for another half hour or so? I need to run home and let Latte out real quick since I came in so early."

"Not a problem," Sammy said. "And if it stays this busy, the place will be spick-and-span by the time you get back."

"An added benefit." I smiled. I took off my apron and grabbed my purse from the back. "I shouldn't be long." I hurried out and down the street. The break would give me time to think about where else I might be able to find out who Joe had beaten up.

Chapter 20

I ONLY FIGURED it out late the next day, although not through my own ingenuity.

I was alone in the café when Todd came in.

"Hey, Franny," he called as he walked through the door.

"Hi, Todd," I called back. "What can I do for you today?"

"Is your iced tea sweetened?"

"Does this look like Mississippi?" I joked. "I can add sweetener for you if you'd like, but otherwise it's unsweetened."

"A glass of tea then, please." Todd seemed to be in a much better mood than he had been the past few times I'd seen him.

"Not a problem," I replied. I grabbed a glass, filled it

with ice, and poured the tea I'd made earlier in the day over it. As it turned out, iced tea was more popular than I'd expected, and I was already on the third pitcher. I wondered why we'd never put it on the menu before. Tradition, I supposed. "Can I get you anything else?"

"How about dinner?" he asked, leaning across the counter toward me.

I stared at him, completely confused. "Well, we have mozzarella-tomato-basil sandwiches and a tomato salad, but other than those, unless you want a piece of tiramisu or a—"

"How about you come out to dinner with me?" Todd corrected, interrupting me.

"Oh," I said as it was the only thing I could think to say. I thought for a few seconds, debating whether to accept. Matt wouldn't be getting back until the next day, so I didn't have any other plans for dinner. I didn't want Todd to get the impression that I had a romantic interest in him, but he'd asked if I would go out, not if he could take me out, so that might not have even crossed his mind. Finally, I realized that he was sure to know who had been in that kickboxing match gone wrong. "Sure. I don't close up for a couple of hours yet—is it okay if we have a late dinner?"

"Of course!" He grinned. "How about I come back by for you then?"

"Sounds good," I replied.

He drank his tea down quickly, a skill I guessed he had picked up over years of chugging beer.

"That's good," he said, setting the glass down on the counter. He headed for the door, his long legs carrying him quickly across the room. "I'll see you soon!" he called just as he went out the door.

I waved idly at his back. The way he had appeared in the café, invited me to dinner, and disappeared all within five minutes had thrown me off balance. Had he come in just to ask me to dinner? Or had he come in to get something to drink and suggested dinner on the spur of the moment? Whichever it was, it seemed strange. I distracted myself from thinking about it by remembering that I could use the opportunity to ask him not just about the man whose nose Joe broke, but also about some of the other things Melissa had mentioned to me as we talked in the park.

I worked my way around the café, straightening things up so I could leave quickly when Todd came back. I felt as though I was forever wiping down tables, adjusting chairs, and washing dishes, but I supposed that was to be expected. I checked the display cases to make sure they were fully stocked for the next morning, grateful Monica had insisted in bringing a fresh delivery of tiramisu each day—it had continued to sell stunningly well. A couple of customers came in and lingered over cups of coffee before heading back out into the night.

I was wondering where Todd was and was getting ready to lock up when he burst through the door.

"Hey, Franny. You ready to go?"

"Yup. Just about," I replied. I looked around to make sure everything was in order and ready for Sammy to hit the ground running in the morning. Satisfied that everything was in good shape, I took off my apron and grabbed my purse and keys. "Do you mind if we run by my house real quick so I can feed the dog and let him out?"

"I didn't know you had a dog."

"Yup. Just got him a few months ago."

"Sweet. I love dogs."

We stepped outside onto the sidewalk, and I locked up.

"My car's right here." He gestured to a dark-blue convertible muscle car pulled up to the curb. It was a cool 1960's-era car, probably something recognizable to someone who knew more about cars than I did.

I was surprised to see that he'd driven. "Where are we going to eat?" I asked, thinking it must be someplace out of town.

"I thought we'd go to the Mexican place down on the beach. Do you like that place? They have great food there."

"I love that place," I said, wondering why he'd driven his car if that was as far as we were going, but I guessed maybe he didn't think I would want to walk, or maybe he'd driven somewhere else before coming back by. I didn't remember having seen his car when he'd been at the café earlier in the day, but I hadn't really been looking, either. As we got in the car, I thought of yet another possibility—perhaps Todd, too, was conscious of there still being no arrest in Joe's murder. Perhaps Todd was even afraid he might be in danger as well.

Todd revved the engine higher than he needed to and pulled the car away from the curb, making a U-turn in the middle of the street to direct it toward my house. I knew some girls liked it when guys showed off their cars like that, but just as I didn't know one old car from another, I didn't know why revving engines and squealing tires were appealing.

The trip to my house was quick in the car. I was surprised I didn't have to give Todd a single direction on the way there.

"How did you know where I live?" I asked as we pulled into my driveway.

"Same place as in high school," Todd said.

"You knew where I lived back when we were in high school?"

"Course I did," he replied, climbing out of the car. He was almost to the front door by the time I made it out of my seat. I scurried to catch up.

Latte burst through the door as soon as I opened it,

first prancing around our feet and then sniffing Todd intently. I went ahead inside and scooped Latte's food into his bowl. The sound of the bits of kibble falling into the ceramic bowl drew him away from Todd, and he rushed into the kitchen to gobble down his dinner. Todd followed him in.

"Haven't gotten around to redecorating yet, huh?"

"Nope, not yet," I replied. "I'm hoping to be able to spend a little more time on it after the season ends."

"You should. It looks like an old person lives here instead of a beautiful, eligible bachelorette."

I wasn't sure whether I should be offended or flattered, so I laughed his remark off without comment.

"Latte, let's go outside. M—" I cut myself off before referring to myself as "Mommy" in front of Todd. "I'm going out for a little bit." Latte ran back outside and then back in. "We'll go for a walk when I get back, okay?" I said as I closed the door behind me.

"You should be careful walking alone late at night," Todd warned. "You don't know what kind of creeps could be out roaming the streets. A defenseless woman like you would be an easy target."

"I'm not defenseless," I retorted, bristling at his implication. "I lived in New York for years, remember? I know how to take care of myself."

"Yeah, but Joe was a semipro kickboxer, and you know what happened to him."

The way Todd said it made me uneasy, and I was tired of being uneasy, of being always on edge as I wondered who had killed Joe and if it was random and if the guy was still out there. I needed to buckle down and get serious about finding out who was responsible for Joe's death. The time for just poking around was over.

We got into his car, which he drove slowly down the residential street.

"Have you heard anything else from the police?" I asked.

"Old Mikey keeps coming around, making sure I haven't skipped town or anything, but I think he's out of evidence. He's not asking any new questions. Just the same old ones: 'You haven't thought of anyone who can corroborate your story, have you?' 'Has anything come to mind about someone who might have had a grudge against Joe?' I'm getting tired of it. I practically ignore him when he shows up now."

"That doesn't seem like it's the best way to get him on your side."

"Whatever." He scoffed. "I don't even care anymore. Mike can think whatever he wants."

"Even if he thinks you murdered Joe?"

"Nothing I can do to stop him."

I stared at him in stunned silence. If I had been accused of murder, I would do everything in my power to fight it. I'd present every shred of evidence I could find to prove my innocence. There's no way I'd just shrug my shoulders and say the police could think whatever they wanted. Unless, maybe—and I could hardly conceive of it—unless I actually did it.

I stared out the windshield at the orangey-yellow streetlights flickering by as we drove down Main Street. It was the first time I'd really entertained the thought that Todd might be guilty. When I thought about it, it made sense. He had the motive—Joe's months-overdue gym dues. He had the means and the opportunity—he knew better than anybody that the corner of the parking lot where Joe was killed was the poorest lit, that teenagers left their old broken beer bottles there, and that the security-camera system was down. He had a stereotypically bad alibi—home alone, watching TV. Despite the heat, I felt a chill go down my spine.

I might've been sitting in a car with a murderer.

Chapter 21

WE SAT across from each other at a table on the patio overhanging the water. It was late enough that we were the only ones there. Eating there with Matt had been romantic, but I felt uneasy, even afraid, sitting there with Todd. Even though I knew I was being dramatic, I was grateful for the screen enclosing the porch—if Todd tried to throw me into the ocean, I would leave a me-sized hole in the screen for the police to find. I looked around to find any security cameras, hopefully ones that worked.

"What are you looking for?" Todd asked.

"Just looking around," I said quickly.

"Seemed like you were looking for something."

I shrugged. "Nope, just looking around."

Todd seemed to believe me, because he went back to looking at his menu.

I wasn't sure that he had murdered Joe, but I knew this was my chance to find out. We were alone but in a fairly public place. He couldn't do anything to hurt me there, and if he did, plenty of people would hear me scream. It was now or never, but I couldn't just ask him outright. I had to work my way up to it.

"So, I ran into Joe's ex-girlfriend Melissa the other day."

He didn't take his nose out of the menu. "You did, huh?"

"Yeah, at the park. I was there with Latte, and he wanted to play with her little girl—"

"Wait, your latte wanted to play with Emmy?" He looked at me as if he thought I had lost my mind.

"Yeah, and—"

"How does a latte play with a child?"

"No, not *a* latte. Latte. My dog."

"Your dog's name is Latte?" he asked.

"Yeah."

"Huh," he grunted and looked back down at his menu.

I was sure I had said Latte's name in front of Todd earlier at the house, but maybe he had just missed it. "Anyway, I ran into Melissa, and we got to talking, and she said that—"

"I didn't know you knew Melissa," Todd said, interrupting me yet again.

"I didn't," I said, trying to hide my annoyance. "I just met her the other day."

"Oh."

I glared at the top of Todd's head as he continued studying the menu.

"*Anyway*," I repeated, hoping I could finish what I was trying to say that time. "She and I got to talking, and she mentioned that Joe had broken some guy's nose in a kickboxing match a couple of months ago."

"Yeah," Todd chuckled. "Dave Dean. Dude's big and slow. I don't know why he wanted to fight Joe. He knew he'd lose."

"Melissa said that Dave was upset about losing. Like he might do something to try to get back at Joe?"

"You're asking if I think Dave could have killed Joe? I just told you that he's big and slow, and Joe could take him in a fight *easy*."

"Well, yeah, but Joe was stabbed."

"Not by Dave, trust me. Only way Joe let himself get stabbed like that is he didn't think the guy was a threat."

Like if it was his friend the gym owner. I had to take a different tack, though. "What if the guy was a better fighter than Joe?"

"He got stabbed, not beaten to death. Guy wouldn't have to stab him if he was winning."

He had a point there. But nothing he'd said had ruled himself out. As far as I knew, Todd wasn't a kick-boxer, so he wouldn't have been a better fighter than Joe, and he and Joe were friends, so Joe wouldn't have seen the attack coming. Todd had even ruled out my next best suspect, Dave Dean, on the basis of Joe not letting his guard down around him.

I wasn't sure where to go next with my questioning. I didn't think I should outright accuse him or ask more probing questions about Todd's potential motive just yet. I was afraid he would shut me out if I moved too fast. I had to play it cool, even if I found it nerve-wracking to think that I might be sitting across from a murderer.

Fortunately, the waitress came and saved me from having to make a decision just yet. We ordered our food, and Todd got a beer. I ordered my standard margarita. When the waitress left, I decided to ask my next question, also inspired by something Melissa had mentioned.

"Do you know if Joe gambled at all?" I asked.

Todd took a deep breath and dropped his head back to look at the ceiling. I almost thought he hadn't heard me and what I thought was his reaction was just a perfectly timed but completely unrelated action. Finally, though, he answered.

"Yeah, he did." He looked into my eyes. "Did Melissa tell you that, too?"

I nodded. I wasn't sure if he thought it was good or bad that Melissa had told me.

"I figured. You know, some guys—a lot of guys—can do it no problem. They keep to the slots or to blackjack, they play a few games, maybe lose a little money, and they walk away. Some guys who bet sports like Joe just hold off until they can get out to Vegas. Joe though, man... Joey couldn't stop himself. It wasn't something I talked to him about much, but I know he had a bookie, and you know, from some of what I heard, I think he was actually starting to make book himself."

"Make book?" I repeated. "What does that mean?"

"It means instead of him placing bets with someone else, guys were placing bets with him."

"That's illegal, isn't it?"

Todd laughed. "So is placing the bets with someone else."

"Is it dangerous?"

"If you don't have the money to pay out, it can be. The kind of money some of these guys wager on one game could pay for a year of their kids' private-school tuition. You take that bet and can't pay out, somebody's not going to be happy."

"Do you know who was making bets with Joe?" I asked. If what Todd was saying was true, and Joe had gotten in over his head, that might have been what got him killed. But that didn't do me any good unless I knew who was placing bets with him.

"No," Todd said emphatically. "I stayed out of it. I made sure he knew I didn't want that stuff going on in my gym, and then I walked away. Plausible deniability. If he ever got caught, I wasn't going down with him."

"Did you tell the cops?"

"I did. I hope they're looking into it. I guess they haven't found anything."

Another dead-end lead—at least for the time. I thought I could still find a way to figure out who else was involved in the betting, even if the cops hadn't. But that only mattered if Todd wasn't the one who killed Joe. And that was something I still had to figure out.

The waitress brought out our drinks. As I sipped my margarita, I thought about how I could bring the conversation back around to Todd himself and his involvement, or lack thereof, in Joe's murder. My fingers danced on the stem of my glass as I thought.

"You all right there?" Todd asked. "You look a little anxious."

I looked up from my glass at him, sitting across from me. His deep-blue eyes met mine unflinchingly. I was struck by the sadness there that I hadn't noticed before. I wondered whether Joe's death or maybe the investigation was getting to him—or perhaps I was seeing his regret over having killed Joe.

"I'm okay. Are you?" I asked, hoping my tone conveyed a genuine question, not idle small talk.

It must have worked. His eyes held mine for a moment longer and then turned down to his beer bottle. "It's been a rough week," he said hoarsely.

"You've had a lot to deal with," I agreed.

"You don't even know. The girl I was seeing broke it off with me because she said it was too stressful knowing the cops are investigating me."

"That's kind of..." I paused, searching for the right word. "Crummy of her. I didn't even realize you were dating anyone. It's too bad you weren't with her the night of the murder."

He looked up at me, his face utterly stricken.

"Oh my God, you were! Why didn't you tell me? Have you told the police?"

"No." He looked back down at the table.

"Why on earth not?"

"I didn't... I wanted to protect her."

"But Todd, you're being investigated for murder! What could you possibly be protecting her from that's worth a murder charge?"

"I never thought it would go this far. I thought they would've figured out who really did it by now and it wouldn't matter."

"But it has gone this far," I exclaimed. "You have to tell them."

"I can't. I can't do that to her! I promised!"

"So what? She already broke up with you. What's going to happen if you tell the police you were with her?"

"I don't know… I mean, I don't want…" he stammered. "Her parents—"

"Wait, what?" I interrupted. "Her *parents*? She's not a teenager, is she? Please tell me she's out of high school." I thought of Becky and Amanda, the high schoolers who worked for me at the café, and prayed that the girl wasn't either of them—and also, if it was, that they hadn't met Todd in the café. I'd feel so guilty.

"She's out of high school," he said. "She's nineteen."

"Well, at least there's that." I shook my head and took another sip of my margarita. Suddenly, something clicked. I caught my breath. "It's Karli, isn't it? You're dating Karli." It made so much sense—Todd's enthusiasm for Karli's work, her distress at the repeated police business.

Todd hung his head. "I *was*," he muttered.

I didn't know what to say. She was so… young. And, in comparison, Todd and I were not. Todd was practically old enough to be her father, if he'd been a teen dad. Finally, I managed to focus my brain on the critical issue, Todd's alibi. I took a deep breath.

"So the issue was that you were afraid of her parents finding out that she was with you that night?"

Todd nodded. "She told them she was at a girl-friend's."

"Did they not like you two seeing each other, or did you just not want them to find out?" I asked, momentarily distracted again by the sordid details of Todd dating a teenager.

"They had an idea that we were going out, and her dad especially made it clear that he didn't like it. He didn't like that I'm closer to his age than to hers."

I bit my tongue to keep from muttering what I was thinking, which was *No kidding.* When I thought of something more polite to say, I spoke.

"Her parents don't have to know just because you tell the police. She's over eighteen. She can talk to the police without telling her parents a thing about it."

"I don't know... I mean—" Todd started.

"Todd! This is your *life.* You have to tell them. Now, whether they believe you or not since you've been lying to them all this time, I don't know. I mean, it's not like you have a hotel receipt or anything to prove you were out of town."

Todd dropped his head to stare at the table again.

"You're not serious," I said. "You have a receipt? Why didn't you just show it to them? You could have gotten yourself off the suspect list a long time ago."

"It has charges for room service," he replied. "The

cops would've known I was there with somebody and wanted to talk to her."

"This is ridiculous." I buried my face in my hands and wondered if, despite Todd's apparent business prowess, the dumb-jock stereotype was true and he just really didn't understand what was at stake here and how weak his excuses were. I didn't want to debate it anymore. If Todd was going to act like a child, I was going to treat him like one. "Todd, this is outright ridiculous. You have to go to the police. Tomorrow morning, you're going to call Mike and tell him that you have new information, and you're going to take that hotel receipt and show it to him. Do you understand?"

He nodded reluctantly.

"You'll be lucky if Mike doesn't throw you in jail just for being a numbskull."

He nodded again. The waitress brought out our food, providing me with a convenient distraction from continually mulling over Todd's stupidity.

"You know," Todd said after a couple of bites, "I could really use a woman like you in my life—someone who doesn't take any nonsense, someone with a good head on her shoulders, someone my age."

Fifteen years ago, I would have given my right arm to hear him say that. But now? After the conversation we'd just had?

"Thank you, Todd. I take that as a compliment. But it's not going to happen."

"What? Why not?" His face had a sad-puppy-dog look on it that even a few hours before might have set me weak in the knees but presently held no sway over me. I got the sense that he didn't have much experience getting turned down.

I shook my head. "I just don't think we're right for each other."

"It's Matt, isn't it?" he asked. "I've heard you and him have a little bit of a thing going. Maybe if that goes south…"

I put aside my surprise that there were rumors about Matt and me going around Cape Bay—it was a small town, so what did I expect?—and focused on making sure he knew my rejection wasn't about Matt—not really, anyway.

"You're just not the right guy for me, Todd. A good friend, yes, but I'm not interested in you romantically."

Todd looked glumly at his plate. "Well, if you ever change your mind…"

"Thank you, but I don't think I will."

We focused on eating for the next few minutes and slowly picked up a conversation that was mercifully unrelated to Joe Davis or my romantic inclinations. When we were finished, Todd paid because he said he "owed it to me for smacking some sense into him." I wasn't going to argue with that.

When we got back to my place, he parked his car in the driveway and walked me up to the door.

"Thank you, Franny, for helping me realize I needed to tell the cops the truth." He reached down and enveloped me in a warm hug, holding me close for longer than strictly necessary before slowly letting me go. "I guess I'll see you around."

"Yeah, since you won't be getting thrown in jail for murder now."

"Hopefully, Mike isn't too hard on me for holding out on him for so long."

"I'm sure he'll be fair with you."

"All right, well, I'd better get going. Bye, Franny." Todd headed down my front walk and hopped into his car. It roared to life, and Todd backed it out of the driveway.

As it disappeared down the street, I heard footsteps coming toward me from across the neighbor's lawn. Every muscle in my body tensed as I tried to figure out if I could get the door unlocked and get inside before whoever it was could get to me.

Chapter 22

THE FIGURE CAME into the light, and I saw with relief that it was Matt, home early from his business trip. I tensed up again as soon as I realized what he must have just seen.

"Franny? Were you just on a date with Todd?"

"Matt," I exclaimed. "I thought you weren't getting back until tomorrow."

"So you figured it would be a good time to go out on a date with Todd?" Matt asked.

"No, that's not what it was—"

"Really? It's not? Because I could see you pretty clearly in the porch light there, and that hug looked pretty cozy."

"Well, yeah, but—"

"But what?"

"But it wasn't a date!"

"Then what was it?"

"Todd just asked me to go to dinner with him."

"So it was a date."

In the spirit of the evening, I realized that it was utterly ridiculous for us to be standing in my front yard after ten o'clock at night, debating whether or not my dinner with Todd qualified as a date. I heaved a sigh. "Just come inside, okay?"

I unlocked the door and pushed it open for Matt to go in. Latte, of course, came rushing out, eager both to greet me and Matt and to empty his bladder. When he'd completed the latter, I called him back inside and shut the door behind the three of us.

Matt was standing in my living room, arms folded across his chest, looking rather unhappy.

"It wasn't a date," I said.

He just looked at me, silently daring me to convince him.

I walked into the living room and flicked the light on so we weren't standing in darkness. I sat down on the couch and motioned for Matt to join me. He instead sat down in an armchair off to the side.

"Todd came into the café today and asked me if I wanted to go get dinner tonight," I said.

Matt's glower didn't change.

"I said yes because I didn't see why not. I thought

you were out of town"—Matt started to say something, but I raised my hand to stop him so I could finish —"which meant I didn't have any plans, and I had some new leads I wanted to ask him about. It seemed like a good opportunity. And it was. I got a lot of good information."

"All of which makes Todd look completely innocent, I'm sure."

"Actually, on our way over to dinner, he had me pretty convinced that he was guilty."

"I take it that didn't last," he said snidely.

"Well, no, not after he admitted he had an alibi."

"'Admitted?' Having an alibi isn't something people usually 'admit' to. They usually offer it up the first time the police so much as look at them."

"Yeah, well, Todd's kind of dumb, at least about this."

That got a laugh out of Matt.

"Yeah," I said. "He even has a receipt to prove where he was."

Matt's eyes widened in amazement. "And why didn't he tell the police this?"

"Because," I said then paused for dramatic effect, "his teenage girlfriend didn't want her parents to find out she was with him and not at her friend's house."

Matt stared at me open-mouthed for a few seconds, as incapable of processing what I'd just told him as I had been when Todd told me earlier in the evening. Then the look changed. "It's not—" he started then stopped. "You don't know her name, do you?"

I nodded, not sure why he was asking. "Karli."

He closed his eyes briefly and shook his head. "You've got to be kidding me."

"You know her?" I asked.

"The receptionist at Todd's Gym, right?"

"Yes, but how do you know her?"

Matt shrugged. "I've been going to the gym some."

"You have?" I asked, incredulous.

"Yeah, you know, I figured it would be good for me to get in shape some. That and I figured I might be able to pick up some gossip about what happened to Joe."

"And have you?"

"Actually, yeah. Apparently, he was pretty deep into betting on sports."

"That's what I heard, too!" I exclaimed. "Joe's ex-girlfriend Melissa and Todd both told me that he was involved in it. Melissa told me that a couple of days before he died, he came and gave her two thousand dollars. He didn't say where he got it, but she was guessing it was gambling money."

"He must have won pretty big to have gotten that kind of money out of it."

"Todd said he thought Joe was starting to take bets himself, from other people."

"I heard that too," Matt confirmed. "Somebody would have had to win *really* big to have made Joe that much money."

"Any idea who?" I asked.

"Not a clue."

We sat there for a few minutes, and I thought about whether there was anything else I knew that I needed to share with Matt. I assumed he was thinking along the same lines until he spoke up.

"I'm sorry I accused you of going on a date with Todd," he said.

"Yeah, what was with that?" I asked. "That was weird."

Matt shrugged and looked at the carpet. "I just don't like the idea of you going out with him."

"Even as friends?"

"No, friends is fine. I mean, as long as he knows that's all it is."

"Trust me, he knows."

Matt looked at me with an eyebrow raised, obviously questioning my assertion.

"He knows, Matty," I repeated firmly.

"But what about you, Franny?" He moved from the armchair over to the couch, beside me.

"Well, I'm the one who told him, so yeah, I think I know." My lips twitched as I held back a smile.

"Are you sure?"

"Yes, I'm sure."

A smile played at Matt's lips, but before he could say or do anything, Latte hopped up on the couch between us and leaned into Matt. He shoved his head under Matt's hand and snuffled until Matt started petting him.

"How are you, boy?" Matt asked Latte. "Were you good for your mommy while I was gone?"

I laughed at Matt referring to me as "Mommy." There were times that I thought Matt loved Latte every bit as much as I did, if not more.

"I thought you weren't coming back until tomorrow."

"I wasn't," Matt replied between tousles of Latte's ears. "But our last meeting of the day was canceled, and the one before it ended early, so I called the airline to see if they had any seats available on an earlier flight. And, what do you know, here I am! It'll be good to get to sleep in my own bed. Besides, I missed you."

I stared at him for a moment, scarcely believing what I'd just heard. We'd been tiptoeing around defining our relationship for several weeks, and I was pretty sure his saying he'd missed me while he was in Virginia was the closest he'd come to actually coming out and declaring his feelings for me.

"Matteo Cardosi, did you just admit that you missed me while you were gone?" I asked.

"Hmm?" Matt looked up at me innocently. "Oh, no,

I was talking to Latte." He looked back down at Latte before his smile could totally betray his feigned innocence.

Matt played with Latte for a few minutes, the two of them eventually graduating to playing fetch with a stuffed rabbit toy while my thoughts drifted back to Joe.

"So where do you think we should go next in the investigation?" I eventually asked Matt.

He fought the toy bunny away from Latte and tossed it across the room. "Well, if I were talking to anyone but you, I would say we forget about it and let the police take care of it. But since I am talking to you, I'm not sure what we do. Is the gambling thing the only lead you have?"

I nodded. "And I don't really know where to go next with that. I don't have any names or anything."

"I could try to ask around at the gym a little more," Matt offered. "See if any of the guys know anything."

"Oh, they're 'the guys' now, huh?" I teased.

"Well, they're not girls," he shot back.

"I think you talking to them will be a good plan. I'm kind of at a loss otherwise. I might try talking to Sammy, but I've been trying to keep her out of it since Joe was her friend."

Matt nodded in agreement. We were both uncomfortable knowing a murderer was on the loose, but we were fully aware of how much worse the situation was when the victim of said murderer was a loved one. He looked over at the clock on the wall and cringed when he saw the time.

"I better get going." He stood. "Just because I wasn't supposed to be back until tomorrow afternoon doesn't mean they don't expect me at the office bright and early."

I was a little disappointed that he couldn't stay longer, but I understood and knew I probably needed to get to bed before long myself. I stood up and gave Matt a hug.

"Welcome back," I said softly. "I missed you."

"Don't tell Latte, but I missed you too," he replied.

I walked him to the door and said good night.

Chapter 23

I DIDN'T TALK to Sammy at the café the next day, partly
because I couldn't quite bring myself to ask her about
her friend's gambling habit, which she may not have
even known about, and partly because the café was
steadily busy and we were never alone. The topic wasn't
something tourists would find particularly appetizing.
Eventually, work started to slow down, Sammy's shift
ended, and my chance to ask her any questions was gone
for the day.

I was alone when Coach Snyder came in again. I
wanted to thank him for inadvertently getting me to put
iced tea on the menu, but he was on his phone, seeming
rather anxious as he talked to whoever was on the other
end. I served him his tea and sandwich, took his money,
and let him sit and eat in peace.

As I worked around the café, cleaning up stray dishes and wiping down tables, I found I couldn't help but over-hear bits and pieces of Coach's conversation. I tried my best to ignore it, but every time I walked by, he was telling the person on the other end of the line something loudly enough that I couldn't help but hear it clearly and without any effort.

Coach had apparently been out of town recently and unexpectedly. Wherever he went, he sounded unhappy about how expensive it had been because he kept complaining about money he was never getting back. I sympathized with the sudden expense and wondered if he'd been able to make it to Joe's funeral. He was Joe's former coach, and I imagined he would have made it if he could.

He finally hung up and put the phone down on the table with a sigh. He rubbed his right hand anxiously.

"Everything all right there, Coach?" I asked from behind the counter as I made a fresh pitcher of tea. "You sounded a little stressed."

"You were listening?" he asked, sounding angry and alarmed at once.

I was momentarily flustered by the accusation, but I smiled politely. "I wasn't listening, no, but I could tell that you seemed upset."

"Oh, well, no, no, I'm fine," he insisted, still rubbing his hand.

"Is your hand okay?"

"Hmm? Oh, I, uh, punched a wall the other day."

I raised my eyebrows in surprise.

"When I found out about Joe," he added. "I just hate to see a waste of a young life like that."

"I definitely agree with you there."

"I need to go," Coach said, standing up quickly.

"Thanks for coming in!" I called to his back as he hurried out the door. His sudden exit seemed strange to me, and I wondered if my question about his phone call had offended him.

Over my years working at the café as I grew up, I'd learned that people were generally flattered when I showed I was paying attention to how they were carrying themselves. Whether people were happy or sad, my interest usually made them feel as though they weren't just anonymous customers. Every once in a while though, someone took it the wrong way, and I felt as though I was prying. Between his strained phone call, his hurt hand, and Joe's death, Coach Snyder seemed to have taken my question the wrong way. That bothered me, sure, but I wasn't going to spend a lot of time dwelling on it.

Business for the rest of the evening was steady but nothing I couldn't handle on my own. I served people drinks, moved them in and out, and straightened up in their wake. The time flew by, and I was pleasantly surprised when I looked up from the drink I was preparing to see Matt standing on the other side of the counter.

"Hey! What are you doing here?" I asked.

"Figured you'd want an escort home," he said. He glanced around the café. "I didn't expect it to still be this busy in here."

I looked up at the oversized wrought-iron clock on the wall and noted in surprise that it was closing time.

"I didn't even realize it was that late," I told him. "Could you go flip the sign on the door?"

I finished the drink I was working on as Matt walked back to the door and flipped it from Open to Closed. On his way back, I noted with gratitude that he picked up some dirty dishes to carry into the back.

"Thank you," I mouthed to him as we crossed paths, me on my way to deliver the final drink of the day to a customer, and him on his way to the back room with the dishes. Without my even asking, he stepped in to work right beside me, busing tables, wiping them down, and slowly making it clear to the remaining customers that it was closing time. I would never kick someone out, but I wasn't going to unnecessarily prolong my work day by not cleaning up until the last person was gone, either.

"So you work here now, huh?" I asked Matt as he joined me behind the counter after he had flipped the last of the unoccupied chairs up onto its table. I was fiddling with the espresso machine, making sure it was clean and ready for Sammy to use first thing in the morning.

"Eh, you know, gotta help where I can," he replied with a wink. He drummed his hands on the counter. "What else can I do?"

"Can you make sure the display is full with tiramisu? The fridge in the back has more if you need it."

Matt checked the display and then headed into the back room so he could restock. When he opened the refrigerator, he turned toward me, his eyes wide. "You've been holding out on me!"

I laughed and shrugged. "Monica keeps me well stocked." I saw the look in his eye and held my index finger up in warning. "Don't you even think about eating any of it, either."

Matt put a playful pout on his face but left the pieces of tiramisu in their containers.

We worked on like that, teasing each other on and off as Matt helped me get everything in order for the morning until the last customers finally trickled out. I locked the door and turned out the lights in the front of the café before heading to the back to take my place at the sink next to Matt so we could finish washing the dishes. We chatted amiably for a few minutes as he washed and I dried. I wanted to ask if he'd been to the gym and whether he'd found anything out, but I didn't want him to think I cared only about his investigative skills, so I let the conversation wander to Matt's trip and his work and funny stories from the past few days at the café before I finally brought it up.

"Did you get to talk to your boys today?" I asked.

Matt laughed. "Yes, I did get to talk to 'my boys.'"

"And?" I prompted.

"I don't know if it's all that helpful, but they did mention that one of the guys who's usually around disappeared for a few days right after Joe died. He didn't show back up until a couple days ago."

"Maybe he went on vacation?" I suggested. "It is the middle of the summer, after all."

"Well, I guess he's not really the type to just take off like that. He always makes sure everybody knows when he has something planned, like he's showing off or something. Plus, when he came back, he wouldn't talk about where he'd been. You know, the guys were just asking the way people do—'Hey, man, where you been?'—and he got all offended like they were asking him a really personal question—the color of his underwear or something. I don't know. Like I said, I don't know if it's anything useful, but it was the one thing they seemed focused on."

"So they didn't mention anything else?" I asked, feeling slightly deflated, as if my only remaining lead was about to go up in smoke.

"They did mention he was at the gym the night Joe died and that was unusual. At least, he wasn't usually up with the kickboxers. He was asking Joe about some money Joe owed him or something. It sounded like it was a lot. The guys won't come right out and say it, but it's pretty clear they think it's pretty suspicious."

"Huh," I said thoughtfully, wiping a cup with a cloth. "That might be something. Did they mention the guy's name?"

"Yeah." Matt laughed, passing me another cup. "Get this, it was Coach Snyder from high school. Remember him?"

Chapter 24

THE CUP FELL from my hands and shattered on the tile floor.

"Are you okay?" Matt asked.

I wanted to answer, but my mouth felt frozen by the chill that ran down my spine. Everything suddenly clicked into place—the money Joe had given Melissa just before he died, him having been attacked by someone he wouldn't have seen as a threat, the way Coach had reacted when Sammy mentioned Joe's death. He'd gone on an unexpected trip right after Joe died. I'd thought the cost of the trip had been what he was complaining about never getting back, but I realized the subject was the money Joe had owed him. It even explained why Coach had been rubbing his hand so much—it probably still hurt from his deadly fight with Joe.

"Franny, are you okay?" Matt asked, grabbing my shoulders and trying to catch my eye.

"Coach Snyder killed Joe."

"What? Franny, those guys are meatheads. I wouldn't take anything they say too seriously. I certainly wouldn't base a murder accusation on something they say."

"No, you don't understand," I said, finally making eye contact with him. "Coach Snyder was here. Today. And a couple of days ago. And he was really agitated both times. When Sammy mentioned Joe's murder to him, he had a physical reaction."

"That happens. Joe was on his team all through high school. He probably—"

"No, listen!" I interrupted. "He had a physical reaction and then he could barely get out a response. Today, he was on the phone when he came in, talking about how he'd had to go out of town unexpectedly and he was talking about *money*… that he'd never get back."

"Franny—"

"Joe gave Melissa two thousand dollars a couple of days before he died. Where do you think he got that money?"

"From Coach. But Franny, just because Joe gave some money to Melissa that he should have given to Coach, doesn't mean that Coach killed him."

"No, but his hand!" I explained to Matt about how Coach had been rubbing his hand as though he had hurt it, how he'd been so on edge during his phone call and angry when I asked him about it. I told him all about how Todd was absolutely confident that Joe wouldn't have seen the person who killed him as a threat. I went over every detail I had learned and observed over the last several days. By the end of it, even though I could tell he wasn't quite as certain as I was, Matt agreed with me that it seemed as though, more likely than not, Coach Snyder had killed Joe.

"We have to call Mike," I said.

"Franny, you remember what happened last time."

"Yes, but this time is different."

Matt looked at me skeptically, but I was absolutely sure it was time to tell Mike what we had found out. I had complete faith in his ability as a detective, but Matt and I had both uncovered information that we wouldn't have if we hadn't happened to be in the right places at the right times. Maybe he knew some of it—Melissa would surely have mentioned the money to him—but since Coach Snyder had been in my café only hours earlier acting nervous and angry, I was sure Mike didn't know everything.

Matt finally nodded. "Okay," he said simply, holding his hands up in surrender.

"We need to talk to him in person," I said.

"And you want to do it tonight?"

"Yes. I don't think it should wait."

Matt sighed. "Do you want to call, or do you want me to?" he asked.

I thought about it for a few seconds. Normally, I wouldn't have any issue making that kind of call, but given my recent history with Mike, I thought Matt might have been the better candidate to call him up and tell him we had important information about his case.

"You call," I said.

"All right." Matt pulled his phone out of his pocket and tapped on the screen to pull up Mike's number.

Realizing I needed to direct my nervous energy somewhere, I set about cleaning up the shattered porcelain on the floor. It would never be a functional cup again, but after being glued back together, it could join the legion of others adorning the shelves around the café.

Saving the broken dishes had been another of my grandmother's cost-saving decorating tips. She never worried too much about getting matching sets but simply bought whatever was available and recycled everything into the décor when it had completed its useful life. She thought it made customers feel better too, when they accidentally broke something, if they knew she still had a use for it. As I picked up the broken bits of ceramic and placed them carefully in a cardboard box, I kept one ear on Matt's conversation.

"Hey, Mike. How's it going?" he started. There was

the expected pause as Mike answered him. "Nothing much. I'm just here at Antonia's with Franny, and we were talking about Joe Davis's murder… Uh-huh. Uh-huh. Uh-huh. Well, listen, you know, I was talking to some of the guys at the gym today… Yeah, Todd's Gym. And anyway, when I mentioned it to Franny, it reminded her of something she'd overheard in the café, and, well, after talking it over, we both think it's something you should hear. Uh-huh. Uh-huh. Thirty minutes? Okay, sure. Okay, see you then. Bye."

"Mike won't be here for half an hour?" I asked. I was antsy and wanted to tell him what I'd figured out right then, not in thirty minutes. I wondered whether it would be faster to meet him at his house or the police station. But I was also a little nervous about leaving the café. Whether it was logical or not, I was nervous that Coach Snyder might have thought I'd overheard enough of his phone call that he was lurking outside, waiting for me to leave so he could kill me too.

"Mike won't be to my house for half an hour," Matt corrected. "We're meeting him there."

"But what if Coach Snyder is waiting out there to kill me?" I asked, giving voice to my fear. I couldn't help but realize that it sounded even more ridiculous out loud than it had in my head.

Matt made every effort not to laugh, but he obviously wasn't too concerned about retired baseball coaches lurking in the shadows. "I think we'll be okay," he said. And then, with a grin: "I've been working out, remember?"

I laughed, and some of the worry lifted off my shoulders.

By the time we finished washing the abandoned dishes and locking up the café, we had to walk quickly to get to Matt's house so we wouldn't leave Mike waiting. That suited me just fine because my nervousness came back as soon as we stepped out into the night with only the streetlights keeping the darkness at bay. I tried to be subtle, but we had barely walked half a block when Matt noticed how I was turning my head to study every shadow, looking for Coach-shaped threats hidden in their depths. Matt reached out and took my hand in his, squeezing it gently and then not letting go. I have to admit, the warmth and strength of his hand did distract me from my fears.

We walked up to Matt's house just as Mike pulled into the driveway. I noticed that he was in his personal car instead of his patrol car, and I wondered if that meant he wasn't taking this revelation seriously. I hoped it was just that he was currently off duty and didn't want to be compelled to do any extraneous police work that would keep him from getting back home.

"Hey, guys," he called as he climbed out of his car. "I was going to apologize for taking so long putting the kids to bed, but it doesn't look like I held you all up any. You want to go inside and talk?"

He was already halfway to the front door by then. Matt and I hurried up the front walk after him.

Inside, Matt offered to make coffee, but Mike and I both declined—Mike on the basis of needing to get back home as soon as he could, and me on the basis of having tasted Matt's coffee before. I didn't tell him that was why, of course, but based on the look he gave me, I think he knew.

The three of us settled down in the living room, Matt and me on the couch and Mike in an armchair opposite us. It was an unsettling repeat of the last time the three of us had gathered in that room on the day Matt's dad died.

Mike pulled a small notebook out of his back pocket and flipped it open. "So, what've you two got for me today?" he asked.

Matt and I looked at each other as Mike looked between the two of us. Finally, I took a deep breath and launched into a detailed explanation of everything I'd learned about the circumstances of Joe's murder over the past several days. Mike nodded as he listened, jotting down notes along the way. He asked a few questions here and there, which gave me confidence that he at least felt as though my story was plausible. When I finished, I looked at him expectantly, waiting for him to congratulate me on a job well done. Instead, he leaned back in his chair and tapped his pen against his notebook.

"Well, Fran, you've brought me some interesting information. It's not enough to make an arrest, but it's enough to make me want to have a little chat with Coach Snyder. I'll go see him first thing tomorrow and see if we can't have a little chat." He glanced down at his notebook again, scanning his notes. "Is there anything else you want to add before I go?"

I thought over everything I'd told him and then shook my head, satisfied I'd said everything I'd wanted. "Nope, that's everything."

Mike scooted forward in his chair. "Well, then, I'll get out of here and go make sure the kids actually went to sleep and aren't driving Sandra up the wall." He stood up and shook our hands. He looked me in the eye as he held onto my hand. "Thank you, Fran. Seriously. This is good information."

"Thank you for coming out so late," I replied.

"A cop's job is never done," he said as he headed for the door.

I watched Matt walk him to the door, and I hoped the information I'd given him was enough.

Chapter 25

COACH SNYDER SANG like a bird as soon as Mike brought him down to the police department. Mike was too much of a professional to say anything, but rumor had it that Coach even cried during the interview, and not just tearing up and sniffling—word was he was full-on sobbing almost as soon as Mike started asking questions. I almost felt bad for the guy. Almost. He had killed someone, after all.

The story turned out to be more or less what I had figured out. Coach placed a bet with Joe and won, but Joe had been feeling guilty about not paying child support, so instead of paying out as he was supposed to, he gave the money to Melissa. Coach went to the gym the night of Joe's death to try to talk to him and get his money back, but they got into a scuffle. Joe was younger, stronger, faster, and better trained than Coach, so in the heat of the moment, Coach picked up the first thing he could find on the ground that he could use as a weapon, one of the broken beer bottles the teenagers who hung out in the parking lot had left behind. Coach brandished it at Joe just as Joe lunged at Coach. The bottle punctured Joe's chest in the worst possible way and killed him. When Coach saw Joe crumple to the ground, he hurried to his car and left town for a few days, hoping the case would have died down by the time he got back. Little did he realize that skipping town would be one of the key pieces of information that led me to him.

Coach's arrest meant, of course, that Todd was completely off the hook. When he heard I had passed some of the critical information to Mike that led to the arrest, he came by the café to thank me personally for taking the time to investigate the case. He did not, I noticed, bring or send flowers. I took that as a sign that he understood I'd been serious when I told him I wasn't interested in a romantic relationship. I wouldn't have complained about more flowers, though.

In a lucky twist of fate, Joe had a life-insurance policy that gave Melissa enough money to get Emmy some pretty, frilly clothes like she wanted, with plenty left over to save for Emmy's future. The money didn't make up for the loss of Joe in Emmy's life, but it gave Melissa some peace of mind so she wouldn't spend every waking moment wondering how she was going to feed and clothe her daughter that month. It gave her the freedom to focus on being the best mother she could be.

Melissa thought about using some of the money to pick up and move somewhere Emmy wouldn't have to be known as a murder victim's daughter, but at least for the time, she decided to stay in Cape Bay where she and Emmy could be surrounded by friends and family who could keep Joe's memory alive for the little girl. I knew all of that partly because Sammy filled me in and partly because Melissa had started making it a point to stop by the café and say hello every few days. She and I would talk for a few minutes if I could. Making new friends and putting down new roots in my hometown felt good.

Melissa was in the café one day, talking to Sammy and showing her something on her phone, when Sammy called me over from where I was organizing supplies behind the counter.

"Hey, have you seen this?" she asked.

"Seen what?"

I walked over toward them, and she held out Melissa's phone. On the screen was a picture of a latte that, if I hadn't known any better, I would have sworn I'd made. It was a beach scene with a palm tree, something I was sure thousands of baristas were perfectly capable of making, but instead of looking as though it had been poured by some anonymous hand, it looked exactly like what I would pour if I went to the espresso machine and attempted to make the same design that very minute. When I looked more closely, the cup even looked like one of ours. I took the phone from her and scrolled down to see if it had a caption.

Beachy latte art from Antonia's Italian Café in Cape Bay, Massachusetts

"What is this?" I asked, looking up first at Sammy and then at Melissa.

"Scroll down," Sammy said.

I scrolled all the way down to the bottom of the article, resisting the urge to stop and read as I went. There, at the bottom of the page, just above the comments, was the smiling face of a man who looked very familiar. I couldn't quite place him until I read the biography next to his picture.

Jack McAllister is a born-and-bred Southern boy with a taste for travel and delicious food. He has an unnatural fondness for Hawaiian shirts.

I looked up at Sammy, my jaw hanging open.

"He's a food blogger," she said.

I looked back down at the phone and then up again at her.

"Don't worry. It's a good review. He only has excellent things to say about you and the café," Melissa said.

"He mentions me?" I asked. I scrolled up to the top of the article. There were several more pictures along the way that I hadn't noticed him taking, including an artistic one of Monica's tiramisu. Aside from his avowed love of Hawaiian shirts, I now understood the reasoning behind the stereotypical tourist garb—no one would ever be suspicious of someone dressed like that taking pictures of restaurants. Someone who looked like a journalist—whatever a journalist looked like—was more likely to draw attention. But a tourist? Tourists take pictures to remember every second of their vacations, especially in the age of social media.

"He talks about how you're really warm and friendly and how you delivered his drinks right to him and spent time talking to him. He talks a little bit about your grandparents, too," Sammy said.

"Wow," I murmured, reaching the top of the article and starting to read. I leaned against the counter. I had just finished the first paragraph when Sammy loudly cleared her throat. "What?" I asked, looking up. I looked back down and realized that the phone in my hand wasn't mine. "Can you send me the link to this?" I asked Melissa, handing her phone back.

"Sure," she replied. "But I don't think that's what Sammy was referring to." She nodded toward the door.

I turned to see a man approaching the counter with a large vase of lilies covering his face. I wasn't sure how he could even see. A smile spread across my face when he set them down and I saw that their bearer was Matt.

"Hi," I said shyly.

"Hi, yourself," he replied.

Ever since the night Matt had held my hand, walking home from the café, we'd been getting closer and closer. I was even now almost willing to call him—*dare I say it?*—my boyfriend, even though our conversations still skirted around the subject.

"You brought me flowers," I said, my lovestruck brain incapable of saying anything beyond the obvious.

"Lilies," he said.

"My favorite."

"I know. Why do you think I brought them? Oh, and the florist assured me that these have no smell whatsoever, so they won't interfere with the smell of the coffee. I sniffed them myself, just to make extra sure."

I smiled, about to walk around the counter to give him a hug, when I noticed an envelope stuffed among the flowers.

"What's this?" I reached in to get it.

Matt shrugged innocently. "You have to open it to find out."

I gasped when I peeked inside. "Is this what I think it is?" Several weeks earlier, after his dad's death, Matt had sold his house and moved back into his childhood home —the one just down the street from my own. When he told me, he'd also announced his desire to use some of the money to take a dream trip to Italy before investing the rest. The best part was that he'd invited me along.

I slid the sheet of paper out of the envelope and unfolded it on the counter. Matt leaned across so he could see it too.

"It's our itinerary. I wanted to surprise you with the plane tickets, but you just print those online now, so it didn't seem as special. This way, you get to see everything that we're going to do."

I scanned down the list. We were due to leave in mid-October, after the tourist season ended. It would be a long stay—two weeks—but we'd get to see most of the country, from Venice and Verona in the north, down to Rome and Naples and even Sicily in the south. It really was a dream trip. I could barely contain my excitement. I ran around the counter and threw my arms around Matt. He slid his arms around my waist and lifted me up into the air for a second, as though we were in a movie. And when he set me back down, he leaned in and very gently kissed me on the lips.

Recipe 1: London Fog

Ingredients:
- Earl Grey tea bag
- Milk
- Vanilla extract
- Sugar

Brew a strong cup of Earl Grey tea. Strain the tea and combine it with steamed milk. Add a dash of vanilla and your desired amount of sugar (or sweetener).

Recipe 2: Tiramisu

9 servings

Ingredients:
- •6 egg yolks
- •1 1/4 cup mascarpone cheese
- •1/3/4 cup heavy whipping cream
- •1 cup sugar
- •2 seven-ounce packages Italian ladyfingers
- •1 cup cold espresso
- •1/2 cup coffee-flavored liqueur
- •1 tbsp. cocoa for dusting

Combine egg yolks and sugar in the top of a double boiler, over boiling water. Reduce heat to low. Cook for

10 minutes, stirring constantly. Remove from heat and whip yolks until thick and lemon colored.

Add mascarpone to whipped yolks. Beat until combined. In a separate bowl, whip cream to stiff peaks.

Gently fold the whipped cream in the mascarpone sabayon mixture and set aside.

Mix cold espresso with the coffee liqueur and dip the ladyfingers into the mixture just long enough to get them wet. Don't soak them. Arrange ladyfingers in the bottom of a 9-inch square baking dish.

Spoon half the mascarpone cream filling over the ladyfingers. Repeat the process with another layer of ladyfingers and cream.

Refrigerate 4 hours or overnight. Dust with cocoa before serving.

Book 3: Margaritas, Marzipan, and Murder

Chapter 1

"TO SAMMY!" Dawn said, lifting her margarita glass in the air for a toast.

"To Sammy," I echoed, clinking my glass against Dawn's and Sammy's. "To her freedom!"

"Hear, hear," Dawn cheered as Sammy blushed.

The three of us—me, Sammy, and Dawn, Sammy's best friend since preschool—were gathered on the oceanfront deck of Fiesta Mexicana, Cape Bay's best and only Mexican restaurant, to celebrate Sammy's breakup with her longtime loser boyfriend, Jared.

They'd been together for ten years, since their senior year in high school, and Jared had been refusing to move their relationship beyond boyfriend-girlfriend status for almost as long, always claiming that it would break his mother's heart if he left her to get married.

Even so, Sammy had held out hope for a ring for their one-year anniversary, then their five-year, then their ten-year anniversary a few weeks ago. In the last case, the big surprise he'd promised her turned out to be an evening of go-karting. When that happened, even I, who hadn't known her well for all that long, asked her what she was still doing with him. She said it was because she loved him. I let it go. But Dawn didn't.

"God, I'm glad I finally convinced you to break up with him," Dawn said, coming up from a long drink from her glass. We had been at the bar less than half an hour, but she had ordered a second round, despite Sammy and me having made nowhere near the impact on our drinks that she had. I'd never gone out with Dawn before, but I could already tell she was either going to be a lot of fun or no fun at all. She was that kind of girl.

"Fran did some convincing, too," Sammy said, nodding in my direction.

I looked at her with my eyebrows raised as I swallowed the sip I'd just taken. The margarita was made just the way I liked it: a little tart, a little sweet, a little salty, and exactly the right amount of burn from the tequila. "I did?" I asked after the liquid had made its way down my throat.

"You did."

"What did I say?" I asked.

"It wasn't so much what you said as the fact that you said it. It was one thing when Dawn told me I needed to break up with him. I mean, she's been saying that for years."

"Nine and a half years to be exact," Dawn interjected. "Maybe nine and three quarters."

Sammy rolled her eyes with a smile and a shake of her head at her best friend. Clearly, they'd had the same conversation more than once. "Anyway, I've been hearing about it from Dawn for years, but when you said something after we've only really known each other for a few months…"

I looked down at my glass, embarrassed that I'd been so blunt. It was very un-New-England-y of me. Well, being blunt was very New England, but sticking my nose in someone else's business wasn't. Who someone else chose to spend their time with was none of my concern, even if I did think they were making a huge mistake. "I'm sorry," I said. "I shouldn't have pried into your personal life."

"Don't be sorry," Sammy exclaimed.

"Please," Dawn chimed in. "If that's what it took to get the girl to see reason, I'm glad you said something!" She tipped her glass up and emptied it.

"Still—" I started.

"Still nothing," Sammy said, looking me dead in the eye. "I'd been with him for ten *years*, Fran, always telling myself it didn't matter that he didn't want to get married, that it was fine if he never wanted to go away for a weekend because his mom would be all alone, that birthdays and anniversaries weren't really that big of a deal so it was okay if he never wanted to do anything special to celebrate. Ten years! Do you know how many of my friends I've watched get married and have kids in that time?" Sammy's face was getting flushed as she ranted.

"Do you know how many times I've been asked when we were getting engaged?" she went on. "And I couldn't even be one of those people who just says they're not the marrying kind or something, because I *am* the marrying kind. It's all I've wanted for ten years! Jared just kept saying he wasn't ready." She waved her margarita glass in the air.

She was so worked up that she didn't even notice that some of it sloshed over the side and fell onto the deck floor. I reached out, took it from her hand, and placed it on the table. She kept going without missing a beat.

"I had to keep telling people we were waiting until we were a little older, a little more established, had a little more money. It was so embarrassing! And then when I had to tell you that my big anniversary date was go-karts? Ugh! I wanted to sink into the floor and disappear! And what was my excuse? That I loved him? When that's how he treated me?" She stopped and shook her head. "I'm just glad I finally realized it before I wasted any more time on him."

I was surprised and impressed by Sammy's outburst. It was so far out of character for her. Sammy's usual disposition was as sunny as her blond hair. She smiled a lot, laughed a lot, got along with everybody, and made customers at the café smile. She rarely got worked up about anything, and on the incredibly rare occasion that she did, she never had that much to say about it. I liked seeing that kind of spunk and passion from her.

Not knowing what else to say, I raised my glass toward Sammy. "To getting out and not wasting time on losers!"

"I'll drink to that!" Dawn said, clinking her glass against mine and Sammy's.

The waiter had brought the second round while Sammy was venting about Jared. Dawn tipped it back and drank so much I felt reasonably confident we'd be on to the third round soon. Of course, if we kept going at our current pace, she could just drink Sammy's or mine. She'd be ready for her next one long before we were.

"You know, I gotta say, Sam, I am glad you're finally done feeling sorry for yourself about the breakup. Jared was a loser and not worth all the crying you were doing over him, was he, Fran?" Dawn said.

The native New Englander in me wanted to make a

noncommittal grunt, but apparently my opinion had meant something to Sammy before.

"I can't fault you for crying. I know I cried my share of tears when I found out my fiancé was cheating on me. But it's definitely good to see you getting past the really depressed phase. He didn't deserve you, and you deserve to be happy."

Sammy gave me a small, grateful smile. I knew from my own recent experience that Dawn's tough-love attitude was sometimes exactly what the doctor ordered, but other times, you needed someone to tell you that whatever you were feeling was fine and that they were there for you no matter how long it took you to get back to normal. Between the two of us, we had Sammy's emotional needs covered. But that, I suspected, was why I'd been invited along.

The night out on the town had been Dawn's idea. She'd come into the café the evening before, after Sammy had gone home but before I closed up shop. I didn't know Dawn personally, but she came into the café sometimes after Sammy's shifts to hang out with her.

She burst through the door unceremoniously, calling out before she even had the chance to see that I was standing right at the counter.

"Fran!" she bellowed. "We have to do something about Sammy!"

"We do?" I asked.

"For God's sake, yes!" she said, slamming her hands down on the counter. "She's been moping around, crying her eyes out for a week now. I can't take it anymore!"

You can't take it anymore? Sammy's the one with the broken heart. But at the same time, I understood where she was coming from. Sammy had been doing okay at work—not breaking down in tears or anything like that, at least not after the first day or two—but she definitely wasn't her normal, cheery, ebullient self.

"What do you want me to do?" I asked Dawn.

While I considered Sammy a friend, she was also my employee. I'd known her for a long time but had only really gotten to know her personally over the past couple of months since I'd returned to Cape Bay from New York City. I really wasn't sure I was the right person to help break her out of her funk.

Dawn looked at me as if I was stupid. "We need to take her out. Like, to party. Girls' night out. I know that's not just a Massachusetts thing. I watch TV. They have girls' nights out in New York."

"Even if they didn't, I'm from Massachusetts."

She didn't look as though she believed me.

"Really!" *She knew that, didn't she? That I'd moved back to Cape Bay to take over the café after my mother died? That I grew up here?*

"I know," she replied coolly. "You were just away so long, I thought maybe you forgot."

"Forgot the girls' nights out that we also have in New York?"

She gave me that "are you stupid?" look again then shook her head as if she couldn't be bothered. "We need to take Sammy out," she said, giving up on explaining the concept of "girls' night out" to me.

"Do you really think Sammy would want me there? I mean, I'm her boss."

"And her friend. Of course she would want you there. Are you free tomorrow night?"

Even though I knew it would take Sammy some time to get over the breakup since she'd been with Jared for so long, I couldn't help but think that it would do her some good to get out, have a little fun, and remember that there was a big world out there as soon as she was ready to rejoin it. So I had agreed to Dawn's plan for a girls' night out.

And that was how we'd ended up on the deck of Fiesta Mexicana, tipping back margaritas and breathing in the salty sea air. It was the last week of the summer tourist season, and you could already feel the chill creeping into the air. Labor Day was coming up on Monday, the kids would go back to school on Tuesday, and Cape Bay's tourist traffic would be confined to the weekends for the next six weeks until Columbus Day, when it essentially ground to a halt.

There would be a few tourists over the holidays and Valentine's Day, but it wouldn't be anything noteworthy until the spring breakers invaded in March, after which it would stop again until the season started on Memorial Day weekend. After the emotionally and physically exhausting summer, my mother's sudden death, and the long hours I'd been working at the café, I was more than ready for the slower pace of winter.

Dawn downed the last of her drink and stood up. "I'll be back. Gotta hit the little girls' room."

I watched her walk away then looked over at Sammy, who was staring out at the ocean. The sun had long since set, but the full moon lit the water up brightly enough that the people walking along the beach didn't bother turning their flashlights on to light their way. It was a perfect late-summer night, but I could tell from Sammy's face that she wasn't really enjoying it.

"You okay?" I asked her quietly.

She nodded without taking her eyes off the water. The light from the neon beer sign behind her shone down on her hair, creating a halo effect. It wasn't the first time the word "cherubic" had come to my mind in relation to Sammy, although it was usually the smiling cherubs I thought she looked like, not the tearful ones.

"It'll get better," I said. I knew from experience. It

had only been a few months since my then-fiancé had broken the news that he was leaving me for the girl in his office he'd been cheating on me with. The first couple of weeks had been agonizing, and then when I wasn't looking, the cloud began to lift.

She turned away from the water and looked at me, the corner of her mouth twitching up while her eyes stayed sad. "Promise?"

"Promise," I replied. "It might seem like forever, but things will be looking up before you know it."

The door from the deck to the patio opened, and Dawn walked through. She moved slowly, and I thought I detected a wobble in her step as she passed the table next to ours. I nudged Sammy and nodded in Dawn's direction. Sammy's eyes got big, and she started to stand, but before she could get up, Dawn lunged into the chair closest to her.

Dawn's head tipped back, coming so close to the woman sitting at the table next to us that it nearly rested on her shoulder. Sammy and I looked at each other again. I wasn't sure what was wrong with Dawn, and from Sammy's expression, I guessed that she didn't either.

"Dawn, are you—" I started, leaning across the table toward her.

Her head snapped forward, and one finger flew to her lips. "Shhhhh!" Her eyes were round and intense as she looked at me then at Sammy. After a few seconds, she leaned back again and turned her face upward.

I leaned over to Sammy and whispered, "Is she okay?"

Sammy shook her head and shrugged, no surer of Dawn's condition than I was.

I looked back at Dawn, who was still inexplicably staring at the ceiling, her shoulder-length, rust-colored hair actually falling over the back of the other woman's chair. The people at that table had just been seated, and they were chatting as they looked over their menus, too absorbed in what they were doing to notice that Dawn had practically joined their party.

I had no idea what was going on with her. She had seemed fine before she left the table. And she'd seemed okay—strange, but fine—when she'd sat up and shushed us. She'd only had two drinks, and she'd been right there with us until she'd gone to the bathroom.

No one except the waiter had come near us. I didn't think she'd had enough alcohol to be drunk, and unless someone had intercepted her on her way to the bathroom, I couldn't imagine that she'd been drugged. That wasn't even something I would have worried about going out with girlfriends in New York, let alone sleepy little Cape Bay.

Something was very wrong; I just didn't know what.

Chapter 2

I WATCHED Dawn for what seemed like an eternity but was probably only a few seconds. Sammy was still watching Dawn and looking as confused as I was. I tucked my long brown hair behind my ears to try to hear better what Dawn was listening to, but with the chatters of the restaurant patrons around me, I still couldn't make out the words.

Finally, I decided I couldn't just let her sit there all limp and not do anything. I reached out toward Dawn to see if I could get her attention by tapping on the table.

Before I could even tap once, she popped up and leaned her elbows on the table. She stared at me as if I was crazy for having my arm stretched across the table. I pulled it back, knowing it wasn't worth trying to explain that we thought she had passed out.

"Did you hear what they're talking about?" she whispered.

So that was what she had been doing—eavesdropping on the neighboring table. It almost made sense, though it would have been less weird for her to have told Sammy and me what she was doing.

From what I knew of Dawn, eavesdropping was something she would do. She seemed to have a constant expectation that everyone around her should understand what was going on in her head. I certainly didn't. Maybe Sammy did, based on how unfazed she seemed by Dawn's return to the land of the living. But then again, maybe Sammy was just used to Dawn's quirks.

When neither of us admitted to eavesdropping on the conversation next to us—perhaps because we were distracted by Dawn's strange behavior—she filled us in. "They found a body!"

"They did?" I asked, gesturing toward the other table.

"No, not them," Dawn said, looking disgusted. "They," she repeated, making air quotes. "Like, people in general. A body was found."

"Where?" I asked. "Here in Cape Bay?"

She rolled her eyes. I was convinced she thought I was too dense to tie my own shoes. "Yes, here in Cape Bay! Where else?"

"I would prefer anywhere else," Sammy said.

I lifted my margarita glass and tapped it against hers. I could drink to not finding a body in Cape Bay. We'd had enough of those lately—first my boyfriend Matt's father and then a local kickboxing student. It would be fine by me if no one found another dead body in town ever again.

"Where?" I asked. "Where in Cape Bay, I mean?" I clarified before Dawn could lose her eyeballs in the back of her head.

"Right next to Mary Ellen's," Dawn said. Mary Ellen's Souvenirs and Gifts was located on Main Street, just a couple of blocks from my café. "They said the cops are still there. You wanna go check it out?"

"The body?" I asked.

"Yeah! Why not? Have you ever seen a real crime scene before, like not on a cop show?"

"Yes," I replied.

I had the unfortunate distinction of being the one to find my neighbor's body—my now-boyfriend Matt's dad —when he was murdered, and I had been there when they processed the scene. Of course, they hadn't known he had been murdered at first, so it hadn't been like on TV at all, but I still wasn't too keen on seeing another corpse.

"Oh yeah," Dawn said.

I could see the wheels turning in her head as she tried to think of another reason for us to visit the crime scene. I finished my drink as I waited for her to land on another idea.

"Do you think Mary Ellen needs us?" Sammy asked.

I immediately realized I wasn't going to win. If Sammy was on Dawn's side, there was no getting out of it, especially since I thought Sammy had a good point. If somebody had been found dead next to Mary Ellen's shop, she'd probably be pretty freaked out.

In a small town like Cape Bay, we all supported each other, especially the shopkeepers. I knew if a body was found next to my café, Mary Ellen would be right there to help me in any way she could. Still, I couldn't concede my point that easily.

"Sammy and I haven't even started our second drinks, and you already ordered a third round," I pointed out. "We can't let all that money and perfectly good alcohol go to waste."

Dawn didn't miss a beat. She stood and picked up the two untouched glasses from the table. She turned around and placed them on the table she'd been eavesdropping on.

"Here you go, ladies! We've been unexpectedly called away and won't be able to finish our drinking. Here are two delicious, untouched margaritas for you to enjoy. This one is your classic margarita on the rocks, and this pretty pink frozen one here is strawberry."

One of the women looked as if she wanted to speak.

Before she could, Dawn spotted the waiter coming with our third round perched on his tray and bellowed, "And just in time, here's the rest of them! Put them right here, Alberto." She gestured for him to place them on the strangers' table. "We have another classic on the rocks, another frozen strawberry, and this one here"—she picked up the drink she'd ordered for herself—"is top-shelf and mango. Who wants it?" She glanced around the table, her gaze landing on the woman closest to the window. "You? You look like a girl who appreciates fine liquor." She set the drink down in front of the woman and immediately reached in her own jeans pocket, pulling out a few bills. She handed them to Alberto. "Keep the change, my friend." She turned back to us. "You ready to go?"

"Guess so," I said, standing up. Dawn had made my one solid objection disappear in the blink of an eye and had managed to convince a group of women that drinks from a stranger's table were suitable for consumption. It was kind of impressive and, I suspected, evidence of how good Dawn was at her bartending job.

Sammy swallowed the last of her drink, grabbed her purse, and stood up. "All right, let's go."

Even though it was Sammy's comment about Mary Ellen that convinced us to head to the crime scene, I couldn't tell whether she was actually happy about going or not. I had a feeling she wasn't exactly enjoying herself and was just ready to leave.

We headed out of the restaurant and made our way into the heart of town. Fiesta Mexicana was situated at the end of the mile-long boardwalk that ran the length of Cape Bay's beachfront.

Main Street ran perpendicular to the beach at the middle of the boardwalk. Mary Ellen's shop was a couple of blocks up from the beach, and my café was a little beyond that. It wasn't a long walk, especially on such a nice night.

If I'd had my way, I would have gone down and sat on the beach to watch the waves crash under the moon. But between Sammy and Mary Ellen, I knew I was needed elsewhere.

Soon, we could see the flashing red and blue lights of the police cars and an ambulance parked outside Mary Ellen's shop. It looked like the entirety of Cape Bay's police force—all nine of them—was out to aid in the investigation.

To be fair, it was still tourist season, so the police department had an extra handful of officers on staff as seasonal help, but the group was still only a fraction of the size of what would have been assembled in New York City for the discovery of a body. The ambulance wasn't even ours—it was from the county EMS station in the next town over.

From what I could see, the police also had a spotlight shining into the alley next to Mary Ellen's store. The light actually belonged to the town. I remembered seeing it set up during Cape Bay's annual Founders' Day celebration.

A big crowd of people was gathered around the group of police cars blocking the road.

Dawn was shameless and walked right past the police cars up to the crime scene tape, which was strung from the corners of the buildings on either side of the alley and around parking meters at the road. A swarm of blue uniforms blocked our view, but Dawn angled and craned her neck to see between them.

"I can see him!" she hissed back at us.

"And?" I asked, not sure I wanted to know.

"Pretty sure he's dead."

It was my turn to roll my eyes. The phrase "a body" didn't typically refer to a living body.

"Would you idiots stop standing there and try doing some police work?" someone shouted from behind the police tape. The voice was familiar, but between my years in Cape Bay and my work at the café, I knew just about everyone on the police force.

"What do you want us to do, Detective?" one of the officers asked.

The detective sighed heavily. "Oh, for the love of..." Heavy footsteps moved toward us. "You," the detective said. "Get a camera. Take pictures. Get everything from every angle. Use a ruler so we know how big things are. You, go with him. You, call the medical examiner's office and find out when somebody's going to be here. I want this body off my street."

The officers gradually dispersed to their different tasks, revealing the scene in the alley. Just as Dawn had said, there was a body, presumably dead as evidenced by both the fact that the paramedics weren't attending to it and that it was covered by a sheet. I was grateful for that.

There were little yellow tents scattered around, marking bits of evidence that mostly seemed to be rocks and bits of trash you'd expect to find in an alley. I remembered seeing on one of those police procedurals with the hot older man lead detective that the police had to consider all trash important until they could be sure it didn't have any blood or footprints on it. I was glad I didn't have that job.

On one side of the sheet-draped body—a man's body, I guessed, from the size and shape of it—was a plastic bag full of…something I couldn't identify. A chill went up my spine when I saw what was on the other side of the body—a gun.

Sammy must have spotted it at the same time. "Was he shot?" she whispered.

I instinctively reached one hand back toward her.

Judging by how tight she gripped it, I knew the sight bothered her as much as it did me.

Dawn, however, seemed mostly unaffected. "Yeah, I think so." She got up on her tiptoes and leaned to her right. "I think that's blood over there." She pointed toward the body.

"Okay, that's it, let's go," I said. Still holding Sammy's hand, I turned and pulled her along with me back through the police cars and over to the grassy median a block away, near where the ambulance was parked. Sammy's face looked pale in the yellow-orange streetlight,

"Are you okay?" I asked.

"Yeah, just…" She stopped and shuddered. "Another murder."

"Actually, it looks like a suicide," a man's voice said. The dark-haired police officer had been standing just around the corner of the ambulance out of our view but apparently well within earshot. He stepped toward us. "So nothing for you to worry about," he said with a smile at Sammy and me. As he looked at each of us, his eyes lingered for just a second longer on Sammy. "You all right, miss?"

"Yes, I'm fine."

"Are you sure?" His brow furrowed. "You need to sit down? Here, let me help." He popped open the handle on the back of the ambulance door. "Sit down here."

"I'm fine, really. I—"

"Sit down," he repeated firmly. "Don't want to have another body on the ground."

Sammy and I both looked at him, startled by his comment.

"No, I-I mean… sorry, cop humor. I just meant that you looked like you might pass out. And then you'd be…" He gestured toward the ground then shook his head. "Sorry, bad joke."

Sammy sat down on the back of the ambulance. "It's okay. I make coffee jokes sometimes when I'm stressed at work."

The cop chuckled and ran his fingers across his close-cropped hair. "Yeah? You work at a coffee shop?"

"Just up the street," she said, pointing in the direction of the café. "Antonia's Italian Café. I work with Fran here. She owns the place." She motioned to me.

"Oh yeah?" he replied with a smile. "I haven't been there yet. I'll have to come by sometime and see you."

Sammy looked at him curiously, and I knew she was wondering the same thing I was: how had a Cape Bay police officer not been into Antonia's?

The officer must have read her expression, too, a handy skill for someone who had to suss out criminals for a living. "I'm new," he said. "Just moved here from Buffalo."

"What brings you to town?" I asked.

"Family. I grew up in Plymouth. I've been out in New York for a while and just wanted to get back home."

"Well, welcome to Cape Bay! Come into the café any time. Between me and Sammy, one of us is almost always there. We'll get you a cup of coffee on the house."

"Don't let her fool you," Sammy said before he could reply. "Police and firefighters always get free coffee."

I gave her a dirty look for blowing my secret.

The cop laughed. "Well, thank you… Fran, was it?"

"Francesca Amaro," I said, extending my hand. "And we're happy to do it. It's a long-standing family tradition." Back when my grandparents started the café nearly seventy years ago, they gave free food and coffee to the police and firefighters who protected the town as a way of not just thanking them for what they did but also to establish Antonia's as part of the community.

"I'm Ryan Leary," he said, shaking my hand. His hand was huge and strong, and his handshake was just on this side of uncomfortable. I suspected it was a carefully practiced technique. He gave Sammy a questioning look.

"Samantha Eriksen," she said, reaching her hand up to him from where she was still sitting on the back of the ambulance. "Sammy."

"Sammy," he repeated with a smile. "You look like your color's coming back a little."

I wasn't sure whether it was that or if she was blushing, but she did seem to be getting some pink back in her skin.

"Leary!" someone bellowed.

"Right here, Detective," Ryan called, turning and raising one hand in the air.

Detective Mike Stanton stalked into view, and the second he saw me, I knew I was in trouble.

Chapter 3

MIKE'S STARE probably only lasted a few seconds, but it seemed like almost an eternity before his eyes shifted to Sammy. Ryan stood by uneasily, obviously confused about why his boss had gone from urgently demanding his presence to silently staring at Sammy and me.

"You okay, Sam?" Mike finally asked.

"Yeah," she said, standing up quickly from her seat on the ambulance. She dusted her hands off on her jeans. "Just, uh, just needed to sit down for a minute." She managed to flash him a weak smile.

Mike studied her for another few seconds and then turned to me.

"So you two were just walking by when Sammy—what?—started to feel lightheaded and needed to sit down?"

"Sort of. We're actually here with Dawn. We were having a girls' night out—" I started to explain.

"Dawn?" Mike interrupted. Based on his tone, I was almost surprised he didn't pull his little investigator's notebook out of his breast pocket and start taking notes.

"Dawn…" I tried to pull her last name from the dredges of my memory.

"There you are!" Dawn shouted, bounding over to us. "I've been looking everywhere for you guys. You just took off, and I was standing there talking to myself like a weirdo!"

"Oh, *Dawn*," Mike said, clearly realizing which Dawn I was referring to and, I guessed, putting together how our girls' night out had turned into a girls' night at a crime scene.

"Yes, *Dawn*," she repeated. "How are you doin', Mikey?" She punched his arm affectionately, and I wondered if it was legal to hit a police officer in uniform, even if it was playful. I also wondered when someone had last called him "Mikey." He and I had gone to school together from kindergarten all the way through high school, and I couldn't remember anyone calling him "Mikey" after about second grade.

"I'd rather be home with my wife and kids, but other than that, I'm good, Dawn. How are you?" Mike replied, ignoring both her punch and her nickname for him.

"Good! You know, girls' night out tonight. Cele-brating Sammy's breakup!" Dawn bounced as she spoke, and I wouldn't have been surprised if she took off to run a lap or two around the ambulance. I wondered if alcohol always made her so energetic.

Sammy flushed at the mention of her breakup. Ryan looked at her as if he thought she was going to need to sit back down.

"Well, if that's cause for celebration, then congratu-lations, Sammy," Mike said hesitantly. As a Cape Bay native and a longtime regular at Antonia's, Mike should have known Sammy had been seeing Jared practically forever and that the breakup wasn't the easiest thing for her.

"Thanks," she said quietly.

Mike kept his eyes on her as he nodded. For a second, I thought he was going to walk away without asking me any more questions, but then he looked right at me. "So you were just walking by?"

"Actually," Dawn interrupted, oblivious to the fact that Mike was talking to me instead of her, "we were down at the Mexican place." She waved her arm wildly in the general direction of Fiesta Mexicana and almost smacked Mike in the face. "I overheard the table next to us talking about how somebody found a body down here, so I thought we should come and check it out."

"You heard there was a body, and your first thought

was to come and investigate?" Mike asked Dawn, even though he was looking at me. I tried to keep my face perfectly neutral, even though I knew what he was getting at.

"Yeah, basically," Dawn replied. "Why not?"

"Fran?" Mike said, ignoring Dawn.

"It was Dawn's idea," I said, hearing how childish I sounded.

Mike stared at me stoically.

"I didn't want to come down here. I would have been perfectly happy keeping up with my margarita drinking. I've had enough dead bodies for a few decades."

"Have you now?"

Before I could respond, Sammy interrupted. "It was my fault. Dawn said they found the body next to Mary Ellen's, and I thought she might need some moral support. Fran really didn't want to come."

Mike looked from me to Sammy and back again. Then he lifted one hand and made a beckoning motion. "Come here a minute, Fran."

I followed him around to the front of the ambulance. He folded his arms across his chest and looked at me without saying anything.

I tried to wait him out, but I finally couldn't take it anymore. "Really, I just wanted to stay at the restaurant and hang out. We were supposed to be celebrating Sammy's breakup. I don't want anything to do with another body." It was true, but I couldn't blame him for being suspicious.

After each of Cape Bay's two recent murders, I'd done a little bit more investigating than Mike would have liked. Which was to say, he wanted me to stay out of it completely and leave all the investigating to the police. But it was hard when each of the cases directly affected friends of mine.

To my credit, I'd found the key evidence that led to the murderers' arrests in both cases. Mike didn't like to admit it, but if pressed, or if under the influence of a beer or two, he'd begrudgingly give me credit. I knew because his wife Sandra had told me.

Mike stared at me a few more seconds and then sighed heavily. "Just...try to stay out of it this time, okay?"

I nodded. "I'll do my best."

He eyed me and shook his head. "It's a suicide anyway. There's not much that needs investigating."

"That's good. For you, I mean. It's not good that someone's dead."

"Never is," Mike said and turned to walk away. He'd made it a few steps when I thought of something.

"Hey, Mike?"

He turned around, looking weary already. "Yeah?"

"Who was it?"

Mike paused for a second, and I felt tension grow in

the pit of my stomach. Cape Bay was a small town, the kind of place where everybody knew everybody, if not by sight then by name. Everybody in this town was somebody's mother, son, girlfriend, husband, sibling, or best friend. Whoever's body was in the alley, somebody would be walking into my café tomorrow brokenhearted over it. I just didn't know if that person would be me.

"We don't know," he said finally.

I gasped. My mind went straight to the worst—that the body was unidentifiable.

"He's not a local," Mike said.

I almost burst into tears from relief.

"Nobody recognizes him. We're waiting for the ME's office to get here so we can move the body and check for a wallet."

"So he was a tourist?" I asked. My initial reaction of relief quickly shifted to concern as I realized that a vacationer getting shot in our town would be extremely bad for our tourism business. Not that that compared to how awful it would be for whoever he was vacationing with.

"Depends on whether you consider everyone from out of town to be a tourist. If you do, then yes. If you mean a vacationer, well, I don't know yet."

I looked at Mike curiously.

"He—" he started, then stopped and seemed to debate how much he wanted to tell me. I knew he thought giving me too much information would get me interested in the case, but I wasn't going near this one. I was done involving myself in police investigations. Finally, he gave in. "He wasn't dressed like a vacationer."

"No Hawaiian shirt and camera around his neck?" I asked, thinking of the most stereotypical tourist outfit I could. Of course, the last time I'd thought that, I'd been wrong, but it was still an outfit that screamed "Tourist!"

Mike chuckled. "No. More business casual."

Mike was right. Business casual clothes didn't sound much like what you packed for vacation.

"Mike!" someone called from somewhere in the direction of the alley.

"On my way!" Mike yelled back. He turned and looked at me. "Duty calls. Stay out of it, Fran, okay?"

"Trust me, Mike. I have no interest in this case."

He grunted and stalked off around the ambulance. I walked back over to Dawn and Sammy, who were still huddled at the back of the ambulance. Ryan was gone, probably off to wherever Mike was.

"So you're not under arrest?" Dawn asked.

"No. Why would I be?" I retorted.

"We're at a crime scene, and a cop wanted to talk to you. Makes sense to me."

"It's not a crime scene," I said.

Dawn looked at me with the predictable "are you stupid?" look on her face that she seemed fond of giving me. "Um, the dead body over there would say different,"

Dawn said, after apparently deciding that my stupidity wasn't going to resolve itself.

"It was a suicide," Sammy said quietly. I could tell the sight of the body was still bothering her. Not that I could blame her. It was still bothering me, too.

"Well, whatever. What did ol' Officer Mike want?" Dawn asked.

"Nothing important," I said. I wasn't sure if Dawn knew about my involvement in the previous cases—it wasn't like the CBPD had broadcast the news that a civilian was solving their crimes—and I didn't want to fill her in now if she didn't.

"Telling you to stay out of it?" Apparently, Dawn did know.

"Maybe," I admitted.

Dawn laughed, a big, loud laugh. A couple of the officers turned around and gave her the eye. Laughing noisily probably wasn't the most tactful way to behave in the presence of a dead body.

"Maybe we should leave," I suggested.

"We haven't seen Mary Ellen," Sammy said.

As much as I didn't want to hang around any longer, Mary Ellen was the only reason we had come there in the first place. Leaving without seeing or talking to her would completely defeat the purpose of having left our comfortable seats on the patio of Fiesta Mexicana.

"Okay, let's go find her," I said.

"How are we going to do that in all this mess?" Dawn asked, gesturing at the crowd of people, cops, and police cars.

I knew Mary Ellen had only been an excuse for Dawn to get us to come there, and it annoyed me that she was trying to get out of seeing her now. "We just start looking," I said.

"Start with her store," Sammy said.

It was so blazingly obvious that I didn't know how I hadn't already thought of it. "Of course," I said. "Let's go." I started off through the crowd toward Mary Ellen's shop, with Sammy and Dawn trailing behind me.

Sammy hurried to catch up. "Did Mike say who it was?" she asked as quietly as she could in the noisy crowd of people.

I shook my head. "They don't know yet. Out-of-towner, they think."

Sammy nodded in acknowledgment as we walked to the front of Mary Ellen's shop. I don't know what I expected to see, but I was surprised all the lights were off. Logically, it made sense. It was long past closing time, and Mary Ellen wasn't the type to open just so tourists could come in to buy morbid mementos of the time a body was found in their vacation spot.

"It's all closed up," I said.

I wondered if maybe Mary Ellen had gone home and didn't need our moral support at all.

"I don't know if we'll be able to find her with all these people hanging around," Dawn said. "We could always go back to the restaurant and get our drink on. You guys can come find her tomorrow. Tonight was supposed to be about Sammy, after all." She bumped her denim-clad hip into Sammy's.

Sammy glared at her. "The light's on in the back," she said. I leaned toward the front window of the store and realized a light I'd thought was reflected from the street was actually coming from deep inside.

Dawn looked too. "She's probably back there with the cops or something."

Sammy rolled her eyes at Dawn and walked over to the glass door. She knocked on it rapidly, paused, and then knocked again. I watched the patch of light in the back to see if I could detect any movement.

Sammy had just raised her hand to knock again when I saw a head peek through the lit doorway. I put my hand on Sammy's shoulder to get her attention and then pointed to the head. She framed her eyes with her hands and leaned up against the glass.

"Mary Ellen? Mary Ellen!" she called through the door. "Mary Ellen!"

The owner of the head moved fully into the doorway. The person was completely backlit, so I couldn't be sure, but the hair looked an awful lot like Mary Ellen's.

"Mary Ellen!" Sammy called again. "It's me, Sammy! And Dawn and Fran."

The person began to move through the store toward us. When she finally reached the front of the store, the light from the street caught her face and her curly blond hair, and I saw it really was Mary Ellen. I breathed a sigh of relief. Even though I knew the body in the alley was a suicide, I was still a little creeped out and uneasy about a shadowy figure approaching us.

Mary Ellen unlocked the door, and Sammy stepped aside so she could push it open.

"Ladies, come in," she said, motioning us to enter.

Mary Ellen Chapman was older than the three of us, closer to my mother's age than mine, but still young enough to have been impossibly cool in my youthful eyes. For one thing, she was the only adult in town who had let us call her by her first name when we were children. She'd said if her first name was on the front of her store, there was no sense in the kids calling her "Mrs. Chapman."

As an adult, I wondered if it also might have had something to do with her being widowed shortly before she moved to Cape Bay. Maybe she didn't want to be reminded of her husband's death by constantly being addressed by her married name.

In any case, my mom and the other parents begrudgingly accepted us using her first name, as long as we put a "miss" in front of it. So she was "Miss Mary Ellen" all through my childhood and up until I graduated college, when I casually dropped it despite the glares I received from my mother as a result.

"Mary Ellen, we heard about the body and—" Sammy started as soon as we got inside.

"Let's go in the back," Mary Ellen interrupted. She locked the door behind us. "Too many strange ears out there."

I glanced over my shoulder as we followed her toward the back room, wondering who was out there that she didn't want overhearing our conversation.

Chapter 4

MARY ELLEN INVITED us to sit down at the little table in the back room of her store. The space was bigger and far less crowded than the back room at my café. Shelves lined the wall, full of supplies and extra stock. A computer sat on the desk. Handmade jewelry was scattered across the table next to the desk, surrounded by four chairs.

"Sorry for the mess," Mary Ellen said. "I was just sorting through some new pieces one of the local jewelry designers brought in. Can I get you ladies anything?"

Sammy and I shook our heads. "No, thank you," we both said.

"You have any beer?" Dawn asked with a laugh.

"No, I don't." Mary Ellen pulled the last chair out

from the table, but Dawn interrupted her before she could sit.

"Water, then."

Mary Ellen stopped mid-sit and pushed herself back up. As soon as she turned to walk to the little refrigerator under her desk, I shot Dawn a glare. She made a face at me. Mary Ellen brought a bottle of water to the table and placed it in front of Dawn. "Anything else I can get you?" she asked.

"No, this'll be fine, thanks," Dawn said.

I breathed a sigh of relief, grateful she hadn't decided to ask for a snack.

Mary Ellen sat down and spread her hands out on the table. She took a slow, deep breath as she stared blankly at a point somewhere in the middle of the table.

"How are you?" Sammy asked.

Mary Ellen turned her head toward Sammy, looking startled, as though she'd already forgotten we were there. "What was that, Sammy? Did you say something?"

"I asked how you're doing. You know, because of..." Sammy waved her hand in the direction of the alley.

Mary Ellen took a deep breath. "I'm fine. Certainly better than the fellow out there. I just..." She sighed heavily and shook her head, not bothering to finish the sentence.

Sammy reached out and took one of Mary Ellen's hands. Mary Ellen grasped it tightly. Her big blue eyes were tearful, and I thought she might erupt in sobs at any second. Not that I could blame her, given the circumstances.

"I'm sorry," Mary Ellen said. "It's just so hard to believe. Someone killed—so close—just steps away." She brought her other hand to her mouth and held it there for a second.

"Mary Ellen—" Sammy started, then stopped while she waited for Mary Ellen to look at her. "Mary Ellen, it wasn't murder. He killed himself."

Mary Ellen looked at Sammy with confusion in her eyes. She opened her mouth a couple of times as though she wanted to say something, but each time, she stopped herself, looking more confused than before. Finally, she managed to put a sentence together. "Is that what the police said?"

Sammy nodded. "There didn't seem to be any doubt."

Mary Ellen's eyes drifted away from Sammy's face. I couldn't tell what she was thinking, but she seemed troubled.

"Will you be all right alone here tonight?" Sammy asked. I was impressed by her compassion for Mary Ellen. It had been a deeply upsetting night, which was supposed to have been a celebration of Sammy's freedom. The way she put all that aside and concerned herself with only Mary Ellen's well-being made me proud to be her friend.

Mary Ellen's eyes widened, and she glanced out through the darkened store to the brightly lit street beyond. Her apartment was upstairs from the store.

All the shops on Main Street had apartments on the second floor, except the few that had been converted for another purpose—a studio for one of the local artisans, extra sales floor space for a downstairs shop, and a whole separate store.

When my grandparents had first moved to Cape Bay, they'd lived in the apartment above the café while they waited for children to come along. Mary Ellen had lived in the apartment above her own shop since she'd arrived in town twenty-five or so years earlier. Whatever was going on outside was impossible to ignore while she was sleeping—or trying to sleep—upstairs.

"Do you want me to stay with you tonight?" Sammy offered.

"No, tonight's supposed to be about you," I said. "Mary Ellen, I'll stay with you if you don't want to be alone."

"Fran, you have Latte to worry about. I'll stay," Sammy replied, referring to my beloved café-au-lait–colored Berger Picard dog. He was a stray I'd adopted a couple of months earlier after he found me in the park.

"He's with Matt," I said. "He can keep Latte overnight."

"It's fine—"

"Ladies!" Mary Ellen interrupted, stopping Sammy and me from debating the matter any further. I noticed Dawn hadn't jumped in at all. "Ladies, I am a grown woman, and I have been living on my own for twenty-five years. I certainly don't need one of you to stay here and babysit me just because there are a few police cars outside. And you said yourself, Sammy, there's no murderer on the loose that I need protecting from." She must have realized she was still clasping Sammy's hand because she dropped it quickly.

"Mary Ellen, really, I don't mind—" Sammy started.

"Any of us would be happy—" I said at the same time as Sammy.

Dawn made a face, which I was glad Mary Ellen hadn't seemed to see.

"Girls, I will be fine!" Mary Ellen said, emphasizing the word *girls* and, with it, how much younger than her we were.

Sammy gave me an imploring look, and I shrugged in response. If Mary Ellen didn't want us, we wouldn't be able to convince her otherwise.

"If you're sure…" Sammy said cautiously.

"I'm sure. I appreciate you all coming by to check on

me, but I'll be fine on my own tonight. The doors all have locks, and besides, I have a feeling the police will be out there for half the night anyway." She nodded toward the street.

She was probably right. Mike and his team did seem to be taking their time.

"Would you like us to stay a while, or should we go?" Sammy asked.

"Don't ruin your night's fun for me," Mary Ellen said. "It sounds like you were having a bit of a girls' night. Is it your birthday, Sammy?"

"No—"

"We were celebrating her breakup with her loser boyfriend," Dawn said, finally finding something in the conversation she cared about.

"Jared?" Mary Ellen asked, looking surprised. "The two of you had been together for quite a while, hadn't you?"

"Ten years," Sammy said.

"Ten years too long!" Dawn interjected.

"And this is cause for celebration?" Mary Ellen asked.

"I guess," Sammy said at the same moment Dawn exclaimed, "Yes!"

"We wanted to show Sammy our support," I said to Mary Ellen. "And take her out to have some fun and get her mind off things."

"Well, don't let me stop you from going out and enjoying yourselves," Mary Ellen said.

"You heard the lady." Dawn stood up. "I can hear the margaritas calling me."

"We're not going back for more margaritas," Sammy said. "Well, I'm not, anyway. You're welcome to."

"Then what do you want to do? Go out to the bar? Go back to your place and make our own drinks? Find a movie with some hot shirtless guys we can watch?"

"I don't care what you do. I'm staying here with Mary Ellen if I can convince her to let me. Otherwise, I'm going home—by myself—and going to bed. I've had enough celebrating for tonight."

Dawn looked annoyed as she sat back down in her chair.

"Mary Ellen," Sammy said, looking over at her, "since you wouldn't be getting in the way of any celebrating, would you like us—me—to stay a while or go?"

Mary Ellen looked between us as if trying to decide whether she wanted any of our company. I wouldn't have blamed her if she'd asked us to go just for fear of Dawn staying. "Well, if you really want to stay, I could use some help getting this jewelry sorted and tagged for sale."

"I'd be happy to help out," Sammy said.

"If you don't mind, I'll stay, too," I said. "It'll give

me a chance to look all this stuff over and figure out what I'm coming back to buy."

I recognized the jewelry on the counter as the work of Marti Bowman. She mostly worked with silver, making delicate filigree pieces I'd loved for years. My mother had made it a tradition to buy me a piece or two for every Christmas and birthday. Between those pieces and the ones I'd inherited after my mother's death, I had a fairly sizeable collection. That made me even more eager to see all her newest pieces.

Dawn withered and sank lower in her chair.

"You don't have to stay," Sammy said to her.

Dawn shrugged, and I silently wished for her to go. "I'll stay," she said. "I like Marti Bowman's stuff. It'll be cool to look through it."

I was surprised. I had been almost certain she wouldn't want to stay. But then I realized that if she was Sammy's best friend, they had to have something in common. Sammy was quiet and mostly a homebody, while Dawn was one of the most boisterous people I'd ever met, and she went out every chance she got. But they had to meet in the middle somewhere, and apparently tonight, that was the back room of Mary Ellen's shop.

Mary Ellen spread the jewelry out so we could reach it easily and dropped a pile of tags in the middle of the table with a price list. She explained briefly what she needed us to do, and the four of us settled in to get the jewelry ready for sale. As my grandmother would say, "Many hands make light work." It turned out to be surprisingly fun. We laughed and chatted as we sorted and tagged the pieces. Even Dawn perked up and seemed to enjoy herself, despite the lack of slushy, citrusy alcohol.

It took a little over an hour to finish everything Mary Ellen needed done.

"Thank you, ladies!" she said as we stood in the back room, getting ready to leave. "This would have taken me a week if I had to do it on my own. I'll set up the display in the morning. I know Marti will be happy it's out there so quickly."

"We're happy to help." Sammy smiled.

"I appreciate you giving up your girls' night out to do it." Mary Ellen leaned over to hug Sammy.

"To be honest, finding out the police were investigating a dead body kind of put a damper on things, so this was a good distraction," Sammy replied.

"For me, too."

We said our goodbyes and headed for the front door. We would normally have gone out the back instead of making our way through the darkened store, but we could tell by the spotlights still shining in through the plate glass windows that the police were still set up outside, so the alley would be closed.

Dawn and I had just stepped into the darkness of the store when Mary Ellen reached out and touched Sammy's arm.

"Oh, Sammy!" she said. "I have something for you." She turned to Dawn and me. "You two go on ahead. Just turn the bolt to unlock it. You know how to do it, Fran. It's the same as yours."

Dawn and I went ahead and waited on the sidewalk for Sammy. The entire CBPD was still milling around. Flashes of light came from the alley, where one of the officers was still taking pictures. A couple of the others were taking notes as they talked to people in the crowd. Mike and Ryan were huddled together near one of the police cars. I realized with relief that the ambulance was gone, along with the man under the sheet.

Sammy emerged from the store as Mary Ellen held the door open for her.

"Thank you again, ladies!" Mary Ellen called out with a wave. "Be careful going home." She waved again as she closed and locked the door then disappeared toward the back room.

"What did she have for you?" Dawn asked.

Sammy raised her hand to her throat and held out the sparkly bauble dangling there. It was a tiny three-dimensional heart made of intertwined silver-and-gold filigree, with the twisted silver-and-gold chain emerging from the center as though it were two strands. It was obviously one of Marti's pieces and one of the prettiest things I'd ever seen.

"It's called 'Full Heart,'" Sammy said. "Mary Ellen said she wanted me to have it as a reminder that my heart is whole, even without Jared."

"That's so sweet," I said.

"It's gorgeous. I'm jealous!" Dawn bumped her shoulder into Sammy's with a smile.

Sammy smiled back, looking the happiest I'd seen her since the breakup. I knew her well enough to know it wasn't the gift or its value that made her happy but the sentiment behind it.

We lingered for another minute or so, admiring Sammy's necklace and Mary Ellen's generosity, then made our way down the road toward Sammy's and Dawn's apartments.

They both lived in apartments above shops on Main Street. When I'd first found out they were best friends but didn't live together, I was a little surprised, but as I got to know them both better, I came to understand they were probably smart to live apart. They loved each other, but they wouldn't have lasted long sharing a living space.

We left Dawn at her apartment first then headed for Sammy's.

"Are you going to be all right walking home alone?" she asked when we reached her door.

"Sure, I'll be fine," I assured her.

"Really? I can drive you if you want."

"No, I'll be fine. Promise."

"Okay, if you say so." She hugged me. "Thanks for a good night."

I laughed. "I don't know if I really did much to make it a good night."

"You were there. That meant a lot."

"I'm glad I could be there for you."

I watched to make sure Sammy got in okay then headed for Matt's house on a road off Main Street. The street lights were shining, but after the brightness of the police spotlights outside Mary Ellen's, the road seemed dim and shadowed. Once I got onto my street, where the lights were spaced farther apart, I found myself walking a little faster.

"There's nothing to be afraid of," I told myself. "It was a suicide, not a murder. There's nothing to be afraid of." Still, the shadows seemed ominous.

Chapter 5

BY THE TIME I turned onto Matt's front walk, I was barely able to keep from breaking into a jog. I should have taken Sammy up on her offer to drive me home—if only so that anyone who happened to be looking out their window and saw me scamper by wouldn't think I had lost my mind. But then I remembered that Matt and I were the two youngest residents on a street mostly populated by people a generation older than we were.

Our neighbors seemed to go to bed at nightfall, so no one was likely to see me rushing by. That thought made me even more nervous, and I ran the last few steps to Matt's door. I rapped quickly on the door then grabbed the knob. It was locked, so I knocked again.

Matt pulled open the front door, and I flung myself into his arms.

"Matty!" I exclaimed, my childhood nickname for him bursting from my lips.

He hesitated for a moment then hugged me close.

"What's going on?" he asked, clearly confused. "Are you okay?"

Latte poked his nose at me, trying to figure out where my hands were and why they weren't scratching his head. Giving up, he popped up on his back legs and leaned his front legs against me. I released Matt and reached down to rub Latte's ears. Matt leaned out the door and looked around.

"You just miss me that much?" he asked after determining there was nothing outside.

I nodded, suddenly feeling silly for letting imagination run away with me. "Yeah, you and Latte. Latte mostly."

Matt cast another glance outside then closed the door. "How was your girls' night?"

"Okay." I walked into the dimly lit living room, with Latte following along. Matt had one of the late-night talk shows on TV. I walked to the kitchen and flipped on the light before glancing at the back door to make sure it was locked. I decided it was overkill to cross the kitchen and turn on the bathroom light just for the sake of soothing my overactive imagination. Instead, I grabbed a glass from the cabinet and went to the sink to pour myself a glass of water.

"Just okay?" Matt asked, standing in the entryway to the kitchen.

I nodded as I chugged the water then put the glass on the counter. "A little short."

Matt made a face and looked at the clock over the sink. "It's after midnight."

"Yeah, well…" I stopped and sighed.

Matt looked at me with his eyebrows raised. Tiny Cape Bay didn't have its own news broadcast, and the one from Boston had things to report other than the goings-on of a little resort town over an hour away. News travels fast in a small town, but mostly during daylight hours. Matt had no way of knowing about the interruption to Sammy's celebration.

"They found a body," I said.

"They *what?*"

"That's right—dead body."

"Who? Where?"

"I'm not sure who. In the alley next to Mary Ellen's store. Mike said it was a suicide."

"Mike was there?" Matt asked.

"Of course he was. You think no one called the police about a body in an alley?"

Matt shot me a dirty look. "Smart mouth," he muttered.

"You sound like my mother."

"I'll take that as a compliment."

I rolled my eyes. He always could get the better of me.

"Is that what you're so spooked about?" he asked.

"Spooked? I'm not spooked." Now that I'd had the chance to calm down in the bright light of Matt's kitchen, my earlier panic was starting to feel silly.

Matt's lips twitched, and his eyebrows rose. "Oh really? So you were just that happy to see me?"

"Mm-hmm." I nodded.

Matt shook his head. He knew I was trying to brush off my anxiety, but he was a good enough guy that he let me.

"You want to talk about it?" he asked.

I shook my head, shrugged, then nodded. "Maybe."

"Glass of wine?"

"Please."

Matt crossed the tiled floor and grabbed two wine glasses out of the cabinet. He pulled a bottle of red wine out of the rack. I handed him the corkscrew, and he popped the bottle open. He poured out two generous glasses and handed one to me.

He wedged the cork back in, picked up the bottle with one hand, took his wine glass in the other, and gestured toward the living room. I followed him, and Latte followed me.

Matt sat down on the far end of the couch, putting the wine bottle on the end table. I kicked off my shoes and curled up on the opposite side. Latte settled in between us, resting his paws on my feet. Though Latte obviously loved Matt, I never doubted that he was completely devoted to me.

"So somebody killed themselves in the alley next to Mary Ellen's store," Matt said.

I nodded.

"Weren't you going out for margaritas?"

I nodded again.

"Those two places are at least half a mile apart. How did a body at Mary Ellen's mess up your night out at Fiesta Mexicana?"

"Dawn."

Matt's forehead wrinkled. I could tell he was trying to figure something out, and I finally realized what it was.

"Sammy's friend. Dawn…" I paused while I tried to think of her last name. I still couldn't come up with it. "Dawn, Sammy's friend. Not sunrise dawn."

"Ohhh," Matt breathed, realization setting in. "Oh," he said again, this time in the same tone Mike had used. I had a feeling a lot of people used that tone when they realized Dawn was involved in something. It was remarkable how just telling people that I'd been with her explained how the whole night had gone off in an unanticipated direction.

I sipped my wine as he paused for a minute.

"So, she overheard someone talking in the restaurant about the police finding a body and then dragged you and Sammy over there to check it out?" he asked. I wasn't sure if he thought that was the most logical or most ridiculous possible course of events, but with Dawn, the most ridiculous was probably also the most logical.

"Yup, that's it."

"Really?" Matt asked. Apparently, he had been leaning toward the ludicrous end of the spectrum.

"Well, almost. We never did find out who found the body. Just that it was found."

"Semantics. I'm still right."

"Of course you are." I took another sip of my wine.

"I wonder who did find the body."

I shrugged.

"You said it was in the alley? Behind a dumpster or something?"

"Nope. Just in the middle."

"So you saw it?" Matt looked confused.

"Well, it was covered by a sheet. There wasn't much to see, except—" I remembered Dawn saying she thought she saw blood.

"Except?" Matt prompted.

I shook my head. "Nothing. There wasn't much to see."

"But you talked to Mike?"

541

"Yup."

"I bet he was happy to see you."

"You could say that," I said, trying not to choke on my wine or spit it across the couch at Matt.

His eyes twinkled. It didn't take any great imagination for him to guess how Mike felt about seeing me anywhere near a dead body.

"What did he say?" Matt asked.

"Just told me to stay out of it," I said. "But it's a suicide. There's nothing to stay out of."

"And they thought my dad's death was natural."

I narrowed my eyes and looked at him. "What are you saying?"

He shrugged and sipped his wine. "Just that things aren't always the way they seem at first."

"You want me to get in trouble with Mike, don't you?" I poked at him with the foot Latte wasn't lying on. Latte snuggled closer to me.

Matt laughed and batted my foot away. "No, I'd actually prefer you didn't. I was just saying."

"Just saying what? Huh? Huh? Just saying what?" I kept poking at him determinedly.

He kept swatting my foot away. "Just saying you should stop doing that before I spill my wine all over the couch!"

I pulled my foot back and tucked it under me. "Good point. That would be a terrible end for good wine." I took another sip. "This is good wine, by the way. Where'd you get it?"

He told me, and we debated for a few minutes which places nearby had the best selection. After we'd come to a consensus, Matt topped off our glasses.

"So did Sammy enjoy the part of the girls' night she did get to have?"

"She seemed to. I mean, she's still feeling kind of sad, but I think she's starting to cheer up a little."

"The breakup was her idea, right?"

"Well, I think it was Dawn's idea, but Sammy's the one who did the actual breaking up."

"Dawn." Matt shook his head.

"Sammy actually said it was partly me, too, because I asked her why she was still with him if he treats her so poorly."

"Fran," Matt said in the same tone he'd used earlier, shaking his head again. I poked him with my foot. "Remind me to never take you go-karting for our anniversary."

"Remind me not to date you for ten years with no sign of commitment."

"Oh, that might be a problem," Matt said. "I wasn't planning on showing any signs of commitment until I'm at least forty."

"That's only six years away."

"Are we that old?" he asked.

"Yup, thirty-four," I replied.

"Wow, when did that happen?"

"Almost a year ago."

"I'm getting old, man. No wonder I've been getting so sore from all that working out I've been doing. See? This spot, right here." He slid the sleeve of his T-shirt up on his wine-holding arm to show me the increasing definition of the muscles there. "All those weights I've been lifting are hard on an old body." He'd been going to the gym lately and liked to point out its effects to me.

I liked to tease him and downplay it. "I don't think lifting a wine glass from your leg to your lips counts as lifting weights."

"It does if you keep it as full as I do." He poured more wine into each of our glasses. "So what was it that had you so spooked earlier?" he asked after we spent a few minutes watching the late night show's new host interview some B-list celebrity about his awful-looking movie premiering that weekend.

I shrugged as I debated whether I should 'fess up or keep playing it off. Matt probably wouldn't let it go until I told him the truth, so I decided to get it over with. "It's stupid," I said, then waited to see if he would pursue it.

He did, of course. "When I was six, I got scared because I found my dad's car doors locked. I was scared of *locked car doors*. Since my dad never locked his doors, I was convinced that meant there was somebody hiding in the trunk who had locked them to throw us off. You can't tell me that whatever scared you was stupider than that."

"You were a kid. Kids are allowed to be stupid."

"It was five years ago."

I laughed even though I was pretty sure I actually remembered that happening when we were kids. Unless it was an oddly persistent fear, I doubted it had happened that recently. Still, it made me feel a little bit better.

"I'm not really sure why I was so on edge," I said. "I think it was just seeing the body and then walking home alone in the dark. The streetlights aren't very bright out there. There's no one out on the street. Most of the time, it's great how quiet Cape Bay is. When you get scared about something, though, suddenly every shadow seems sinister, like there's someone lurking where you can't see them. At least in New York, there were enough people around that you could pretend someone would come help you if you were attacked."

Matt laughed.

"You said you wouldn't laugh!"

"I never said that," he replied. "But I wasn't laughing at you being afraid. I was laughing at you not even trying to pretend someone would actually come help you in New York."

"It's true."

"I know it is. That's why it's funny."

I shook my head and turned my attention back to the late night show. There was some band on I'd never heard of. Based on how they sounded, I wouldn't have minded never hearing them. They sounded like a lot of loud noise. I felt very old.

"Man, these guys suck," Matt said.

"You're not kidding."

"Apparently, they're very popular with the preteen girls, though."

I turned my head slowly from the TV to Matt, and my eyebrows shot up about as far as they could go. "I was not aware you spent a lot of time with preteen girls."

"A guy I work with took his daughter and a bunch of her friends to one of their concerts. He said he could barely hear the next day from all the high-pitched screaming in his ears."

"Was that from the girls or the band?" I asked as the lead singer launched into the screeching falsetto of the song's chorus.

"You know, I'm actually not sure," Matt said, rubbing his ear.

The song and the show finally ended, and the next one came on. I pretended to pay attention to the host's monologue, but my mind kept drifting back to the body in the alley. Something about it—besides the obvious— was bothering me, but I couldn't quite figure out what.

"What?" Matt asked, staring at my face intently.

"What?" I asked back.

"You look like you're trying to solve the Hodge conjecture."

"The what?"

"Never mind, it's a math thing. You look like you're thinking about something."

"Nothing in particular," I said, turning back to the TV. Well, nothing I could put my finger on, anyway. Whatever it was that was bothering me was still lurking at the edge of my brain, just beyond what I could consciously comprehend. I tried not to focus on it.

Just as the monologue ended and the band broke into the generic glorified hold music they all played, it came to me. I inhaled sharply.

"What?" Matt asked, looking at me as though he thought something was wrong.

"Matty, I don't think the man in the alley killed himself."

Chapter 6

"FRANNY!"

I wasn't sure whether Matt was annoyed or amused by my declaration. He was clearly surprised.

"What?" I tried to sound neutral.

"The one thing Mike told you to do was stay out of it."

"I know, but then I started thinking about it…"

Matt smiled and shook his head. At least he wasn't annoyed.

"You're the one who said things aren't always what they seem."

"It wasn't a suggestion to go looking."

"I know. I just—something about it was bothering me, and I couldn't figure out what it was."

"Maybe that someone killed himself in an alley?"

"I don't think he killed himself, remember?"

Matt rolled his eyes. "So, what then?" he asked. "Dropped dead and managed to make it look like a suicide just to throw off the cops? Or, oh God, you think it was murder, don't you?"

I looked away from him, not trying very hard to hide the fact that I did, indeed, think it was murder. The wine was making me feel a little silly.

"You really can't leave it alone, can you?"

I smiled and shrugged.

"So what was it? What got you thinking?"

"He had a bag," I said.

"A bag? A bag means he didn't kill himself?"

"It does when it's a bag of souvenirs."

Matt eyed me. "He had a bag of souvenirs?"

"Yup. From Mary Ellen's." I had seen the bag lying on the pavement next to the sheet-covered body. Its logo had looked familiar, but it wasn't immediately obvious where it was from. If it had been Mary Ellen's old logo, the one she'd had when she opened up her shop, I would have recognized it instantly. But she had recently put a new design on her business cards, ads, and bags she put her customers' purchases in. Her graphic designer niece had created it—clean and modern with Mary Ellen's initials intertwined in a swirl. It looked good, but I wasn't used to it yet. That little thing had prickled at the back of my mind. When

I finally placed the logo, a red flag waved high in the air.

"So a bag of souvenirs means he didn't commit suicide?"

"Well, yeah. Why would you buy a bag full of souvenirs and then walk straight outside and kill yourself?"

"Your family would still get the stuff. The police don't keep it forever."

"Well, yeah, but why would you risk..." I thought back to the sight in the alley and lowered my voice before I continued, even though we were the only two people in the house. "Why would you risk getting blood on everything?"

"There was blood?"

I hesitated and made a face. "I'm not sure. There was a gun, though. I saw that." I realized the gun was the other thing bothering me—the violence of it. It wasn't just the loss of life but how aggressively it had been taken. That someone could do that to another person, or even to themselves, upset me more than the death itself.

Matt grimaced. I could tell he hadn't put much thought into the *how* of the death until that moment. "I guess maybe you're right," he said.

"So you agree? You think it was murder?"

"I didn't say that. I said you had a point about the

souvenirs."

"Thank you." I sipped my wine.

"But are you sure there were souvenirs in the bag? Did you actually see them or just the bag?"

I rested my glass against my lower lip. I wasn't sure. I only saw the outside of the bag. Anything could have been in that bag. So my theory wasn't as sound as I'd thought, but the bag from Mary Ellen's shop was full of —something or other. Souvenirs made the most sense, but that wasn't the most logical possibility. "I only saw the bag," I admitted. "But when we saw her, Mary Ellen was acting so strange."

"You talked to Mary Ellen?"

"Yeah. I didn't tell you that?"

"Nope."

"Sorry." I shook my head in an attempt to gather my thoughts. "I'm all over the place, aren't I?"

"It's okay." Matt reached out his sock-covered foot and rubbed it against my bare one. "You've had a rough night." He rested his foot on mine. Between him and Latte, my toes were toasty warm.

"The whole reason we actually went to the scene was to check on Mary Ellen. Sammy thought she might be upset and we should check on her. She was upset, but even more than I expected. She seemed—rattled."

Matt didn't say anything, but I could guess what he was thinking from the look on his face. It made just as much sense for Mary Ellen to be rattled by a suicide as a homicide.

"I don't know. Maybe I'm wrong. But something about that scene just didn't feel like a suicide."

Matt looked at me, his face twitching slightly as though he wanted to say something but was doing his best to hold back.

"Go ahead."

"As soon as I say this one thing, I'm going to tell you to go with your gut and go talk to Mary Ellen. See if the guy had been in her shop and find out why she seemed so upset about it. But first, I just have to ask: do you really think your instinct on this is more likely to be right? I mean, better than the instinct of a cop who has as much experience as Mike does?" Matt paused to let the question sink in then smiled. "But if you really feel strongly about this, you know, Franny, you should just go."

I smiled back at him. I knew he thought I was crazy for even considering that I might have caught onto something the police hadn't, but beyond a cautious warning or two, he wasn't going to say anything about it. He tolerated me investigating murders, and I tolerated him spending so much time watching football and baseball.

"I don't know," I said. "Maybe Mike was trying to keep it quiet. Maybe he was tired and didn't notice.

Maybe I have a sixth sense for these things and should become a detective. Or a private eye. Or a psychic."

Matt laughed. "I think maybe you've had enough to drink."

I looked into my glass. "Nope, still some in there."

"Still some in the bottle, too." Matt reached for the wine bottle and poured the last of it into our glasses.

"I will take your suggestion, though."

Matt wrinkled his forehead, apparently having forgotten what he'd just said. I wondered if the wine was hitting him, too.

"To talk to Mary Ellen," I clarified. "I'll go by her shop tomorrow before I go to work and see if I can find anything out."

"Sounds like a plan." Matt stifled a yawn.

I looked at the cuckoo clock, which had belonged to Matt's mother and had hung in the same spot for as long as I could remember. Over the summer, Matt, like me, had moved back into the house where he'd grown up, and neither of us had redecorated. Not that the clock would move even if Matt did redecorate—his mom had died when we were kids, and I knew the clock was a special memento of her, which told me it was almost two in the morning.

"I better get going. You had to work today. You must be exhausted."

Matt stifled another yawn. "I'm fine. We can keep

talking." He looked pitiful and adorable. The lids of his big brown eyes were heavy, and his dark hair was every bit as messy as I would have expected since he was going on twenty hours of awake time.

"No, I think I'm all talked out."

"You sure? I don't mind."

"I believe you, but I think you might fall asleep on me if I try to keep you up much longer."

"Me? No. I'm really okay." He closed his eyes and leaned his head against the back of the couch.

I pulled my foot out from where it was still tucked under his and kicked him.

"Ow!" he cried, popping his head back up.

"Walk me home." I wiggled my toes until Latte moved off my other foot. I stood up, stretched, then downed what was left of my wine. Matt finished off his glass and handed it to me. I took them to the kitchen, rinsed them out, and left them in the sink. Matt was barely pulling himself up off the couch as I put my shoes back on and started for the door.

"Hold up." He slowly got to his feet. "I'm coming." He shuffled over to the door, where he had a pair of slippers, and slid them on over his socks.

I looked at him in his warm-up pants, T-shirt, socks, and slippers, and shook my head. "You look like an old man."

"It's this street. This is how I see everybody dressed

when they go out to get their papers in the morning, and I start to think this is how everyone dresses."

"In that case, you're missing your robe."

"You're right." He made a move for the bedroom.

"No!" I grabbed his arm to hold him in place, and he grinned at me. I knew he was just messing with me, but I also knew he wouldn't hesitate to actually wear the robe to walk me home. Then he could tease me about the time he walked me home in a robe after I said he looked like an old man, probably for the rest of my life.

Matt hooked Latte's leash to his collar. The leash was just a formality. Neither of us was likely to actually hold onto it. Only one house stood between Matt's and mine, and Latte knew the way home. Matt and I could stand on our respective front steps, and Latte would run between us if we told him to.

The three of us stepped outside. Matt didn't lock his door because it was Cape Bay, and our neighbors thought it was strange the two of us locked our doors when we went to work each day. Except, apparently, for murder, Cape Bay was a safe town.

Looking out at the street, I remembered how anxious I'd been walking to Matt's. The shadows were every bit as creepy right then as they had been before. Matt slipped his hand into mine, and we cut across our neighbor's lawn just as we'd done as kids. We had always said there was no sense in going all the way to the sidewalk when we could save a few steps. Our parents had disagreed, but the Williams family who lived in the house in between us never seemed to mind. So as long as our parents weren't looking, we would beeline across the grass.

Mr. and Mrs. Williams—I never could bring myself to call them by their first names, even though they'd assured me it was fine—still lived in the house, though I hadn't seen much of them since my return to Cape Bay. I'd seen even less of their son, Chase, though he came into the café from time to time.

He always seemed to come in when we were completely slammed, and I couldn't steal away to talk to him for even a few minutes. The best I could manage was a fond hello, a "What can I get you?" and a "Here you go!" He was a couple of years younger than I was, so he'd never been much of a playmate, but he was still someone I thought of with fondness when I looked back on my school years. I'd known one of his older sisters a little better because she was only a year older than me, but I hadn't so much as laid eyes on either her or her older sister since I left for college. They both had moved away, one to Boston and one to San Francisco. I would have to ask Chase or his mom how they were doing the next time I saw one of them.

We reached my front door, and I unlocked it then reached inside to flip on the light. Matt held my hand as

Latte trotted over behind the big oak in the yard to take care of business.

"Are you sure you're going to be all right tonight?" he asked.

I nodded. "Yup, I'm sure." A little tightening in my abdomen made me wonder if he was fishing for me to invite him inside, but then I remembered how he'd almost fallen asleep on the sofa just five minutes earlier and decided he was just asking because he was a nice guy. Besides, if that's what he wanted, he could have asked me to stay instead of walking me home.

In any case, I wasn't sure if I was ready for that. I wasn't looking for any more emotional turmoil. Even though Matt was taking me to Italy with the money he'd made from the sale of his previous house, we had agreed to take things slow. We'd been friends for a long time, and neither of us wanted to mess up our friendship by getting too serious too fast.

"Okay, well, lock your doors, and don't worry about waking me up if you get scared and want to call me. I can be down here in about ten seconds, and if I run really fast, my robe will fly out behind me, and you'll feel like Superman is coming to your rescue."

"Yeah, well, you might want to trade those slippers for some sneakers unless you're actually planning on going flying through the air. Those things don't look like they have much traction."

Matt slid his foot back and forth across the surface of the step. "You may be right. I'll put my sneakers by the door. Or maybe I'll just run over barefoot. Isn't that supposed to be good for your knees or something?"

"I don't think it matters that much when you're running a couple hundred feet across grass."

"Then I'll just pick whichever's fastest."

I smiled. "You do that."

Latte ran past me into the house. I heard him lapping up his water in the kitchen, then he came back, nudged my hand, and went to stand on the stairs leading up to my bedroom.

"Looks like somebody's ready for bed," I said.

"That makes two of us."

"I thought you said you weren't tired!"

"I never said that. I said I would stay up and talk to you if you wanted. That just means I'm a good boyfriend, not that I'm not tired."

"Ah, I see."

Matt pulled me toward him. "Goodnight, Franny." He kissed me softly.

"'Night, Matty." I smiled.

He leaned around me and looked at Latte on the stairs. "Goodnight, my furry friend."

Latte blew out his breath and licked away some droplets of water that were clinging to his nose.

"I'll take that as a goodnight." He pulled me in for

another quick kiss then released my hand and stepped off the front step. "I'll see you tomorrow."

"See you." I turned and went inside, locking the door behind me. I knew Matt wouldn't leave until he knew I was safely inside with the metaphorical hatches battened down.

I patted my leg as I stepped past Latte on the stairs, beckoning him to follow me. He trotted after me obediently. In my bedroom, he jumped onto my bed and flailed around, trying to get the quilt arranged to his liking. He stopped, and I thought he had everything the way he wanted it, but then he flailed again, rolled over, and flailed some more before he finally calmed down and rested his head on the spare pillow. The bed was a mess, but at least he was comfortable.

I changed my clothes, lay down, and turned out the light. Latte floundered around until his body was pressed against mine. I reached out to pet him, and he snuggled into me. In a few minutes, his slow, steady breathing told me he had fallen asleep. I tried to close my eyes, but they seemed determined to pop back open. Despite the ridiculously late hour and all the wine I'd drunk, my mind raced, and sleep eluded me. I couldn't stop thinking about what was in the bag lying beside the dead man and whether it would convince me more or less his death wasn't a suicide.

Chapter 7

LATTE NUDGED me awake far earlier than I would have liked given my late bedtime, but as soon as I was awake, there was no going back. The small part of my mind that had actually woken up went straight back to the dead man in the alley.

I pulled myself from bed. Latte perched on the edge of it, his eyes trained on me, watching and waiting for me to make a move toward the stairs. I could practically hear his little doggie thoughts: "Food. Food. Food. Food. Food. Food. Food. Food."

I rubbed my hands over my face a few times, reached back, and pulled the elastic out of my hair. The thick mass of dark waves fell down my back. I glanced in the mirror over the dresser. I hadn't realized how long my hair had gotten. I'd have to find time to get it cut. I didn't even know where to go. There was a salon down the street from my café. It had been there for about ten years, but I'd been in New York all that time and didn't know if it was any good. I'd have to ask Sammy about it.

I gave my scalp a quick massage and then pulled my hair back into a tight chignon. I changed into a T-shirt and a pair of flared yoga pants suitable for taking Latte on his morning walk and headed downstairs. Latte seemed to teleport from the bed to his bowl in the kitchen. He sat eagerly with one paw in the air, looking ready to explode with excitement. I scooped his food from the container in the pantry and refilled his water bowl as he practically inhaled the kibble.

When he was finished, he ran to the front door, picked up his leash, and resumed his "I can hardly wait" stance. I made him wait until my coffee was ready, not out of cruelty but because he probably wouldn't want me passing out halfway through our walk.

When my coffee was ready and safely poured into my travel mug, I grabbed his tennis ball and headed out. I was tempted to deviate from our normal path along the tree-lined residential streets and head to Main Street just to see if there was any activity in the alley next to Mary Ellen's, but Latte was a creature of habit, and he guided me to the left instead of the right. Just as well. I'd be seeing the alley later when I went to talk to Mary Ellen anyway.

My mind wandered as we walked. My thoughts predictably went straight to the body in the alley. Who was he? How had he died? Was it murder or suicide? Whichever one it was, why was the body right in the middle of the alley? Wouldn't it make more sense to hide in a corner somewhere? Why kill yourself, or someone else, practically out in the open where anybody walking by could have seen? Why didn't anybody see? Or did someone?

I found myself walking faster, leading Latte instead of letting him walk ahead of me like I normally did. We were almost past the park when I felt a tug at the leash and realized he had stopped to stare longingly at the fenced-in expanse of grass that served as the rec league playing fields and dog park.

Miraculously, at this hour on a beautiful weekend morning, the fields were empty. I wondered whether it was an oversight or a mix-up in scheduling. Or maybe there was a reason unknown to single, childless women like me why there were absolutely no sports being played on the fields on this particular Saturday morning.

But it didn't really matter why the fields were empty, just that they were. As distracted as I was by the body, and as anxious as I was to go talk to Mary Ellen about it, I couldn't say no when Latte looked at me with those sad puppy dog eyes.

We crossed the street into the park and headed into

the enclosed fields. I made sure the gate was closed behind me then hurled the ball as far as I could across the grass. Latte took off like a shot, his little legs going so fast that it almost looked as though he were flying.

I chuckled as I thought about the night before when I'd warned Matt he would probably go flying if he tried to run across the grass to my house wearing his slippers. I could just see it—Matt running, his robe flapping in the air, his foot slipping, and him falling ungraciously into the bushes. In my scenario, he wouldn't have any injuries beyond a few scratches from the holly bush and the more significant one to his pride. I actually giggled as I thought it over.

Latte brought the ball back and dropped it at my feet. I tried not to cringe when I picked it up and drool covered my hand. I threw the ball and wiped my hand off on my shirt even though I knew it would be wet again as soon as Latte brought the ball back. I couldn't bring myself to just stand there with a drooly hand while I waited to throw the ball.

My thoughts were light for the rest of our playtime. We played chase a little bit. The game started out with Latte running behind me and ended up with him sprinting back and forth across the field as I trailed behind. From my understanding, the family Latte had lived with before I adopted him had kids, and I had a feeling his love of chase was from time spent running around with them. Those little legs of his could really go, and my sneakers kept slipping in the dew-covered grass. Matt really would have gone flying if he'd tried to run in his slippers.

When Latte finally lay down in the grass, panting heavily, I picked up his leash so we could walk back home. His fatigued pace kept me from moving too fast, even though my mind was back on Mary Ellen and the mystery of the body in the alley. I wondered if Mike felt this way when he was on a case, as if every mundane life task was spent preoccupied with pondering the questions of a murder—or suicide, as the case may be.

Latte and I got home, and I left him to drink his water and sprawl out on the cool tile floor while I went upstairs to shower and get dressed. I thought about making myself a quick brunch but decided I would just grab a sandwich at the café. I tried to get Latte to go outside. He stared up at me from the floor as if I had lost my mind, so I bent down and scratched him behind the ears.

"I'm going to work now, but I'll be back to check on you in a little bit, okay? You're a good boy, aren't you? Yes, you are! Yes, you are! Mommy loves you!" I'd had the dog barely a couple of months, and I was already baby-talking him. I would have been embarrassed, but I was devoted to him to the point that I didn't care what anyone else thought. I kissed him on his little doggie nose and headed out.

It was a short walk to Mary Ellen's, down the street and then up a few blocks. I arrived at the alley in a matter of minutes. All signs of the previous night's events were gone. No police tape, evidence markers, or stains on the pavement. Nothing at all to indicate a man's body had lain there twelve hours earlier. Not even a bouquet of flowers to memorialize him. To me, that was even more tragic—no one seemed to miss the man at all. Unless, of course, the people who would miss him didn't know about his death yet—or they were the ones who'd killed him.

I walked past the alley and paused in front of Mary Ellen's. If I went into her store, I would be deliberately disregarding Mike's direction to stay out of it. Did I want to do that? Did I really want to get involved?

"Curiosity killed the cat," I heard my mother's voice say in my head.

"But satisfaction brought it back," I whispered in response. I pushed the door open, the bell overhead jingling to announce my presence. Mary Ellen, normally the type to greet a customer as soon as they walked in, didn't appear. "Mary Ellen?" I called. "Mary Ellen?"

My overactive imagination ran away with me, and I started worrying that Mary Ellen had been felled by whatever villain had killed the man in the alley. I glanced around for a weapon.

"Hi! How can I help you?" Mary Ellen called, emerging from the back room. A smile spread across her face when she spotted me. "Oh, hello, Francesca."

"Hi, Mary Ellen. How are you?"

"I'm well, and yourself?"

I waited a moment for her to register that I wasn't just politely trying to exchange idle pleasantries. I had been there the night before and knew how upset she'd been.

She sighed when she finally realized. "I've been better."

"I can imagine. Do you have a minute to talk?"

Mary Ellen motioned around the shop. "Saturday mornings aren't a very busy time for me. Most people come get their souvenirs before roll-over day." All the weekly vacation rentals rolled over on Saturdays. With the previous week's renters going out and the following week's renters coming in, it made sense that everyone would get their souvenirs before the day they were desperately trying to beat the traffic out of town.

"We usually get slammed for about two hours on Saturday mornings—everybody trying to get coffee before they hit the road. In fact, it's probably pretty crazy over there right now."

"Sammy holding down the fort?"

"Yup. Becky and Amanda were scheduled to work, too, so she's got plenty of helping hands."

"You can't fit much more than three people behind the counter, can you?"

"Not if anyone wants to be able to move."

Mary Ellen chuckled. "Ah, well, why don't you come into the back with me, and we can chat?"

I followed her to the back and took the same chair I'd sat in the night before. The table was now covered in an assortment of knitted items. I picked up an impossibly soft scarf and ran my hands over it.

"Did you make this?" I asked, knowing she was an accomplished knitter.

"I did," she said proudly. "Do you like it?"

"It's beautiful. Even nicer than some of the stuff I saw in Bergdorf's back in New York City."

"Oh, I doubt that."

"No, really! I'd swear it was cashmere."

"That's probably because it is," Mary Ellen said. "Would you like a cup of tea?" She poured tea from the kettle she had sitting on a hot plate into a mug decorated with a beach scene and "Cape Bay!" in a scrawling script.

"No thanks, I'm fine."

She eased herself into a chair to my right from which she could see out into the shop in case anyone came in.

"So what did you want to talk about? Is it safe to guess you have your investigator's cap back on?"

Did everybody in town know about that? "Well, I wouldn't go as far as that. It's just been on my mind. It's so mysterious. Who was he? What was he doing in Cape Bay? Why would he kill himself practically out in the open like that?" I stopped and shook my head. "I don't know. It just bothers me."

Mary Ellen nodded and shifted in her chair. "Death is upsetting," she muttered as she raised her mug to her lips.

I studied her for a moment. I suspected her mid-length curly blond hair got both its color and texture from a bottle. She didn't wear much makeup, just a little around her eyes and a touch of red on her lips. She'd aged well for the most part. Other than a few scattered wrinkles, she looked almost exactly as she had when she'd first arrived in town. But at that moment, there was something else in her eyes—a guardedness, perhaps? Sadness? Fear?

"Were you here when the man, uh, died?"

"I was," she said simply.

I waited for her to elaborate, but she didn't. I'd hoped it would be easier to get her to volunteer information without much prompting, but our conversation didn't seem to be going that way. "Did—did you hear it?" I asked, lowering my voice as though that would somehow make my question less horrifying.

She fixed her pale-blue eyes on me for a second, her mug held in both hands at her mouth, then shifted her gaze back to the door. Her head bobbed in the slightest nod.

"It was a gunshot?"

She paused then flicked her eyes to me, a scant smile playing at her lips. "For someone who's not investigating, you certainly have a lot of questions."

I blushed and looked down at the scarf I was still absently petting. "Mike told me to stay out of it."

"I haven't stayed single for a quarter century by obediently doing whatever a man tells me to do. Now tell me what you really want to know."

I looked at her, silently trying to judge whether she was really going to answer my questions just on the basis of female solidarity. Based on her expression and my previous experience, I decided she probably was, so I went straight to my real questions.

"When I—briefly—saw the body in the alley, I saw a bag on the ground next to it. A bag with a bunch of stuff in it that looked like it was from your store."

Mary Ellen nodded.

"Did he come in here?"

She nodded again.

"Just before he died?"

A third nod.

"Tell me."

She took a deep breath and a sip of her tea. "It was just before closing. He came in, looked around a while, gradually selected some items, paid, left, and died."

Well, that was one way to say it. I tried to think like a cop. What would Mike ask? What had Mike probably already asked when he had surely interviewed Mary Ellen himself? "What did he buy?"

"Oh, a bunch of things. A couple of those little key chains we have—the cheap, plastic ones, not the nice metal ones—a pair of earrings, a little stuffed bear, some of the Mason jar soups Sue Hodges makes, some marzipan, and, uh, I think that's it."

My mouth started watering at the mention of soup and marzipan. Sue's Mason jar soups were perfect single-size servings of a wide variety of classic soups—chicken, tomato, vegetable, and, of course, New England clam chowder—that she made at home, pressure canned, and sold in a few local shops. They were divine.

And the marzipan! Mary Ellen got it from a local pastry shop. It was sweet and almondy and came in the cutest shapes.

There were the plain square-shaped, chocolate-covered ones, of course, but there were also flowers, hearts, and every kind of animal I could imagine. The designs were only limited by the skill of the person molding the dough. My favorites were the fruit and vegetable shapes. Biting into something that looked exactly like a tiny banana, carrot, or lime but tasted like candy always made me happy.

The thought made me hungry. I hadn't eaten breakfast, and it was creeping up on lunchtime. If I could have raided Mary Ellen's display case right then, I could have put away ten or so of those little candies.

"Francesca?"

"Hmm?" I looked up to see Mary Ellen looking at me expectantly.

"Are you there?" She smiled. "You look like you're a thousand miles away."

"Oh, sorry. I got distracted by the marzipan. Skipped breakfast this morning."

Mary Ellen chuckled and stood up. She walked to a shelf and pulled down a plastic container. She brought it over to me and opened it. Inside were about four dozen tiny marzipan figures, and most of them were the fruits and vegetables I adored.

"Oh, no, I'm fine. Really." I couldn't take my eyes off the perfectly crafted little apple at the top of the container. A little leaf with delicate veins etched into it sprouted from the stem.

"Take it!" Mary Ellen pushed the plastic box closer to me.

Reluctantly, I took a piece of candy and sank my teeth into it. It was every bit as good as I'd hoped.

"So was that all you wanted to know? What the gentleman bought?"

"No." I swallowed. "Although I am impressed that you remembered all those things he bought."

Mary Ellen shrugged her slender shoulders. "He turned out to be a rather memorable customer."

"I can see how that would happen." I certainly would remember every detail about an encounter with a customer who died moments after stepping outside of my café. "Was he here with anyone?"

Mary Ellen shook her head.

"Did you see anyone outside?"

She shook her head again.

"Did you hear anything before the gunshot?"

Mary Ellen paused and then nodded.

I took a deep breath. I was about to find out something very important or be very annoyed. "What did you hear?"

"I heard the man yelling. I couldn't understand all of it, but he was saying 'no' to someone. I don't know who. I didn't see. There was more yelling and then the gunshot. I didn't go out to look. I didn't even go to the door to lock it. I just closed myself in the back room and called the police."

I didn't blame her. No wonder she'd looked so

shaken. I picked up a tiny marzipan carrot, complete with leafy stems. "So there was definitely someone else out there? You heard them?"

"Yes. Well—"

"What is it?"

"Like I said, I never actually saw anyone. And I heard yelling, but I don't know if it was one voice or two. I can't be certain."

"Is there anything else, Mary Ellen? Anything you saw or heard that might not have seemed significant at the time? Anything at all?"

She thought for a moment as I nibbled on my "carrot," feeling a bit like Bugs Bunny. Finally, she shook her head. "No, that's all."

I was disappointed. I don't know what I'd hoped—maybe for Mary Ellen to tell me exactly who the dead man was. Who killed him and why. But all I'd gotten was confirmation he'd been in her store and bought souvenirs right before he died.

"I'm sorry I can't be of more help, dear."

"It's fine, Mary Ellen." I smiled. "I appreciate you talking to me. And the marzipan. I could eat this stuff all day."

"Well then, why don't you take some with you?"

"No, no, it's fine. I've had plenty."

"It's on the house, Fran. I'm not going to charge you for a little box of marzipan."

"I was actually thinking of buying a jar or two of soup anyway."

"Just take them. Consider it a thank you for you girls coming to check on me last night. I do appreciate it."

Mary Ellen put a small assortment of the marzipan figures into a box. She put the candy and the soups I'd picked out into a bag and handed it to me. I was halfway to the door when a thought crossed my mind.

"Mary Ellen, the souvenirs the man bought last night —how did he pay for them?"

"By credit card."

My heart pounded. I took a breath. "A real credit card? Not a gift card? Did it have his name on it?"

"Yes."

Chapter 8

I TOOK A DEEP BREATH. Mary Ellen had the most important piece of information in the case so far, and she hadn't volunteered it. Had she told the police? Had Mike known who the dead man was when I'd talked to him the night before? Was there a reason he was keeping that information to himself? Was there a reason Mary Ellen hadn't told me?

"What was his name, Mary Ellen?"

"Abraham Casey."

"Are you sure?"

"Of course I'm sure! I'll never forget that man's name or his face." She walked to the cash register and punched a few buttons to open it. She pulled out a receipt and handed it to me. "See? Abraham Casey."

I took the receipt and studied it. Abraham Casey's

signature was a mess, the way a doctor's looks on a prescription pad. He'd signed his name with an A, squiggles, a C, and more squiggles, including one that dropped below the signature line. I gave the receipt back to Mary Ellen but didn't let go when she put her hand on it.

"Actually, do you mind if I take a picture of it?" I caught her curious gaze and shrugged. "I don't know. Seems like it could be important."

"Certainly." She withdrew her hand, and I laid the receipt down on the counter. I pulled my phone out of my pocket and snapped a few pictures of the receipt, focusing on the signature at the bottom.

"Thank you," I said, slipping my phone back into my pocket. I turned to go and then turned right back around to Mary Ellen. "What did he look like?"

"He was nice looking. A little older than you. A little taller than me." She gestured a couple of inches above her head. She was tall, probably close to five foot ten, so I guessed the man was about six feet. "His hair was short. Dark. He had brown eyes and little wire-rim glasses." She curled her hands around her eyes to mimic glasses. "A beard." She rubbed her cheeks. "Just a short one. He wore a navy blue polo shirt and a pair of khakis. Very neat. Very well groomed. He seemed like a nice man." She shook her head. "It's a shame."

I nodded in agreement. "Thank you, Mary Ellen.

For everything." I lifted the bag to indicate I meant both the food and the conversation.

"Come by any time. I enjoy your company."

I turned to go again then thought of another question before I made it out the door. If I were a detective, I would either be exceptionally bad at my job because I would only think of the most critical questions after I left, or I would be incredibly good at it because I would wear the suspects down, and they would confess just to keep me from coming back repeatedly with more questions.

"Mary Ellen?"

"Yes?"

"One more thing—did you give the police the man's name?"

Mary Ellen hesitated. "No, I didn't."

"Why not?"

"Well, they didn't ask."

I was surprised. I'd noticed Mary Ellen seemed reluctant to volunteer information to me, but I hadn't thought she'd be the same with the police. I wondered if she was hiding something.

"I was so shaken up when they were here, I didn't even think about the credit card receipt. I only thought of it late last night."

Well, at least that explained why she didn't tell the police—if she was telling the truth, that is.

"So, are you going to tell them?"

Mary Ellen smiled, apparently noticing my concern that she hadn't shared all the information with the police. "I called the officer this morning and left a message."

"Mike?"

"No, it was a young man. He interviewed me yesterday and left me his card. I can find it for you if you'd like."

"Was it Ryan? Leary?" I remembered the new-in-town officer Sammy and I had met the night before. "Tall, broad shoulders, dark hair, crew cut?"

"No, that wasn't him. Do you want me to find that business card?"

"No, it'll be all right. I was just curious. Thanks again."

I finally managed to leave Mary Ellen's then headed to the coffee shop. I snuck in the back door and peeked into the café. It was busy, but nothing Sammy and the girls couldn't handle.

Sammy looked up and caught my eye. I motioned that I was going to eat, and she nodded. Back in the stock room, I selected a tomato soup Mary Ellen had given me and heated it up in the microwave.

The soup was every bit as delicious as I expected. The broth was smooth and had the flavor of delicious, fresh, summer vine-ripened tomatoes. I probably could have eaten a gallon of it. Instead, I opened the box of marzipan and scanned through it, looking for which piece I wanted to indulge in.

I spotted a little tomato and smiled. What better dessert than a marzipan tomato after a lunch of tomato soup? I ate it and left the box open on the counter so Sammy and the girls could have some. I considered not sharing, but my grandfather's voice in my head reminded me to be kind to my employees.

I pulled an apron over my head, tied it behind my back, and went out front to the café.

"Where do you need me?" It was my café, but the girls had a good rhythm going, and I wasn't going to mess it up just because I was the boss.

Sammy looked around as she prepared a cappuccino. "Um, dishes? Or you can take over here after I finish this one, and I can wash dishes."

"Up to you." I much preferred to be behind the espresso machine, but I wasn't going to kick Sammy off if that's where she wanted to be.

She looked at me. "Nobody comes in here to see my latte art."

"Doesn't matter what the picture is if the coffee's bad. And you make good coffee."

"Yeah, but I'm not the one who earned a write-up in a food blog. Here." She stepped back from the machine, the cappuccino she'd been working on in a saucer in her hand. "I'll take this to the customer. You make the next one. Latte, double shot espresso. Gentleman in the corner, blue shirt."

I stepped up to the espresso machine, and Sammy walked around the counter to deliver the drink she'd just made. I checked the machine over quickly to make sure everything was ship-shape then started pulling the espresso shots.

While the machine worked, I began steaming the milk to pour into the cup. As I worked, I thought about the design I wanted to put into the latte's foam. I liked to start slow and not make anything too complicated until a few drinks in. I thought about a butterfly but decided on a star. Women tended to get more excited about butter-flies and hearts, so I usually saved those designs for them.

The espresso and milk were ready. I leaned over the cup and began my pour. Once the dot of milk was in, I picked up the small metal etching tool and began drawing in the star. It only took a few seconds, and the star was beautiful when it was done. My grandfather would have been proud. It had always been his motto to "Make your food delicious, and make it beautiful." The delicious came first then the beautiful, but both were important.

I carried the cup and saucer to the blue-shirted man in the corner then returned to the espresso machine.

There was no one else in line. The rush was over. I wiped down the machine and the counter.

Amanda was bussing the tables and taking the dirty dishes to Sammy in the back. Becky had started refilling the food in the display case without anyone requesting her to. I made a mental note to put a little something extra in her paycheck. Another thing I'd learned from my grandparents when they'd run the café was to reward people when you caught them going above and beyond.

I finished wiping everything down and went to help Sammy with the dishes. She had a stack of clean dishes that needed to be put away, so I worked on those.

"Sorry about your night out getting ruined last night," I said.

Sammy shrugged. "When you go out with Dawn, you have to expect things to go a way you didn't expect. It would have been more fun if it had turned into a spontaneous road trip to New York, though."

I didn't really think a trip to New York was as exciting as she did, only because I'd lived there for so long, but I had to agree it would have been preferable to checking out a crime scene. "Maybe we can try again next week. We'll be on fall hours then, so we'll have more time."

Like most businesses in Cape Bay, we basically ran three schedules—summer hours, spring/fall hours, and winter hours—depending on the expected amount of tourist traffic. With school starting the next week, we'd be closing earlier on the weekdays, finally giving us a chance to catch up on our personal lives.

"That sounds good. That mango margarita Dawn got right before we left sounded pretty good. I'd be up for going to get one."

"Tuesday night?"

"That'll be perfect!" She flashed me a sunny smile and seemed like her old self.

"What can I work on?" Becky stuck her head through the door. Her red curls were typically frizzy, the result of spending a morning over steaming cups of coffee. Amanda was hovering behind her also awaiting orders.

"How are we on sandwiches?" I asked.

"Good. Display case is fully stocked, and there are a few more in the refrigerator."

"What about tiramisu?"

"All filled up. Cupcakes and muffins are, too."

"There's some marzipan on the table over there," I offered.

"Where do you want me to put it?"

"No, for you. You and Amanda take some."

Becky approached the table cautiously and looked into the box. "What is it?"

"Marzipan." Then, I realized she had no idea what that was. "It's like candy."

"Oh, okay." She and Amanda peered at the figures in the box. "The animals are all too cute too eat." Becky picked up a heart instead.

Amanda and I both watched her face as she bit into it slowly. She looked very serious as she tasted it. Then she smiled. "It's good!" She pushed the box toward Amanda, who picked out a pine tree. Amanda smiled when the marzipan hit her tongue.

"Why don't you two each take a couple of pieces and go home for the day? Enjoy your last weekend before school starts. It's going to be dead in here the rest of the day anyway." Out of the corner of my eye, I saw Sammy make a face at my choice of words. The girls didn't seem to notice it, though.

"Awesome! Thanks!" They each picked out a few pieces and wrapped them in napkins. After they hung their aprons and fished their purses out of drawers, they waved goodbye and headed for home, or wherever else they spent their time when their parents thought they were at work.

Sammy and I went back to washing dishes. My mind returned to the man in the alley.

Chapter 9

I SPENT the afternoon itching to get online to see if I could find information on an Abraham Casey, preferably one with short dark hair, dark eyes, a trim beard, and glasses. I was lucky the café was slow and I didn't have to concern myself too much with customers, although thinking about something else for a few minutes probably would have done me some good.

Half an hour or so before Sammy was due to leave, I ran home to let Latte out and play with him for a minute. When I got back, the café was just as empty as when I'd left, with just a couple of local moms lingering in some comfy armchairs, chatting quietly and enjoying the break from their kids. Having witnessed them come in before with their kids, I didn't blame them for wanting some time to themselves.

I greeted them with a wave and went in the back to put my apron on. I found Sammy slipping the last bite of a marzipan bunny into her mouth.

"Sorry," she mumbled around it. "I got hungry."

"With all the food in this café, you had to take my marzipan? I'm kidding—I left it there so you guys could eat it."

"That's what you said, but I know how you feel about marzipan."

I laughed. "And I thought I kept that so well hidden."

She smiled and slid her apron over her head. "Guess I better get going."

"Big plans tonight?" I hoped for her sake that she wasn't planning on spending the night at home on the couch with a pint of ice cream and a cry-your-eyes-out movie.

"I'm going over to help my mom with some canning while my dad watches college football and yells at the TV."

I thought that sounded less depressing than the movie and ice cream on the couch. "Well, have fun."

Sammy laughed. "I'll try. After a day spent over hot drinks and a hot dishwater and an evening spent over boiling water, sterilizing jars for preserves doesn't exactly sound like a great time, but I'll survive."

She slipped out the back door, and I looked around

for something to occupy me until the café's traffic picked up again around dinnertime. That was when all the vacationers ventured out to see the town and when the locals who had been out running errands all day stopped in to pick up a quick sandwich or coffee to get them through the evening.

As usual, Sammy had left everything in immaculate condition. All the dishes—except the ones being used by the two women out front—were cleaned and put away, the display cases were fully stocked, and every last table and counter had been wiped down. I was grateful, of course, for her attention to detail, but it didn't leave me much to do to keep busy.

I let my hair down from its perpetual summertime chignon and ran my fingers through it. I noticed again how long it was and wished I had remembered to ask Sammy for a recommendation on a good place to get it cut. I'd have to remember to ask when I saw her tomorrow. I twisted my hair back up off my neck and secured it.

I was tempted to sit down at the computer and start researching the late Mr. Casey, but I restrained myself. My research could wait until I didn't have a business to run. Instead, I decided to roast a batch of coffee beans. It never hurt to have extra beans roasted. Unfortunately, roasting coffee beans didn't take much time or effort since the machine did most of the work, but it made me feel productive.

I stood and looked around the café. Mismatched chairs and tables lined the exposed brick walls. A few comfortable armchairs sat in the corner for people who liked to spend a little more time lingering over their drinks. A chalkboard menu, covered in Sammy's flawless handwriting and artful drawings, hung above the counter. It looked almost the same as it had when my grandparents were alive. It was warm and cozy and felt like home. I suspected it did for a lot of our customers, too, based on how often they came and how long they stayed.

The two women left, and I went into the back storeroom to organize. The bell over the door would let me know if someone came in. I managed to kill the rest of the afternoon until the evening rush started. I had a busy hour or so, but nothing I couldn't handle on my own. Of course, Chase Williams was in and out as I worked busily on making drinks. I waved hello, took his order, made his drink, and waved goodbye. I'd try to talk to him again next time.

I was grateful for the brief rush not only for the revenue and the fact that the increase in customers kept me busy for a while, but also because it stopped my attempts at organizing the storeroom. I'd managed to make the back room look messier than it had when I'd started. Sammy would have a fit when she saw it. Matt came in just as the rush subsided and saved me from doing any more damage.

"How's it going?" He walked up to the counter.

"Doing okay." I smiled. "Been pretty slow until the last hour or so." I shrugged. "But that's normal for a Saturday."

"You mind if I hang out for a while?" he asked.

"No. Why would I?"

"I was being polite."

"You're such a gentleman."

"A hungry gentleman, at the moment."

"And what can I get you, sir?" I asked in my politest café-owner voice.

"A latte, please." He leaned back to look into the display case. "And is that my favorite dark chocolate cupcake I see in there?"

"You know I make a point to always have it for you."

"The day I don't ask is the day you don't have it."

I slid open the door of the display case and pulled out one of the dark chocolate, peanut-butter-filled cupcakes he adored. I put it on a plate and handed it across the counter to him. "Go sit down. I'll bring your latte over in a minute."

Matt took the plate and settled at a table in the back corner. I turned to the espresso machine and started working on his coffee. The motions of preparing the drink were so familiar that I was reasonably sure I could do it in my sleep. I was glad because I needed to focus most of my mental faculties on deciding what design to put into the foam. I made Matt coffee so often that I always had trouble coming up with what to create.

I varied between the extremes of a simple rosette and the most complicated, creative, or quirky design I could think of. The time frame to decide was so short—only seconds from the time the espresso was ready until I had to start pouring—there wasn't really time to dwell on what I wanted to do. I smiled as the idea came to me and started pouring the milk.

There was no one else in line, so I quickly prepared a drink for myself and decorated it with a simple swan then carried both over to Matt's table.

"Mind if I join you?" I set the cups down. I made sure Matt's was angled just right so he could fully appreciate my hard work the instant he looked at it.

"Not at all," he said around a bite of cupcake. He gestured toward the chair on the opposite side of the table.

I sat down and waited while he chewed. He took so long that I started getting antsy. I was probably a little too excited about my design, but I thought it was really clever.

He finally looked down. He squinted his eyes a little, cocked his head, and smiled. "Latte?"

"Of course! That's what you ordered!" My lips twitched as I tried to keep a straight face.

"I didn't specify I wanted Latte in my latte."

"I figured I'd go literal." I smiled. I'd named my dog after the drink because they were the exact same color. It seemed only natural to recreate the dog in the drink.

"I gotta hand it to you, it looks exactly like him. I have no idea how you make something like this out of milk and coffee."

I resisted the urge to correct him and point out that a latte is made with espresso, not coffee. I had learned a long time ago the average person didn't care about the intricacies of the coffee world. I still had to bite my tongue to keep from correcting people, though.

Matt hesitated as he looked at the cup. "I hate to ruin it." He shook his head.

"There's no point if you don't drink it." I'd told him a hundred times before, and I'd probably have to say it a hundred times more. I loved how much he appreciated my creations, and I'd be a little disappointed the first time he didn't hesitate to ruin it.

Matt tipped the latte back and took a drink. "Delicious as usual."

I smiled with pride and took a drink from my own cup.

We sat peacefully for a few minutes, enjoying each other's company in silence. My mind cleared as I sat with Matt, and I didn't think about Abraham Casey for a change.

Finally, Matt spoke up. "Get the chance to talk to Mary Ellen today?"

"I did." I sipped my coffee. I felt a surge of excitement when I remembered what I had to tell him, but I held it in, or tried to.

"And?"

"He was in her shop right before he died."

"Buying souvenirs?"

"Buying souvenirs," I confirmed.

"So you were right."

"Yup, I was."

Matt looked at me, his eyes narrowed, and I fought back a smile.

"What else?"

"He paid with a credit card."

Matt thought for a minute. "So…" He paused. "He doesn't carry cash? He has a tough time at vending machines?"

"What's on a credit card?"

"A number. An expiration date. A verification number. Uh…"

I looked at him, wondering if he'd gone dumb or was just playing with me. "Really? Matty, come on. Under the number. Think about it, *Matteo Cardosi*." I emphasized the syllables of his name. "Are you really telling me, *Francesca Amaro*, that you can't think of anything else that might be on a credit card?"

I could practically see a light bulb turn on over his head. "A name!" And then he realized the significance of that. "You found out his name?"

"I did. Abraham Casey."

"Abraham Casey," Matt repeated. "Do you know anything else about him yet?"

"Yet? You just assume I'm going to keep investigating?"

Matt chuckled. "Well, I have met you."

Clearly, I was too predictable. "No, I haven't looked him up yet. I thought I should focus on running the café. Not that I'm doing a very good job of it right now." I motioned to a few tables scattered with dirty dishes. "I'll look him up later tonight."

"I'm impressed with your restraint." The corner of Matt's mouth twitched as he sipped his coffee.

I rolled my eyes, stood up, and downed the last of my latte. "But that reminds me—it's getting close to closing time. I should get to cleaning up."

"I guess I could help," Matt said, mock-reluctantly.

"You better get to it if you want to help me research one Abraham Casey later tonight."

"Oh, well, when you put it that way!"

Matt got up and helped me clear the tables, wipe everything down, and clean the dishes. By closing time, we had everything neat, clean, and ready to go for when Sammy opened up the next morning. The back room I'd turned into a chaotic mess would have to wait.

I locked up, and Matt and I started the walk home. We had gotten about halfway there when my stomach rumbled, and I realized I'd barely eaten all day.

"I need a lobster roll," I announced.

"Right now?"

"I've had a bowl of soup, some marzipan, and coffee today. I'm starving."

"Sandy's?"

"Yes." I turned on my heel and headed toward Sandy's Seafood Shack before Matt had a chance to react. After realizing I hadn't eaten, I seemed to get hungrier with every step.

"You really must be hungry." Matt hurried along beside me.

"I am." I paused. "Are you?"

"I could eat."

"That's not exactly convincing."

"I'm always up for lobster."

Sandy's was at the opposite end of the boardwalk, so it took us a little while to get there, but I wasn't complaining because I knew the warm, buttery lobster would be totally worth it.

When we got to Sandy's, we sat at one of the picnic tables on the back deck. Through the window screens, we could hear the ocean waves crashing. I took a deep breath of the tangy salt air. Since Cape Bay was a seaside town, the salt air was evident almost everywhere in town, but Sandy's deck literally hung out over the ocean, so the aroma was all encompassing. I loved it. It smelled like home.

We both ordered a lobster roll and a beer, as well as an order of fried clams to split between us. It was the best food I could imagine eating on a Saturday night in New England. Nothing compares to fresh-caught seafood.

Matt was in the restroom when the waitress brought the food to the table. I politely waited for him to return before digging into my lobster roll, but I went ahead and started popping the clams into my mouth. I told myself they were more like an appetizer than part of the actual meal, so it was okay to start without him.

"You gonna save some of those for me?" Matt asked as he returned to the table.

"If I have to." I was practically inhaling the crispy, delicious bits of clam.

He reached for one, and I swatted his hand.

"Do I have to fight you for them or something?"

"Or you could ask nicely." I shoved another piece into my mouth.

"May I please have some fried clams, Francesca,

darling?" He batted the long lashes that encircled his warm brown eyes.

I took the clam that was almost in my mouth and put it in his outstretched hand. "You may have one."

Matt placed it delicately in his mouth then chewed very slowly.

I finally laughed. "Here, take them before I eat them all." I pushed the paper bowl toward him.

"I'll be fine if you just want to eat them."

"No, we got them to share."

"But if you're that hungry, I don't mind. I have plenty of lobster here. Unless you're planning to eat that, too."

"I'm not. I think I have enough on my own. But thanks for the offer." I lifted my lobster roll to my mouth and ate. It was perfection.

Despite my protests that I'd eaten more than half the food, Matt paid the bill when we finished, and we started the walk back to our street. Now that my stomach was full, the only thought on my mind was finding out just who Abraham Casey was.

Chapter 10

BACK AT MY HOUSE, we set up camp at opposite ends of the couch. Matt turned on a football game I couldn't have cared less about. I didn't even know they played football on Saturdays until he turned it on, although I did remember Sammy mentioning something about it earlier in the day.

When I asked Matt about the game, he launched into a lengthy explanation of the different types of football and their relative merits. I zoned out somewhere around "No, that's the NFL. This is college," which was almost immediately after he started talking.

Latte lay on Matt's lap because his hands were free for petting except when he used them to change the channel to a different game or for his beer-to-mouth weight-lifting exercises. Fortunately for Latte, Matt's intermittent activities only required one hand. My hands were occupied with my laptop. I was searching for Abraham Casey.

A surprising number of men had that name. I was glad his name wasn't John Smith or Mike Jones. I scrolled through the pages of search results, trying to figure out which one he might be. I ruled out the one who was born in 1783 and died in 1817 as well as his son and grandson. Several results just happened to have the words Abraham and Casey on the same page, including an article by someone named Casey Johnson about the biblical Abraham.

Another article featured an actress who played a character named Casey in a new movie, and someone with the last name Abraham had commented on it. I found it difficult to stay focused on my research because so many other things caught my attention.

"How's it going?" Matt asked when his game stopped for a studio-based segment with a bunch of brawny men and one busty blond woman wearing a dramatically low-cut shirt.

"Not great. I found a bunch of people named Abraham Casey, but I don't know how to narrow it down or figure out which one is the guy I'm looking for."

"Want me to help?"

"No." My stubbornness had kicked in, and I was determined not just to figure out who he was but to do it on my own. I felt as if I were so close, and if I just tried a little harder, there he would be. I tried my search again with Abraham Casey in quotes so it would only return results with both words next to each other.

"Any luck?" Matt asked later when another pretty blonde in a revealing top was interviewing a large sweaty man in football pads.

"No," I groused.

"Did you try social media?"

I shoved the laptop toward Matt. He perched it on the arm of the couch to keep from disrupting Latte.

"So what have you tried so far?"

I scooted next to him and listed off the things I'd tried. I'd been at it for so long, I knew I was probably forgetting half of it.

Matt clicked around and did a few general web searches then searched a couple of different social networks. I rested my chin on his shoulder as I watched him work.

"I can find a couple guys..." he murmured as he typed and clicked and scrolled and clicked and typed.

"A couple of guys?" I repeated when he didn't finish his sentence.

"A couple of guys who are at least sort of local. I figure they're the best ones to start with. There's one in

Boston and one down in Hartford."

"You think either of them's him?"

"I don't know. The one in Boston's a pharmacist. The one in Hartford's a..." He scrolled and peered at the screen. "Mechanic."

"Mike and Mary Ellen both said the guy was dressed business casual. Can we check out the pharmacist first? Can we find out more about him?"

"Hold on one second." Matt typed in the search box again. He scrolled down the page and then back up. "You said Mary Ellen described him to you?"

I nodded without moving off his shoulder.

"Ouch! You have a pointy chin!" He pulled out from under my chin.

"Yes, she described him." I put my chin back where it was. He let me leave it there.

"What did he look like?"

"Brown hair, brown eyes, beard, glasses."

"That should narrow it down." I was reasonably sure he was being sarcastic, especially since brown hair and eyes described the majority of the world's population.

"Let me know if you see anyone who looks right." He pulled up a screen of people whose pictures were somehow associated online with the words "Abraham Casey." I was slightly embarrassed I hadn't thought to try that, but he didn't say anything, so I didn't either.

I looked at the screen. The first image looked as

though it was from the article about Abraham in the Bible by Casey Johnson because it was an image of an old man with a long, flowing beard, a long cloak, and a shepherd's staff. The second picture was the actress who played Casey. The next few people were definitely not the man in the alley—too old, too young, too female. I let my eye wander down the page and gasped.

Matt saw it a second after I did. "This one?" He pointed at the image of a friendly-looking man staring out at us from the middle of the screen.

"Yup." The man had short brown hair, brown eyes, a trim beard, and glasses. He looked as though he were about five or ten years older than me.

Matt clicked on the picture, and we were taken to a social network we'd searched earlier to no avail. In the vast expanse of social media users, we hadn't been able to find the Abraham Casey we were looking for. But now he was smiling at us like he'd just been sitting there, waiting for us to show up. Above him on the screen was another picture of him. In this picture, a woman and child smiled beside him. His wife and son, I assumed.

"Wow," Matt said.

"What?"

Matt clicked around on the screen, flipping between tabs that showed a variety of information about the elusive Mr. Abraham Casey. His birthday with the year, his hometown, his current employer, previous employers, his wife's name, his son's name and birthdate, his friends, his interests, places he'd been—almost everything you could want to know about him.

"This guy is not concerned with privacy. Look." He clicked to the Friends tab. "No mutual friends. If we can see this, that means everyone can see it. Every detail of his life out here for anyone to see."

"Is that bad?"

Matt craned his neck to look at me since I was still leaning on his shoulder. "Are you serious?"

"Yes?"

"Oh, Franny." He navigated away from Abraham's page and clicked on a menu. He scrolled down, clicking more menus here and there. "Well, yours aren't as bad as his, but they could use some tightening up. Do you mind?" He hovered the mouse over one of the settings.

"Go right ahead. Fix me up. As long as I can still see the pictures of all my friends' vacations to exotic places, you can do whatever you want."

Matt clicked around for a couple of minutes. "There. Now you won't have strangers looking at your profile because they came across your name on the Internet somewhere and wanted to know everything about you."

"Thanks." Matt clicked back on Abraham's profile

page. I noticed the little link to his wife's profile and pointed over his shoulder. "Can we go look at her page?"

Matt clicked on the blue text, and we were taken to her profile. It was empty except for a picture of her smiling next to Abraham and holding their son. It looked like it was from a professional shoot.

"At least someone in that family had some sense about privacy," Matt muttered.

"Can we go back to his page?" He clicked over, and I leaned in to get a better look at the screen. "Scroll down."

Abraham Casey's entire life was laid out in front of us in pictures and short lines of text. Romantic dinners he'd had with his wife. Vacations they'd taken with their son. Funny bumper stickers he'd seen while stuck in traffic. The annoying thing the woman in front of him in the grocery store line had done.

I was transfixed by the bits and pieces of a stranger's life. A stranger I still wasn't entirely sure was the man in the alley. I'd have to print out his picture and take it to Mary Ellen to see if she could confirm whether it was the man who had come into her store. Then something caught my eye as Matt scrolled down farther.

"Stop!" I put my hand on his arm. "Go back. Up. Up. There!" I looked at the screen in shock.

"Oh, Abraham," Matt whispered.

On the screen was a picture of Abraham Casey's

driver's license with the caption, "Took 3 hours at the DMV, but I'm renewed!"

Along with his picture, his address, height, weight, and all the other information on a driver's license, Abraham's signature was at the bottom.

I looked around at the couch, the end table, the floor, and stuck my hand between the couch cushions.

"What are you doing?"

"Looking for my phone." I got up on my knees and felt my pocket. The hard rectangle was on the left. I pulled it out and unlocked it. I tapped furiously, trying to get to what I wanted.

"Now what are you doing?"

"Looking for something." I finally found it and held my phone up to the screen. The signature was the same on the driver's license and the credit card receipt.

"It really is him." Matt sounded vaguely surprised. To be honest, I was, too. A part of me hadn't thought we'd actually find him and that maybe Abraham Casey was a pseudonym, but there he was. If the name was a pseudonym, it was the one he used in his everyday life. This really was the Abraham Casey we were looking for.

I sank back down onto the couch. "Okay, even I wouldn't put my driver's license online like that."

Matt laughed. "Well, at least you know that much." We stared at the screen, stunned that we'd trapped our quarry. "Now what? Do we call Mike?"

I shook my head. "Mary Ellen already called the police."

"She did? Then what did we do all this searching for if the police already know his name?"

"I wanted to know who he was. Like, really. Who the man was and what got him killed."

"And did you find that?"

"I think I know who he was," I said slowly. "Or at least I will after I stay up half the night reading down through his page. But no, I don't know why he was killed."

"And you're sure now that he was murdered?"

"Mary Ellen heard him yelling 'no.' He was either murdered or wanted someone to think he was."

"Maybe he had a life insurance policy that doesn't pay out for suicide. He wanted to kill himself but wanted his wife and kid to get the money."

I thought about it for a few seconds. "I don't know. It still doesn't make sense to me. He bought a lot of stuff at Mary Ellen's. If he just wanted to get souvenirs to make it look good, why buy so much stuff? If he bought things he actually wanted his family to have, why risk them getting messed up or his family not getting them at all? I still think murder makes more sense. I just have to figure out why."

"Do you have any ideas?"

"Well, in New York, I would have said mugging gone

wrong, but we don't really have a lot of muggings in Cape Bay, so that's probably out. Revenge? Vendetta?"

"Lovers' quarrel?" Matt suggested.

"You think Mrs. Casey—what was her name? Leah? —you think Leah killed him?"

"Or his lover. Or hers."

"Crime of passion. It's a possibility." I thought about it. If Leah had killed him, had she come to town with him? Or was he here to meet a lover and she'd caught them together? Or maybe Leah was the one in town for a tryst, and Abraham had interrupted them. But then why would he have bought souvenirs? What if it actually was random? A chill ran down my spine. A random murder was frightening to think about. "I need to find out why he was here and who he was with. That's what I need to know before I can figure out the rest."

Matt nodded and scrolled quickly to the top of Abraham's page. "Nothing since Tuesday." He scrolled down slowly, then faster, slowed down, sped up, and slowed down again. "And that seems unusual for him. It looks like he usually posts every day. Sometimes two or three times a day even."

"He only died last night, though."

"So something happened before that to make him stop posting."

"What's the last thing he put up?"

Matt scrolled up. Abraham had posted a picture of

himself with his wife Leah and their son, sitting at what looked like a restaurant table.

"Dinner at Woodman's," I read off the screen.

"They look happy."

I leaned against the back of the couch. Why did he stop posting? What had he been doing that he couldn't —or didn't want to—post? I stared at the screen, thinking through the possibilities. I needed to find out what he had been doing in Cape Bay. He'd had dinner with his family in Boston on Tuesday and died in Cape Bay on Friday. I had to find out what happened between those days.

"So what are you thinking?" Matt asked.

"I'm going to find out why he was here."

"And how are you going to do that?"

"Well, we know he didn't spend a whole week here, so he probably wasn't staying in a rental house."

"So, the Surfside?"

"That's where I'll start."

The Surfside Inn was the biggest and most popular lodging place in Cape Bay, although that wasn't saying much. The inn had about twenty-five rooms, which was a lot compared with the next-largest places, a couple of six-room bed and breakfasts. In other words, it wasn't hard to be the biggest.

The inn was a nice enough place as far as I knew, although I'd never stayed there. I crossed my fingers that

Abraham Casey had. I hoped the clerk remembered him and wasn't feeling shy. If I couldn't get any information, I would have to hit the ten or so bed and breakfasts in our town and the next.

But first, I was going to the Surfside Inn.

Chapter 11

LATE THE NEXT MORNING, I stood outside the Surf-side Inn. True to its name, it was located right on the beach and boasted that each of its rooms had an ocean view. I was pretty sure the majority of the rooms only had an ocean view if you leaned over the edge of the balcony and tilted your head a certain way.

The inn was a two-story, U-shaped building that looked as though it had been blue and white at some point but now was more grayish-blue and gray. All rooms opened to the exterior and shared a walkway that circled the building. A pool was located in the interior of the U, but that was on the ocean-facing side, and I was on the road-facing side. "Surfside Inn" was emblazoned across the marquee in large white letters with blue waves on either side. Predictably for Labor Day weekend, the "No" was lit up in the No Vacancy sign.

I took a deep breath, crossed my fingers, opened the front door, and walked inside. A bored-looking teenager slumped at the front desk, poking at his phone on the counter with one hand and resting his head in the other.

"Sorry, we're full," he muttered, not even looking up at me.

"I'm not looking for a room. I'm looking for a person."

He raised his eyebrows to look at me without having to change the angle of his head. I waited, but he didn't say anything.

"I think he's a guest of yours?"

He pointed with his cell phone-poking finger over at a phone in the corner. He managed to do it without changing his elbow's position on the table. It was quite a feat of stillness. "You can call his room from there. Just dial the room number." He went back to tapping at his phone.

I took a slow, deep breath through my clenched teeth. I stepped closer to the counter. "I don't know his room number. That's why I came in here."

"Oh. Well, can't you call his cell or something?" he asked without looking up.

Most of the time, I didn't feel much older than the

teenagers I encountered, but this kid was making me feel every bit of our nearly twenty-year age difference.

I suddenly understood what my grandfather had felt when he called the more disrespectful teenagers he encountered "little twerps." This kid was a little twerp, and I was done with him. I placed my hands firmly on the counter and barely restrained myself from slamming them down as hard as I could. He finally looked fully up at me.

"Excuse me, young man, but I am asking you to please stop messing around on your phone long enough to help me with one simple request. Since that seems to be beyond what you are willing to do today, could you *please* go get your supervisor for me. And don't even try to tell me that you're the manager, because if you are, I want to see the owner. I have lived in this town long enough to be quite certain you are not that."

Before the little twerp could say anything, a middle-aged man came through a door behind him. He was balding slightly with a sizable paunch. Warm brown eyes shone out from behind the wire-frame glasses perched on his nose.

"Hi, I'm the owner. Can I help you?" he said kindly, stepping up to the counter. He completely ignored the little twerp, who leaned back in his chair and glared at me. I glared right back. He may not have known it yet, but I was winning this.

"Hi," I replied, just as nicely. The little twerp would see how customers and business representatives were supposed to interact. "I was wondering if you could help me with something. I'm looking for someone who I think might be a guest of yours." I cast a glance twerp-ward. "Would you mind if we spoke in private?"

"Of course. Come back around into my office here with me."

I stepped around the counter and went into his office. He gestured for me to take a chair and shut the door behind us. He sat down across the desk from me.

"Thank you for seeing me, Mr...."

"Martin. Edward Martin. And you, I believe, are Francesca Amaro."

"Yes, I am," I said, startled. "How—"

"You're Carmella's daughter."

I nodded.

"I've been too busy to make it over to Antonia's much this summer, but I usually make it up there quite a lot during the off-season. Your mother was a lovely woman. Her passing was quite a loss to the Cape Bay community."

"Thank you." His kind words made my throat tighten up.

"Of course, from everything I've heard, you're doing quite well yourself. A real honor to her memory. So, kudos."

"Thank you."

"Now, you said you're looking for a guest of mine?"

"Yes." I took a deep breath. I needed to get my mind off my mother and back on the case. "A Mr. Abraham Casey."

"Abraham Casey," he repeated. He turned in his chair toward his computer and punched a few buttons. After a moment, he nodded. "Yes, Room 205. But I don't think you asked to speak privately just to find out his room number."

I took a deep breath. I was worried about convincing him to give me information. I wasn't with the police, and I wasn't a friend or family member of Abraham Casey. I was barely an acquaintance of Edward Martin. He had no reason at all to give me the information I was looking for. To complicate matters, I didn't even know if the police had told him about the man's death. I certainly didn't want to be the one to break it to him.

"Is anyone staying here with him?"

"Just how do you know Mr. Casey, Francesca?"

"Fran, please. Call me Fran."

"And you can call me Ed." He paused, and I thought I was off the hook.

"How do you know Mr. Casey, Fran?"

I closed my eyes for a second and took a deep breath. I was at a crossroads. I could lie to this fellow local business owner, whom I would probably see around town on a regular basis, and risk any potential goodwill that might exist between us. Or I could tell the truth and risk not getting the information I was looking for. The little twerp out front certainly wasn't going to help me out. I needed to preserve my reputation in Cape Bay, but I needed the information, too.

I took a deep breath and opened my mouth, still not certain what was going to come out.

"I don't." I waited for him to kick me out.

"May I ask why you're inquiring after him?" he asked kindly.

There was something in the way he asked that made me willing to go out on a limb. "I think you may already know."

Ed leaned back in his chair and took off his glasses. He pinched the bridge of his nose and sighed. "I was afraid of that."

Afraid I was asking because I was nosing around a murder case? Or afraid Abraham Casey was the man in the alley everyone in Cape Bay had heard about?

"You're sure? That Casey is the dead man?"

"Reasonably so, yes."

"And you're asking about him because?"

"Because apparently it's what I do." I immediately realized how strange it must sound.

"Ah, yes, I'd heard about that." He slid his glasses

back onto his face and leaned his elbows back on his desk.

Really? Everyone in town!

"It's nothing lurid, I promise. I'm not going to publish the information anywhere or anything. I just have questions. And if that gets people thinking and helps the police solve the case a little faster, then that's a good thing."

"It was a suicide, though, wasn't it?"

"It may have been." I stopped, wondering how much I should say. I didn't really know Ed, so as genial as he seemed, I decided it might be best to play some of my cards close to the vest. "Someone," I said, carefully omitting Mary Ellen's name, "heard shouting from the alley just before the gunshot. Maybe it was a suicide. But if it wasn't, it would be an injustice to let a murderer go free."

Ed nodded thoughtfully. He rubbed his hand over his balding head and sighed. "He was here alone," he said finally then made a face. "He checked in alone. One adult on the reservation."

I noticed the careful way he phrased it. "But?"

"The other night, uh, Thursday, I was here late taking care of a maintenance issue in 207—a clogged toilet—some college kid shoved a towel down in there and still thought it should flush. Dumb kids. Anyway, I was going out when Casey was coming in. I was the one who checked him in, so I knew he was alone. Except he wasn't alone." Ed paused and fidgeted uncomfortably in his chair. "He was with a young lady." He held up his hands quickly. "Now I'm not one to judge. A man can do whatever he wants with his time. In my hotel, as long as you're not breaking the law or disturbing the other guests, you're free to do what you please. Heck, for all I know, she was Mrs. Casey. He wore a wedding ring, you know."

I did know. I'd seen it in some of his many pictures online. And I'd also seen Mrs. Casey in some of those pictures. "Can you describe the woman he was with?"

"Are you sure you're not working for the police?" He chuckled.

"I'm sure." I smiled. "Just want to figure out who else I should talk to."

"Sure. She was young. A little older than the college girls who stay here a lot. Maybe in her mid-twenties, maybe a little older. She was a pretty girl. Blond hair, very tan. She looked like she spends a fair bit of time on the beach. Her outfit didn't leave much to the imagination. She was very..." He cleared his throat and looked away from me. He lowered his voice to barely more than a whisper. "She was very well..." He paused again. "Very well endowed." He looked like he was beyond embarrassed. He paused, and I waited to give him time to get past his discomfort. "You know, come to think of it, I don't think she was his wife."

I choked back a laugh. The buxom blonde ten years or more his junior wasn't clean-cut, fastidious Abraham Casey's wife? No kidding! I supposed there had been more ridiculous pairings. Part of my disbelief likely had something to do with having seen pictures of the actual Mrs. Casey, who was beautiful in her own right, but much more of what you might expect the wife of a pharmacist from Boston to look like. Leah Casey was also blond but looked more the type to slather on sunscreen each day and wear sweater sets.

"What makes you think that?" I managed to ask and hoped I didn't give away how preposterous I found the very thought.

"Well, I just realized that I've seen her around town before. I think she's a waitress over at the Sand Bar."

Dawn bartended at the Sand Bar. If Ed was right, and Abraham Casey's mystery woman was a waitress there, Dawn might be able to tell me who she was. It was a lucky break.

"Was there anything else you noticed about her? Or him?"

Ed looked up toward the ceiling thoughtfully and drummed his fingers lightly on the desk. "No, no, not that I can think of. Is there anything you had in mind? Something in particular?"

"Did either of them say anything to you?"

"Not a word. Casey looked at me, but he didn't say anything. They both seemed pretty tipsy. She was hanging all over him, saying something about how she had been so stressed out and low on money and just needed to relax and was so glad she'd run into him. That was all I heard."

The interesting information certainly painted a different picture of the man than his social network postings.

"When he checked in, did he say why he was in Cape Bay?"

"He didn't. Most people come for vacation. I assumed he was here for that reason also."

"Did he have a reservation, or did he just show up?"

"Reservation." He punched a few buttons on his computer. "Made three months ago."

"For how long?"

He peered at the computer again. "Wednesday through Saturday."

"So not the whole weekend?"

"No."

"Is that normal?"

"Not at all. Wednesday through Saturday is a very unusual reservation span. We're not as structured as the houses, but for the most part, people stay a whole week, or Friday through Sunday, or sometimes just a night or two in the middle of the week. But Wednesday through Saturday, that's unusual."

I had asked every question I had come in planning to ask, but I took a moment to think. I wanted to make a smoother exit from the Seaside Inn than I had at Mary Ellen's the day before when I tried to leave three times before I finally ran out of questions. I didn't want Ed Martin's first impression of me to be that I was scatter-brained.

"What did you think of him? Abraham Casey, I mean," I asked finally. "What was he like?"

"He seemed like a nice man. Kind, friendly. Tried to offer me a tip just for checking him in. He didn't even need help with his bags. He kept his room very tidy but left generous tips for the maids each day. That's actually when I first suspected that it was him in the alley— Amelia mentioned that his bed hadn't been slept in and there was no tip. Now, don't get me wrong, it's not like they expect a tip each day. It's just that Casey had left a ten, clearly labeled as being for the maid, both of the previous nights. When nothing was disturbed Saturday morning, and there was no tip, but his bag was still there —well, I was concerned."

We sat for a moment and reflected on the dead man. Ed had met him personally and seemed to like him. I was just putting together a picture of him through his social media and the reflections of others. But both of us felt saddened by his passing.

"Well, I've certainly taken up enough of your time." I scooted to the edge of my chair. "Thank you, and it was a pleasure to meet you." I extended my hand across the desk, and he shook it.

"Thank you for coming by. You certainly jogged my memory. Do you think I should call the police to let them know that Casey was staying here?"

"They haven't been by yet?"

"No. I was holding out hope that it meant the man in the alley wasn't our guest."

I wondered if that was the case. Everything I'd found pointed in Abraham Casey's direction, and it would be an unbelievable coincidence if the dead man were someone else. "It can't hurt to call."

"You're right. I'll do that."

We stood, and he walked me to the door.

"Oh, one other thing." I nearly kicked myself for doing the exact same thing I'd done at Mary Ellen's. I stopped for a moment, trying to figure out how best to phrase what I wanted to say. "The young man at the desk—"

"My sister's kid." Ed cut me off. "I'd fire him if I could, but I'd get such a guilt trip about it from my mother. I just haven't worked up the nerve. I try to schedule him when there's not too much foot traffic in the lobby so I don't inflict him on too many people."

"I can't say I blame you for that." I bid Ed Martin farewell and went into the lobby. The little twerp didn't even glance up at me as I walked by. He made me glad I was an only child.

Chapter 12

ON THE WAY to the café, the weight of my thick hair reminded me to ask Sammy for a stylist recommendation. "Ask Sammy about hair. Ask Sammy about hair. Ask Sammy about hair. Ask Sammy about hair." I mentally repeated the phrase.

When I walked through the back door, Sammy was pushing the boxes I'd moved back to where they belonged on the shelves.

"Did you do this?" she asked immediately. She was very possessive of the storeroom organization. She considered it a personal point of pride that she knew where everything was and could produce it in seconds.

"Ask Sammy about hair," I said out loud.

"What?"

"Sorry, I've just been reminding myself. Yes, I did that. I'm sorry. I was trying to organize and—you know how when you try to clean up a room, sometimes it gets messier before it gets cleaner?" The look on Sammy's face indicated she was not familiar with that phenomenon. "Well, that's what happened. Also, can you recommend a good stylist? My hair is getting long, and I don't know who to go to."

"Everything was organized just fine before you went on your little…" She looked around as though baffled by what I'd done. "Your little rampage here. Don't do that again or at least tell me if you do. I can't find the napkins for the life of me. And Chase Williams down at Beach Waves. I've been going to him for years."

"Chase does hair? I had no idea." Why had no one ever mentioned my childhood neighbor had grown up to be a hair stylist? "And the napkins are over on the left side of the third shelf. P for paper."

Sammy looked at me blankly.

"I alphabetized everything. A through G is on the top shelf, H through N on the second, O through U on the third, and V through Z on the bottom."

Sammy blinked. She opened her mouth and closed it. She held up one finger. "Why not N for napkins?"

"I thought all the paper products should be together."

"And alphabetized under P."

"Uh-huh."

Sammy looked at me, and from her expression, I couldn't tell if she wanted to hug me, pat me on the head, or cry. "Please do not organize."

I laughed. "That bad, huh?"

"Yes. That bad."

"I thought it kind of worked."

"Oh, Fran."

"No?"

"How many supplies do you think we have that can be categorized as V through Z?"

"Water?"

"We get that from a tap," she whispered, sounding somewhat exasperated.

"Good point."

"Please don't organize again." I was now certain she wanted to pat me on the head.

"Yes, ma'am."

"You better be glad I love you." She gave me a hug then looked at my face and shook her head.

"You better be glad you're great at your job. You couldn't get away with talking to your boss like that just everywhere, you know," I teased.

"Is that a threat?" she joked back.

"No, the café would go under without you. It was just a statement of fact."

Sammy laughed. "Come over here and help me put everything back where it belongs."

I tilted my head to see how Becky was doing out in front. It wasn't very busy, and she looked as though she had everything under control. "Do you think Becky's doing okay? I could go out there and help her," I said just to irk Sammy.

"No!" She laughed. "You will stay here and fix what you messed up, young lady!" I hadn't seen her in such a good mood in weeks, and I wondered if the time spent canning with her mother had done her good or if it was something else.

"Yes, Sammy." I gave in to my fate of straightening up. I let Sammy direct me for the most part, and as we worked, we actually came up with a better organizational system. I made a mental note to point out that my messing with things had turned out for the best after all. But at the moment, I had something else I wanted to bring up.

"Hey, do you know if Dawn is working tonight?"

"I think so. Labor Day weekend. People will want to go out and party more than usual for a Sunday because of the holiday tomorrow. Why?"

"I just wanted to ask her about something. I figured I may as well try to catch her at work."

"You want to talk to Dawn about something?" She

knew full well Dawn and I really only socialized because of her.

"Yeeaah." I drew the word out. I hadn't told Sammy about my investigation into Abraham Casey's death, although I knew she probably wouldn't be surprised based on my recent track record.

Sammy studied me like a parent looking for signs of a lie in her child's face. "Are you investigating again?"

"It just didn't make sense to me that it was a suicide. I started looking into it, and the man was seen with a girl who may work at the Sand Bar. I thought Dawn might know her."

"You've figured all that out in a day and a half? While still working here, and I'm going to guess sleeping once in a while?"

I nodded.

"Have you ever thought about giving up coffee and joining the police force?"

"Do you really think Mike would let them hire me?"

"Good point." We moved boxes for a few more minutes before Sammy thought of something. "Oh, if you want to get Chase to cut your hair, you should probably go ahead and call over there. He books up really fast. It may be a while before he can get you in. He's really good, though. It's worth the wait."

I grimaced like a pouty child who didn't want to

wait, but in the interest of getting my hair done as soon as possible, I called the salon.

"Good news!" I said to Sammy when I got off the phone a few minutes later. "He had a cancellation for Tuesday morning and got me in!"

"Must be your lucky day!"

It certainly seemed like a good day so far. I'd gotten a great lead from Ed Martin on Abraham Casey, and I'd gotten an appointment in less than forty-eight hours with my old neighbor who was now apparently the top hair stylist in the bustling metropolis of Cape Bay. I only hoped my luck held out, and I would be able to find out from Dawn the identity of the woman Abraham Casey had taken to his hotel room.

I didn't have much time to dwell on my luck the rest of the afternoon. The café got busier than I'd seen it on a Sunday afternoon. Predictably, Chase Williams breezed in and out during the busiest time. I began to wonder if he somehow did it on purpose. Maybe he wanted coffee but didn't want to talk to me. If that were the case, he could just come when I wasn't there. Of course, for all I knew, he did.

The rush lasted an exceptionally long time, and both Sammy and Becky ended up staying long past the time they were supposed to leave. Everything finally calmed down near closing time, and I managed to shoo them out.

"Take tomorrow off!" I joked as they left. Antonia's, like every other locally owned business in Cape Bay, would be closed for Labor Day. We closed for most holidays—Easter, Memorial Day, Fourth of July, Labor Day, Columbus Day, Thanksgiving, and Christmas at a minimum. We had never decided to open those days when so many other businesses across the country had. It was a point of pride for us that we cared more about our workers and our community than the added revenue we would earn from opening on holidays.

Matt came in just as Sammy and Becky left. He put his hand on my waist and kissed me lightly. "How'd your day go?"

"Busy! I don't know where all those people came from. It was like every single person in town for the weekend suddenly felt compelled to get some coffee. Did you get over to my house to take care of Latte?" Partway through the afternoon when I realized I wouldn't be able to get away long enough to run home, I'd texted Matt and asked him to feed Latte and let him out.

"You know I did. We had a good time. Took a walk and everything."

"You're a good boyfriend." I stood on my tiptoes to kiss him on the cheek. He wasn't much taller than me, but it was enough that I had to make an effort.

"You know it. What about your trip to the Seaside?"

It took a second to realize he was referring to the

motel, not the oceanfront. One of the downfalls of living in a beach town was half the businesses had a beach theme in their name—Seaside Inn, Sand Bar, Sandy's Seafood Shack, Beach Waves. It was as if we just couldn't stop ourselves.

"Better than I expected," I said after I figured out what he meant.

"Yeah? He was staying there?"

"More than that." I filled him in on everything I had found out in my meeting with Ed Martin.

"So I take it we're going out drinking tonight?" he asked after I told him I wanted to ask Dawn about the blonde Ed saw at the motel.

"You can drink. I have interviews to do."

"You're so professional," he teased.

I didn't have much left to do before closing the café. We had gone from incredibly busy to completely empty —a usual occurrence for the café. Sammy had refused to leave until everything was completely in order—as much as it could be, considering we were still open. Becky wouldn't be outdone and stayed right along with her. When closing time officially rolled around, Matt helped me shut the machines down and stow the food away. I grabbed the box of marzipan from the table in the back. I had found myself craving the sweet treats the night before and thought it would be prudent to bring them home with me to snack on during my much-anticipated day off.

"You want to run home to change?" Matt asked as we left the café.

"What? You don't like my stylin' work clothes?" I gestured to my outfit and struck what I considered a vaguely modelesque pose.

"They're fine. I just thought you might want to get changed before we went out."

"It's not really 'going out,' is it? I mean, I'm just going over there to ask Dawn who that girl is."

"Up to you." Matt shrugged.

We walked along a little farther before I abruptly turned down a side street.

"Where are you going?" Matt hurried after me.

"I decided you were right. We're going out. I can put on something that doesn't have coffee stains on it. Besides," I said, holding out the box of marzipan. "If I carry this into the bar, I might have to share it. Can't have that."

"Bar-goers are known for how much they enjoy a nice piece of marzipan with their tequila shots," he deadpanned.

I greeted Latte as I hurried into the house then left him to play with Matt while I ran upstairs to change. I didn't have time to take a shower as I would have liked before a date, but I changed into a cute pair of jeans and a nice top before touching up my makeup.

I let my hair down but didn't like the way it looked and tied it right back up again. I declared my reflection in the mirror more than satisfactory and headed downstairs to Matt and our date at the Sand Bar.

Chapter 13

"WOW."

"What?"

"You look nice." Matt smiled.

"Thanks!" I was glad I had put extra time into my makeup and kind of wished I'd left my hair down. I knew it wouldn't have lasted, though, and I would have put it back up almost as soon as we walked out the front door. "You look...the same as you did when I went upstairs." We both laughed. "Handsome, though. I don't think I told you that earlier."

"Thank you."

I bent down to scratch Latte's head. "You be a good boy while I'm gone, okay? Did Matty give you a treat? Do you have a chewy?" I looked to Matt for answers since Latte wasn't exactly the most forthcoming with information.

He shook his head. "I didn't give him anything."

"Well, somebody needs a treat then, doesn't he?" Even as the words came out of my mouth, I couldn't believe I was baby-talking Latte in front of Matt. But it was probably a good sign for our relationship that I felt so comfortable with him.

I got Latte a treat and a rawhide from the kitchen. We went through his commands—sit, speak, lie down, roll over—and I rewarded him with his treat. Just before Matt and I walked out the door, I gave Latte the rawhide. "Now, you be a good boy while Mommy's gone! I love you!"

"You spoil that dog," Matt muttered as we walked toward the street.

"Oh, and you don't?"

"You're around him more than I am. My spoiling is like a favorite uncle. Yours is like, I don't know, an overly indulgent mother. Sorry, not a very good analogy."

"I don't think that was an analogy at all."

"I'm an engineer, not an English teacher."

We walked along Cape Bay's dimly lit streets, bantering back and forth about whatever mundane thoughts sprang into our minds. I felt remarkably safer with Matt than I had just two nights before when I had walked this path on my own. And then, I'd thought the man in the alley had killed himself. Now, I was reasonably sure he'd been murdered. By most measures, I should be much more nervous walking around now that I knew there was a murderer on the loose, but I also knew Matt would do whatever he had to do to keep me safe, and that made all the difference in the world.

We got to the Sand Bar in about ten minutes. While most of Cape Bay was deserted—there were barely any cars out driving around, and every business that wasn't a restaurant was closed—the Sand Bar was packed. The parking lot was full, and cars lined the street for at least a block in each direction.

"Is it always like this?" I asked.

Matt shrugged. He wasn't the barfly type.

We walked into the bar past the crowd spilling out the front door. It smelled like stale beer and hot, sweaty people. A band was set up on the stage, playing so loudly I couldn't even tell what the song was. I could feel the beat in my chest and thought if I tried hard enough, I might be able to pick out the song just based on that.

I hated when bands turned their amplifiers way up when they played in a relatively small place, like in restaurants, where you had to scream at the server just to give your order. Amps needed to be turned down lower in those situations. I sometimes wondered if bands kept them loud because they'd ruined their hearing over the years and honestly thought they were playing at a reasonable volume.

Once in a while, we had musicians play at Antonia's, and our long-time policy was that those musicians would play acoustic. It had started back in my grandparents' time when their friends would come in, sing, and strum the same guitar they played for their children at home. Electric guitars weren't as popular then as they'd become over the years, so it may have been that, also. Pianists were the one exception to the rule. We obviously didn't have a piano in the café, so piano players had to bring a keyboard, which they were allowed to plug in. It's hard to hear the melody from an unplugged keyboard.

"Why are they so loud!" I screamed in Matt's ear, the volume of my voice so high that it was impossible to make it actually sound like a question.

"So you can't tell how bad they are!" he yelled back.

That seemed like a distinct possibility, and I wasn't exactly going to give them a ringing endorsement based on the ringing I'd have in my ears long after their performance ended.

"You want to get a table!" Matt hollered.

I nodded, grateful that yes and no could be communicated without actual speech. He took my hand and led me through the maze of tables to a high-top table on the far wall.

"How's this!" he shouted.

I nodded again.

"I'll go get our drinks!"

I shook my head.

He crinkled his forehead and leaned his ear in to my mouth.

"I need to talk to Dawn!"

He shook his head, still not understanding.

"She's the bartender!"

He turned his head so that his mouth was next to my ear.

"Is she here?"

I stood on my tiptoes, balancing myself with a hand on Matt's shoulder, and craned my neck toward the bar. I could see Dawn darting between the shapes of people sitting on barstools. I pulled Matt down toward me. "Yes!"

"Are you going to be able to hear her over all this!"

He had a point.

I opened my mouth to bellow that I didn't know, when the band's noise came to a crescendo so loud I couldn't possibly yell over it. The guitar player wailed on his instrument. The drummer seemed to have his sticks on every single drum at once. And then it all stopped.

"We're going to take a break, but don't go anywhere 'cause we'll be right back!" the lead singer shouted into the microphone. I wondered if he understood how microphones worked.

"Depends on whether or not her hearing has been permanently damaged by all the noise yet," I said in what I hoped was a normal tone of voice. I could only hear the reverberations of my voice through my skull, so I couldn't actually be sure if I was whispering or screaming.

"Get me a beer?"

"Sure thing." I hurried away before he could realize that if I was ordering the drinks, I was the one paying for them. Who paid when we went out was a long-standing battle between us—each of us vying to treat the other. We once talked about each paying our own way, but the first time we went out with that intention, we both tried to slip the waitress our credit card within the span of roughly two minutes. We went right back to openly competing.

I wedged in between two tough-looking guys who had stationed themselves at the bar and tried to catch Dawn's eye. She was working the side of the bar I was on, and a rather nice-looking guy was working the other side. He wore a tight white T-shirt and tight black jeans. Dawn wore a deep scoop-neck tank top and a tiny pair of shorts.

I wondered if she got so hot working behind the bar that she had to wear skimpy clothes to keep cool. Then I saw the way the guys at the other end of the bar waved her over even though the other bartender was closer, and

I realized her outfit was probably more to improve her tips than her comfort. When the other bartender came down to take my order, I realized the system worked both ways.

"What can I get you?" He put an elbow down on the bar, which I suspected he did mostly to give himself the opportunity to flex his bicep.

"Her." I pointed at Dawn.

He looked surprised. "Oh, all right."

"She's a friend," I said hurriedly.

He shrugged his muscular shoulders. "Dawn!"

She turned around, and he pointed his thumb over his shoulder at me. I smiled at her and waved. She rolled her eyes when she spotted me but moved toward me. Muscles made his way back to the other end, where there was a shortage of girls but plenty of thirsty guys.

"What do you want?" Dawn made a face as though she thought I wasn't cool enough to be at a bar.

I almost gave her a line about how she owed me a drink to make up for my ruined girls' night out but decided it wouldn't help my case. I needed her to want to talk to me. "I need to ask you about something."

She looked up and down the bar at the mass of people that had gathered. Apparently, I wasn't the only one who thought the band's break was the best time to get the bartender to hear you. "Can it wait? I kinda got a full crowd right now."

"Sure." I hoped she wasn't going to make me wait until after the bar closed.

"When the band comes back on."

She must have seen the concern in my face as I wondered how on earth we'd hear each other. "We'll go in the back."

I agreed.

"That it? You gonna order a drink, or are you just taking up my tip-earning time?"

"A beer. And can you make a margarita?"

She rolled her eyes. "Regular, on the rocks only. Frozen takes too long."

"That's fine."

She stared at me, waiting for I didn't know what.

"What?" I asked finally.

"What kind of beer?"

"Oh, um, I don't know. It's for Matt. Whatever you think he'd like."

She rolled her eyes again. I thought about saying what my grandmother would have—if she didn't stop rolling her eyes, they'd get stuck like that—but I thought wiser of it. She walked away. I waited, cash in hand, for her to come back, then handed her my money and told her to keep the change.

"Thanks." She looked less than impressed. I wondered if I should have tipped her more or if she would have reacted the same no matter what I gave her. I decided it didn't matter and went back to find Matt.

"Find out what you wanted to know?" he asked as I set his beer down in front of him.

"She told me to come back when the band starts back up."

"She really doesn't want to talk to you, does she?"

"I don't think so, but she said we'd go in the back."

Matt tasted his beer. "This is good. What is it?"

"I don't know." I shrugged. "I told Dawn to just give me something she thought you'd like."

"No wonder she doesn't want to talk to you."

I sipped my margarita, slightly afraid she might have poisoned it, but it turned out to be really good. Maybe Sammy wasn't the only reason she tolerated me after all.

After only a few minutes of relative quiet, the band reappeared on stage.

"Are you ready for some music!" the lead singer screamed into the microphone. He really didn't know how they worked. "Let's go!" The band struck their first note, and I resisted the urge to cover my ears.

Matt pointed past me toward the bar, and I turned to see Dawn beckoning me to follow her. I waved to Matt because it wasn't worth destroying my voice to tell him what he already knew then picked up my margarita. It was too good to leave behind on the table to get watered down as the ice melted.

Dawn pulled keys out of her tiny shorts and used them to unlock a door that was labeled "Employees Only."

"We had to start locking it because the drunks kept coming in and crashing on the couch." She closed the door behind us. The noise from the bar was suddenly deadened. "Sound proofing," she said when she saw my surprised look. "So what's up?" She flopped down on the couch.

"This is really good." I indicated the margarita. "And Matt liked his beer, too."

"That's what you wanted to talk to me about? You just knew you'd want to thank me for a drink you hadn't even ordered yet?"

"I was being nice."

"Sorry. Thanks. I actually kind of like it sometimes when people ask me just to get them whatever. Gives me a chance to get creative."

"You're good at it."

"Thanks. So what did you want to talk about?"

"Well, I've, uh, I've been kind of looking into that suicide the other night."

Dawn laughed her biggest, fullest, Dawn-est laugh. "Oh, I love it. Mike tells you to stay out of it, and the first thing you do is go poking your nose into things. You know, I think you're cooler than you act, Fran."

"Thank you?" I wasn't sure if I was supposed to take that as a compliment.

"It's a good thing." She answered my unspoken question. "But I'm guessing you're not here just to fill me in on that fact."

"Well, no." I sat down on a chair opposite her. "First thing, I don't think it was a suicide."

"There wouldn't really be anything for you to investigate if it was, would there?"

"Not really. The reason I'm here, though, is that I found out who the guy was and talked to somebody who saw him with a girl the other night."

"Wasn't me," she said immediately.

"No, I know it wasn't you. But I think she might work here."

Dawn raised her eyebrows but didn't say anything.

"Mid to late twenties, blond, really tan, busty. Dresses kind of provocatively. Well, at least when she's going back to a guy's hotel room. The person I talked to said he thinks she's a waitress here."

"Who'd you talk to? Eh, it doesn't matter," she said when I hesitated.

I took a sip of my margarita and swallowed hard. "So, do you know who she is?"

Dawn narrowed her eyes at me and pursed her lips. "Yup."

Chapter 14

"YOU DO?" I couldn't believe Dawn would be able to identify the girl I was looking for based on a description that probably fit fifty different girls in Cape Bay.

Dawn nodded. "You think she killed him?"

I opened my mouth to say no then reconsidered. "Maybe. I don't know her. Do you think she could kill a man?"

Dawn thought for a minute. "Depends on what he did to her."

I let that sink in. I hadn't put much thought into why Abraham Casey was murdered, just who he was and why he was in town. I still wanted to know why he was in town, but now that I was talking to people who had interacted with him, I needed to be on the lookout for potential suspects. And potential motives. If Abraham

Casey had taken a girl up to his hotel room, maybe under duress, coercion, or something worse, she might have a motive. But I wouldn't know until I talked to her.

"I need to talk to her, Dawn."

She stared at me for so long that I was sure she was going to say no. Then she sighed. "Her name's Suzy. Suzy Frazier."

"Is she here tonight?"

Dawn nodded. "I'll point her out to you."

"Could you introduce her to me?"

"You're pushing your luck."

"Sorry."

"Oh, come on. Of course I'm going to introduce you to her. You're going to tell her I told you who she was anyway, right? I may as well be there to make sure she knows you're not some stark raving lunatic or the dead guy's wife or something."

"Thank you."

She shook her head and rolled her eyes again. I watched in hopes they would stick, but they didn't. They went right back to their normal place in her head.

"You ready?"

"To talk to her?"

"No, to go to the mall. Of course to talk to her." It was painfully obvious that even if Dawn was willing to defend me against a potential suggestion that I was a lunatic, she was completely convinced I was the dumbest person she'd ever met. But for some reason, probably Sammy, she was nice to me.

"Yes, I'm ready."

Dawn reluctantly got up and walked to the door. With her hand on the doorknob, she turned and looked at me. "Get ready." She opened the door, and the screaming music blared into the room. It was so much worse than I remembered. She gestured for me to follow her, and we made our way across the barroom floor. I waved and smiled at Matt as we passed. He tipped his beer glass at me.

Dawn walked up to a girl who fit Ed Martin's description of the woman he'd seen almost exactly. The only thing I would have added was that she wore a lot of makeup. But I expected he hadn't been paying that much attention to her face.

Dawn put her mouth to Suzy's ear and gestured at me. Suzy looked at me and nodded a couple of times, listened again, and nodded some more. I couldn't imagine what Dawn was saying except maybe, "Take pity on her. She's stupid, but she's my best friend's boss." As long as Suzy talked to me, I didn't care what Dawn told her.

Finally, they walked back in my direction. Dawn breezed by me, but Suzy came up to me and assumed the now-familiar mouth-to-ear position.

"You want to go outside?" she bellowed into my ear.

I nodded and followed her outside, pausing to drop my now-empty margarita glass at the bar as I went. She walked a short distance past the people gathered outside the door, most of whom had cigarettes between their fingers or dangling from their lips. Once we were out of earshot, Suzy stopped and leaned against the building. She pulled a pack of cigarettes and a lighter out of her pocket. "Want one?" She held a cigarette out to me.

"No thanks." My voice sounded very strange in the relative quiet of the outdoors after all the noise inside the bar.

Suzy put the cigarette in her mouth and lit it, taking a long draw. "So, Dawn said you want to talk to me?"

"Yeah, if you have a minute."

"I got about ten." She held out her cigarette and nodded at it.

"I'm Fran." I figured my name was a reasonable place to start.

"Suzy."

"Hi Suzy." I smiled.

"What is this? AA?"

"Sorry," I muttered. I felt like we were already getting off on the wrong foot. I took a deep breath. "Look, let me cut to the chase. I heard you might have gone back to a guy's hotel room with him Thursday night."

"So what if I did? You his wife or something?"

"Dawn said she was going to tell you that I'm not."

"She did. She said you're a friend of hers."

"She did?" I was shocked Dawn had called me a friend.

"Yeah, aren't you?"

"Yeah, I guess so."

Suzy gave me her version of the look Dawn liked to give me—the "are you stupid?" look. "You guess so? You don't know who your friends are?"

"No, I do, it's just that Dawn-I-well, never mind. We're friends. I'm not the guy's wife. I just want to know if you're the girl who went up to his room, and, if you are, maybe you could answer a few questions for me."

"You police?"

"No."

"Then why you asking questions?"

"Curious, I guess."

"About whose hotel room I'm going to."

"No, I'm curious about the guy. He—you know the guy they found in the alley the other day?"

"Yeah?" Of course she did. Everybody did.

"I think that was him. The same guy. The guy whose hotel room you went to, I mean. If that was you." We were back on the wrong foot, and I was struggling to get things back on track. It seemed as though her cigarette was disappearing into thin air right before my eyes. Which I guess, in a way, it was.

"Hmph." I couldn't tell if she didn't care, wasn't surprised, or was glad he was dead. Two of the three possibilities interested me. One concerned me.

"So, it was you?"

"Yeah, it was me."

"Did you happen to know his name?"

"What are you trying to say?"

I realized how my question must have sounded. "No, I just mean—I want to make sure it was the same guy. And I'm curious as to whether he gave you his real name."

She looked at me through narrowed eyes as she took a long drag from her cigarette. "It was the same guy."

My heart thudded. What was she saying? "How do you know?"

"You wouldn't be here if it wasn't. You didn't find me by accident."

I wasn't sure if her answer made me more or less suspicious of her. I tried to refocus her on my questions, and I was now uneasy enough that I knew I needed to pay close attention to her reactions. "What did he tell you his name was?"

"Abe. He didn't offer a last name, and I didn't ask. Wasn't like I told him mine either."

Abe. I wondered if that was what he went by all the time, what his wife called him. "Did you know he was married?"

She shrugged. "Didn't care."

"How did you meet him?"

"Here. He came in looking for a buzz and a good time. I was waiting on him. He was flirting pretty hard. Stayed around until closing time and asked me what I was up to after. I didn't have any plans, so I went back to his room with him."

"And did you—" I started to ask, then stopped. "Never mind, I don't want to know."

Suzy looked at me out of the corner of her eye and smirked. I got the feeling she thought I was as much of an uptight prude as Dawn thought I was a dumb bore.

"I mean…just never mind." I took a deep breath. "What was he like?"

Now Suzy smiled for real. "He was real nice. Real friendly. A charmer. Knew how to make a girl feel good about herself. And he threw around money like it was nothing."

"Really?" I was surprised even though her statement was consistent with what Ed Martin had said about Abraham Casey's tipping habits.

"Yeah, only wanted the top-shelf stuff, bought a round for the whole bar, gave me a tip that was more than I usually make in a whole night. Nice guy. Real shame."

The way she spoke, I couldn't tell if she honestly thought his death was a real shame, or if she meant it the way movie mob bosses said "it would be a real shame if something happened to that nice new car of yours."

"Did he tell you anything about himself? About his family?"

"What, do you think we sat around and talked all night?" She rolled her eyes.

I wondered if eye rolling was something the bar taught in its new-employee orientation. I decided it was more likely part of the interview process.

"No, he didn't talk about his family or anything. I knew he was like a pharmacist or something because he —" She paused and cast a sideways glance at me. "Because he mentioned it. And he didn't have to tell me he was from Boston because I could hear it when he talked. Southie, I think. Could be wrong about that, though."

Her cigarette was almost gone, and I searched my mind frantically for other important questions to ask. I got the feeling there would be no doorknob questions— no turning around at the last second to ask one more thing. When Suzy Frazier was done with her cigarette, she was going to be done with me.

"Did he mention anyone who might have wanted to kill him?"

"You mean other than himself?"

"He told you he wanted to kill himself?" If that were true, then the whole murder theory might be dead in the water. A man who said he wanted to kill himself and then died, apparently by his own hand, looked an awful lot like a suicide, no matter how many souvenirs he bought just before his death.

"No, but he did, didn't he? Kill himself?"

"I think it was murder."

"Oh, you do, do you now? And what makes you think that?"

"He bought a bunch of souvenirs just before he died. A big bag of them. Stuff for his wife and kid. Why would a man buy presents for his family and kill himself right after?"

Suzy seemed to go pale, though it was hard to tell from the dim parking lot lights. "He didn't say anything about anyone wanting to kill him. Until just right now, I didn't hear anything about anything but suicide, okay? I can't help you with that."

"Okay, okay, I'm sorry. I didn't mean to upset you."

"I ain't upset."

"I'm—I'm sorry," I said again. "Can you just tell me one last thing?" I asked as she dropped her cigarette and ground it out with the toe of her worn boot.

"What?"

"Did he tell you why he was in town?"

She stared at me, and I could see her tongue working around in her mouth. She was either debating with herself whether she wanted to tell me something or trying to get something out of her teeth. "No. He didn't say. Like I said, we didn't talk much."

I decided to make one last effort. "Is there anything else I should know about him?"

She stared at me again for an uncomfortably long period of time. Finally, she closed her eyes and sighed. She shook her head. "He could help you relax. If that was something you needed. And that's it. That's all I got to say to you. I got to get back to work." She brushed past me and headed for the door.

I stared after her for a second, not sure what had happened or what she meant. She had taken offense at almost everything I had said and seemed to be lying or hiding something in her responses. I didn't know if there was actually something to it or if she just didn't like me.

Slowly, I walked back into the bar. The music was louder and worse than I remembered. I wound my way through the tables to Matt. He was halfway through what I guessed was his second beer based on the fresh margarita sitting across from him.

I hopped into my seat and took a sip of the drink. It was as delicious as the first one. "Thank you," I mouthed to him, lacking the energy to scream after my conversation with Suzy. He pointed past me in the direction of the bar.

I turned around and saw Dawn looking at me. She raised her eyebrows and gave a thumbs up. Understanding that she was asking how the drink was, I smiled and gave her a thumbs up in response. Maybe she knew I would need another drink after talking to Suzy, or maybe we really were friends.

Matt and I finished our drinks without trying to talk. When we were done, he pointed toward the door, and I nodded. We slid off our chairs then made our way through the bar with me in the lead and Matt following with his hand gently brushing the small of my back. When we got outside, he took my hand.

"How did that go?" he asked loudly.

"I don't think you have to talk that loud," I said at what I thought was an appropriate volume.

"What?" he asked, even louder this time.

"Shh!" I whisper-shouted. I pulled him down toward me. "You're going to wake up the whole town," I said into his ear.

"Sorry." He spoke more quietly this time, but still on the loud side. "How did it go?"

I gave him the highlights of my chat with Suzy in as loud a voice as I dared. He nodded at appropriate parts, giving me the impression he understood at least most of what I was saying.

"There's something more to the story she's not telling you." His voice was a much more appropriate volume now. I was glad, not just because I didn't want him waking up the neighbors but also because I had been starting to worry about long-term hearing damage.

I agreed with him. "I just wish I knew what it was. Or at least whether it's important or not. I mean, it could be anything from she stole twenty dollars from him to she killed him. I just don't know."

"Add that to your list of things you have to figure out."

That list was getting pretty long.

Chapter 15

AS I LAY in bed that night with Latte by my side, I was unable to fall asleep for the life of me. I just couldn't get the information I'd learned about Abraham—Abe, according to Suzy—out of my head. I'd started the day with my perception of him completely shaped by his social media profile—an outgoing, open, gregarious type of guy, a clean-cut family man. Now that I'd talked to a couple of people who had actually interacted with him while he was in Cape Bay, I was getting a completely different perspective of him.

He still seemed outgoing, open, gregarious, and generous with his money to boot, but perhaps he wasn't as much of a family man as he'd made himself out to be. The realization was unsettling and made me question even more strongly what he had been doing in Cape Bay.

It was clear his visit hadn't been an end-of-summer family vacation. He was here alone. He was living it up, unhindered by his wife and family obligations. He was drinking high-end alcohol and hooking up with a bar waitress he'd only just met and hadn't even given his last name to. Just two nights before, he'd been out to dinner with his wife and young son. And a day later, he was dead. Had his activities while he was away caused his death? Or was it whatever had brought him to Cape Bay in the first place? And why didn't I know what that was?

I tried to clear my mind and allow the sandman a chance to come, but it wasn't working. Something about my conversation with Suzy was bothering me. In all honesty, a lot of it bothered me, but there was something in particular I couldn't quite put my finger on. I tried to remember what it was, but my mind was going so fast over the facts of the case that I couldn't pin it down.

Just relax, Fran. You need to relax.

And there it was: *relax*. That was what had been bothering me. Suzy had said Abraham could help you "relax." Ed Martin had mentioned her saying something similar when she was at the hotel with Abraham—that she was stressed out and needed to relax. Was waitressing really so stressful?

As soon as that thought crossed my mind, I

dismissed it as ridiculous. My old New York friends would ask the same thing about working at the café—is working at a coffee shop really so stressful? Yes. Yes, it was.

But I didn't go around talking about how I needed to relax. And what did Suzy mean when she said he could help her relax? Suzy didn't seem like the type to beat around the bush about much. So what was she trying to hide? Something illegal? Drugs? I knew more about drugs from watching TV than I did from personal experience, but I did remember from my middle school health teacher that some drugs were called "uppers" and "downers."

Was Suzy saying Abraham Casey had given her some kind of drug to help her relax? Even with what I'd learned about him, I had trouble fitting that idea with the straight-laced pharmacist I'd seen in so many pictures online.

Even if he was a cheating, unprescribed-drug-dispensing pharmacist, what was he doing in Cape Bay, and why didn't anyone know? As friendly and outgoing as he was, why hadn't he told anyone why he was in town? It seemed out of character for the man who had posted his every move online. Had his wife known where he was? Was she okay with him going off to the beach for a few days while she stayed home with their small child? He'd clearly planned the trip, but for what purpose? Did the odd scheduling have something to do with it? Was that a clue?

The answers weren't coming to me, and staying up half the night thinking about it wasn't going to help. At that point, I wasn't sure any amount of thinking would help. Suzy hadn't suggested anyone new for me to talk to, and unless I was going to contact Abraham Casey's wife, which I had no intention of doing, I was at a loss for where to go next. If I could clear my mind and fall asleep, maybe some brilliant idea would pop into my head by morning. Or maybe I would dream the answer. I wasn't optimistic.

I rolled over, laying my arm across Latte's warm little body. I felt his soft fur beneath my fingers and the steady rise and fall of his belly as he slept, completely unaware of my internal turmoil. Gradually, the comfortable rhythm of his breathing lulled me to sleep, and his tongue on my face woke me the next morning.

"Hey there, buddy," I murmured as I tried to drag myself from sleep. I scratched him behind the ears and hoped it would distract him from his true goal—breakfast. I just wanted to lie in bed a little bit longer.

I felt him shove his head under my hand and realized I must have fallen back asleep. "Okay, okay." I rolled over to check the time. It was long past time for me to get up. I pulled myself into a sitting position then stumbled downstairs to let Latte out and feed him. I went back upstairs as he ate and made my way through my morning routine.

I didn't know what to do next in my investigation of Abraham Casey's murder. It seemed as though I were at a dead end. I wondered if Mike was doing any better. I was sure he was. He was a professional at this, after all. I resolved to put the whole thing out of my mind, at least until some new piece of information fell into my lap or some previously overlooked connection appeared in my mind. Unfortunately, I wasn't very hopeful about either of those prospects.

Latte and I went for our walk, and I fixed myself a light, early lunch. One of Matt's coworkers was having a Labor Day cookout, and we were invited. Dinner was scheduled for early and promised to be large. With the likely menu of burgers, hot dogs, chips, dips, pretzels, and sweets, I knew I would be stuffed by the end of the evening. A light lunch was exactly what I needed, and I followed it with another long walk, just as a preemptive measure against the quantity of food I expected to consume later.

After the second walk, which was complemented by a rousing game of fetch and an extended race around the playing fields, I showered and changed into cookout clothes—shorts, a T-shirt, and a pair of sneakers. I was inspired by Matt's warning that a game of softball was likely to break out sometime during the afternoon.

He picked me up promptly at three o'clock and drove us to his coworker's house in the next town.

"So, whose house is it we're going to again?" I asked as we cruised out of Cape Bay.

"His name's Brant. I've worked with him for about five years."

"And his wife?"

"Mindy."

"What does she do?"

"Not sure. Something medical, I think."

"'Something medical.' You've worked with the guy for five years, and you don't know what his wife does?"

He shrugged as he kept his eyes on the road. "Doesn't really come up."

I sighed. "Are they from here?"

Matt thought for a minute. "I don't think so."

"Where are they from?"

"I'm not sure. It's not something that has come up."

I rolled my eyes and wondered if this was what Dawn felt like when she was talking to me—like she was speaking to someone from another planet whose customs were nothing like her own. Customs like actually speaking to your coworkers about their lives and families. "Kids?" I asked.

"Yes."

"Are you sure? That's something that actually came up?"

"He has pictures of them at his desk."

I wanted to ask if he was sure the kids were Brant's and not nieces and nephews or much-younger siblings but decided that particular line of questioning would serve no purpose but to frustrate me, and in all likelihood, the pictures probably were of Brant's kids.

Brant and Mindy did not have kids.

I was getting fresh lemonade from the pretty, excessively decorated glass drink dispenser that even had lemon slices floating in it when Mindy came up.

"Are you enjoying yourself?" She flashed a gorgeous smile with brilliant white teeth. She was impeccably dressed in a white sleeveless collared top, white tennis skirt, and white tennis shoes. I was reasonably certain her skirt and top had been ironed more recently than they'd been worn to play tennis. Mindy's long, lush brown hair was pulled into a high ponytail.

"I am." I felt woefully underdressed. "The lemonade is delicious." I tried not to be jealous.

"Thanks, my mom made it." She gestured in the direction of an immaculately groomed older woman, who looked and was dressed just like Mindy, except her hair was shorter and shining white. "I have no culinary skills whatsoever."

I chuckled and was secretly glad I at least had one thing up on her.

"The outfits are also all my mom. Her twist on

white not being worn after Labor Day is that it's the only color that actually can be worn on Labor Day." Perhaps Mindy wasn't quite as perfect as I thought.

"Are those your kids over there?" I gestured with my lemonade glass, which managed to be frosty cold despite the end-of-summer heat, at a group of kids running around who were also dressed in immaculate white. I suspected their clothes would stop being white long before the party ended.

"Oh God, no!" Mindy exclaimed. "Nooo. No, no, no. No kids for me."

"Are they Brant's?" I thought perhaps they were her stepchildren, and her mother insisted on them also being dressed in white.

"No." She looked confused. "They're my sister's. Brant and I don't have kids."

"But Matt—" I started then stopped, realizing what had happened. "Matt's an idiot."

"Let me guess, no clue about any of his coworkers' personal lives beyond the most basic details?"

"Not a one." I paused. "Your name is Mindy, right?" I dreaded the answer.

She laughed. "Sure is. And you're Franny?"

"Well, most people call me Fran. Or Francesca. Whichever. Franny's fine, too, though."

"Men." she laughed again. "You're a chef?"

"I own a coffee shop. Antonia's Italian Café, over in Cape Bay."

"Oh, I love that place! The best coffee I've ever had. And your desserts! Seriously, I wish I could bake like that."

"We bring most of it in. I've been known to make a cupcake or two, though."

"Still jealous." She smiled.

"Matt said you do something medical?"

"Pharmacist."

My heart skipped a beat. I forced myself to focus on the lovely conversation I was having with Mindy and not on the other pharmacist who'd recently been occupying my thoughts.

"That must be interesting."

"It is. Although you wouldn't know it from the convention I just came from."

"Convention?"

"Pharmacist convention over in Providence. I genuinely love learning about new medications and reading the literature, but, my God, the presentations were boring. I hardly even know why I go except to see a couple old friends I rarely get to catch up with."

"You said you just came from it?"

"Well, I got back Saturday afternoon. Drove out to Providence on Wednesday, had a reception that night, seminars all day Thursday and Friday, a couple more Saturday morning, then came home. I thought about just driving over there every day instead of staying in the hotel, but it's just far enough that I didn't want to do that, you know?"

I nodded absently. Wednesday through Saturday. She'd gone to Providence for a pharmacy convention and stayed from Wednesday through Saturday. The same days Abraham Casey, the pharmacist, had been booked at the Seaside Inn.

I wondered if that was the excuse he'd given his wife for his trip out of town. It made so much sense. What better excuse? And it would have been easier than years ago when she would have caught on if she called the hotel and he wasn't there. No, she would just call his cell phone, which he could answer from, and say he was, anywhere.

"You don't happen to know a guy named Abraham Casey, do you? He's a pharmacist, too. I think he was supposed to be at that convention, now that you've mentioned it." I felt safe saying his name without her connecting it to the body in the alley in Cape Bay. It hadn't been printed in the paper yet—neither the Boston paper nor the local one—and as far as I knew, it wasn't public knowledge.

Mindy thought for a moment. "No, can't say I do. Is he a friend of yours?"

"An acquaintance. Just thought it was worth a shot asking. It's a small world and all, you know?"

"Oh, I know. You wouldn't believe the connections I make—I once filled prescriptions for years for a woman before I found out she was the wife of my very first boyfriend back in middle school. It's always worth asking."

"Well, I'm glad that you don't think I'm crazy."

"Not at all. Crazy is making your thirty-five-year-old daughter dress in tennis whites even though she hasn't picked up a racket in almost twenty years."

"Mindy! Franny!" someone called. We both looked up in the direction the voice had come from. Brant was standing across the lawn waving his hands over his head, a softball bat in one and a glove in the other.

Matt was beside him also waving his arms in the air. "Softball!"

"So much for relaxing in the shade," Mindy said. She dropped her glass into a bucket of soapy water and motioned for me to do the same.

"Do you have enough glasses to get through the day?" I wondered who had that many glasses and how they kept up with the dishes.

"More than enough. Mom rents them and pays her friend's granddaughter to wash them and cycle them through the freezer throughout the day."

"Wow." I was impressed at the effort her mother

made for what was otherwise your average Labor Day cookout.

"Yeah, wow."

As we headed across the field toward where Matt and Brant were trying to figure out how to anchor a paper plate to the grass so it could serve as home plate, I thought about the remarkable coincidence of Mindy being a pharmacist and virtually laying out Abraham Casey's excuse for getting out of town.

Chapter 16

"LOOKED like you were having a good time with Mindy," Matt said as we drove back to Cape Bay.

"I did!" I was pleased to realize I meant it. After our talk about the pharmacy convention, we'd chatted for the rest of the evening, laughing through the softball game about how useless we were as we swung and missed balls our significant others said we should have hit, and we failed to come within roughly a mile of balls hit in our direction in the field. We were both pretty sure we would have gotten kicked out of the game if they'd had enough players to replace us.

"What'd you two talk about?"

"A little of everything. How useless you and Brant are at accurately learning and sharing personal information about each other. Fun fact: they do not have any children."

"They don't?"

"No, they don't."

"Then who were all those kids running around?"

"Really, Matty?"

"What?" he asked innocently.

"They belonged to any of the other people who were there."

"Yeah, I guess."

I gave up and decided to bring up the other significant piece of information I'd acquired. "Anyway, Mindy is a pharmacist."

"Oh yeah? I thought it was something medical."

"She went to a pharmacy convention this week. Wednesday through Saturday."

"Sounds dull."

"She said it was." I paused and waited to see if he'd figure out what I was getting at. When he didn't, I chose to be glad he was paying more attention to the road than to what I was trying to tell him, as the alternative would probably not turn out well for anyone. "Can you think of anyone else who's a pharmacist?"

"Um, I think my pharmacist's name is Bill or something. Bob maybe."

"Anyone else?"

"Who am I supposed to be thinking of?" He clearly

did not have much patience for my quizzing. Again, I chose to see it as a good thing.

"Maybe someone who was found in an alley?"

"Casey?"

"You got it."

"Did she know him or something?"

I decided to lay it all out for him. Trying to get him to figure the whole thing out was going to exhaust my patience. "I think the conference she went to was what he used as a cover story for his wife. The dates line up perfectly. Ed Martin said he booked his room three months ago, which is about the time you'd register for a conference."

"How do you know he didn't actually go to the conference? Maybe he just doesn't like staying at the same hotel as everybody else."

"Providence is an hour and a half away, Matty. It's closer to Boston than it is to Cape Bay."

"So why would he even book a hotel? Why not stay at home and just drive down every day?"

"That's the point. What if he told his wife he was going to the conference and had to stay there so he could network or go to all the activities or whatever? At the conferences I've been to, interacting with your peers is more valuable than the actual sessions. Besides, would you want to drive from Boston to Providence in time for a session at eight in the morning?"

Matt visibly cringed at the thought of the traffic that would be involved. There was a reason he didn't live in the city even though he could easily have gotten a more lucrative job in Boston than the one he had. It wasn't as though Bostonians were particularly known for their superior driving skills, and anyone who both lived and worked in the city would take public transportation if they needed to commute farther than they could walk. No, travelling from Boston to Providence and back again each day for a conference was a ridiculous idea. And so was travelling from Cape Bay to Providence.

"Okay, you have a point," Matt conceded. "But why did he come here? If he was using the conference as a cover, he could have gone anywhere."

"I don't know," I admitted. "But I have a feeling whatever it was is what got him killed."

"You sure it wasn't his wife? She found out that he wasn't at the conference after all and came after him?"

"Just for going on vacation without her? There would have to be more. I mean, you couldn't blame her for confronting him, but killing him? Seems a bit much."

"What if he got violent, and she fought back? Self-defense?" he suggested.

"So she shot him and made it look like a suicide to cover it up? I don't know."

"Think about it—they have a kid, right?"

"Yeah."

"If she kills him, she goes to jail, and then what happens to the kid? Besides, you can't benefit from a life insurance policy if you cause the death."

I turned my head slowly to look at him. "And why do you know that?"

He grinned. "TV. I swear."

"I hope so." I settled back in my seat. I thought over Matt's suggestion. It seemed plausible. It was one of the first theories we'd had—a lovers' quarrel. Since I'd found out about Abraham's rendezvous with Suzy, it seemed even more plausible. Maybe Leah Casey had found out her husband lied about going to the conference then came to Cape Bay to confront him. Maybe she caught him with Suzy. Maybe she confronted him. Maybe she was so angry she killed him. Or maybe he got violent when she confronted him, and she defended herself. Matt's points about jail and insurance both seemed valid.

I wondered if I should call Mike and fill him in on what I'd learned. I didn't really want him to know I'd blatantly disregarded his direction not to get involved, but I couldn't very well keep information from him that could be critical to solving a murder. It had been one thing when I had some lingering questions—who the victim was, who killed him, why they killed him, why they arranged it to look like a suicide. I hadn't meant to go this far. I had just been curious and had a few questions. Mike would likely be furious if I came clean, but I didn't see what choice I had. For all I knew, withholding information was a crime of its own. Maybe that's what my mother had meant when she said "curiosity killed the cat." Once I gave in to my curiosity, I was doomed no matter what.

Matt parked the car in his driveway and walked me home. He stood with me while Latte ran around the yard, then kissed me goodnight. Latte and I went up to bed. I expected to be up again half the night thinking about what I was going to do with my information, but apparently now that my questions had all been answered, my brain and body were both ready for rest. My head had barely hit the pillow when I fell sound asleep.

I woke up early the next morning, knowing I had a big day ahead of me. I had an exercise class, a haircut, work, and a night out with Sammy. Somewhere in there, I had to contact Mike Stanton and fill him in on everything I'd learned. I took solace in the fact that even though he might be mad at me, he probably couldn't arrest me.

Latte and I hurried through our morning routine, leaving me just enough time to walk to the gym before my class started. I was taking a kickboxing class, something I'd long resisted. I'd never liked all the hitting and kicking involved. It felt too aggressive, even if it was just a punching bag I was attacking. I preferred to alleviate my stress by curling up on the couch with a nice glass of red wine. I wondered if I should recommend that method of relaxation to Suzy but decided she was probably familiar with the effects of alcohol.

The young, perky front desk clerk at the local gym had extolled the virtues of kickboxing, encouraging me to sign up, even if just for one month to see how I liked it. When I declined, she suggested water aerobics. I signed up for kickboxing. After I'd paid for the class, I wondered if she had deliberately manipulated me into it. But since I was already signed up, and I'd only committed to a single month, I stuck with it and eventually even found that I liked it. Perky Karli smiled every time I walked past her on my way to class, and she was kind enough not to say anything when I signed up for a second month.

After kickboxing, I headed home to take a shower. I felt slightly ridiculous washing my hair less than an hour before paying someone to do it for me, but I couldn't handle the thought of going into Beach Waves with sweaty, gross hair. It was a catch-22. I could get a shower before I got my hair done and have someone rewash my already clean hair, or I could wait and shower after my cut and ruin the blowout with the humidity. Double washing my hair was less of a blow to my dignity.

After my shower, I went ahead and put on my work clothes so I didn't have to come back home. I took Latte out and threw his tennis ball for him a few times. I felt the lightest and happiest I had in days. Abraham Casey's murder was all but solved, I had drinks with Sammy to look forward to, and I was finally getting my hair cut. I must have gotten carried away with Latte because by the time I checked the time, I was running late.

"Here you go!" I sang, giving Latte a treat. "Love you! See you later!" I let him lick me on the nose a few times then shut the door and headed for the salon.

"Hi. Fran Amaro," I said as I stepped up to the front desk.

The pink-and-purple-haired girl staffing the counter made me wonder exactly where we found so many bored teenagers in such a small town. Then I realized it was the first day of school, and instead of sitting in a class-room, she was sitting in a salon, so she had to be older than I thought. I wondered whether I was just getting too old to accurately guess the ages of people younger than me. The thought was not encouraging, especially knowing another birthday was on the horizon.

The girl looked at me blankly.

"I have an appointment." I tried to be polite.

"Who with?"

With whom, I mentally corrected. "Chase Williams," I said instead, deciding civility was a more important lesson for this girl than grammar.

She clicked her computer mouse a few times. "Okay,

have a seat." She managed a level of monotone I hadn't realized possible.

I took a chair and picked up a magazine featuring a celebrity wedding on the cover. It was at least a few months old because I happened to know the couple was already divorced. Still, I flipped through it, looking for my favorite feature, "What's In Your Bag?" where they emptied out a celebrity's purse and took a picture, then annotated the contents with prices and some inane bit of information about why the product was in the celebrity's bag. "She loves this lip balm ($25 for 0.25 oz.) for how silky soft it makes her lips!" "Q-tips ($2 for 250) are a must for quick makeup fixes on the go!" "This luxurious hand crème ($225 for 0.75 oz.) is essential for maintaining the health of her nails and cuticles! Use it to smooth flyaways, too!" I couldn't say whether I loved seeing the products or the prices more.

"Fran?" an assistant asked, poking her head around a corner.

"That's me!" I stood up and reluctantly parted with the magazine. I hadn't yet gotten to the "Who Wore It Best?" feature, which was another favorite. I saw the assistant's face as it went from a happy smile to a look of concern as she saw my still-wet hair wrapped up in a bun.

She politely waited until I was next to her before she

commented. "You know you don't have to wash your own hair. We do that for you."

"I know. I had a kickboxing class this morning and—"

"Oh, say no more! I totally understand!"

She took me to the shampoo bowl and rewashed my hair. At least the salon's products were high quality and didn't make my hair feel as dry and awful as the cheap stuff. She finished with a quick scalp massage, wrung the excess water out of my hair, and led me to Chase's chair.

"Have you ever been here before?"

"Nope, first time."

"You're in for a treat. Chase's haircuts are amazing."

Chapter 17

CHASE STOOD BEHIND ME, flipping my hair, which had been cut, dried, and styled, over my shoulders, pulling it back, tucking it behind my ears, and tousling it up. "Do you like it?" he asked.

I nodded. "My head feels so light!"

"Shake your head. Run your fingers through it. See how it feels."

I did as instructed. "It's so soft." I thought it was probably the best haircut I'd ever had, better even than the astronomically expensive ones I'd had in New York. It was exactly what I wanted—what I'd already had, but better.

He flipped it back and forth again then rested his hands on my shoulders as he looked at me in the mirror.

"It was so nice to finally get the chance to catch up with you."

"I know! It's been forever, hasn't it?" As long as it had been, he hadn't changed a bit over the years. He still had the same sandy blond hair and the same pale blue eyes. Admittedly, the stubble on his chin hadn't been there in high school, but whenever I'd seen him in passing since then, it had grazed his face. He'd grown taller and broader since school, but the grin was still the same, as was the easy surfer-dude voice and the laid-back mannerisms. At his core, he was the same old Chase even after more than fifteen years.

"Probably high school since we've had a real conversation."

"You know, you're probably right."

"I think every time I come into the café, you're so busy. I see you behind the counter, making drinks for everyone, rushing around. It's not stressing you out too much, is it, Fran? Too much stress isn't good for you."

I was touched by his concern. I'd always felt having my hair done was like a form of therapy—you come in, sit down for an hour, talk to a professional, and when you leave, you feel fresh and rejuvenated. Like yourself, only better. And stylists like Chase only proved the point. Not only was he great at doing hair, he was great at reading his clients.

"I'm doing okay." I smiled at him in the mirror. "We

have our busy times, but we have our slow time, too. You just always seem to come in when there's a rush."

"Don't I know it," he laughed. He touched the ends of my hair again, arranging them just so. "But, you know, seriously, Fran, if you ever get to feeling like it's too much, let me know. I have some stuff that can help you relax a little."

"What? Like scissors and a comb? Haircuts do always make me feel better." I laughed nervously. I was almost certain that wasn't what he meant.

"Well, there's that," he laughed. "But I meant I have something else. To help you relax." He paused and looked at me for a second. I tried to keep my face perfectly neutral. "Just let me know, okay?"

I nodded and tried to give him a little bit of a smile. Not enough to encourage him, but enough to let him know I wasn't going to run straight to the police to turn him in for offering me...whatever he had just offered. Drugs? A gift certificate for a massage? Essential oils?

As we walked toward the front counter, I chided myself for assuming the worst. Chase could quite possibly be offering me some kind of herbal supplement. Matt or Sammy could have said the exact same thing, and I never would have questioned it. The situation with Abraham Casey had me jumping to crazy conclusions. I needed to find Mike as soon as possible and fill him in on everything I'd learned over the past few days so I could get back to my normal life and stop assuming my friends were trying to sell me drugs.

"I'll check her out," Chase said to the bored, punk-haired teenager at the desk.

"Whatever." She sighed and rolled her chair back from the computer.

Chase leaned over the computer and punched a few buttons. "I'll give you the friends and family discount." He winked at me. He clicked the mouse a couple of times and told me the price. The salon's rates were already reasonable, especially in comparison to what I was used to paying, but the number Chase gave me was a forty-percent discount on top of that. I tipped him generously in exchange.

I was giving him a quick hug goodbye when I glanced out the window and saw Mike on the other side of the street, walking down the sidewalk in the direction of the salon. It was perfect timing. I could go talk to him, tell him everything, and still make it to work on time. I waved goodbye to Chase and hurried outside to catch up with Mike. I stepped out between the parallel-parked cars and glanced down the street to check for oncoming traffic. It was all clear, so I crossed to the median.

"Mike!" I called out, waving my hand as he passed me across the other lane of traffic. "Mike!"

He stopped in front of the miniature golf place and turned around to see who was calling him. His face grew stern when he saw it was me. I wondered if he'd heard about my investigation.

"Hi, Mike!" I caught up to him on the sidewalk. He was wearing a suit and tie—his detective clothes. When he was just patrolling the streets, he wore a regular uniform. The fact that he was wearing his investigating clothes didn't bode well for me.

"Hello, Francesca." Whatever he looked so serious about wasn't good if he was using my full name.

"How are you?" I tried to sound cheerful.

"I've been better. In fact, I was better this morning before I went over to the Seaside Inn to interview Ed Martin."

I swallowed hard and tried to play off my apprehension. "Oh, did it not go well?"

"It went very well, actually. His recollection of the events in question was quite good. Apparently, someone came by the other day and helped refresh everything for him."

"Oh?"

"Fran..." The warning tone in his voice unmistakable.

"Yes?"

"I told you to stay out of it."

"I know. I'm sorry. I didn't mean to get involved."

"But you did."

I nodded.

"You need to tell me everything."

"Can we go somewhere to talk? Instead of…out here?" I waved my hand around to indicate the very public nature of Main Street. The idea of going into detail about my findings while standing where anyone could walk by and hear me was incredibly unappealing, as was the idea of enduring Mike's reaction.

"You mean like my interrogation room?" he suggested.

"I was thinking more like my café."

Mike grunted, turned, and stalked off in the direction of the coffee shop. I took that to mean he was agreeing to my suggestion and followed him.

He pulled open the café door and let me go in first.

"Hey!" Sammy exclaimed. "You're here early. I didn't expect you for—" She stopped suddenly when she saw Mike and his sullen expression. "Hey, Mike." She barely succeeded at sounding cheerful.

I made a move to sit in an armchair in the corner, but Mike had other ideas. "Back room," he barked as he blew past me. He managed to flash a smile at Sammy. "Black coffee, please, Sam. Large. And could you bring it to me in the back?"

"Sure thing, Mike." She raised her eyebrows and made her eyes big as I walked past her. The code for both was "what did you do" and "you're in trouble."

I grimaced and followed Mike into the back. He shut

the door behind us and sat in a chair. He crossed his legs, ankle over knee, and folded his arms across his chest. He was a tall, muscular man, quite imposing in the small room. I edged past him and sat down in another chair facing him.

He didn't say a word, which only served to make me more nervous. He kept his eyes on me, and I waited. There was a knock on the door.

"Come in," Mike called.

"I have your coffee." Sammy stuck her head in.

"Thanks, Sam." He reached up and took the coffee from her without breaking eye contact with me.

Sammy mouthed "good luck" and slipped back out, pulling the door closed.

Mike took a sip of his coffee. "You may as well get started," he said.

"Well, that night—the night of the murder—"

"I'm sorry?" Mike interrupted me.

"The night of the murder."

He leaned forward and put an elbow on his knee. "How do you know that?"

"Know what?"

"I told you it was a suicide. Why did you just say murder?"

"Oh, um, I just sort of…figured it out. Suicide didn't make sense to me, so I thought it was probably a murder."

"Suicide didn't make sense to you." He shook his head. "Go on."

"Well, that was the first thing. I went home and talked to Matt about it and realized it was probably a murder. So the next day, I went and talked to Mary Ellen to see what she could tell me about Abraham Casey."

"Wait, how did you find out his name?"

"Mary Ellen."

"Mary Ellen told you?"

I nodded. "Is that not okay? She didn't know if it was okay or not."

"It's not okay when she's giving you information she's withholding from the police."

"But—she wasn't withholding it. She told you as soon as she remembered she knew it."

"And what makes you think that?"

"She told me."

"When?"

"Saturday."

"*Saturday?*"

"Yes. She told me she remembered it during the night and called the officer who interviewed her first thing in the morning. She left him a message."

Mike stared at me for a second. "Son of a—" he muttered under his breath, followed by another, even less polite word. "She called Bradshaw?" he asked in a normal tone of voice.

"That's what she said. He didn't get the message?"

"He either didn't get it or just didn't bother to tell anyone. Do you know how many hours we wasted trying to figure out this guy's name when we could have had it first thing?"

A horrible thought occurred to me. "You don't think Mary Ellen lied to me about calling, do you?"

"I don't think so. I've had issues with Bradshaw before. Never like this, though." He shook his head, and I could tell he was trying to contain himself. "How did Mary Ellen know his name?"

"It was on his credit card receipt."

"He paid with a credit card?"

"Yes."

"He paid with a credit card," he repeated, seemingly pained by the words. Mike leaned back in his chair and rubbed his forehead vigorously. "I'm going to fire him," he said, again under his breath. "He's fired. I'm firing him."

"So, wait—if you didn't get Mary Ellen's message, how did you find out his name?"

"His fingerprints came back from IAFIS yesterday." He must have noticed the blank look on my face. "Integrated Automated Fingerprint Identification System. It's an FBI system. Lets you compare a set of fingerprints against a huge pool of them. Casey had to get fingerprinted to get his pharmacy license." He paused. "I assume you already know he was a pharmacist." He sounded weary.

I nodded.

"Of course you do. You're a better detective than half the guys on my force, and it's not even your job." He pointed to me. "Don't you ever tell anyone I said that."

I grinned. "I won't."

"Tell me what else you know." He pulled a little notebook out of his pocket. He flipped to a blank page and poised his pencil over it.

I ran quickly through the other information I'd gathered during my nearly three-day head start—his wife and child, the pharmacists' convention, and my conversation with Suzy. Mike scribbled down notes as I spoke.

"So, you think there's a drug angle to this?" Mike asked.

"I don't know if I think there's a drug *angle*. I think there are maybe some drugs involved. Lovers' quarrel makes the most sense to me, though. His wife found out he didn't go to the conference, came here to confront him, caught him with Suzy, and things got violent."

"So you think the wife did it? What's her name..." He flipped the pages in his little notebook, looking for her name.

"Leah," I offered.

"Of course you know that."

I smiled. He didn't. I guessed he was still annoyed his officer had dropped the ball.

"You think Leah Casey did it?"

"I'm not really *sure* she did it." I didn't want him to think I had more evidence than I did pointing in her direction. "And even if she did, it could have been self-defense. He might have attacked her first."

"And have you spoken with Mrs. Casey?"

"No! Of course not. I'm not going to call up a grieving widow and start asking her questions about her dead husband."

"If you'd called her before last night, you would have been the one breaking the news to her."

I cringed, grateful I'd decided not to contact her. "I'll leave that stuff up to you. I'm not the police, remember?"

"Oh, I remember. I'm just not so sure you do."

I looked down at my hands in my lap.

"So, since you seem to know everything about this case, can you tell me why he didn't actually go to the conference? He was registered, you know."

I didn't know, and I could have kicked myself for not having thought to check whether he'd been registered. "I figure he just wanted a break from his everyday life. He probably booked the conference so he'd have a cover and then decided to just go to the beach for a few days, get away from it all."

"Hook up with a waitress he met in a bar," Mike added. "Anything else you've noticed? Anything that seemed unusual?"

"No, I think I've told you everything."

Mike nodded and drummed the eraser of his pencil against his notebook. He looked as though he was thinking hard about something. "Well, Fran, I have to tell you, you've done some good work here. I still don't approve." He looked at me pointedly. "But it's good work. The lovers' quarrel is a solid theory. I gotta say, though—I think there might be a little more to it than that." He shifted forward in his chair and looked at me. "We've known for a while that there are drugs coming into Cape Bay. Not street drugs. Pharmaceuticals. We've been keeping it quiet until we could put the pieces of the puzzle together. Not just who's selling it here but how they're getting it in. With Casey being a pharmacist and Suzy hinting that he had drugs he was sharing, I don't think we should dismiss the drug angle just yet."

Chapter 18

MIKE and I sat in the back room and talked about the case for a few more minutes. He told me about all the proper procedures they'd followed, and I told him about all the gut instincts and logical leaps I'd followed. He shook his head every time I told him about something I'd figured out on my own that had taken the police department way more time to learn.

He finished his coffee and tossed the paper cup in the trash. "I guess I'd better get going. I have some leads I have to follow and an officer I have to chew out."

"Good luck with both of those. I'd tell you not to be too hard on Officer Bradshaw, but he probably deserves it."

"Damn right he does. Could have blown the whole investigation. And it wasn't just not relaying the message from Mary Ellen—he shouldn't have needed to get the message in the first place. He should have asked to see the receipt when he was there Friday night." He shook his head, obviously disgusted with the incompetence of his officer. "I can't believe we had to wait three days to get information we should have had immediately."

"I feel bad. I mean, if I had called you Saturday to let you know—"

"To let us know information you thought we already had? That's not your fault, Fran. You had no way of knowing we—well, one of us, anyway—would overlook something so obvious."

"Besides, you probably would have shut me down right then."

"You better believe it. Not that it probably would have done much good."

I shrugged then nodded. "Probably not."

Mike shook his head at me. "Well, thanks for the information, Fran. If you think of anything else or come across anything at all, even if you think we already know—"

"I'll call you right away."

"That's not an invitation to do any more investigating."

"I know. And I'm done, anyway. I've had enough of this case."

"I hope so." He reached to open the door.

"One thing—"

"I'm not even out the door, Fran!"

"I know!" I smiled sheepishly. "But how did you find out it wasn't a suicide? I assume it was based on more than a feeling you had."

"Autopsy. No gunshot residue on his hands. And the bullet's angle of entry was wrong. Straight on instead of at an angle." He twisted his hand to show how hard it would be to shoot yourself dead on.

"So it wasn't hard to figure out?"

"Not once we had the medical examiner's opinion. Whoever did it is either not very good at murder or was just hoping to get a couple days' head start on us."

"Anybody see Leah Casey in the past few days?"

"That's what I'm about to go check with Boston PD on. They did the death notification."

"Well, good luck."

"Thanks. The way this case has been going, I'm going to need it." He opened the door and let me precede him into the café.

A few customers were scattered around enjoying their drinks and, from the looks of most of the tables, their lunches. Most of the people were locals, a stark difference from the crowd that had filled the place a week ago. I had a sneaking suspicion a lot of the locals avoided spending much time in the shops during the tourist season, preferring to wait for the calm of the off-season and the company of each other.

Sammy was leaning over the counter, talking to someone I couldn't see. I almost couldn't believe my ears when I heard her laugh. She sounded so happy and carefree. I angled my head as I walked around the counter to see who she was talking to.

"Leary! What are you doing here?" I heard Mike call.

Finally reaching where I could see who Sammy was talking to, I saw Mike shake Ryan Leary's hand and slap him on the back.

"Hey, Mike!" Ryan replied. "Just stopped in for some coffee and a bite to eat before my shift."

"Come by and see me when you get into the office. I have some new information about the case I want to share with you."

"Yes, sir. I should be there in an hour or so."

Mike nodded and turned back to the counter. Before he could even ask, Sammy handed him a large to-go cup and a bag that probably contained his usual of a mozzarella-tomato-basil sandwich and a piece of tiramisu.

"You know me too well," Mike said with a smile. "Thanks, Sam. Thanks to you, too, Fran."

"What's a guy gotta do to get that kind of service?" Ryan asked as Mike walked away.

"You gotta come in a lot. Like, a *lot*," Sammy said. I saw a twinkle in her eye that hadn't been there for weeks. "How often does Mike come in, Fran?"

"Few times a week!" Mike called from the door.

"More than that!" I retorted.

"Don't tell my wife!" He pushed the door open and waved once before he disappeared down the sidewalk.

"Almost every day," I said to Ryan. I looked at Sammy for confirmation. She nodded vigorously.

"I might be able to manage that," Ryan said. "The food's good. The drinks are great. The company couldn't be better. I could get used to coming around." He flashed a brilliant smile our way.

"We could get used to having you," Sammy said with a smile. She was good at engaging customers, connecting with them, and charming them into coming back, not just for the coffee, but also for the pleasant company.

The bell over the door jingled as a customer came in.

"I'll get her," I said before Sammy could even look up. She seemed happy talking to Ryan, and I knew happiness was something she needed right now.

I got the customer's drink, and the next, and the next. We had a slow but steady stream of customers, enough to keep from getting bored but not so many that it was overwhelming. The café started to empty out, Ryan left, and Sammy joined me at the register.

"Sorry about that," she said. "We just kind of got

started talking, then you seemed like you were handling it and—"

"You're fine." I cut her off. "You were enjoying yourself, and I had everything under control. You do enough around here. You're entitled to slack off a little every now and then."

Sammy looked uncomfortable. She was a hard worker and a perfectionist, and she didn't like the suggestion that she wasn't working her hardest. She worked incredibly hard the vast majority of the time, which earned her a chat or two with a customer, especially since I was there to take care of the café's patrons.

A pair of customers got up, and Sammy hurried to clear their table before I could so much as flinch in their direction. I hadn't intended to guilt her into working even harder than usual, but apparently, I had done just that. I'd have to avoid the words "slack off" the next time I said something like that to her.

The café gradually emptied out, and Sammy and I found ourselves alone.

"You can go home if you want," I offered. "I don't think it'll be too busy the rest of the day."

"Okay, thanks." But Sammy didn't make a move for the door. She just stood at the counter, swaying slightly, and not quite making eye contact with me.

"What?" I asked finally, deciding there was something on her mind she didn't want to bring up.

"What happened back there with Mike? When you two went back there, he looked furious, but by the time you came out, the two of you were laughing and joking. What happened?"

I ran through the morning's conversation with Mike briefly for Sammy—how angry he was that I had been investigating the case, how his officer's major screw-up had basically gotten me off the hook, and some of the information I had shared with him, including my theory that Leah Casey, the victim's wife, was somehow involved.

"Wow," Sammy said. "You're like a regular part of the police force now."

"Well, I wouldn't say that, and Mike definitely wouldn't. I think it's more that he was just glad that I had a little information he could use."

"Mm-hmm, sure," Sammy teased. "He's going to call you up and hire you tomorrow. 'Fran, I know you're busy with the coffee shop and all, but we've had a rash of people waking up to their lawn ornaments being rearranged, and I need your expertise.'" Sammy lowered her voice and did her best impression of Mike's gruff cop demeanor. It was terrible and hilarious.

"I can only hope Cape Bay's crime goes back to just having that kind of stuff."

"I know, right?" Something outside caught Sammy's

eye, and she reached around her back to untie her apron. "Still okay if I head out?"

"Do you see any more customers than we had ten minutes ago?"

"Nope." She pulled her apron over her head. "Are we still on for tonight? Drinks at Fiesta Mexicana?" She was headed for the back room, barely glancing at me as she spoke.

"Yeah, of course. Where are you going?"

"Home. I just—remembered I had something I had to do. I'll see you tonight. Bye!" She grabbed her purse and disappeared out the back door so fast I barely understood what was going on.

Just as the back door closed, the front door opened. I put on a big smile to greet the customer and turned around, immediately realizing why Sammy had suddenly hurried out.

"Francesca!" Mrs. D'Angelo exclaimed. "Oh, Francesca, how are you?" Mrs. D'Angelo, as unfamiliar with boundaries as ever, came around the corner and enveloped me with her arms and her heavy floral perfume. "It's been ages since I've seen you!"

"Actually, Mrs. D'Angelo, I saw you just last week. Remember? You came in." Mrs. D'Angelo's visits were a predictable weekly occurrence. I tried to refresh her memory about her last visit, but for that to work, she'd have to stop talking long enough to hear what I was saying. With Mrs. D'Angelo, that was unlikely.

"You look tired! Are you sleeping well, dear? Of course not, how could you when there are bodies turning up all over town? It's awful, just awful, isn't it? And the last one so close to your shop! Just down the street! Why, it must be just terrible for business. Just look around! There's no one here!"

"Well, it's the off-season now, so things are a little slower. We had a good crowd a little while ago, though." I knew it was useless to really get a word in, but I had to try. I couldn't just stand there.

"Oh, dear, you know it will be all right. Antonia's has been here for fifty years now—"

"It's actually closer to seventy, Mrs. D'Angelo."

"It's weathered far worse storms than this, and I'd venture that it will weather plenty more. You have a good head on your shoulders, dear. Your mother and your grandparents raised you well! You will survive this!"

The bell rang, and a customer came in. I wanted to go to the register to help him, but Mrs. D'Angelo held me fast, her sharp red nails pressing into the flesh of my upper arms. I managed a glance over my shoulder and a weak smile before Mrs. D'Angelo pulled me into another hug.

"You will survive, Francesca!" She pushed me back at arm's length, keeping her nails firmly implanted in my skin, and stared into my face. "I see your grandmother in you. You have her strength." She nodded once then released me. I reflexively rubbed the sore spots on my upper arms. "Now, is Samantha here? I heard she and that boy she was with split up, and I wanted to give her some words of encouragement."

I happened to know that Mrs. D'Angelo had already offered Sammy quite a few words of encouragement in the weeks since her breakup. "Oh, you just missed her. I'll tell her you stopped by, though."

"Please do, dear." She glanced at the delicate gold watch on her slim wrist. "My heavens! I have to go. Now that the busy season is over, the Ladies' Auxiliary is planning a trip up the coast to look for potential sister cities for Cape Bay, and I have to work out all the sleeping arrangements."

"Aren't sister cities usually overseas?" I went against my own better judgment by asking her a question when she was already halfway out the door.

"Yes, but we think it would be lovely to have some in New England so we can all be closer. Goodbye, dear! Remember, you will survive!" She breezed out the door, leaving only the scent of perfume in her wake.

Chapter 19

I FINISHED my shift without too much trouble. People wandered in throughout the afternoon, enjoyed their drinks and snacks, then headed off to wherever they were going next. The after-school rush returned with the first day of school but was sort of the anti-rush. Kids as young as elementary schoolers stopped in on their walks home. They all took their time studying the menu, inevitably choosing something either frozen and fruity or chocolatey.

A few tried to show how mature they were and ordered coffee. I looked at them with my eyebrow raised and my finger poised over the buttons on the register until they, afraid the all-powerful grown-up would tell on them to their parents, corrected themselves and requested something more age appropriate. I didn't bother telling them that I didn't recognize most of them enough to know who their parents were. The silent threat was enough.

The teenagers who came through were less adorable. They ordered their complicated drinks with multiple additions and modifications in the most disaffected, blasé tones they could muster, desperately trying to show me and their friends how impossibly cool they were. I didn't tell any of them that the harder they tried, the less cool they actually looked.

Becky came through with a group of her friends, greeted me with a bright smile, and ordered directly from the menu. Most of her friends ended up being friendlier than the vast majority of their peers.

The after-school rush bled into the dinner rush. Maybe twenty or thirty people stopped in, mostly single adults who wanted to pick up something quick and light for dinner on their way home from work. A few people stayed and ate at a table, some took their orders to go, and all of them were gone by closing time.

I straightened up the café, washed dishes, restocked the display cases, and made sure all the chairs were arranged properly at the tables. I wiped everything down and swept up so the café would be ready for Sammy the next morning.

At the last second, I remembered I had promised to bring dinner to Matt. I grabbed a bag and slid a sandwich and salad inside. Then I put one of his favorite chocolate cupcakes in a to-go box and laid it carefully on top of the other food items.

It felt luxurious to lock up an hour early. It wasn't even completely dark out when I turned the key in the door and left the café behind.

Sammy and I had planned to meet a little later so I'd have time to change and take care of Latte. I had arranged to bring the dog to Matt before I headed out for the night so he wouldn't be lonely. Latte, that was, not Matt. Although I supposed Matt probably appreciated the company as well.

Latte dashed out to greet me as soon as I opened the door. I bent down to scratch his ears and give him a good rub all over. He licked my face as though it had been more than a few hours since he'd last seen me. I rubbed his head one last time and stood up.

He ran out into the yard then ran back inside, making a beeline straight for the kitchen. He stood politely next to his bowl, paw in the air, waiting for me to serve his dinner. I scooped the kibble then went upstairs to get dressed.

It took a few minutes of staring into my closet to figure out what I wanted to wear. So much of my wardrobe was black, a popular color from my New York City days, but tonight was supposed to be a fun night for Sammy, and I wanted to wear something a little brighter.

I spotted a cornflower blue shirt that had been my mother's and perfectly complemented my eyes. I pulled it on with my favorite jeans and checked out my reflection in the mirror. It was a good look, except for my hair, which I'd put back up in a chignon during the day. I let it down and shook it out around my shoulders. I ran my fingers through it a few times until it lay just right. I touched up my makeup until I was satisfied I looked girls' night out-ready then went back downstairs.

I had a message on my cell phone from Sammy.

You almost ready?

I tapped out my reply quickly.

Just have to drop Latte off at Matt's and then I'll be on my way! Looking forward to it!

I slid my phone into my purse and slung it over my shoulder. I picked up Latte's leash.

"Latte! Come here, boy!" I called, patting my leg. Latte came running, having heard the sounds he associated with going for a walk. "You're going to Matty's for a little while, okay, boy? You'll have so much fun. Yes, you will! Yes, you will!"

I didn't even bother putting the leash on him, just held it in my hand with Matt's dinner and opened the door. Latte ran out, and I locked the door behind us. Latte did a couple of laps around me, excited to be going somewhere, then fell obediently into place beside me.

I started across the Williamses' lawn. Their house was dark. It wasn't that late, so I wondered if they were out of town. They hadn't mentioned anything, but I didn't see them that often. The sun was all the way down, and it was completely dark. On our tree-lined street, the streetlights did nothing to illuminate the paths up to our houses. I walked through the grass toward Matt's house more by memory than by anything I could see.

Now that the Casey case was all but solved and the likely murderer was long gone from Cape Bay, I didn't have the slightest inkling of fear. I only felt excitement and anticipation for my night with Sammy. Even though we saw each other every day at work, we almost never got to spend time together in a strictly social setting. This night was special and would be fun. And it was just the two of us—no Dawn to turn our night in a direction we never expected—so it should be relaxing as well.

Just as I passed by the Williamses' front door, something caught my eye at the side of their house—a movement, or a shadow the slightest bit darker than the air around it.

I hesitated, straining my eyes to see what it was. Was it a tree in the distance? A shrub at the corner of the house? I tried to picture the Williamses' landscaping, but I couldn't remember if they had a tallish shrub anywhere.

I stepped forward slowly, trying to chalk whatever it was up to my overactive imagination. And then it moved. Definitely. I was sure. The shadow moved out from the corner of the house. If it was a shrub, it was on wheels.

I stopped in my tracks. Latte stopped beside me. I didn't take my eyes off the shadow, and I was certain Latte didn't either. I heard none of his usual happy noises—his panting, the jingling of his collar, his feet tramping on the grass—but I knew he was there, which meant he was just as focused on the figure as I was.

I tried to think of what to do. I couldn't see well enough to know whether it was a person, although I couldn't think of what else it might be. It wasn't moving toward me. It wasn't moving away from me. It wasn't moving in any direction at the moment. I didn't even know if it was facing me at all. I didn't know if it could see me.

The shadow moved farther out from the house. It was definitely human. I could tell by the way he or she walked. The shadow moved farther this time, stopping directly in my path. It had to see me.

A sickening feeling came over me. What if I had been completely wrong about Abraham Casey's murder? What if it was random? What if this was his murderer striking again? Would Matt find me dead in the Williamses' yard when he came to find out why I hadn't brought Latte over yet? Oh God, what if the person hurt Latte?

I still hadn't moved, keeping my eyes fixed on the shadowy figure. I thought about my options. The Williamses' house was closest, but it was dark. If no one was home, no one could help me. I could try to run to Matt's house, but I would have to run past the figure. The shadow was far enough ahead of me that it would certainly catch me, even if I tried to run around it. I could run back to my house. But the door was locked, and unlocking it would kill any head start I had.

My only choice was to run for the street and hope Latte followed me. I would scream. The evening was early enough that the old folks on the street would still be awake and would hear me. They could look out their windows and see me running down the road, which was illuminated by the streetlights. They would call the police. I would run to Main Street if I had to. Eventually, someone would see me. I would run until someone saw me.

I tensed all my muscles, getting ready to make a break for it while trying not to let the figure see which way I was going. I counted down in my head. Three...two...one...

"You just couldn't stay out of it, could you, Fran?" The figure spoke. The voice was familiar, male, but in my panic, I couldn't place it. I didn't run. I tried to speak, to apologize to the figure for getting involved, to beg him to leave me alone, but the fear paralyzed my vocal cords, and nothing came out.

"You just couldn't leave well enough alone." He took a step toward me now. I stepped backward, not wanting to let him get any closer than he already was. He kept coming toward me. "You had to tell everything to Mike, had to go running your mouth to him. I should have known better, but I didn't realize quite what a little tattle-tale you are."

His long legs were bringing him toward me faster than I could back away. His walk was familiar, too, as was the way he carried himself. His identity flitted around my brain but wouldn't stop long enough for me to catch it.

His arm moved to pull something out of his jacket pocket. I heard a nauseating click that I had never before heard in real life, only on TV: the sound of a gun safety clicking off. "It's too bad, you know." He stepped quickly toward me. "I always liked you."

And then I knew who it was. I recognized the laid-back tone of the voice, now tinged with aggression, and the casual swaying walk that suddenly seemed so menacing.

"Chase, please, you don't have to do this." I finally found my voice.

"Oh, I don't? You're about to bring the law down on

me, and I don't have to stop you? That's where you're wrong."

"I didn't tell him it was you! I swear! I didn't even know you had anything to do with it! Why would I think that?"

"You expect me to believe that?"

"Yes! You have to! It's the truth!"

"I may be a criminal, but I'm not an idiot, Fran."

He was an arm's length away from me now. I had to do something, or I would be another case file on Mike's desk.

I did the first thing that came to mind. I kicked him. Then I hit him, just the way we learned in kickboxing class—plant your feet, twist with your hips, drive through your first two knuckles. I kicked him again. I screamed with each blow just like our teacher had taught us.

Chase was stumbling back now, likely more surprised by the attack than he was injured by it. But if surprise was what I had going for me, I was going to use it.

I kept coming, hitting and kicking. I heard the gun fall to the ground with a thud. I heard Latte barking frantically. I kicked Chase again and landed another punch. I remembered something I should have thought of sooner and, with my next kick, planted my foot firmly in his groin. He fell to the ground, clutching himself. I kicked him again to make sure he wasn't faking it. Latte ran past me toward Matt's house then flew back my way, barking all the while. He circled me then took off toward Matt's again.

I looked at Chase on the ground and tried to figure out what to do next. If I ran, he might get away. Instead, I planted my foot on his throat with just enough force to make sure he knew it was there. He whimpered but didn't move.

Latte made another lap, and I felt in my pocket for my phone to call the police. I came up empty-handed and realized I'd put it in my purse, which I'd dropped at some point in the confrontation. I opened my mouth to scream for help, but before I could make a noise, Matt's front light came on, and his door opened.

"What the hell?" He stopped as he caught sight of me standing over Chase with Latte barking furiously in his face.

"Latte, hush!" I commanded. Latte stopped barking but kept a low growl going in Chase's direction. I looked at Matt, whose bewildered expression I could see in the light from the house. "Could you call the police? And, if you can, could you let Sammy know I'm probably not going to make it to our girls' night?"

Chapter 20

THREE NIGHTS LATER–A week to the day after our first attempt—we finally managed to have our girls' night out, which had expanded a little from our first two attempts.

The group of us—me, Sammy, Matt, Dawn, the guy bartender from the Sand Bar, Mike, his wife Sandra, and Ryan—had taken over the back deck at Fiesta Mexicana. Appetizer plates were scattered across the tables, intermixed with bowls of chips, salsa, queso, and guacamole. We each had drinks planted in front of us: beers for Matt, Mike, and Ryan; tequila shots for Dawn and her bartender friend; and margaritas for Sammy, Sandra, and me.

"I'd like to propose a toast!" Dawn announced, lifting her shot glass in the air. Bartender Guy raised his glass with her, and the rest of us quickly followed. "To Sammy! To her freedom and to second chances at celebrating it."

"Um, third chance," I corrected her.

"It only counts as the second because you guys didn't invite me to the last one!" Dawn said in the exact same tone she'd used for the toast. "To Sammy!" she repeated.

"To Sammy!" we all echoed and took a drink.

Dawn nudged me. "Your turn," she said.

I looked at her in confusion, but she gave me a "hurry up" look, so I raised my glass. "Uh, to Dawn! For arranging this night out!"

"To Dawn!" everyone repeated.

Dawn looked at Matt. He thought for a minute then raised his glass again. "To Mike! For not arresting my girlfriend for beating the crap out of a guy!" We drank.

"To good times with good friends!" Sammy offered without prompting.

"To Cape Bay!" Ryan declared.

"To Fran, for catching the murderer!" Sandra said. I blushed. Mike rolled his eyes, but I saw the hint of a smile on his face as he glanced at me.

"To not having any more murders for Fran to meddle in!" Mike toasted, his slight smile breaking into a grin.

"I can drink to that," I muttered.

Dawn nudged Bartender Guy next to her when it

became clear he wasn't going to realize it was his turn. "Go!" she hissed.

"To tequila!" he said, and we drank. "Excuse me," he said, standing up. "I gotta hit the head."

I watched as he left the patio then leaned over to Dawn. "Hey, what's his name?"

"You don't know?"

"You didn't introduce him."

"It's Dave."

"Ah, okay." I gestured back and forth between Dawn and Dave's empty chair. "Are you and Dave, uh, seeing each other?"

Dawn made a face. "No, Dave's gay."

"But I saw him flirting with all the girls at the bar the other night."

"You get better tips when you flirt." She smirked.

"I guess that makes sense." I leaned back in my chair.

"You get better service when you flirt, too," she said as the waiter came out with another round of drinks. "Thank you, Javier," she cooed then smiled and batted her eyelashes a couple of times.

"I brought you some empanadas." He set the plate down. "On the house."

"Aren't you the sweetest!" Dawn looked at me knowingly as he walked away. "See, I told you." She took a bite of empanada.

I shook my head and took an empanada before offering the plate to Matt.

"So, Mikey," Dawn said a few minutes later after Dave had returned from the restroom. I saw Sandra's eyes get big as she glanced at Mike. Clearly, she was just as surprised as I had been the first time I'd heard Dawn call him that. Mike narrowed his eyes a little bit in Dawn's direction but otherwise let it go. "I know Chase killed the guy in the alley, and Franny beat the snot out of Chase, but there's a lot of other things in that story I don't know. How about you fill us in?"

Mike glanced around the table then shrugged. "It's not like it won't be in the paper soon enough anyway." He inhaled deeply then blew out a breath. "So, we've known for a while—"

"Wait, who's we?" Dawn interjected.

"The Cape Bay Police Department," Mike said sternly, apparently not fond of being interrupted. I almost wanted to warn him that it would probably not be the last time Dawn jumped into the middle of his story, but I had a feeling that would come as no surprise. "So, the Cape Bay Police Department has known for a while that there were drugs coming into town—I told Fran this back before we made the arrest. Pharmaceutical stuff, mostly painkillers, but some benzos and barbiturates."

"Some whats?" Dawn asked.

Mike took a breath. I guessed he was resisting the urge to say something unkind to her. "Benzodiazepines and barbiturates." Dawn looked at him blankly. "Valium and sleeping pills."

"Oh, okay," she said. "Go on."

Mike took another deep breath. "It's been fairly steady for a while now, but there have been some spikes and drop-offs here and there. Most recently, we confiscated some during an arrest that the lab said were so long expired they were basically placebos. Sugar pills!" he added before Dawn could say anything.

"I knew that one." She smiled, and I saw Sandra stifle a giggle.

"Anyway, we knew the drugs were coming in from the outside, and, at the quantities we were seeing, they weren't just people with legal prescriptions selling off the individual pills. This had to be organized. There had to be a source—a drug manufacturer or a sales rep—or as it turned out in this case, a pharmacist. The Boston PD is still looking into how Casey managed to get the quantities of drugs that he did and move them through his pharmacy without alerting the feds to what was going on. But he was the source of the drugs, and Chase Williams was the local dealer. The kingpin, really—he sold them all down the coast and out on Cape Cod. Those rich kids apparently have quite a taste for this stuff."

"How did Chase and Casey know each other?" I asked, risking the wrath of Mike.

"Good question!" Mike said. Dawn shot me a dirty look for getting Mike's approval on my question. I gave her back my best teacher's pet smile. "It turns out," Mike continued, "that Casey used to work in the same hospital as Chase's sister Cheryl. Cheryl took Chase with her to a holiday party once before she was married, and that's when he met Casey. They've been working together for years now. Chase used his work at the salon as a front— no one would ever question him singling out a special bottle of 'shampoo' for a customer or giving them a sample of a product. He'd put the pills in a baggie and slip them into the shampoo bottle or the sample container, and the customer would pay him cash or include it in his tip. Apparently, he was really good at cutting hair, so no one thought twice about him making a lot in tips."

Around the table, the women nodded. "If I wasn't married to his arresting officer, I'd say that losing Chase as a hair stylist is a real blow to the community," Sandra said. Mike looked at her as though he thought she had lost her mind. "But I am married to him," she rushed to say, "so I understand fully how important it is that he's off the streets." Mike nodded and looked away from her. She leaned back in her chair so he couldn't see her, made a sad face, and wiped a mock tear from her eye.

Sammy, Dawn, and I all looked away so Mike didn't see us laugh.

"Anyway, I had mentioned that the worthless batch had been circulating around town. Chase realized that it was bad, and when Casey came to deliver the next batch, Chase confronted him about it and told him that he wasn't paying this time since he'd paid the last time and gotten a bad product. Casey refused, they argued, then they parted ways. The next day, Chase came looking for Casey for another attempt at 'negotiations.' This time, he brought a gun to try to be a little more persuasive. Casey still wouldn't back down, and Chase shot him. Says it was an accident, but I'm not so sure about that."

"What was with the suicide thing?" Dawn asked.

Mike didn't even seem to flinch at this interruption, now engrossed in telling his story. "Chase knew that Casey had lied to his wife about where he was going. He knew Casey had hooked up with Suzy from the Sand Bar the night before. He figured there was enough evidence along those lines to make suicide plausible, as long as no one looked too close, so he put the gun in Casey's hand and walked away. Why he thought we wouldn't do an autopsy or check for gunshot residue, I don't know. As long as he kept his drug trade going, you'd think he'd be a little better at covering up his crimes, but I guess his incompetence is just something for us to be grateful for."

"So, did you know it was him before he attacked Fran?" Matt asked.

"Not a clue. We were pursuing other leads. We might have figured it out eventually, but I can't be sure. If he hadn't attacked Fran, he might have gotten off scot-free."

"Why did he come after me?" I asked. "I never told you anything about him. I thought it was the wife."

"Apparently, he saw you talking to me after your haircut the other day. I guess he'd just offered you some pills and thought that you were ratting him out. He thought that if we came after him for that, the whole thing would come crashing down on him, so he decided to eliminate the witness."

"Even though he thought I'd already told you what happened?"

Mike shrugged. "Criminals don't always think the clearest."

"Suzy's going to be mad that her drug supply's dried up," Dawn said.

"I'm sure she'll find a way to get them," Mike said. "There's too much of a demand for stuff like that for the supply to dry up for too long. All we can do is keep it off the streets the best we can."

We all sat and let Mike's information sink in.

"So," Sammy said thoughtfully, "Fran really is kind of responsible for the case getting solved. If she hadn't gotten involved, you might never have figured out who the murderer was."

"We would have gotten it eventually," Mike said.

"But you solved it faster because of Fran."

"Civilians should leave police business up to the police." Mike cast a look in my direction.

"I can't help that I get curious!" I said. "I just saw that souvenir bag and knew there had to be something more to the case. And then Mary Ellen told me about the marzipan and—well, who buys marzipan without planning to eat it? That stuff is delicious!"

"She has good instincts. You have to give her that," Ryan said.

Mike shook his head and looked at me. "And I don't care how good your instincts are. I'm not inviting you to work on a case any time soon."

"She was helpful, though, wasn't she, Mike?" Sandra prompted.

He looked at Sandra for a second as though she'd just shared with all of us what kind of underwear he preferred. She smiled a lovely smile at him. He turned back to me. "You were helpful, even if it was by accident."

I smiled at him, accepting his indirect compliment. I knew better than to push my luck.

"I think I'm going to sign up for Fran's kickboxing class on Monday," Sandra said.

"I'll get you a gun," Mike said.

"Chase had a gun," I pointed out. "I just had a few kickboxing lessons and a lot of adrenaline."

Mike grunted.

Our conversation faded into silence.

Matt took my hand. "I'm glad you're safe," he whispered and lifted my hand to his lips.

I smiled at him and took a sip of my margarita. It was perfect. It was served on the rocks, just the way I liked it. Between that, the cool salt air blowing in off the water, and the friends surrounding me, I didn't think I could be any happier.

Recipe 1: Marzipan

Makes 12 ounces

Ingredients:
- 1 ½ cups almond flour/meal
- 1 ½ cups powdered sugar
- 2 teaspoons pure almond extract
- 1 teaspoon food-grade rose water
- 1 egg white

Pulse almond flour and sugar in a food processor until fully combined with no lumps. Add almond extract and rose water. Pulse again to combine. Add egg white, and process until a thick dough is formed. If the dough is still wet and sticky, add more sugar or ground almonds. If the dough is flimsy, it will become firmer after refrigeration.

Knead almond marzipan on a work surface. Shape into a log. Wrap in plastic wrap and refrigerate. It will keep for a month in the fridge or up to six months in the freezer.

Marzipan can be dipped in chocolate. If you're artistic, you can shape marzipan into fruits, vegetables, figurines, or anything you'd like.

Recipe 2: Classic Margarita on the Rocks

Ingredients:

- 2 ounces tequila
- 1 ounce Cointreau
- 1 ounce fresh lime juice
- Salt for garnish

Combine tequila, Cointreau, and lime juice in a cocktail shaker with ice. Moisten the rim of a cocktail glass with lime juice or water. Hold the glass upside down and dip into salt. Strain drink into glass and serve.

Recipe 3: Frozen Strawberry Margarita

Ingredients:

- 3 ½ cups strawberries
- 2 ½ cups crushed ice
- ½ cup tequila
- ½ cup fresh lime juice
- ¼ cup sugar
- 3 tablespoons Cointreau
- Lime wedges (optional)

Combine strawberries, ice, tequila, lime juice, sugar, and Cointreau in a blender. Process until smooth. Pour margaritas into four large glasses. Garnish margaritas with a lime wedge, if desired.

About the Author

Harper Lin is the *USA TODAY* bestselling author of 6 cozy mystery series including *The Patisserie Mysteries* and *The Cape Bay Cafe Mysteries*.

When she's not reading or writing mysteries, she loves going to yoga classes, hiking, and hanging out with her family and friends.

For a complete list of her books by series, see her website.

www.HarperLin.com

www.ingramcontent.com/pod-product-compliance
Lightning Source LLC
Chambersburg PA
CBHW030737030726
47497CB00001B/15